His keen gaze wandered over her languid posture on the chaise longue, and caressed her face as she lay back on the cushions.

"You are in much pain?" he asked gently, his deep voice lowered so that only she could hear him.

She nodded, her eyes searching his face.

"Your will is stronger than your body," he said, still softly. "You have a cruel, stubborn will. I wonder that you bend to anyone else's commands—or wishes. . . ."

Their gazes met. His eyes were gray and fathomless, but not cold. Not tonight . . .

HIDDEN FIRES

HIDDEN FIRES

A Regency Romance by
Janette Radcliffe

A DELL BOOK

Published by
Dell Publishing Co., Inc.
1 Dag Hammarskjold Plaza
New York, New York 10017

Dell ® TM 681510, Dell Publishing Co., Inc.

ISBN: 0-440-10657-5

Printed in the United States of America

First printing—May 1978
Second printing—July 1978
Third printing—August 1978

To Beverly Lewis
For her friendship and encouragement

CHAPTER ONE

Deborah Stanton had led small Frederick and Jenny from the church aisle out to the portico, and then beyond to the churchyard. The children were restless, and she firmly held her nephew's and niece's hands as they impatiently waited for their parents. The squire and his talkative wife were often delayed by friends and neighbors.

Deborah gave a slight shake of her gray bonnet as little Jenny started to hop up and down on one foot.

"It hurts and buzzes," whispered Jenny. "I sat still so long and was so very good!"

Deborah returned her smile, and pressed the child's hand. "We shall be home soon, darling. Then you may play in the garden for a while. It is not so cold today."

Deborah's sister Alice was emerging from the church surrounded by three admiring young men. Deborah's gaze dwelt fondly on the younger girl's round fair face, with the large blue eyes, the dimples, the curly blonde hair escaping around the brim of the pale blue bonnet. What a lovely girl she was. Deborah felt an almost maternal pride in

Alice, for she had brought her up since their mother died seven years ago. Now Alice was eighteen, her good nature unaltered by the flattering attention she received wherever she went. Old enough to marry, said their elder sister Gertrude.

Deborah's face shadowed at a sudden memory. Seven years ago, she herself had been eighteen, ready, eager to marry. But it had not happened. It was not meant to be, she told herself, suppressing a sigh. Family pressure had been part of it, but the rest had been her own sense of duty to her sister, only eleven then, and as shattered as Deborah by the death of their beloved mother. Their father had been away at sea as usual. There was nothing for it, Gertrude had said briskly, but that Deborah give up her plans and assume the care of Alice.

"Miss Stanton!"

Deborah turned around, and a smile of genuine pleasure brightened her weary face. "Mrs. Dexter, how do you do?"

The woman looked so excited that Deborah's heart gave a leap. Could it be—another letter from Morgan? More news of him? There had been so little of late.

From childhood Marion Dexter had worked at the great estate of Treverly, county seat of Viscount Treverly. Now middle-aged and married to the gamekeeper of the vast property, she had become housekeeper and manager of the lovely home that waited for its new owner, successor to the long-ailing viscount who had died some months before.

"Miss Stanton, such good news!" the woman confided in a whisper. "Soon all the neighborhood will know, but you must be the first. His lordship is coming home this week!"

"His lordship?" Deborah asked blankly.

"Yes, yes, the new Lord Treverly," said Mrs. Dexter, with a significant smile and a keen look at her friend's face. "Mr. Morgan!"

"Oh—oh, I had almost forgot. Of course, he is now master of—oh, dear, is he really coming home? Is he really?" A chill raced through her, then she felt quite warm, even feverish, in the snapping March wind. "When—when does he come?"

"Sometime this week. He comes with his young cousin, Mr. William Vaughan. His leg is much improved, writes Lord Treverly, and he is able to travel at last."

"Oh—thank God, thank God," whispered Deborah. She had released the children's hands, and now her own small hands in the worn gloves were clasped fervently together, as though in prayer. "I was much concerned."

"Aye, and so were we all. That wound so fierce—However, he has sold his commission and makes his way here shortly. He means to make his home here and take hold of matters. Is that not splendid?" The good woman was beaming her joy and relief.

"Oh, yes, truly splendid! I am so glad—so glad for you. You have carried such a burden since the old viscount died. And all his sons dead before him—it was so sad."

"Yes, yes, but Mr. Morgan, he was always my favorite," the housekeeper confided, her lips close

JANETTE RADCLIFFE

to Miss Stanton's ear. "I should not say it, but Lord Treverly's sons were too fond of gaming. Might have lost the whole place. Now Mr. Morgan —Lord Treverly, I should say—he is another matter entirely. Sober and industrious and used to command, him being a colonel in his regiment, and covered with honors, you might say."

"Oh, yes, indeed, you are perfectly correct, Mrs. Dexter."

Someone was coming toward them. The housekeeper half-turned, then whispered, "And *you'll* be mighty pleased to have him home again, Miss Stanton!" Her eyes shone with secret knowledge.

Deborah blushed vividly, her face coming to embarrassed life. "Oh, you will not say—you will not tell him—about my asking after him, and your letting me read his letters—"

"No, no, not a word! It is our secret. So I promised, and so it shall be. Unless, of course, he should especially ask!" Mrs. Dexter laughed and, turning to her neighbor, began to chat animatedly.

Deborah scarcely noticed when her older sister Gertrude came up to her. "Deborah!" The reproachful voice sharply recalled her attention. "Where are Frederick and Jenny? You have let them go!"

Deborah anxiously looked about and spied the two children racing each other about the graveyard.

"Oh, dear, I shall fetch them!" Deborah started after them.

"You should be more careful!" Gertrude's reproof rang as harshly as if she were addressing a naughty nursemaid. Several people turned to stare.

Deborah bowed her head in embarrassment and went soberly in pursuit of the children, to scold them and take their hands again. Sometimes Gertrude seemed to forget they were sisters, she thought, and that she helped out with the children for love of them, not for pay. She tried to suppress her annoyance as they reached the carriage, where the nursemaid waited with the two younger children, Tommy, two and a half, and Susan, a sweet-tempered child of one year.

They waited more than fifteen minutes before the squire, Clarence Frome, drew his wife Gertrude and his young sister-in-law, Alice, with him to the carriage. "We must be off! You should not be standing in the cold, my dear Deborah!" His good-natured rebuke was accompanied by a kind smile, and he offered his hand to help her into the carriage.

The squire, at forty, was big and hearty and honest, with a shrewd common sense that made him a favorite in the district. Gertrude still counted herself fortunate that he had singled her out, among all the eligible women, seven years ago. Now they were blessed with four children and lived in an ample manor house just inside the village.

Deborah sat alongside the nursemaid and the squire, their backs to the horses. The nursemaid held Susan, Deborah held squirming Tommy, Gertrude took charge of Jenny and Frederick, and Alice sat unencumbered, her face soft and dreamy-eyed. Deborah doubted that Alice was thinking of the sermon, on the life to come and the fearful dangers of hell. More likely she was recollecting the young men who had gathered about her on the church steps afterwards.

The ride was not long. They were home and in the comfortable house within twenty minutes. Deborah shuddered with pleasure at the warmth, for she had felt chilled standing in the churchyard. Jenny and Frederick at once dashed into the garden. Gertrude called after them, "Come right back in a few minutes, my darlings! I will not have you take cold!"

Deborah started for the stairs, to go to her room and remove her cloak and bonnet. The Fromes had invited guests for luncheon, and the squire disappeared into the drawing room to make sure all was ready. Alice was halfway up the stairs when Gertrude called Deborah back.

Deborah returned, studying her sister's plump, impatient face. Gertrude had always been rather spoiled, and her husband adored her and spoiled her all the more. Her blue eyes could be hard sometimes, yet whenever Deborah was inclined to think her sister callous, she reminded herself of what a careful mother Gertrude was.

"Deborah, I wish you would take care of the children this noon, rather than take your luncheon with us. I do not think you would enjoy the company, and the children do not eat properly unless someone watches them closely. Nurse does not exercise enough discipline, as you know."

Deborah gazed at her sister. More and more over the past two years Deborah had been relegated to the nursery and the schoolroom. Before that she had spent long years nursing her father and bringing up a younger sister. But at twenty-five she still did not feel like a spinster.

"I should like to come down to luncheon, Gertrude," she said quietly. "You know I always enjoy Reverend Plummer and his wife's conversation. Pray do not deny me this."

"You can talk to them any day of the week," Gertrude snapped, an angry flush appearing on her fair face. She was as blonde as Alice, but without the doll-like prettiness of the young girl. Next to her, however, Deborah felt sallow and plain. "You have tea with them every week, and you can see your beau, Mr. Irving, whenever he comes to call!"

"Philip Irving is not my beau. I wish you would not refer to him so. We merely have some interests in common." Deborah felt vastly annoyed. Whenever Gertrude wanted to tease, she spoke of the schoolmaster, Philip Irving, as Deborah's suitor. The man was tall, gaunt, and earnest. Deborah felt sorry for him, but she did not much care for him. His advances made her feel cold and distant.

"Well, well, then, why do you need to come down?" Gertrude repeated impatiently. "Really, Deborah, you can be so difficult! I give you hours off to do your painting, which will lead nowhere, as you well know, and now you show blatant indifference to the children!"

"I was not aware that they were fully in my charge," said Deborah drily. "I thought Clarence had invited Alice and me to live here as his guests, until we should marry."

Gertrude's pale blue eyes shifted away from her

sister. "Oh, very well then. I can see you are going to have your way, and our guests are coming at any minute. But I shall not enjoy a moment of our luncheon, knowing that the children are not eating properly!"

When Gertrude's voice became a whine, Deborah knew she might as well give in. She sighed to herself and said, "Very well, I shall remain with them, if you wish it. But, Gertrude, please remember I am not their nursemaid! I am glad to care for them, as I love them dearly—"

"Then that is all that matters! Thank you, Deborah. I knew I could depend on you."

Soon Frederick and Jenny returned from their romp in the garden, and from the nursery at the top of the house, Deborah could not even hear the voices of the arriving guests. Automatically she presided over the luncheon of the three older children, while the nurse fed the baby and put her to bed. Gertrude really should hire another nursemaid for the four of them, but she had put it off, saying that with Deborah there, the expense of another mouth to feed and more wages to pay was unnecessary.

She really must put her foot down, thought Deborah, absently removing the spoon from Tommy's hand as he happily spattered his porridge. She fed him without really looking at his cheerful round face or Jenny's small wise one. She was thinking of what Mrs. Dexter had said.

Morgan was coming home.

Morgan. Her darling, her dearest. And safe and well now, though he had been badly injured, one leg nearly shattered. He was well enough to come home.

He had sworn to love her forever. He had kissed her in the garden that moonlit night in July, before he departed. He had asked her to marry him, and she had gladly consented. On his first leave they would be married. . . .

When the children were settled for a nap, she retreated to her own room. Gertrude had placed her in a room near the children's, so she might hear them at night. She curled up in the window seat, still in her good black dress.

The fickle March wind had turned and was rending the leaves from the bushes. She gazed out over the fields, toward Treverly. On this gray March day, with the trees barren and the fields not yet plowed, she could see across to the stately former abbey that loomed atop a hill above the village, visible from miles away. She studied lovingly the beautiful turrets and towers formed of gray-yellow Cotswold stone. Even at this distance, she could see the sunshine glinting off its immense mullioned windows.

Morgan was returning! Of course, he had not written to her all these years. He had been furious with her for refusing to marry him. Yet he had sworn to love her always—before the chaos of the parting, the pain of the farewells.

Deborah sighed and put her cheek against the cold windowpane. Her head ached vaguely, a small echo of the ache in her heart. All those years. If she had not been able to read the letters, curt and few though they were, that he had written to Mrs. Dexter, she would have died of grief. Not a word from him—not a line, not a message.

And he had adored her. He had sworn it!

She thought of him, and he was as real to her as though he stood before her. She saw his blond curly hair, deep gray eyes, his tall and supple body. So handsome in his regimentals. So aristocratic, so arrogant, that she had sometimes teased him about being vain.

She remembered the night he had proposed to her. They had attended a dance at the village hall. He had stood up with her again and again, his eyes watching her gravely, never leaving her face. Her own had shone up at him. She had known she looked her prettiest, only eighteen years old, with dark brown hair curling above her shoulders, wide brown eyes shining with hope and love. She had worn a rose gown with little milk roses she herself had sewn on the bodice and skirt. He had picked up one that fell off and refused to return it to her though she had laughed and pleaded with him.

He had taken her home in the carriage. Her mother was gravely ill, so they had not gone indoors for fear of disturbing her fitful rest. But in the garden, they had paused.

Her father was away on a mission for the Navy, this one lasting a full year, as was often the case with his work. He sketched machines and ships, ports and naval yards, and even portraits of important officers. Deborah's trunk was full of mementos of her father, his sketches and portfolios. And her own fingers had inherited his talent.

In the garden, with the night scents close about them, Morgan had taken her by the shoulders. "Deborah, I love you," he had said simply. "I want to marry you and take you with me."

"Oh Morgan!" Her heart had been bursting with joy. She had gone into his arms like a homing bird into its nest. His lean arms had closed about her slim body, he had held her tightly, his chin resting on her hair. "I—I love you also," she whispered. "Oh, I do love you so!"

"And you will marry me?"

"Oh, yes, yes, my darling!"

His stern face had lightened, there in the moonlight. He had tipped back her face and gazed down at her tenderly. His lips had brushed her cheeks, her forehead, then her mouth. She had felt like fainting when his mouth closed over hers. It had been so hard, so possessive, so strange to her, against her trembling lips. But with his protective arms about her, she knew she could rest against him, and love him, and be with him always.

He had gone away with her promise to marry him on his next leave. Then—then her mother had died. Her father had come home, distraught with anxiety and grief.

Gertrude was about to marry Clarence Frome, one of the most eligible men in the vicinity. To her displeasure, the wedding must now be a quiet one. She would have adored an elaborate affair, but mourning dictated a somber ceremony.

Her father remained home long enough to give Gertrude away to the handsome, jolly squire. Then there was the matter of Deborah and Alice.

Deborah and her father had had a long conversation. "You need not worry about me, Father. I am to marry Morgan Randall," Deborah had told him, radiant and confident.

"Marriage? Nonsense, you are too young!" Captain Dudley Stanton was frankly appalled. "Gertrude is just married! You are not old enough!"

"But, Father, I love him. And I am eighteen."

He had stared at her bleakly, then passed his hand over his eyes in a gesture of dismay. "Not Morgan Randall—Lord Treverly's young cousin? But he has nothing but his small pay from the regiment! What will you live on?"

"We will manage, Father!"

"Nonsense, nonsense. He is not good enough for you. I have scarcely met him! How dared he go to you without my permission? It will not do, it will not do!"

Fear struck Deborah's heart as her father repeated again and again that Morgan would not do. Patiently she told him of Morgan's steadfastness, his integrity. Her father refused his permission. The marriage was beneath her.

"And besides, there is Alice!" Captain Stanton went on. "Who will take care of her?"

"But of course Gertrude will take her," Deborah said simply. "She is married now, and has a fine big house. There will be plenty of room for Alice! And Gertrude is lovely with children."

Captain Stanton snorted. "You will find she is far from willing to take on such a burden, and her just married! Have you asked her?"

Deborah's heart plummeted. "No, but—surely Gertrude—"

When Gertrude and her husband returned from their short wedding trip, Deborah applied to the radiant young matron on Alice's behalf. Gertrude stared at her sister incredulously.

"Take care of Alice? Take care of Alice?" she gasped. "Are you mad? I am just married! What do you imagine my husband would think if I foisted upon him a child of eleven? No, no, you must carry on. Clearly you are best situated to take care of her."

"But I am to be married as well, and I could scarcely take her with me," said Deborah patiently, her cheeks glowing. "I am to be married to Morgan Randall. We shall not have much to live on, but you and the squire—"

"I could never ask him to take her in," said Gertrude crisply. "You must not imagine it."

Dismayed and stunned, Deborah begged her to reconsider. The older sister was final in her refusal. If Deborah would not care for Alice, the girl would have to live alone, in the care of a housekeeper—and how did Deborah suppose they would find anyone suitable for such an important undertaking?

When Deborah returned to her father with the grim news, he offered no comfort. "I told you it would be so. Gertrude is newly married, she wants no child hanging about!"

And then he was off again on his own concerns. He returned from time to time, and he regularly sent his daughters money, but he was rarely home for long.

Morgan returned on leave. Deborah had written to him, a tear-stained letter in which she tried to set out the facts of the case. "If I do not remain with Alice, she will be raised by a stranger, and I could not endure that. She is so gentle, so easily crushed. How could she endure to be abandoned?"

Morgan arrived, hotly angry. They talked in the drawing room, not like lovers, but like strangers arguing.

"If you loved me enough," he said, "you would marry me and forget your ungrateful family!"

"I do love you, Morgan," she had said fiercely, in the face of his cold-eyed scorn. "However, Father will not permit the marriage at this time. Please, please be patient and wait for me."

"How long? A century?"

"Until Alice is grown," she begged.

"Your sister could take her! You are too soft, too lacking in will to assert yourself! Or you do not love me enough. That is probably it. You do not want to run the risks that marriage to me would entail."

In vain she had begged him for patience. He had ridden off, furiously driving his horse, and she had not seen him again, nor heard directly from him.

Now Deborah leaned against the window, her mouth soft and eager, her eyes dreamy. It had been seven years. Now she was free! And so was Morgan. He had never married. She knew that much. He had fought bravely, gallantly—how eagerly she had read of his honors, and with what fear of the battles in which he was engaged. She had prayed for him nightly, fervently asking

God to protect him and bring him home safely—
to her.

And now he was coming. Morgan was coming!

She rose at last and went over to the mirror.
She gazed rather ruefully into it. She was so pale.
She had been a long time recovering from the
strain of nursing her father in his final illness. He
had taken a bad fall from his horse, and for months
had lain in a delirious state. Day and night she
had nursed him, lying in the room next to his,
half-awake, listening for him to stir, to call.

He had died two years ago. The squire had
come to Deborah and said, "We'll sell your house,
and you two girls will move in with us. There's
plenty of room at the manor. I'll take care of
everything."

Deborah had stared at him. "But Gertrude will
not want us about—"

"Of course she will, of course she will!" And
Gertrude, with three small children of her own at
her knees, had welcomed them cheerfully.

Alice had been given a beautiful bedroom on
the second floor, in frilly white and pastel blues,
a bedroom for a princess, Deborah had thought.
Her own plain white room was bleak, but she
was near the children and could hear if they
called in the night. She must not be jealous of
her pretty younger sister, she must not.

Deborah pinched her cheeks to make the color
come. Sleepless nights and days of work had
drained her face of most of its fine color. Even
walks in the fields had been denied her during
the harsh winter. Her only recreation was draw-

ing and sketching, hastily, when she was not needed elsewhere.

But Morgan was coming. He was coming. And all would be well. He had sworn to love her for a lifetime, they were both free now—life would begin for them, life together, full of beauty and happiness.

The thought kept her going that week. Tommy became ill with a sore throat, and Deborah nursed him. Gertrude stayed away for fear of catching his illness and passing it on to the other children.

On Thursday, Deborah went to town in the small carriage. Lowbridge boasted a fine apothecary, who would make up more medicine for Tommy. And Deborah felt the need of fresh air, to be out in the world and see someone besides a sick, fretful child.

So Deborah donned her gray bonnet with the black ribbons, her black cloak—for she was still in mourning—and set off. She felt relieved to be out, and handled the reins of the single-horse carriage briskly. She bowed and smiled to those she met on the street. She had known them all her life, and they lifted their hats or waved their mitted fingers to her.

She got down in front of the apothecary shop and tied the horse to the post there. When she went inside she found that four people were ahead of her, so she sat down to wait her turn.

The apothecary nodded to her. "With you directly, Miss Stanton," he said respectfully. Her father had been honored in the town, and her sister had married the squire. She smiled back.

"There is no hurry, Mr. Hurst," she said.

She settled back to watch the passersby on the street. What a bustle there was, even on this bleak March day. She noted the bloom of the street lamps, the sight of a tall thin man leaning against an equally elongated building. She longed to sketch it. She must buy more sketching materials, she reminded herself. The long winter days had depleted her supplies.

Finally it was her turn, and Mr. Hurst filled the prescription, inquired into the health of the whole family, and told her about his wife's recent illness.

He had other news. "Lady Horatia Torrington has come to occupy her house here. She has not been with us for many years, you know. Her uncle was Lord Torrington, a formidable man in the House of Lords. She was his hostess in London. And now she comes to Lowbridge!"

"Oh, really? I vaguely remember her—"

What she remembered was a tall, eccentric woman, usually gowned in purple silk or taffeta, with an elaborate turban on her head, sometimes with a tall feather sticking from it. And everyone seemed frightened of her.

She longed to ask for news of Lord Treverly, but did not dare. Anyway, when *he* came, all the town would know and she would hear of it.

She paid for the prescription, thanked Mr. Hurst, and went out to the carriage. But perhaps she had time to visit the bookstore after all, where she would obtain fresh crayons and paper.

Half an hour later Deborah emerged from the

bookstore with the treasured crayons, paper, India ink, and paints. She had diffidently asked Clarence for money for them and he had generously given her what she wished. He was a kind man, she thought. And he seemed pleased that she "had such a nice hobby, something to keep you interested," as he put it.

She had just started back toward her carriage when she noted another carriage being tied up near hers, a grand high-perch phaeton, with a crest on the side. And pulled by two beautiful, restless black horses.

Two men were jumping down. One was slim, with light brown hair and merry eyes, and dressed in a fine coat of deep blue and a lace-fronted shirt. He was not very tall, but supple in his movements.

The other—her heart seemed to stop completely, then suddenly catch a beat and race on. The other was taller, with blond curly hair, and he moved slowly, as if favoring one leg. His face was thin to the point of gauntness. And he looked older than the last time she had seen him. But he had the same arrogant manner, she saw, as he lifted his hat to acknowledge a bow from someone. Coming closer, Deborah saw the glint of gray eyes, cold as a winter sky.

Morgan.

She walked, though her heart was beating so erratically that she felt quite faint. The two young men were walking toward her. They could not fail to see her. Over her parcels, her gaze met his. They were coming—closer—

They were past. The younger man had bowed slightly as he passed her, even though he did not know her. But Morgan Randall's eyes seemed to skim over her, her face, the drab bonnet, the black cloak, and move on indifferently.

He had not bowed, he had not spoken.

He had cut her dead.

She heard his voice, cool and unconcerned. "Ah, there's the bookstore I told you about. We should be able to find the book you wanted—"

The two men turned into the bookstore. Deborah set her parcels in the carriage. Numbly she unfastened the reins, stepped up into the carriage, and set the horse moving with a sharp cluck-cluck.

She felt cold as death. He had cut her dead! He had seen her, had not bowed, had spoken not a word, not even in the chilliest tone.

Surely, surely, she could not expect such coldness! What was wrong? Perhaps in the shadow of her bonnet, her face had not shown plainly. Perhaps—

She was almost to the squire's manor house when the answer occurred to her, so crushing to her self-esteem that she thought she could not endure it. He had not recognized her at all. She had changed so much that he had not known her.

CHAPTER TWO

Tommy recovered from his sore throat with the rapidity of which children are capable. One day so pale and wan that one thought the child was going into a decline, the next up and about, impatient to run outdoors. Deborah breathed a sigh of relief.

She could enjoy an uninterrupted night of sleep again, and the first night she slept hard, though she wakened in the morning heartsick from the encounter with Morgan. He had not known her! Was she so very altered?

She peered anxiously into the mirror. Yes, she was pale and drawn, but one did not change so much in seven years. Yet—her hair was closely bound into a chignon at her neck, her complexion was no longer rosy and bright. And the gray bonnet—so unlike the gay ones she had worn as a girl. The squire had purchased black clothes for them all two years ago, at Captain Stanton's death. Deborah still wore her black dresses and gray ones, for they were the newest in her scanty wardrobe.

There were always new clothes for Alice, for she

went out often and was immensely popular. The squire talked confidently to Gertrude and Deborah of the younger girl's prospects: "Alice will marry well, you mark my words," he said. "So pretty, so gentle and kind, and withal intelligent. And such a little housekeeper! Yes, she will marry well."

Gertrude beamed and nodded, and Deborah smiled her pleasure. Alice deserved the best in life, she was so lovely and yet so unspoiled. Her sweetness and modesty were attractive to everyone.

Deborah fingered her dark dresses wistfully this morning. If only she had a new rose dress! Or blue! Morgan had liked her in blue. But all those dresses were old, and most had been discarded long ago. The pretty muslins, the silks that she had worn at eighteen were all gone. Worn out and never replaced.

Deborah had been too busy to consider replenishing her wardrobe—busy making ends meet, keeping up the modest house, providing for the growing Alice, making her father comfortable on his rare journeys home. Then the year of his illness —she shuddered. It had been a nightmare. She had scarcely left the house.

Morgan had come home for the funeral of his cousin, Lord Treverly, and she had not even known of it until weeks later, after her own father's funeral. Mrs. Dexter had informed her of it, and how dear Mr. Morgan had assured her she would always have a post with him. If only Deborah had had the comfort of his presence at that terrible time!

The squire had done much to help, and done

all so cheerfully that Deborah would always be grateful to him. The Stanton house had been sold briskly, and they had been moved into his manor house at once. The money from the sale was invested so that one day some of the income would be Deborah's—after she married, and her husband could control it for her—and some Alice's. Not much, but something of their own. Gertrude had already used her share for new carpets and furnishings for the squire's residence.

On Saturday afternoon there was great excitement. Lady Horatia Torrington came to call, bringing three charming French émigrés with her. She had written to the squire requesting permission to call, and Gertrude had flown into a flurry of housecleaning and preparations.

"Imagine, a viscountess in our home!" cried Gertrude, quite red-faced with her efforts. "Oh, my dears. How grand we are! You know, of course, she was hostess to her uncle, and acquainted with all London society. I believe she's been traveling on the Continent—"

The appointed hour was three o'clock. That meant Lady Horatia would remain to tea. The silver was polished, the best formal china laid out, the servants instructed until they were almost as frantic as their mistress.

Promptly at three o'clock, a huge black carriage drew up. Deborah peeped curiously from the window to see the tall figure clad in purple satin that she remembered from her childhood. A grand cloak of purple velvet swept about her. The purple turban on her head was made taller by the addition of a brilliant peacock feather. The three figures who accompanied her, a lady and two gentlemen, seemed to be swept along in her wake.

The butler opened the door to them, and led them to the drawing room. He announced them carefully, as ordered by Gertrude.

"Lady Horatia Torrington! Madame Marie Andreossy! Monsieur Bernard Houdon! Monsieur Paul Rigaud!" Deborah thought he had not done badly at all with the French names; she herself had coached him.

There were bows all around. The taller woman swept in grandly, extended her hand to the squire, who kissed it, then beamed down at her.

"Well, Lady Horatia. You have not honored Lowbridge for many a year. It is exceedingly pleasant to have you return to us. Welcome, welcome!"

She condescended to look pleased by his welcome, but when Gertrude came up to greet her, she was subjected by Lady Horatia to a keen look and a stiff nod. Then Lady Horatia introduced her companions.

Deborah, hovering in the background, had the chance to observe the introductions with eyes which were sharp and interested. What sketches they would all make!

Only a little golden-gray hair peeped from under the viscountess's purple turban. Her imperious face with its long nose and large chin seemed to tower over them all. It was wrinkled now, but the gray eyes missed nothing as she flicked a look about the room.

Beside her the Frenchwoman looked quite tiny, though plump as a pigeon, as Clarence would say. She was exceedingly pretty, with dark curly hair, gray-green eyes, and pleasingly rounded curves at the bosom and hips. Her red dress seemed to flame in the dim room on that gray afternoon. She was about thirty, Deborah guessed.

Deborah turned her attention to the two men. One was older, perhaps in his mid-forties, with a sharp, rather cynical face, pointed like a fox's. He wore a coat of black velvet and a paisley scarf about his throat, instead of the conventional white stock. Deborah found him decidedly foreign-looking.

Paul Rigaud looked to be in his early thirties, and was a little taller even than the formidable Lady Torrington. He had curly dark hair, dark brown eyes, and handsome features. When Alice, charming in a blue gown, was brought forward to be introduced, he bowed so gracefully it seemed he was about to dance in a cotillion. He wore a dark blue silk coat which fit his broad shoulders neatly, and a small gold and ruby ring shone on his finger, matching the jewel in his intricately folded stock.

Deborah was amused at the Frenchman's reaction to Alice. She looked him over critically, automatically seeing him as a possible beau for her sister. The older man, Bernard Houdon, was too cynical and cold, impossible for Alice. But the younger man—ah, he was different.

The squire beckoned to Deborah. She started, then came forward shyly. She smiled at Lady

Horatia and bowed to her. "So happy to meet you," she murmured. "I used to see you in Lowbridge, when you came years ago."

"I do not recall you," her ladyship said abruptly, looking into Deborah's dark eyes.

Deborah blushed slightly; she felt her cheeks grow hot. "I was but a child," she murmured.

"Ah, yes. I recollect how the children laughed at my costume and the way I rode my horse into town, in my Amazon dress!" Lady Horatia said brusquely.

Deborah greeted the others, who gazed back at her with indifference. She retreated to a chair near the far sofa and continued to watch the proceedings. Lady Horatia sat down on the sofa with Gertrude and commanded that all the gossip of the past ten years be conveyed to her at once.

The younger Frenchman, Paul Rigaud, managed to sit next to Alice and carried on a flattering conversation, to judge by the blush in the girl's cheeks and the flutter of her lashes. The squire talked with Houdon, whose conversation seemed to consist mainly of biting comments on English politics and customs. The squire laughed heartily at some of them.

"No, no, sir, you do not understand us," he said. "We have the finest navy in the world! We fuss among ourselves, but we are proud of our navy. You must disregard those cartoons and the arguments in the House of Lords! Our navy shall endure! Eh, Deborah?"

She started at being so suddenly included in the conversation. "Yes, sir," she said.

"The girls' father was a captain in the navy until his untimely death," the squire explained. "Fine fellow, invaluable to the navy! Went about sketching all the time! Painted portraits as well!"

"Ah, indeed? What did he sketch?" Houdon asked.

The squire was about to answer when Lady Horatia turned abruptly to Deborah. "Young lady, why are you staring at me?"

Deborah jumped. "I beg your pardon—"

"You may beg my pardon all you please, I still wish to know why you are staring at me! You have not ceased for half an hour!"

"Oh, I am so sorry—I did but wish I could sketch you!" Deborah said frankly.

Gertrude frowned and gestured to her sister to be quiet. But the formidable Lady Horatia was not to be halted.

"Now, that remark is open to at least two interpretations. Did you mean that you wish you were talented enough to sketch my portrait? Or did you mean that you have a talent and wish to exercise it? Make yourself clear!"

Deborah was scarlet with embarrassment at being made the object of all their stares—Alice's apprehensive, Gertrude's disgusted, the squire's amused. All the guests seemed to be looking at her also.

"I meant," she said in a low tone, "I have—some talent and wish I had the opportunity to—to sketch you. You have a fine, interesting face and profile."

"I have an ugly face," said Lady Horatia flatly. "I have a huge nose, unfortunately a common

feature in my family. I have a large chin, too big
for a woman. And my forehead is too broad, which
means I have too great an intellect to be pleasing
to the frivolous ladies of society."

"Oh, indeed, my lady, you are the wonder of
London and all England," cried Gertrude anxiously, hoping to redeem the afternoon. "We have
read about you in the gazettes, how you entertain at Brighton and at Bath, how you travel to
Paris and to Rome—"

"Yes, yes, but no young man would offer for
me," said the lady with a grim smile and a sudden
lifting of the chin that set the peacock feather
waving. "Uncle said I should marry when I could
find a man with more intelligence than mine, and
I never found one! *Never!* What do you think of
that?"

The squire laughed, which caused her to glare
at him. "Madam, you are using the wrong criteria,"
he said amiably. "You should have found a man to
respect and care for, as well as you cared for your
uncle. Now, there was a fine man, and you made
him so secure in his home that he could without
hesitation go forth to slay all his enemies—who
were many, because of his honesty and integrity!
Should you have found a husband like him, you
would have married, and done well."

Her face softened, and she even favored him
with a smile. "You are a shrewd man, Squire. Yes,
perhaps I should have done so. But as for this
young lady—" She turned her sharp gray eyes on
Deborah. "Get your pencil and paper, and sketch
me!"

"Now?" asked Deborah faintly, very conscious of her older sister's fury at the possibly disastrous course the afternoon was taking.

"Yes, now! I shall see what talent you have, what you can make of my ravaged features!"

And she sent Deborah from the room with a gesture of her large, almost masculine-looking hands, covered with rings of every description, silver and gold, ruby and diamond and sapphire, and a curious cat's-eye yellow.

Deborah heard Gertrude breathlessly assuring her ladyship that her features were far from ravaged, that indeed she was among the handsomest women she had met. Deborah smiled to herself as she raced up the stairs. Lady Horatia was too shrewd to be taken in by flattery.

Her pulses raced as she ran up to her room, gathered up a sketching block and some crayons. Then she ran down again to the drawing room. The butler was rolling in a huge cart bearing the tea service. It came to rest before Gertrude.

"You may sketch me now," said Lady Horatia, seeing Deborah hesitate. "If my mouth is open and I am popping a tart into it, it shall be seen as a natural portrait. I love to eat! Come now, continue, I shall be amused to see what you make of me!"

Deborah chuckled, and the good lady stared at her in some surprise. "I shall do my best, my lady," she said and resumed her former place, from where she could view the woman's profile. She began to sketch, shaking her head as Alice approached to bring her a cup of tea.

The conversation continued, some of it lighthearted, then turning serious as they discussed the possibility of a French invasion of England.

"We have men who have volunteered to come forward with their weapons, should the French attack us," the squire said.

"Here in Somerset?" Bernard Houdon asked in grave mockery. "You jest, surely! If Napoleon attacks, it will be on the coast opposite to the French channel ports—Calais, Boulogne, and so on. You English should gather there and prepare to repel him. He is a beast, an animal! He will spring from the French ports, to the most direct route, and attack toward London. I assure you, I have studied the matter."

"I am sure you *have* studied it, monsieur. You must be most anxious, with your loyalties torn between your native country and your new home," said Lady Horatia, tactful for once. "However, I am sure all England should be prepared, regardless of where the First Consul might attack. I am glad to learn that preparations are being made even in Lowbridge," and she gave the squire an approving nod.

"Oh, but how wretched that we must endure this fear of attack yet again," sighed Gertrude. "He threatens us, we prepare, then there is peace once more. After all, the Peace of Amiens was signed but a year ago!"

"Napoleon uses peaceful times to prepare himself for more war," said Bernard Houdon, getting up to stroll over to Deborah's chair, standing behind her to view her sketch block. "You should beware of him. A very clever man, who makes promises only to break them. Land was promised to us, to make up for that which was taken from us during the Revolution. We still wait for it, and shall wait until we are dead."

"The émigrés have been treated badly," said Lady Horatia gravely. "The revolutionaries took their lands and homes, all the jewels they could get their hands on. And now Napoleon would keep those lands, offering them as favors to those who fawn upon him. I think you must give up all hope of returning to the France you love, and settle down in England. Here we have no guillotines, no revolutions. Here you will one day be able to restore your former way of life. You will find contentment once more," and she patted Marie Andreossy's hand encouragingly.

Deborah caught the fleeting softness in the viscountess's hard profile, and added a gentler touch to the mouth she was sketching. Houdon hung over the back of the couch, so that she was uncomfortably aware of his presence. She moved restlessly in her chair, and he stood erect at once.

"I beg your pardon, mademoiselle," he said softly. "I am disturbing you. You sketch so well, so swiftly."

"Thank you, monsieur," she murmured, and was relieved when he moved away, to seat himself near the squire. Clarence gave Deborah a little wink of encouragement as though to say, here is a man who appreciates you, my dear!

They did not know there was but one man in the world for her, and she might see him soon. She resolved to look her prettiest when he came, for surely he must come eventually. Surely he would be over his anger by this time. She had promised to wait for him.

Her fingers had stilled over the sketch; she studied it without seeing it. Oh, Morgan, Morgan, she thought. All the years we wasted! But it had been necessary, surely he would see that. They were free now—that was the important thing.

Next it was Paul Rigaud who ambled over to Deborah's chair and glanced down at the pad. "Admirable!" he murmured. "I swear, it is her ladyship to the life!"

Lady Horatia broke off her conversation to turn to Deborah. Her ears must be very quick, Deborah thought.

"Are you finished? I am curious to see what you have produced."

"Not yet, my lady. Only a few more minutes." She set to work again, now acutely conscious of the handsome young man stationed behind her. He did not lean annoyingly close, as Monsieur Houdon had done, but she knew he was watching her nevertheless.

Finally the sketch was finished, and Deborah stood up to show it to Lady Horatia. The woman was animatedly describing a society function she had recently attended, and Gertrude gave Deborah a cold, annoyed look. Deborah sat down again, her pad on her lap.

Paul Rigaud leaned closer. "Mademoiselle? You are the sister of Madame Frome?"

"Yes, monsieur," she murmured. He came to sit beside her on the sofa, rather closer than was polite, she thought.

"You are young to be so talented," he whispered, as though not to disturb the general conversation that went on about them. "And she seems so settled, so—so matronly—is that the word? I long to converse with you. I have a feeling you are intelligent as well as lovely."

She raised her eyes in amazement. Was he teasing her? She was not lovely. On the contrary, she was rather sallow and plain. Gertrude had said so often enough, and her mirror told her the same. But the intense look in this man's dark brown eyes told her he did not jest.

"I—I do not know. You must be teasing me," she said uncertainly.

"I? No. I see below the surface of matters, mademoiselle. A silk dress does not make a lady, nor a diamond ring a virtuous woman." He spoke so solemnly that she could not laugh at him, but a dimple appeared in her cheek, and he gazed at her still more intently.

"You smile at my English? I do not mind, not if it brings that charming mark into your beautiful face. You are lovelier than ever—" he whispered.

"No, no, your English is excellent, Monsieur Rigaud," she interrupted. "Forgive me, I am not accustomed to being spoken of as beautiful. I cannot help but think you are teasing me. It is my sister Alice who is beautiful. And she is good and sweet withal," said Deborah proudly, her wide eyes alight.

"Ah. You praise your sister. That is good. That is as it should be. But she wears a pretty blue dress, and you wear mourning. Is it not so? Why is she not in mourning as well?"

"You see, my father died two years ago," she began.

"How long is the period of mourning?" he asked.

"Why—one year. And another year in gray," she explained. "However, everyone does not observe it."

"I wish to see you in a prettier color—brown like your eyes, or amber, or gold," he murmured.

"What are you whispering about, Paul?" asked Lady Horatia sharply, making them both start. "Are you interrupting her work? Do you dare interfere with work of such importance?"

Deborah understood that the woman was teasing, and smiled at her, but Gertrude looked apprehensive.

"I am finished, my lady. Should you like to see the sketch now?"

"Allow me!" said Paul eagerly, taking the sketch block from Deborah to carry it over to Lady Horatia. She took up her lorgnette in one hand, the sketch block in the other, and examined it keenly for some moments.

Gertrude seemed to be holding her breath. Even the squire lost his smile. If the woman was displeased—

"Good!" pronounced her ladyship, setting down her eyeglass. "I should like to keep this, child. You show much promise—no, you have shown you are *beyond* promise. Yours is a talent which you have sharpened with use! In little more than one hour you have done better than a portrait painter in London who took five weeks to come up with some miserable sketches of me!"

Gertrude let out her breath in relief. The squire smiled again. Deborah could not conceal her pleasure. "Thank you, my lady, you are most kind."

"Do you ever work in oils?"

"Why—I have in times past, my lady. Now I have little time for it, but only sketch."

"Little time? But you must make time! You have an important talent. I wish you to paint my portrait," said Lady Horatia decisively. "Let me see. Come to my house on Monday, and I shall sit for you."

Gertrude recovered first. The squire could only stare. Much as he admired Deborah's little talent, as he called it, he had not thought of her as a painter of portraits, certainly not of subjects such as the grand Lady Horatia Torrington!

"But Deborah is not free to come, my lady, I beg your pardon! She gives lessons to the older children during the week. They are learning most rapidly under her," Gertrude said complacently. "Frederick and Jenny are quite intelligent."

Lady Horatia lifted her lorgnette to examine Gertrude's face. "You must be jesting," she said, letting the eyeglass fall again to her lap, her fingers toying with the stem. "Your sister, a governess in your own home? And she with such a magnificent talent?"

There was a long awkward silence, which the viscountess finally broke. Alice was blushing with embarrassment for her older sister, and the squire looked deeply thoughtful.

"You must hire a governess, Mrs. Frome," said Lady Horatia firmly. "Deborah shall come to me on Monday and Wednesday, to sketch my portrait. I am determined on it. Anyone can become a governess. It takes a true talent to come up with something like this—" And she tapped the sketch block with long fingers that shone with her many rings. "And only an hour to do it. Dear me, I am remaining too long, though. I must take my leave of you all. You should not entertain me so well—I am quite spoiled with your kind attentions! And the tea was excellently brewed. I shall send you a box of some of the tea I received recently from India. A fine brew!"

She stood up, ripped the page of her portrait from the pad, and returned the block to Deborah with a shrewd look and a smile. "You will come to me on Monday at ten o'clock, Miss Deborah," she said. "We shall explore your talents further!" She turned to Madame Andreossy. "Come, Marie, come with me. You have said little today. I hope you understood all the conversation? Your English is excellent, and I know that you did!"

Sprinkling compliments lavishly among her hosts, she herded her own guests to the door and out into the garden. "A lovely place, you have my compliments, Squire Frome. I shall look forward to seeing it in the spring."

After the black carriage had departed, Gertrude let out a long breath of outrage. "Well—of all the impossible—what a truly dreadful woman! Telling me to hire a governess! She will have me turn out my own sister from my home!"

"No, indeed," said the squire. "She but complimented our Deborah on her talent. A fine thing, indeed."

"*Father* was talented! *He* had a superior position in the navy," Gertrude went on. "But Deborah— her sketching is only a small diversion to amuse the children. A portrait indeed! Lady Horatia would be sorely disappointed should it ever be done! If it is done honestly, it will show her sour features and her long nose which she pokes into other people's business! Do not think of going, Deborah. I will not allow you to be so humiliated!"

"I do not feel humiliated," said Deborah mildly. "And I should like to do her portrait. She has magnificent features, a truly fine face, with much experience stamped upon it. The portrait would be a challenge."

"You are mad," sniffed Gertrude. "Where are my children? I do not hear them. What is that nurse doing with them? Deborah, go up and see about them!"

"They are having tea, Gertrude," said Deborah patiently. "I should like to do another sketch of Lady Horatia from memory, so that I shall be more prepared on Monday when I go to her."

Gertrude shut her mouth in an ugly line and stamped back to her sitting room, where she proceeded to give the housekeeper a bad time of it.

Alice put her arm about Deborah's waist as they climbed the stairs to the upper hall. "Oh, dear, Deborah, do you really wish to do that dreadful woman's portrait? She seems so stiff and formal! And her temper—" She shuddered at the memory.

"I should like it immensely. She does not frighten me," said Deborah with a smile. She pressed a kiss on her sister's pink and white cheek, so like a peach, she thought. "You did very well this afternoon, my dear. You conversed quite animatedly with the guests. Did you understand any of the French?"

Alice's face lighted up. "Oh, I did. In fact I spoke in French for quite a time to Madame Andreossy. She was so amiable as to correct me twice for my accent, then praised me that I spoke so well. I told her you had taught me yourself, and she wondered at us both."

Deborah continued on to her room, where she proceeded to sketch until dinner time. She quite forgot the children, and besides, the nurse was with them. Her young face glowed as she worked alone, recalling the woman's features. She would like to do the portrait; she could visualize the perfect setting for it: Lady Horatia posed among such exotic items as ivory elephants, a Persian carpet on a rosewood table, a Japanese screen behind her splendid head. . . . It quite occupied her thoughts all the evening, and she scarcely noticed Gertrude's ill-humor.

CHAPTER THREE

Gertrude needed the carriage on Monday, so Deborah could not have it for her "frivolities," as Gertrude said. Deborah, not to be deterred, walked to Lady Horatia Torrington's home to begin her work. The good lady was scandalized.

"You *walked?* It is a full mile, my dear!" she exclaimed when Deborah appeared at the door of her drawing room in muddy boots, carrying her sketch pad and pencils. "Come in, come in! You may be sure I shall send you home in my carriage. But first, sit down and let us become acquainted."

She was entirely amiable with Deborah and appeared to find pleasure in describing her life in London, her late uncle, the famous diplomat, and the problems, both grave and amusing, of entertaining for a man of his standing.

Deborah watched her expressions and, observing the changes that came over her face, could not resist making a number of sketches. She tried to capture the swift humor that came first to the fine eyes, then turned up the corners of the generous mouth. Lady Horatia had a caustic wit and used it freely, making Deborah laugh often.

"Good, good, you understand me! You are not afraid of me!" said Lady Horatia as Deborah made ready to depart, following an elegant lunch and an interesting afternoon of conversation. "You will come again on Wednesday. Do not let your sister stop you—you promise you will come?"

"I promise," Deborah said simply, knowing it was a promise she could not resist keeping. Indeed, she had been treated with more respect by this formidable woman than by her own sister, these past years!

She pondered that observation as she rode home in the beautiful black carriage that conveyed her so quickly and lightly.

Alice asked her anxiously how the session had passed, and Deborah was full of enthusiasm.

"She treated me so well, Alice, you would not believe how generous she was! I admired some items about the room, and she insisted I should examine them and hear their histories. She showed me pieces of ivory and jade and some porcelain that came from China, a miniature tree of crystal hung with leaves and flowers of many precious gems. Truly, she has magnificent taste. She said that later, when she had finished unpacking, she would show me garments she had worn in Arabia and in India. Imagine!"

Alice's eyes opened wide with wonder. "Oh, she has obviously taken to you, Deborah. I am so glad for you! I should be terrified of her myself. Fortunately, it is you she favors."

"She is a good woman, and I think very unhappy at the death of her uncle. Not only has she lost a loved one, but her position in society as well," said Deborah thoughtfully. "She told me she was accustomed to being much sought after. Now she is nobody, and she decided she had to leave London, she felt so humiliated."

"How can people be so cruel?" asked Alice, who had no experience of cruelty directed at herself. Hers was a sympathetic nature, though her understanding of others was shallow. Her good heart led her to believe all people were like herself, and she attributed shows of malice to some illness or temporary affliction.

Deborah smiled affectionately at her younger sister. When she thought of the threat that had hung over Alice, of being virtually abandoned by her family, left to the care of a stranger, she shuddered. No, no, that would never have done. Surely, Morgan had by now comprehended that Deborah had only done what she had to do, seven years ago. Surely he would call on her soon! At the very least, he must pay a duty call on the squire. She had not attended church on Sunday, since Jenny had seemed on the verge of coming down with Tommy's ailment, and she had stayed with the restless child all day, trying to keep her from exerting herself.

On Tuesday afternoon, Deborah was sitting peacefully in the drawing room. It had rained much of the day, so hard at times that they expected no callers. She wore a simple gray dress, while Alice was in blue muslin, the ribbons tied under her slight breasts, and her hair loose. Alice sat before the fire, toasting her wet toes. Her slip-

pers had become damp when she went out to secure a few early daffodils for the table—"to make
us more cheerful," as she had said, arranging
them deftly in a blue vase.

Deborah had taken out a recent portfolio of her
sketches. She turned them over thoughtfully. She
had not done much sketching in recent years, but
here were some of Alice, and some of her father,
erect and fine in his uniform. These must have
been done on his last visit home before the dreadful accident.

In the bottom of the portfolio she found some
sketches she had made of a port they had visited
together. On her father's infrequent holidays at
home, he had rarely wished to remain for long. He
would pack up Alice and Deborah and carry them
off on a "working holiday," during which he would
sketch ships and various ports. He had entry
everywhere. Deborah had always been enchanted
by the ships, so graceful and romantic.

Even raw sailors had bashfully sat for her, and
she had made sketches of their faces and of their
poses as they hung in the rigging, remaining mo-
tionless for quite half an hour while she drew.
She paused at one scene of a port with the ship
just coming in. It showed the beautiful background of hills, the wide channel, the busy port
with small figures darting about to secure the
ship. It was not bad, she thought. Perhaps she did
have more talent than her father had realized.
His own talent, recognized by all, had overshad-
owed her burgeoning one. She must get out
his sketches one day, the maps of the harbors and

ports, the pictures of ships, the rough drawings for portraits he had completed later.

She was lost in her thoughts when the butler came to the door, a little flushed and disturbed.

"Miss Stanton?" he said.

"Yes, what is it?" She looked up absently from her work.

"Monsieur Paul Rigaud is here, and begs permission to see the ladies."

"Oh, dear!" Gertrude was not at home; the squire was absorbed in work in his study and hated to be disturbed when he was doing the accounts. He dealt splendidly with people, but accounts drove him into a frenzy of confusion, he always said. She looked at Alice, who stood up hastily, straightening her dress. "I—I think you should show him in. And inform the squire we should be pleased if he will take tea with us—at about four, if you will."

"Yes, Miss Stanton."

The butler bowed, and disappeared to return shortly with the cheerful, but rain-soaked young Frenchman. He at once burst into apologies.

"I was walking on the grounds nearby and was caught in a rain storm. At once I thought of my friends here, and so I beg your indulgence. If I might but dry myself before your fire—"

Deborah rose and went to him, her hand outstretched. His embarrassment at his appearance made him seem younger, more awkward, than the charming man of the world she had met several days before. He must be quite a dandy, she thought, to be so upset by his imperfect appearance. "Pray, come in and seat yourself by the fire. We were but warming ourselves. Such a gray, rainy day—I must apologize for our weather."

"How kind you are!" His big hand clasped hers warmly, a little longer than necessary, and his gaze dwelt on her flushed cheeks, her bright eyes. "You are as gentle of heart as you are lovely of face, Miss Stanton. No wonder Lady Horatia praises you without ceasing."

She blushed more hotly at this, his boldest compliment yet. She withdrew her hand gently and gestured to her sister. "You remember my sister, Miss Alice Stanton?"

"How could I forget such loveliness?" He bowed deeply to young Alice, who blushed in turn and bobbed a curtsey. He was full of compliments; it was probably the French way, thought Deborah.

She gestured him to a chair near the fire, but he protested that his damp clothes would spoil the fabric. "No, no, I shall stand here near the fire and steam myself dry. If you do not object? How cosy it is here! How fortunate to have a home of one's own, to feel secure!" And he suppressed a sigh, though his eyes shadowed for a moment.

She recalled that he was an exile from his own country, probably deprived of a splendid home by the Revolution. What a bitter blow to him that bloody time must have been!

The butler and a maid brought the tea which Deborah had ordered immediately after Paul Rigaud's arrival. The squire had sent his apologies. "He begs you to excuse him for another half hour, Miss Stanton. He will finish the column then, he asked me to inform you."

Deborah smiled and nodded, then turned back to their guest. "The squire is wrestling with his accounts, sir. I do beg you to excuse his seeming discourtesy. It is the one task he puts off as long as possible. When it can be postponed no longer, he sighs like the north wind, pulls a long face, and confines himself to the study until the task is done."

"But I shall excuse him gladly. How could I complain when I have two lovely ladies to entertain me? I am the lucky man today!"

And indeed he did seem to be in high spirits, amusing them with light tales of his travels, emphasizing the humor of them rather than the discomfort and danger. And he showed considerable enthusiasm for Deborah's sketches.

"Ah, your good work, Miss Stanton. May I look at these?" She nodded, a little reluctantly. He picked up the folder from the desk and went to sit beside her on the sofa. He looked long at each drawing, smiling over the ones of Alice. "Your love for your sister shows! How charming she was at—what? Fifteen, sixteen?"

"Yes, at fifteen, sir."

He raised his dark eyebrows at the sketches of the sailors and officers. "They posed for you?" He spoke in French, so surprised was he. "How marvelous, yet how strange! They must be fond of you indeed!"

"They were aware of my father's rank, I think, sir," said Deborah wryly. "However, they were very amiable about it. Father was also sketching at the time, for a portrait of the Admiral of the Fleet. The painting now hangs on the flagship."

"Indeed! How proud you must be of him! And how proud he must have been of you," he added gently, looking through the next sketches. "You have inherited his magnificent talent. These are fine, fine."

"You are very kind, sir."

"No, no, I am not kind. I am cruel when it comes to art," he said earnestly. His dark eyes met hers. "You see, I care too much about beauty, about art and music, to take them lightly. When a young lady such as yourself says that she sketches, I think immediately of the immature daubs of the young ladies of my acquaintance, who take up art because it is 'done,' but have no more talent than a cow in the field. They take up music, and the din of it is excruciating to my ears! They attempt to read poetry, and I wish to scream 'Stop, stop, you are killing the muse!'"

Both Alice and Deborah burst into laughter at his grimace. Paul Rigaud smiled at them his eyes twinkling.

"Laugh if you will, you know what I mean. But you must promise not to betray me the next time I am forced to sit through one of these exhibitions of non-talent and have to keep a grave face. What a pleasure it is, then, to look at your work and know that here is rare ability."

"You are most kind, sir."

He shook his handsome head at her. "Not kind, I refuse the word 'kind.' I know what I like to see. I know when lines are drawn with a kind of genius, capturing an expression swiftly, or the beauty of a ship—ah." He paused, turning to the last sketches, those of the ports, and the ship coming into harbor. "What is this place?"

"It is on Bristol Channel," said Deborah. "I sketched a ship just as it came in. The sailors are so quick and nimble, it was difficult to catch them in action. Do you think I succeeded?"

He gazed so long at the sketch, she thought he was not going to answer. He finally looked up with a sigh, his face grave and alert. "You did very well, very well, Miss Stanton. Do you often sketch such scenes?"

"Oh, she has done so for years," said Alice, joining in shyly. "Whenever Papa took us on a trip with him, Deborah would also sketch. He would do his work, and Deborah would fill hundreds of pages with her sketches of the ships and the ports and the people. She did two oil paintings for me, which hang in my bedroom. They are so beautiful, one would think the ships were sailing right at one!"

"I am honored that you have shown these to me. Might I see more of your work, Miss Stanton?" Paul Rigaud asked gravely. "I cannot tell you how much I admire this."

"You are—most generous in your praise," she was beginning, when the butler came to the door again. Once again he appeared to have lost his usual equanimity.

"Yes?" Deborah asked.

"Miss Stanton, two more gentlemen have arrived! May I bring in—" he almost gulped—"his lordship, Viscount Treverly, and his companion, Mr. William Vaughan?"

Deborah could only stare at the butler. Her heart seemed to stop, then plunge on again. Morgan—he was here! Morgan—

She stood up, her hands clasped tightly together. "Pray, ask the squire to attend us at once," she managed to say. "But first show in the gentlemen."

He bowed, and soon Morgan Randall and his friend were at the door. Deborah could raise her eyes only as far as their stiff white collars. "You are most welcome," she said.

She held out her hand to Morgan, and he clasped it briefly; his hand was cold, and she remembered what a gloomy day it was. The coldness sent a chill through her.

"Miss Stanton," he murmured, in a voice like frost.

She managed the introductions of Paul Rigaud and her sister, and was aware of the admiration in Mr. Vaughan's gaze as he looked at Alice. William Vaughan made a less imposing impression than his cousin, but Deborah thought he looked good-natured. He bowed over their hands and murmured something flattering. Lord Treverly merely stood near the fire with his hands clasped behind his back and looked rather bored.

Fortunately the squire hastened in, and all awkwardness was dispelled by his booming cheer. "Good afternoon, good afternoon, how splendid to see you, Lord Treverly! Good of you to call! My wife is out calling on some friends, I'm afraid. How disappointed she'll be when she learns she missed you. Sit down, all. Do get some fresh tea,

Deborah, or perhaps you gentlemen prefer something stronger? I could do with a whiskey myself."

The visitors also chose whiskey, and the squire poured for them all. They sat about, glasses in hand, and the talk turned to hunting. With their attention elsewhere, Deborah was able to steal a furtive look at Morgan. How changed he was, yet how much the same!

He was much thinner, and his tanned face showed lines of pain. Yet his arrogant, almost curt manner was unchanged, unless it had been somewhat exaggerated by the fact that he was now Lord Treverly, not plain Colonel Randall of the Regiment. Fine though that position had been, he was now the possessor of a magnificent estate with a five-hundred-year-old manor house. Also a London townhouse, and other properties.

Paul Rigaud seemed to have little to say to the other men. He listened with interest to their talk of hunting and the horses Morgan had just bought, but all the while he kept examining the pages of Deborah's portfolio, silently admiring her work. Twice he turned to her for a whispered explanation of the subject.

"You met Deborah years ago, did you not? And Alice too?" asked the squire genially, when the hunting topic had been exhausted. "I married their elder sister; I think you knew her also. Fine family! I admired their father deeply."

"Yes. My condolences on his death." Morgan directed the remark in the general direction of Deborah and her sister. His crisp tone seemed to convey no more than conventional politeness.

"Thank you, sir," she murmured. She did not know how she could endure another minute of this agony. He seemed so cold, so unforgiving. Would he never look directly at her? She had borne up all these years, thinking of him, praying for his safe return. Surely he could not have forgotten her completely!

"I believe you remained at home during those years?" asked Morgan, turning the whiskey glass in his hands, gazing down into the amber liquid. It was the first personal remark he had addressed to her.

"Yes, we did, of course," Deborah said. "Father wished us to keep up the house. He meant to retire there, but then his sad accident—" Her voice shook a little.

"Of course, we wanted the girls with us," said the squire cheerfully. "Couldn't see keeping up two households. Plenty of room here, as you can see!" And he waved his glass about, vaguely indicating the vastness of the room. "But Deborah wouldn't hear of it. Her father wished her to remain at home, and there she would remain. I suspect she enjoyed playing housekeeper in her own home. A strong-willed woman!"

"Indeed," murmured Morgan.

Deborah had turned rigid. She could not openly contradict her kind brother-in-law. Was it possible he did not know that Gertrude had refused to give Alice a home, had blighted Deborah's own hopes for marriage? The squire went on cheerfully.

"Soon as their father died, we insisted on their coming to us. Nothing else for it. Sold the house, brought them here. Should have done it long ago. Alice is a joy to have here, so young and sweet, don't you think? And Deborah is a vast help to Gertrude. Can't get along without them!"

Miserably, Deborah had to let him ramble on. Perhaps the squire truly believed they had been offered a home. She finally raised her gaze to Morgan's, hoping he would remember her words of long ago, and believe her. Alice would have been abandoned . . . abandoned. . . .

She watched the twin chips of gray ice that were his eyes. Toward her he showed nothing but cold contempt. She could say nothing, for her throat seemed to have closed up completely.

William Vaughan turned to Alice. "Do you play the piano, ma'am?" Although the question was merely polite, his eyes held more than politeness.

"Only a little," Alice said, with a ripple of laughter. "And after what Monsieur Rigaud has just said to us, I should not dare to play for him!"

"What? Did he insult you?" Vaughan seemed about to spring up and attack the young Frenchman.

Paul Rigaud flung up his hands dramatically. "*Non, non,* but *non!* I was not speaking of Miss Alice. To listen to her play would be a privilege of the most marvelous—"

"That is not what you said a while ago," teased Alice, her blue eyes sparkling. "You said you could not endure it when young ladies were made to perform for you. It was a terrible ordeal for your nerves, because the performances were always so poor! Didn't he say so, Deborah?"

"He—he did not mean—I mean, he was only jesting—"

Her low, faltering words were drowned out by Lord Treverly. "I am sure anything you choose to play for us would be welcome, Miss Alice." And he actually smiled at the young girl, flicking a critical look over her simple blue dress, her flushed face. "Do play. Shall I open the piano for you?"

"Oh please, sir, I could not now," begged Alice, genuinely taking fright.

"Thought you were going to talk to the squire," murmured William Vaughan, giving his friend a significant look. "Didn't you say you had business to discuss about the tenants?"

"Right," said Lord Treverly, setting down his glass. "Squire Frome, I hesitate to break up this pleasant occasion. However, I actually called to beg your advice on a matter of some delicacy. If we might speak in your study—"

Clarence Frome rose at once, pleased at having his advice requested with such urgency. "Of course, of course! Come to my study, and bring your glasses, gentlemen! Deborah, I am sure you need no assistance in entertaining Monsieur Rigaud."

"Of course not," murmured Deborah.

"Mr. Vaughan will come with us," said Lord Treverly, moving with nervous energy toward the door. He paused only to smile down at Alice. "And I hope I have your promise to play for me another time, Miss Alice, when the criticism of Monsieur Rigaud does not cause you to take fright!"

She curtseyed and smiled up at him. He bowed

to her, then more formally to the others, and followed the squire from the room. William Vaughan hesitantly went after them, giving Alice a final look which was not missed by her sister.

Deborah found the next hour almost unbearable. She kept losing the thread of the conversation for she could think of nothing but the icy contempt in Morgan's eyes. He had believed the squire! He did not believe that Deborah had refused him because of family pressure, because of the threat to young Alice. She must convince him somehow, she must make him see how desperate she had been! If only he would believe her! Their love could then blossom as if the seven years they had been separated had never existed.

Yet a doubt crept in. Were all her hopes a mere dream that could never happen? What if he had truly forgotten her over the years? What if some other woman had stolen her place in his heart? Yet he had not married; she had always taken comfort from that.

Paul Rigaud finally took his departure. Gertrude returned soon after, and was greatly irritated that Lord Treverly had called without notice.

"But he came to talk business with the squire. They are still in the study," Deborah assured her. "Perhaps they will remain for dinner, though."

But that suggestion only brought more moaning from her sister. Nothing was prepared that could possibly be offered to his lordship. If only she had had some warning—was one day's notice too much to ask?

They would set the table to include the guests,

Gertrude finally decided, and sent Deborah to the still wet garden to see if there were any flowers that could be used. Then Deborah must hunt out mint-spiced candles, polish the silver epergne, and fill it with something, Gertrude ordered desperately.

Gertrude consulted the cook, who offered some suggestions for amplifying the menu. Deborah and Alice set the table carefully and filled the epergne with daffodils and yellow and purple crocuses drawn from all the vases in the house, and a few last drenched ones from the garden.

The drone of voices still came from the study. Gertrude dashed upstairs to change her afternoon gown for something more stately, probably her dark blue satin. Alice went up to the bedroom and changed to yellow silk with a charming low bodice and a bertha of white lace. Deborah fingered her own gray gown. She had nothing brighter to wear, only other gray dresses and two black ones.

When the squire finally emerged from the study, Gertrude at once captured him and demanded, in a low tone, if the gentlemen would condescend to remain for dinner.

"Well, well, I shall ask them. I'm trying to find the plans for the common and the south acres," he said fretfully. "It seems Lord Treverly means to plow them under this spring. Dear me, whatever did I do with—"

The door to the study was open, and the two gentlemen were talking softly as Deborah slipped past. She wondered if they would remain. She might go up to her room and at least find the strand of pearls her mother had left her, and put them on. They might brighten up her gray dress. After all, Gertrude had put on her diamond choker.

The voices from the study rose slightly, and Deborah caught her own name, and froze.

"Was not Miss Deborah Stanton the lady of whom you spoke to me once, Morgan?" asked his cousin, in a rather compassionate tone. "The one who sent you the cruel letter as you were going into battle?"

Deborah would not have moved from the spot had she been dragged. The cruel letter! As he was going into battle?

"The same," said Morgan flatly. "I fancied myself in love with her. Indeed, we were supposed to be in love, I believe. Love! She knew not the meaning of the term, and I was like any young hothead, about to go off to war. How one deceives oneself!"

She pressed her hand to her breast. She knew she should move on, but she could not. She had to hear every harsh word.

"And now you have returned, wealthy and with a title," said his cousin, with a lightly mocking tone. "Is she setting her cap for you? I rather fancy the younger one myself, sweet and pliable!"

"A charming girl, quite pretty," said Morgan. "Would make a fine wife, I think."

"And you no longer fancy the middle sister?"

There was a pause. Deborah held her breath, afraid to miss a word. "She is—sadly aged," he said finally. "I should not have known her. Gray of face and very thin. I suppose she has worked hard. Well, she could have had a different life with me," he said.

"You have probably had a fortunate escape," William Vaughan said casually. "She was too anxious for security, not the sort of wife a soldier needs. Well—what do you think we shall do with the pasture? Plow it under, or save it for the horses?"

"We must think further about it," said Morgan.

Deborah finally moved now, and once in motion began to run, her hand clutched to her breast. She felt as though she could not breathe. In the privacy of her room, she collapsed on the bed. Her fists clenched the bedclothes in an agony.

She is—sadly aged. Sadly aged.

The words echoed again and again in her ears. She could not seem to understand them. *Sadly aged.* We were *supposed* to be in love, he had said, callously.

Supposed to be! Oh, Morgan! She pressed her fist to her mouth to hold back a cry. Sadly aged. He had never loved her! He had understood nothing! He had not waited for *her*; he had simply not found anyone to make his wife!

Oh, Morgan, Morgan, did I know you at all?

It was some time before she could rise. She straightened her hair, but she did not look for her pearls. In fact, she avoided looking in the mirror at all, knowing she would see a gray face, staring eyes, a frozen look.

She made herself go down, hoping they had

left. But no, they had remained for dinner. Lord Treverly and the squire apologetically continued their business discussion through much of the dinner hour, to Gertrude's barely restrained impatience. There was much to discuss, for the tenants had been neglected for more than two years, since old Lord Treverly had taken sick. The sons had never cared for anything but taking money from the estate.

Lord Treverly spoke of bringing in a stallion and some mares; he would take up breeding, he said. Gertrude muttered a protest; this was scarcely a fit subject for the dinner table. Alice suppressed a grin and met the twinkle in William Vaughan's eyes as he sat across the table from her.

Deborah could not smile, could not even raise her gaze to either of the gentlemen. *She has sadly aged. Sadly aged.* The words rang again and again in her ears, shutting out all other sounds.

After dinner, Gertrude turned to Deborah as they left the table. "I wish you would go upstairs and make sure the children have had their dinners," she said fretfully. "You know, that nurse is not reliable. Do see the children to bed."

Deborah nodded and left the company with a murmured excuse. She was conscious of the cynical look on Lord Treverly's face, the raised eyebrow as she obeyed her sister at once.

He did not know with what relief she left his company. In the children's schoolroom, where they finished their dinner, she automatically corrected Jenny's manners, halted Tommy's mischievous play, and finally saw them washed and put to bed.

The viscount's carriage was just rolling away when she went to her own room. She stood at the window and gazed out at it through the still-falling rain.

"Oh, Morgan," she whispered. "And I waited for you! I wanted so much to see you again! Now I cannot bear to look at you. You hate me, you hate me!"

If only she could bring herself to hate him also.

CHAPTER FOUR

Deborah slept little that night. She brooded over the words she had overheard, bitterly held them up to view, yet could reach no conclusion but that Morgan had come to hate her. He must have received her letter about not marrying him just before he had gone into battle, and the rejection had hurt him deeply.

"Oh, Morgan, Morgan," she would whisper, turning over to bury her face in the pillow, and hot tears soaked the linen before she could sleep even for a time. "I would not have hurt you for the world. I still love you so deeply. And I did wait for you, though you never wrote a word to me."

On Wednesday morning she could scarcely bring herself to set forth for Lady Horatia Torrington's. Gertrude again refused her the carriage, for she disapproved of these "jaunts," as she called them. They could come to nothing, she said. "She is only amusing herself with you. You will see, she will cut off all acquaintance when she becomes bored."

"I promised to come this morning," said Deborah firmly, and set off on foot again, with the great canvas she had primed rolled under her arm. Lady Horatia had promised to supply a stretcher and an easel. She carried her paints and brushes in a hold-all, and before she had gone many steps, the materials seemed heavy.

It was a gray and misty day, and her outer garments were soaked through when she arrived. Lady Horatia instantly showed her disapproval.

"After this, I shall send my carriage for you each morning," she said, shaking her head at the sight of Deborah's drenched feet and cloak. She took the canvas which Deborah had kept dry beneath her cloak. "And you shall keep your materials here. Dear me, I should have thought to send the carriage today."

Deborah apologized for the trouble she was causing. She was so miserable, she felt like apologizing for her very existence. She dried herself before the glorious fire in the great drawing room, but could bring little enthusiasm to the task ahead. After all, she had but a small talent; everyone said so. How dared she presume to paint a portrait of the great Lady Horatia Torrington? Gertrude was right. The woman must be amusing herself.

However, Deborah forced herself to tack the prepared canvas to the stretcher and then set out her paints. She wore an old black dress today, and over it she donned her painting apron with its huge pockets to hold brushes and palette knife. She set out her jars of brushes and oil, the palette and paints, and set to work. She had already given much thought to how she wanted to pose her subject.

Lady Horatia was inclined to chatter at first. Deborah did not mind; she could catch the woman's changing expressions. For today, she would be satisfied to rough in the outline, the full figure of the lady in her grand purple taffeta dress and tall purple turban, with the gold Japanese screen behind her. She was seated in a dark red velvet chair of rounded Queen Anne styling. Her feet, covered by amusing tip-tilted slippers of Moroccan origin, rested on a hassock of red velvet.

She made a striking figure with her alert eyes and proud head. Deborah was soon absorbed in her work, sketching the outline, then beginning to block in some of the colors she would use.

Lady Horatia did not seem to tire; she would stand up and stride about for a time, then relax into the chair again, speaking of some travel adventure, some strange person she had met. Deborah worked until almost two, and Lady Horatia did not stop her, but she studied her little friend thoughtfully.

When the clock chimed, Deborah started and stood back from the easel. "Two o'clock! I thought it was but twelve! I cannot believe—"

"I shall order luncheon to be brought in to us. Come, my dear, sit down and relax."

"Oh, first I must wash my hands and set the brushes to soaking. I had not meant to remain to luncheon today—" Deborah was flustered. She had become so absorbed in her work, she had lost track of time.

Lady Horatia rang for a maid and insisted that Deborah remain for the afternoon. She was glad enough to do so; now that she had stopped working, she realized her neck muscles were tense, and her back ached with the unaccustomed strain. And she had worked nervously, trying to forget about Morgan and his cruel words.

The two women had a delightful luncheon near the fire. Lady Horatia was silent for a time, as they consumed soup, with hot bread, then a delicate veal and rice dish she said she had first sampled in Arabia. Over the chocolate custard, she still spoke very little, seeming to be absorbed in her thoughts.

The maid served coffee, then left them. Finally Lady Horatia looked thoughtfully at Deborah.

"My dear child, you will think I am the most interfering old woman in the world."

Deborah jumped a little, and withdrew her gaze from the blazing fire to stare at her hostess. "My lady, I would never think—" she began. "You are the kindest soul, you have shown me every courtesy—"

"Then pray tell me what makes you so very unhappy today. I cannot but admit I have heard every deep sigh of melancholy you have uttered this morning, even when you seemed most deeply involved in your artistic endeavors."

Deborah flushed and looked down into her coffee cup. "Oh, it is nothing. I mean—something—"

"Your elder sister? Has she been disagreeable again?"

"Oh, yes, but I do not mind. That is, she can be thoughtless, but I *have* promised to look after the children as often as I can—no, no, it's not Gertrude."

"Surely not the squire? He strikes me as a shrewd man, yet very kind of heart. Surely I am not mistaken."

"No, no, he is indeed amiable. He has shown Alice and me every kindness."

"And Alice adores you too much to cause you any hurt," said Lady Horatia, pouring out more coffee. "So it must be someone outside the family. If you do not wish to confide in me, I shall understand. After all, you have not known me very long, and cannot be sure of my ability to keep a confidence. You must believe I gabble about my friends to every chance acquaintance, since I have been so free in my speech to you."

"Oh, no," said Deborah, squirming miserably. "You must not think I hold so poor an opinion of you, my lady."

"I cannot but notice how different you are today from Monday. Perhaps the effort of painting is too much?"

"It isn't that. Oh, believe me—it is Morgan," Deborah blurted out, then clapped a hand to her mouth in dismay. "I mean—I did not mean—"

"Morgan? You mean, Lord Treverly? You knew him before this?" Lady Horatia was mentally sitting up and taking notice, though she still leaned back idly in her chair, her eyes half-closed.

Deborah nodded and again turned her gaze to the fire. "Yes, I knew him. Seven years ago."

"Ah, and you cared for him?"

Deborah gave a great sigh.

"You loved him?" asked Lady Horatia, stirring her coffee.

"I am so ashamed," whispered Deborah.

"Ashamed of loving? Never be ashamed of that. It is a glorious feeling, a heightening of the senses and the mind. It is when we love that we have some little understanding of our great Creator, who loves us. Even when the love is not returned, the emotion is not one to be ashamed of. One carries on, with dignity and perhaps with more compassion for others." And she in turn gave a great sigh.

"But what if—what if he shows contempt and—and does not understand why one did what one did?" Deborah blurted out, pressing her hands to her hot cheeks. "Oh, he must not comprehend—he does not realize—"

"I do dislike a story told back to forwards," Lady Horatia said softly. "Do start at the beginning, my dearest Deborah. Tell me the whole of it. It shall remain in my bosom, I promise you."

With this encouragement, Deborah told her the sad story. "I met Morgan—I mean, Lord Treverly, only he was not Lord Treverly then—I met him here in Lowbridge. He would come to visit his uncle, Lord Treverly. And he was so kind, he seemed so interested in me. We had much in common. We would talk for hours about—oh, history and literature, and his life as a soldier. It seemed that on all subjects we would agree, but even when we disagreed it would only make us laugh. My father seemed to like him too. When—when he declared his love for me, I could only respond that I returned his feelings. We—we swore to love each other forever."

Her voice shook, and she dropped her face into her hands. Lady Horatia eyed the bent head thoughtfully, but said nothing. Finally Deborah resumed the story.

"My mother was very ill, but no one thought she would die. I was so happy, I believe I was not thinking at all. I promised to marry Morgan on his next leave. I did not worry that we would have to get along on his salary—it seemed enormous to me —nor that we would have to move constantly. I wanted to go with him wherever he went, wherever they would allow me to follow."

Her thin hands twisted together as she gazed into the fire, recalling that brief happiness.

"And then your mother died?"

"Yes. Morgan had just left. Father was away, as usual. He was often gone for a year, sometimes two years. He depended on me very much. Gertrude was about to be married to the squire. We were all much involved in the wedding preparations. Then Mother took sick again and, before we knew it, she was gone. We called Father home."

Her slim shoulders drooped.

"And Morgan?" murmured Lady Horatia.

"I wanted to marry him. I saw no difficulty. Rather, it would work out well. Alice would go to Gertrude and her husband. The house could be sold—I did not really think, I fear. I considered only Morgan. Then—then Gertrude said she would not take Alice. She would not bring her sister, still a child, into the house when she had just married. I think, now, that she might not have asked Clarence about it. She wanted only to be alone with him."

"What was to happen to Alice?" asked Lady Horatia.

"Gertrude said a housekeeper would have to be found. There was no money for a governess. Alice would be raised by a stranger. And Papa said he would forbid my marriage. I was too young, and besides, I must take care of the house."

"And take care of him."

"Oh, he was not ill at that time. I wrote to Morgan, explaining the situation. He came home and stormed at me, said I did not love him. I explained the situation with Alice, but he did not seem to understand that Gertrude had refused absolutely to have Alice. Alice left alone, abandoned by everyone she loved! Can you imagine the horror of it for such a gentle girl?" Deborah turned to Lady Horatia, to find the older woman eying her with such sympathy that tears filled Deborah's eyes.

"And so," said Lady Horatia, "you denied yourself your own happiness, sent Morgan away, and continued in the house. Then your father had his sad accident, and you nursed him until his death. And upon the death, the squire sold the house, and you both moved in with him. What did Gertrude say then?"

Deborah frowned a little. "She did not seem to mind then. I suppose because her marriage was not new—"

"*And* she had small children," Lady Horatia added gently.

Deborah nodded.

"But Morgan—Lord Treverly—has returned. And he no longer loves you? Yet, he has not married."

"I thought there was still hope, until I saw him," Deborah whispered miserably. "Then, yesterday, he came to visit with his cousin William Vaughan. I—I overheard them speak of me."

"What did he say?"

"He said—he would not have known me. That I was sadly aged." The bitter words, so familiar now, were difficult to repeat aloud. She forced herself to report the other remarks she had overheard. "He did not understand what I had done. He did not understand at all."

A little silence fell. Deborah felt rather relieved; there was much comfort in talking to Lady Horatia about her problems. She might even have words of hope and comfort to offer. Perhaps she would counsel patience until Morgan once again turned to her.

"Must you wear your hair in that ugly knot?" asked Lady Horatia abruptly.

Deborah turned wide eyes toward her. "Ugly—knot?" she asked, dazed. Her hand went to her head. She had hoped for comfort. Was the lady mad?

"Yes, yes, your hair is quite curly, but sadly flattened by that peculiar style."

Deborah waited. Why was the woman insulting her? Had she mistaken the lady?

"You know, Deborah, gentlemen set great store by appearance. Oh, they say they do not, but nevertheless, I have seen a great beauty with little brains draw an elegant, wealthy gentleman to her, a gentleman, moreover, who professed to hate stupidity! A plain girl must have five times the dowry of a pretty one, and the right connections also, to marry well. That is the way of the world.

You are no longer in mourning, are you, for your father?"

Deborah began to perceive which way the wind blew. "No, but you see, I have only mourning garments, which Clarence kindly bought me. My other dresses grew so old-fashioned that I gave them away."

"Alice does not wear mourning, nor your elder sister," reminded Lady Horatia. "Well, well, I think I know where we shall begin. First, I should like my maid to look at your hair and style it for you. She has elegant taste and good judgment in such matters. Then, I should like your promise that you will come out of mourning. Wear colors, my dear! With your complexion, your dark hair and eyes, you can wear vivid colors. And white would become you also."

"Dresses—but they would be expensive—"

"Do you not have money from the sale of the house?" asked Lady Horatia bluntly.

"Clarence manages it for us. It is invested."

Lady Horatia raised her slim eyebrows slightly. "Then you must ask him for some funds. I would suggest white muslin for day, and for evening wear, a ball gown of rose and white, another of blue crepe—"

She sent for her maid, who was delighted to have a young lady on whom to experiment. Lady Horatia was firm: Deborah was to have curls across her wide forehead, and about her ears. "And throw away those wretched black and gray gowns," she advised. "Or put them in the back of your closet, if you must be frugal. But do not wear them, should you wish to charm your young man again! Think of yourself as a young lady, and you shall be regarded as such."

Deborah went home in a daze of wonder. Lady Horatia seemed so sure. She peered at herself in the mirror of her bedroom. Yes, the hairstyle was decidedly more becoming. And her eyes sparkled with hope. She knew her eyes were her best feature, large and glowing, dark brown, with luxuriant lashes. With more color in her cheeks—Lady Horatia advised frequent strolls in the garden—more sleep and rest, she might regain her looks.

She went down early to dinner, to find Gertrude fretful over her daylong absence. Gertrude stared at her sister, frowning at the new hairstyle.

"What have you done to your hair, Deborah?"

"The style was too severe, Gertrude—suitable perhaps for mourning, but no longer," she said mildly. "I wish to ask you and Clarence for some funds. I have been in mourning for over two years, and that is quite long enough. I should like to purchase some new dresses."

Gertrude took a deep breath, and her face flushed. "You want *what?* Do you think Clarence is made of money? He has just given you a vast sum to purchase paints and canvas. Do you think, miss, that you have but to ask—"

"I could use some of my own money," said Deborah, with the courage of desperation.

"What do you mean, your own money? You are not married, and when you are, your husband will wish to have command of your dowry. Indeed, Deborah, I fear you must have a fever! Or else that woman has put ideas into your head, beyond your station!"

"My station! What is my station, sister?" Deborah's cheeks flushed with anger. Her brown eyes defied her sister.

Gertrude began to speak, then clamped her mouth shut, her blue eyes cold with anger.

"I am not *really* a governess, Gertrude," Deborah said firmly. "Alice and I are guests in your home, here because of the kindness of your husband and you. But I *offered* to help with the children, no more!"

Clarence strolled in, attracted by the women's raised voices. He eyed his wife speculatively, then turned his attention to Deborah, taking note of the new hairstyle, such a contrast to the unbecoming gray dress.

"Dear me, whatever is going on?" he asked mildly.

"I did but ask—"

"She was impertinent!" exclaimed Gertrude. "You were good enough to take her in, and Alice, and now she is becoming insolent!"

"What did you ask, Deborah?" Clarence's voice was patient.

"For new dresses, Clarence," she replied, rather subdued. "I—I am weary of black and gray. It has been over two years now, and Alice has new dresses—she will have another new one for the cotillion this Saturday—"

Suddenly she felt tired and depressed. It was a losing battle. To have to beg for her living! First she had had to beg for household money from her father, even while she slaved away to nurse her mother, care for Alice and the house. Then his pension had ceased on his death and she had nothing, though the house had been left to the three sisters equally.

"It is Lady Horatia who has put grand notions into her head! She will be wanting to be presented next!" sneered Gertrude. "I think that young Frenchman and his compliments have bedazzled her!"

Deborah could only stare at her sister, appalled at the insults her simple request had elicited.

"Well, well," said Clarence. "It does not seem unreasonable. You are young yet, you want amusements and pretty dresses. Why do you not buy them? Go to the dressmaker in town, she will take your measurements."

"Clarence!" cried Gertrude. "We have run up such a huge bill! You said I could buy nothing more until that was paid off!"

"A bill for yourself and for Alice," said Clarence, his voice mild but firm. "Deborah has had no new garments since those purchased for mourning. Yes, my dear, do pretty yourself up. I dislike black and gray. You have my word on it—buy what you will. Some day dresses, and a pretty gown for Saturday —is there time to have one made?"

"Oh, Clarence, you are too good!" Deborah clasped her hands tightly, and beamed at her brother-in-law through tears. "I cannot thank you—"

"Nonsense! It is we who should thank you. How careful you have been of the children! Up all night nursing them. We must make sure you do not get so tired in the future, eh, Gertrude? Deborah must attract a beau of her own. Alice is going to be married off one day also. My word, how the gentlemen will apply to me! I shall quite enjoy it," and he beamed at his wife and sister-in-law.

"Deborah—married? There's been no thought of that for years!" cried Gertrude. "She is too old for that now!"

"Old? At twenty-five? Nonsense. She is of a lovely age, and experienced in housekeeping and the care of children. Some man will find himself quite lucky one day, my dear Deborah." And Clarence patted Deborah's shoulder. "You must think of me as your brother and confide in me, Deborah, should a young man catch your attention. Alice is no problem—except, of course, that I must make sure of the character of the young man, for she is inclined to be flighty. But she attracts all men like bees to honey! But you are inclined to be sober and quiet, and very sensible. I am sure you will choose wisely."

"You are so kind, I cannot thank you enough, Clarence," said Deborah, with genuine gratitude. She suspected Clarence understood quite well why his wife was so angry. Gertrude probably thought her middle sister would remain with them as governess to their children, and take care of them until they were grown, after which she would be contented with a cat and a rocking chair before the fireplace. But Deborah wanted more than that, much more.

When Clarence had left the room, Gertrude

warned that her sister should not take advantage of his kind nature.

"Be careful, Deborah, a dress or two is sufficient! I shall not endure your running up large bills on some mistaken notion that you are still young and flirtatious! And I really do *not* think you need attend the cotillion this Saturday!"

"I really think I shall," said Deborah, her mouth compressed, her eyes flashing.

Alice was equally amazed when she heard that Deborah was going out on Thursday morning, to spend the day at the dressmaker's. "But Deborah, I did not think you cared about pretty dresses," she said simply.

"Not care?" Deborah wanted to snap her sister's head off. "Not care!" But Alice looked so innocently taken aback that Deborah forced herself to calm down. "Of course I care. It is just that—oh, recently, I have been too tired to care. Now I am recovered, I shall go about and dance, and play cards, like all the other young ladies!"

"Oh, that is splendid! What color ball dress shall you buy? I shall wear blue, and Gertrude plans to wear her green."

"Rose, I think," said Deborah, with a deep sigh of pleasure. Morgan had kissed her when she wore rose. Would he remember that? Or was she being as foolish as Gertrude said?

Deborah and Alice walked into town the next day, and chose to visit Mrs. Bertin's shop. Though Lowbridge boasted three dressmakers, Mrs. Bertin had the latest styles and the quickest needle.

Alice seemed to take as great a pleasure in choosing the items as Deborah herself. They pondered earnestly over a white muslin with a rather daring low neck, and another more demure one with a lace scarf. They finally chose the one with lace, and some rose ribbons to tie beneath the breasts. Deborah felt years younger when she put the gown on. She had not realized how shapeless were the dresses she had worn for so long. Mrs. Bertin promised to make her another at once, in a rose color, and still another in pale blue.

Then she asked about a ball gown. Mrs. Bertin pondered, her finger pressed to her lip.

"I received a model gown from London last week, but the lady for whom it was intended decided it did not fit her. We shall try it, you are much slenderer than she."

She took out the dress from its muslin sheeting and held it up. It was a white crepe sheath, simply made in the new Grecian style, with a square neck, short sleeves, and a short spencer of red. Deborah tried it on; the straight lines of the dress set off her charming slim figure, just indicating the rounded bosom. With her hair in curls to her shoulders, she looked lovely, Alice declared.

The gown cost twice what she had planned to pay, but the style was so becoming, she could not resist. She purchased red slippers to match the spencer and two bonnets, one for everyday wear and one for dress.

Recklessly, she even bought new underclothing in chambray and silk, new white mitts in lace and satin. When Mrs. Bertin learned they had not come into town in the carriage, she tactfully arranged for her own carriage to take them home with all the bundles.

Deborah promised to come back the following week to try on the other new garments. "And I shall look out for a lovely Scottish plaid for you, Miss Stanton," said Mrs. Bertin. "I think a lovely red and blue plaid would be charming."

They added a blue velvet cloak, and went home quite exhausted but exhilarated. Gertrude looked over all the purchases grimly, but even her objections were swept away when she saw how Deborah looked, so young and radiant.

Her cool blue eyes softened. "My dear, how lovely you look. I had not realized how dull the gray and black were. Yes, Clarence was right, and I shall tell him so!"

Deborah managed to smile and thank her. She was eager to be alone, however, for she had something else to worry her.

While they had been in the dressmaker's, she had happened to notice several people passing the bowfront windows. Among them was Morgan. Her heart had seemed to burst—until she noticed he had a lady on his arm.

He was bowing and smiling, his lean face unusually animated. And then Deborah saw that the woman on his arm was Marie Andreossy, stunning in a smart red velvet cloak. She was so tiny next to him that he bent, as if devotedly, to hear what she said. Their heads drew very close.

Behind them walked Bernard Houdon, sleek in his black velvet—Deborah imagined it must be his customary attire—and swinging a cane. He obviously accompanied Madame Andreossy, yet he seemed to remain discreetly behind the couple so absorbed in each other.

A pang had struck Deborah's heart. Morgan was not only more experienced than when she had known him, but a prize catch! And evidently he had found Marie Andreossy much to his taste.

Even as the family chattered that evening at dinner, praising Deborah's purchases, teasing her about how fine she would be, Deborah could not banish the picture of Morgan, bent above the beautiful face of Marie Andreossy. Smiling at her! Happy with her! When all he showed Deborah was grim indifference, or icy contempt.

"What if it is all too late?" she whispered to herself that night, as she gently stroked the new garments before setting them away in wardrobe and dresser. "What if all this is in vain? Oh, how shall I bear it then?"

CHAPTER FIVE

Deborah dressed for the cotillion at the Village Hall that Saturday with both hope and fear in her heart. The white dress fit perfectly, and she knew it was very becoming.

"I have a bouquet of beauties in my carriage," the squire said with a smile, as the vehicle rumbled toward the hall. "Deborah, you look charming! You must save a dance for me."

"Thank you, sir, I shall with pleasure."

They were early, for the squire always liked to arrive before the festivities had really begun. This gave him the opportunity to talk with people in an easy manner when they were relaxed and preparing to be entertained, and in this fashion he learned of the problems and concerns of his neighbors. Gertrude hated to wait about, but in this he was firm. Indeed, they were often the first to arrive.

So it was this late March evening. A fresh wind blew from the west, whipping their skirts and the ribbons of their bonnets. March seemed to be making a last show of force before departing for another year. For trees budded, and early lilacs bloomed against the fences; it was almost spring, thought Deborah, with hope blooming anew in her heart.

Reverend and Mrs. Plummer arrived soon after the squire and his family. The Reverend had just been affirmed in the post by the new Lord Treverly, he told them happily.

"What a fine, honest gentleman he is," said Reverend Plummer, and Deborah could have kissed the man. "All concern, I found him. And after the years when the late Lord Treverly could not—um —pay much attention to the needs of the parish."

Rose Plummer chimed in with equal fervor. "And all attention when one speaks of any need in a family! He will not have starving people here, he said very firmly. What do you think of that? He had food sent to them at once, and inquired what work the men could do. I know he has employed four more gardeners and grooms at Treverly, just to provide work."

Deborah's heart swelled with pride at these words. Morgan had often expressed to her privately his dissatisfaction with the way his uncle ignored the villagers under his care and protection. And his cousins had cared for little but gaming— and females of low repute. Morgan was different. How splendid that he had inherited not only the title but the money to carry out his good purposes.

She wished she dared tell him how she admired him for this. But they were no longer close, and might never be again. Depressed by the thought, she turned to smile at the schoolmaster, Philip Irving, who came up to her at once upon entering the hall.

He could not stop staring at her. "Miss Stanton, I should not have known you," he said, in his usual solemn way. "You are splendid this evening. How you have blossomed out!"

He did not seem to approve entirely of her "blossoming out," thought Deborah. He himself was relentlessly serious in nature. Yet he had always liked her, and they had sometimes played as partners at whist, and shared interesting conversations about the politics of the time or books they had both liked.

She accepted his offer to stand up with him and took his hand to be led out for the first dance. She saw that Clarence was leading out Gertrude. He would undoubtedly dance with Mrs. Plummer next, for he was always proper in such matters. Another glance told Deborah that the French party had not yet arrived. Nor could she spot Morgan's tall, elegant figure.

In fact, it was over an hour before Lord Treverly's party arrived. She was sitting in a corner with Mr. Irving when she saw them. Her heart sank to the toes of her red slippers. Morgan had Marie Andreossy on his arm, and Bernard Houdon followed with an attractive young woman, Paul with another. And William Vaughan escorted an older, plump woman who must be a chaperone of some sort, she thought. Morgan must be having a houseparty! Yet she had heard nothing of guests. But then, should anyone have told her of it?

Squire Frome went up to Lord Treverly and his party at once, followed by Gertrude, splendid in pale green. As the leading citizen of Lowbridge, the squire often took it upon himself to act as unofficial host of such functions. Lord Treverly led out Gertrude, but after the first two dances, the party seemed to break up. The gentlemen strolled about the hall, pausing to drink something or to speak to the other guests. There was no coldness about them, no standing apart. They appeared to be cordial to everyone.

Deborah waited and waited. She stood up with Philip Irving again, and then the Reverend Plummer asked her to sit out a dance with him. He rarely danced, but he enjoyed a good chat. And all the while Deborah waited, a smile fixed rather desperately on her face.

Morgan finally approached Alice. He bowed low before her, and took her hand to lead her into the grand cotillion dance. This was the one in which little prizes were awarded, favors from the gentlemen. Deborah watched numbly as Alice received a gold-papered fan and a golden thimble. Deborah did not even participate in the dance, for Philip Irving had deserted her to sit with several young matrons at the side of the room.

She might as well still be in gray, like the mouse she was, Deborah decided bitterly. She turned from the sight of William Vaughan asking for Alice's hand in the next dance. The girl was so popular. Surely Deborah was not jealous of her own beloved sister! *Yes, I am,* she thought to herself. *I have descended so low!*

William Vaughan presently appeared before Deborah and smilingly bowed to her. "I declare, I scarcely knew you, Miss Stanton! I had just about determined that you must be ill and had not attended. Then I asked who the fair stranger was, and to my surprise, Miss Alice said it was you!"

Deborah flinched a little. Had she changed so much? She took his hand, and went to the center of the room. Almost numbly she answered his bows, circled the room, went through the movements of the dance. Morgan was circling the room with one of his pretty house guests. Surely he must look at her eventually! Now, now, he was coming ... at the last moment, his handsome head turned from her; he was smiling down at his partner and did not see Deborah.

She returned to her chair, a dull rebellion rising in her. What must she do to attract his attention? Get up on a chair, whip off her red spencer and wave it in the air? The ridiculousness of the thought brought a genuine smile to her lips, and she relaxed a little. Perhaps Morgan, like his cousin, had thought her to be a stranger.

When Lord Treverly finally came up to her, she was chatting with Lady Horatia Torrington, the latter rather overpowering in a Chinese silk gown of red and gold, with a gold turban on her graying hair. "Here you are, Lord Treverly," said Lady Horatia. "Here you are. You are enjoying yourself, are you not? You have scarcely ceased to dance this evening!"

Morgan bowed to them both, gracefully but a little stiffly. Deborah wondered if his leg still hurt him.

"Good evening, Lady Horatia, Miss Stanton. You look very animated yourself," he said to them both. "Miss Stanton has danced often with the schoolmaster, I believe. Are you serious about him, Miss Stanton? He seems much in earnest." He smiled as though in jest, but his eyes were hard.

"We have much to talk about, sir," she said in a low voice.

"Ah, yes, you have a serious nature also. Your sister informs me that Mr. Irving is most devoted."

Lady Horatia raised her slim eyebrows at Deborah, as though to indicate that at least Lord Treverly was interested enough to observe another man's attentions. Morgan finally asked Deborah to stand up with him.

When he took her hand and escorted her to the center of the large hall, she trembled a little. She had longed for this, but now that the moment was here, she felt dizzy and confused. How did Morgan feel about her now? How could she begin a conversation with him? She longed to talk intimately with him, but judging by his cold expression, she was sure his feelings did not match hers.

"I am happy that you have returned safely," she began hopefully. But someone went by them just then, laughing loudly, and her soft words were drowned. Morgan turned to glance down at her.

"I beg your pardon? What did you say?"

She swallowed nervously, and tried again. "I —I am so happy that—you have returned safely."

"Indeed. I am happy also," he said drily. He handed her to the next man, and she went on to the next. By the time she had returned to Morgan, he seemed to have forgotten she had ever spoken.

She tried once more. "The Plummers are most delighted with your interest in the villagers in Lowbridge."

"I hope I shall always see my duty and do it properly," he said. "However, I do not care to have my actions publicly discussed."

She could only stare at him in dismay. Then the dance was over, and he left her with a bow. She made her way blindly back to the wall, where Lady Horatia soon found her.

"Well, well, it is a beginning," whispered Lady Horatia encouragingly, seeing the downcast face.

"He is so cold, so indifferent—"

"Nonsense. It is the first step. He will ask you again to dance, and you must lead him on!"

Deborah perked up at that. However, Morgan did not come near her. Philip Irving took her in to supper, and they talked for some time about a difficult pupil of his who had much potential but no money for further schooling. Deborah wished she could speak to Morgan about the boy, but knew she could not.

After supper, Paul Rigaud, immaculate in a dark blue silk coat led Deborah out to dance. "How very charming you look this evening, mademoiselle!" he began. "You must not be offended if I say that I did not recognize you when I came in this evening. How lovely you look!"

His manner was so warmly appreciative after Morgan's chilliness that Deborah smiled up at him.

"How can I be offended? I have put off mourning," she said brightly. "I did not realize how dull I seemed!"

"You are like a butterfly coming from its cocoon," he murmured in her ear. "I saw the potential, in your beautiful eyes, your lovely face. Yet even I, who usually scorn fashions and frills, could not help but see how much more beautiful you are in a smart gown. And your hair—charming!"

His flattering attentions, however effusive, were soothing to her wounded sensibilities. She chatted happily with him through the dance and was further flattered when he begged permission to sit down with her and Lady Horatia.

"I have not seen much of you and your compatriots this past week," commented Lady Horatia, fanning herself vigorously with a palm leaf fan. "Perhaps there is some other attraction, eh?"

"Oh, my lady," he said quickly. "We do not ignore you! We had heard you were sitting long hours for your portrait, and when Lord Treverly kindly requested us to make up a party, we did so. He has guests staying at Treverly, you know."

Lady Horatia lifted her lorgnette and gazed critically and long at some of the ladies. "Yes, yes, so I see. Pray, tell me, who are they, Monsieur Rigaud."

"The lady is the widow of Lord Treverly's commander, and the two girls are her daughters. They have been well-acquainted ever since he was a young officer. Indeed, he treats them like his own mother and sisters. I believe they are going on to London for the season."

Lady Horatia let the lorgnette fall to her lap. "May one gossip? Is he more interested in one young lady than another?"

Paul Rigaud tapped his lip and looked mischievous. "He is one to keep his own counsel, I believe, Lady Horatia. However, I am privately of the opinion that he means to marry soon, and who could do better than to choose such a charming young lady as the one on his arm just now? Young, lovely, pliable, she would always yield to his somewhat autocratic will. *And* give him fine sons and daughters. A man might do far worse."

Deborah followed his gaze and gave a violent start. The lady on his arm was her own sister Alice! Deborah watched as William Vaughan approached them, and they paused to speak. But the young man was apparently dismissed and went off to choose another partner. It seemed Lord Treverly meant to dance again with Alice. Deborah watched them with a pang. Alice was so young, so pretty. And he smiled down at her, he *smiled!* Just the way he used to smile at her, so tenderly.

"Yes, yes, you have a beautiful sister," Paul Rigaud murmured into Deborah's reluctant ear. "And she is so young, so pliable! One looks for a girl like that, when one wishes to settle down, *non?* What a hostess she will make for him! Not of your superior intelligence, yet she would not cross him. And he is of a strong nature and firm will. It would be just as well for him to choose such a one."

Lady Horatia had turned away to speak to another woman and did not catch his words. Deborah, however, heard every word clearly, and each bit into her heart like an adder. She felt so dizzy, she was afraid she might faint.

Paul Rigaud offered to bring them some refreshment. Deborah asked for ratafia, Lady Horatia for sherry, and he went off with a good will.

"A nice young man," said Lady Horatia. "I think

he has a *tendre* for you, Deborah! He has been most attentive."

Deborah shook her head, a little blindly, trying to follow the whirl of Alice's blue skirts.

"But I want—" she said in a low, choked tone. Lady Horatia put her hand on Deborah's.

"My dear," she said quietly, "you would not be the first woman to have to settle for second best. It is the man who proposes, and Lord Treverly strikes me as a man who will do his own choosing. If he wishes a wife whom he can mould to his will, let him choose one. I should dislike seeing all the spirit crushed from you!" She tossed her head, as though recalling some experience of her own.

Paul Rigaud appeared with their drinks and proceeded to amuse the ladies with his witticisms and his many stories. He was very attentive to Deborah and quite scowled at Philip Irving when the lanky schoolmaster came up to ask her to dance. Deborah smiled mechanically at them both, and went to stand up in the dance.

Her head was beginning to ache, partly from the warmth of the room, partly from the growing certainty that Morgan did not intend to come near her again. He seemed to hover near Alice constantly, as Gertrude observed to Deborah in an excited whisper when they met later in the evening.

"Our little Alice is quite a success tonight! I knew the blue dress would become her. How elegant Lord Treverly is; look at him bow! One would think he had had the title all his life!"

Deborah could scarcely believe her sister's callousness, until she realized that Gertrude probably did not even remember Deborah's own involvement with Morgan, so long ago. They watched William Vaughan come up to the handsome couple, and a moment later he led Alice away. Lord Treverly looked after them thoughtfully.

"You see, he is jealous of her!" whispered Gertrude happily. "Only observe how he gazes after her, as though he could not be done looking! How lovely she is tonight!"

"Yes, yes, Alice looks beautiful," Deborah said hurriedly, determined not to seem mean-spirited. She noted how William Vaughan also seemed to gaze down into Alice's face, and to hold her carefully, as if to protect her from the couples pressing in all around them. Paul Rigaud claimed her next, then Lord Treverly was back, and Gertrude again must comment on his attentiveness. Deborah sat back in the corner with her sister, marveling that Gertrude had completely forgotten her own role in ruining Deborah's chances of marriage to Morgan. *We could have been married seven years by now,* she thought. *Seven years.* The pain of it almost caused her to gasp.

The evening seemed to drag on and on—the evening which Deborah had anticipated with such joy. Her simple gown now seemed unremarkable next to the lovely gauze and velvet dresses of Morgan's guests, the brilliant scarlet worn by Marie Andreossy. Morgan seemed now to be dividing his attention between the youthful Alice and the mature, sophisticated Frenchwoman. What a contrast! Could he not make up his mind what he wanted in a woman, Deborah wondered savagely, torn with pain. Did he want naïveté or worldliness? Gentleness or assurance?

At any event, he did not want her! For he did not come near her again. She looked about when the evening was nearly over and discovered that Lord Treverly and his party had departed. No doubt to continue their amusements in private, at Treverly Hall.

With the departure of the elegant party from Treverly, the dancing began to break up. Clarence Frome gathered his three "pretty ones" about him and led them out to the carriage.

"Well, well, what a successful, delightful evening," he said happily as they set out, huddled in their cloaks against the now fierce March wind. "Did you enjoy yourself, Gertrude?"

"Oh, very much, as always, Clarence."

"And you, Alice? But I do not need to ask," he added with a laugh. "I do not think you sat out more than half a dozen dances."

"I did enjoy myself," said Alice with a happy sigh.

When Clarence turned to her, Deborah was prepared. "And you, my dear Deborah? Happier in your new finery?"

It would be ungracious to admit how miserable she felt; she smiled and nodded. "Quite an enjoyable evening, Clarence. Several people commented on my gown and praised my new hairstyle. Several even said they scarcely knew me," she added, trying to keep the bitterness from her voice.

"Of course not, of course not, scarcely knew you

myself in your new dress! You may buy another ball gown if you choose, Deborah. Sure to be more occasions now that Lord Treverly has come home. I admire the chap myself, and he certainly has good taste in women!"

He chuckled heartily, and Gertrude automatically chided, "Clarence, do not be indelicate!"

The conversation turned to who had been present, and who had not, and what Lady Horatia had said to Mrs. Plummer, and how the schoolmaster had stood up with Lady Horatia and done creditably.

But the final crushing blow for Deborah came the next day. She had spent the morning with the children, reading them Bible stories suitable for Sunday. The afternoon stretched long before her; she thought she might take a walk.

Gertrude came up to find out how her "chicks" were faring and ordered them all to take a rest. The nursemaid took over, and Deborah left the rooms with Gertrude. Her older sister halted her in the hallway, twin spots of color on her cheeks, blue eyes excited. Her plump form was encased in a splendid gown of silk and gauze, in anticipation of afternoon callers.

"My dear Deborah, I am so happy! Alice has confessed to a great interest in Lord Treverly!"

"What?" exclaimed Deborah, turning pale. "She said—did he say—"

"Of course he has said nothing. It is too early; it would not be proper. However, she showed me the favors he had given her. The bracelet is real gold, my dear!"

Deborah felt rather sick. She groped for the railing of the staircase as they went down together to the next floor. Gertrude seemed to muse, a happy smile on her lips.

"My dear Alice," she said finally, "a viscountess! It could happen, Deborah. Only think of it, our little Alice!"

"Do you think he has—truly engaged—his affections—" Deborah stammered.

"I think so. Only consider how he hovered about her last evening! Everyone remarked on it. And Lord Treverly is not one to be obvious in his attentions, if he is not serious. I am sure he is not a sad flirt. You may depend on it, Deborah, he is becoming serious about our Alice. And he could not find a dearer, sweeter girl! Imagine, she'll be called *my lady!*"

Gertrude left her then, and Deborah rushed to her bedroom. She could not face anyone else today. This was too much. She admitted it—she was sick with jealousy and hurt.

Morgan must have forgotten her completely. He was indeed seeking a wife, but not the girl to whom he had vowed his constant love and affection. He had put her from his mind and heart.

In her bedroom, she wrestled with her sisterly affections, and her deep love. She could not bear it. She wanted the best for Alice, truly, but—but not Morgan! She could not endure that Morgan should turn to her sister!

Her head went down on her arms, and it was so silent in the room that the robin perched on the windowsill dared to try a tentative note or two. The figure did not stir, so he stretched his throat and gave out a beginning trill, busily composing his notes for the coming spring melody.

CHAPTER SIX

The changing weather brought colds and coughs. The children enjoyed running about in the garden, whatever the weather, and soon four-year-old Jenny was down with a severe cough and chest pains. Tommy soon followed and was not nearly so patient as his sister in his illness.

Gertrude hated all forms of illness; she herself was strong as a horse, she often said proudly. However, she dared not risk catching the cold. She must remain fit if she was to fulfill her role as the squire's wife. Would dear Deborah take care of the children?

Numbly, Deborah agreed. What did it matter? Her pretty new gowns hung, untouched, in the closet. Once again dressed in her drab gray gowns, and at night in a warm dark robe, she sat with the children, sang to them, read to them, dealt patiently with their fretfulness.

The nursemaid had removed the baby and Frederick to another section of the nursery, away from the risk of infection. A maid brought meals to Deborah, and tea trays. Gertrude sent up affectionate messages daily.

Lord Treverly and his guests were entertained at dinner one evening by the squire. The maid who brought her meal told Deborah about it excitedly.

"They are all so grand, Miss Stanton! Imagine the gauze and golden scarves, the jewels, the grand manners of them! The table is set for twenty covers! Lady Horatia Torrington is here also, and is wearing a purple satin Chinese robe."

Deborah could hear the chatter and laughter even up on the fourth floor, for the downstairs windows and French doors were open; the early April night had turned rather warm.

Deborah knew that Alice wore white gauze, and Gertrude her green. She had caught a glimpse of them descending the stairs. She had stood like a gray ghost at the top of the nursery stairs and watched for a time, hungrily, hoping for a glimpse of Morgan. But the bend in the stairs hid most of the first floor from her. A child called fretfully, and she sighed, and turned back to her nursing.

The long broken nights and wearying days soon took their toll. She grew thinner and seemed to care about nothing. What did it matter? He had said she was already aged. He had danced but one duty dance with her. He had forgotten her completely.

When one was tired and worn, she thought, the whole world seemed gray and forbidding, and no hope gleamed for a brighter future. It was hard to hold onto one's dreams when the spirit was crushed. She tried to remind herself that she was needed. It was important in the world to be needed, she told herself.

She brushed the tears from her cheeks, scolded herself vigorously, and tried to take some interest in the tea tray the maid had brought up. Alice had arranged on it a vase of spring flowers and sent it up to Deborah with an affectionate note: "How we miss you, dearest Deborah. I long to come to you and have a good coze, but Gertrude forbids it. Do be careful, and do not become ill yourself."

Yes, she was needed and loved. Yet—yet—

Deborah was still young. She still hoped. She thought of Morgan, pictured him strolling with Alice in the garden. Or with Marie Andreossy in his handsome drawing room at Treverly. The fascinating woman with the sad eyes, the provocative accent, the experienced air of a mature woman. Which did he prefer, which haunted his dreams? Or did he sleep peacefully, with no woman to haunt him? Did he think only to marry the woman who could be most useful to him as Lady Treverly? Somehow, Deborah could not imagine him coldly choosing a suitable wife, yet it was done, she thought, it was done.

And then there were the houseguests; either daughter of his former commander might do well. Both girls were handsome, well-mannered, with backgrounds similar to his own. They would know the talk, the gossip, the friends, the battles, the politics.

She tantalized herself with all these thoughts until she could not sleep even when the children rested quietly. And during the following week, when they began to regain their health and high spirits, she slept less than ever. Now they demanded constant attention, or else they would get up and run about and exhaust themselves.

It was more than two weeks before Deborah was free of her duties. She emerged to find that the squire, Gertrude, and Alice had gone to tea at Treverly. Deborah would have been asked, but Lord Treverly understood that she was taking care of the children, Gertrude wrote in a note to Deborah. When they came home, Gertrude learned with delight of the children's recovery but said, "How pale you are, Deborah! You are not getting sick, are you?"

"I don't think so, Gertrude. I have merely missed my walks outdoors."

"Lady Horatia has asked after you frequently." And a little frown drew her eyebrows together. "She seemed to feel I was abusing you! I assured her it was your choice to care for the children, that you are immensely fond of them. She wants to resume the sittings soon, but I told her she must wait."

The next day would be Wednesday, and Deborah could have insisted on going to her session with Lady Horatia. Yet she felt so weary she could not bring herself to think of resuming her work on the portrait. She shook her head. "That can wait, Gertrude."

"I told her so, I told her so! Monsieur Rigaud has also asked after you," said Gertrude cheerfully. She gave Deborah a sly look. "I would think you had a devoted beau. However, he seemed more concerned that you had promised to show him some of your sketches. He admires your artistic talents, it seems."

"He is most kind."

Gertrude finally went away. Deborah wearily went to her room where she propped her chin on her hands and gazed out at the garden. The dusk was settling gently on the spring flowers, the blooming apple tree. How lovely it was. If only there might be spring in her heart. She felt as if she might live in winter forever.

Morgan had come here, but she had not seen him. If the children had not been ill, she might have visited Treverly with the others, seen Morgan in his own setting, admired his possessions. Alice had shown great interest in his treasures from abroad, or so Gertrude said.

How Deborah wished she might have gone. Even though he would have treated her with cold courtesy, she would at least have *seen* him, studied his handsome aristocratic features, heard his stories.

She sighed and dragged herself to her feet. She must rest, or she would be ill herself. It was not like her to allow herself to brood so.

The night brought little relief, though, and the next day she felt she must get outside. She was like a prisoner too long denied the sun. There was no sun today, yet she must find a brief escape.

In midafternoon, she set out wearing sturdy shoes and a dark cloak and bonnet. She felt as gray as the day, and there were new lines on her face. She was indeed aging, she thought wrily.

She walked automatically, and only after half an hour of striding across muddy fields did she realize she was walking toward Treverly. She was daydreaming again, and that was no good. She must forget the past, or she would grow old and embittered before her time.

She continued her walk, but at a safe distance from Treverly. She strode through muddy fields which would soon be plowed. Some apple trees were in bloom, their pink blossoms bright against the gray sky. She looked at the gnarled branches and longed to paint them, with their incongruous pink blossoms. How old and weary they looked— like herself, with the blossoms of one of Lady Horatia's elaborate bonnets set above her drawn face!

She was amused at her own fancies, but felt brighter and happier for getting out, although the wind was now almost too brisk for comfort. She walked on, past Treverly, giving it a shy little glance. She did not want to be discovered near Morgan's home yet could not resist studying the lovely lines of it. It had been built as an abbey more than five hundred years ago, and the ruins had become the foundation of a fine manor house. Cotswold gray walls, turning golden and mellow from long centuries in the sun, rose up three floors. She had heard there was a large center hall, with great rooms opening from it. In the back was a long hall with massive French windows, and a ballroom.

Alice had told her of the decorations in the drawing room—all in plum and gold, she said. Morgan had ordered some changes to be made even before he arrived at Treverly, so that the house he occupied was far different from that of the dreary days of old Lord Treverly. "All is fresh and new, with velvet draperies. He has the heraldry pattern on the walls, two red leopards rampant on a gold field. It is so marvelously executed in woven panels."

The description had excited Deborah's imagination. How she would have loved to help him decorate! However, he did not seem to require any aid, not hers at any rate. She wondered briefly if Marie Andreossy or one of the commander's daughters had assisted him. She pushed the thought away with determination.

It began to rain then, a steady, misty rain that soon wet her cloak and bonnet. Reluctantly she turned back. She must have been gone two hours; they would wonder what had happened to her. Only one of the maids had seen her go out.

She passed the great Hall as the rain began to come down in earnest. If only she could go in and ask for shelter! A beggar maid at the gates, she thought fancifully, and went on, her head lowered against the driving rain, finding some comfort in the fresh, cold spring air. The winter was over, the children were well now, and she would take up her painting again. She must forget Morgan, as he had forgotten her.

A figure in her path startled her so much that her hand flew to her breast. She stared as someone came toward her in the gray mist. She let out her breath in a sigh as she saw it was Morgan.

As though her thoughts had conjured him up, she thought.

He stared at her as they came toward each other on the muddy path through the fields. He was dressed in tweeds and high boots, and carried a gun over his arm.

"Miss Stanton! What are you doing here? Did you come to see me?"

"To see you? No, my lord," she said with a composure which she herself could not help but admire. "I was merely out for a walk."

"In this rain!" He was close enough now to see that her black cloak and bonnet were soaked. He frowned down at her, though his own bare head and clothes were getting drenched.

"Yes, sir, it was not raining when I started out. I felt the need for some air."

She began to go past him. He put out his hand and took her arm. "But you are soaked to the skin!" he said. "You cannot go on like this! It is a good mile to the squire's. Come with me."

"Oh, I thank you, but no. I shall not mind the walk. I told you I wanted the air."

"You are wet through! And you have been nursing two children with colds for weeks. Do you wish to become ill?" He actually sounded angry with her, she thought.

"No, of course not. However, I am quite strong. I merely wished some air—" She began to feel like a fool, repeating her words, when he obviously thought her behavior absurd.

His arm tightened when she would have gone on. He held her to the path before him.

"You will come into the Hall with me, and get dry. You need some brandy to warm you. Then I will drive you home," he said, in quite a human tone, and his eyes seemed genuinely anxious.

"I am in no condition to go calling, Lord Treverly," she said formally, glancing down at herself. She was a little shocked to see how muddy and wet she really was. "As you see, I am not looking my best—"

"As to that—neither am I. I went out to walk— with my gun—never mind. You shall come in by the side door. My guests are amusing themselves with cards in the drawing room, but we shall not disturb them if you do not wish to see them." He sounded angry and impatient, yet concerned for all that.

She began to make excuses again. He shook his head stubbornly and pulled her along with him until she gave up and walked alongside him, his hand still firmly on her arm.

He was as good as his word and led her in by a side door. The butler came to them at once, his eyes wide at the sight of the two bedraggled figures. Morgan said shortly, "Have the fire lit in the sitting room at the back. And have a tray of brandy and hot tea brought at once for Miss Stanton. Do not inform the guests I have returned. We wish to be private."

"Very good, my lord," said the butler and showed them to the room. A footman came at once to light the fire, and a blaze soon burned brightly. Deborah stood before the fire, holding out her chilled hands to the flames.

Morgan set down his gun and laid his hat and gloves on a side table. Then he approached Deborah. "Let me take your cloak," he said, and had his hands on her shoulders before she could refuse.

He took off the cloak and laid it carefully on a

chair near the fire. She would have refused to remove her bonnet, but he insisted.

"It is wet too," he said angrily. Silently, she unfastened the ribbons and took off the bonnet. Her hair was sadly flattened; indeed she felt a wreck. And in her shapeless black dress, the old boots—how he must despise her, she thought.

"Pray sit down when you wish," he said, drawing up a large comfortable chair for her.

She smiled slightly. "I will wait until I am more dry. The hem of my dress is quite soaked," she said, and drew closer to the fire.

"You have not been at home to us these two weeks," he said abruptly. "You do not choose to join the company at dinner, I believe."

She glanced at him in surprise. "Surely Gertrude told you I was caring for the children? They were so ill that the others were kept from them, so that no one else would take cold."

"So she informed us. I found it difficult to believe you were so very fond of—someone else's children!" The sneer in his voice was unmistakable.

She felt her cheeks grow warm and turned her head from him. She disliked seeing the scowl on his handsome features, the black look, she used to call it, when he was angry or displeased.

"I am fond of the children, yes," she said, in a stifled tone.

"And you are still willing to bow down to your elder sister and obey her slightest command! That is what I found so difficult to comprehend. You seem to have intelligence and spirit, yet you meekly give way to her at every turn! She commanded you not to marry, so you would not. She commanded you to take care of your youngest sister, so you did. And your father was as bad—"

Deborah raised her hand to her throat. The attack had come so quickly, she was not prepared.

"Alice would have been abandoned," she said with dignity. "I told you this. And Father—Father disapproved. He would have—have annulled our marriage. He said so."

"Nonsense! You bowed under to them, like a meek-spirited chit!" He was pacing the room now, careless that his muddy boots made marks in the handsome red and gold carpet. "Clarence Frome himself told me that he wished to take you in. He would have cared for you all."

Deborah set her lips in a tight line and gazed in silence at the fire. Morgan glared at her, then turned abruptly as the door was opened. A footman carried in a huge silver tray bearing a tea pot, cups and saucers, a brandy bottle and glasses.

"Good, good, that is what you need," said Morgan.

Deborah felt even a swallow would choke her. So Morgan thought she had lied to avoid marrying him!

"Come and sit down," he ordered abruptly. She wanted to refuse, but under the curious look of the footman, she did not dare cause a scene. In silence she sat in the huge chair near the fire. He poured a glass of brandy for her and set it down on a small inlaid table of rosewood near her hand.

"Will you require the carriage, my lord?" asked the footman.

"In about half an hour, at the side door," said Morgan curtly. The footman bowed and left them.

Half an hour. Half an hour. That was how long she would have with him alone, thought Deborah, the glass trembling in her cold hand. And he was angry with her. She could not speak to him of her hopes, of how she had waited for him. He had obviously not waited for her; he felt only contempt for her.

She sipped at the brandy, and gasped as it burned its way down her throat. Morgan had poured a glass for himself and swallowed down half its contents without any sign of discomfort. He eyed her ironically as she sipped more cautiously.

She set the glass down. "It is too strong for me," she said. "May I have some tea? Then I shall be on my way. I need not trouble you any longer. There is no need to drive me home—"

"No! Do you imagine I would let you walk a mile and get soaked all over again. You have no common sense!" he said harshly, and poured out some tea for her.

She drank it hastily, hot and dark, burning her mouth. She longed to be away from him. He was cruel, cruel. When she had drunk half the contents of the cup, he took it from her and poured brandy into it.

"There, that will do you more good than plain tea," he said.

Then he retreated somewhere behind her. She thought he must have picked up a book or some object to look at. At any rate, he seemed to have nothing more to say to her. She cupped the drink in her hands, letting the warmth penetrate her chilled fingers.

She looked around the room nervously, and her attention came to rest on a painting, above the mantel, of a sweet-faced woman dressed in a costume of about two hundred years before. Above the ruff was a round chin, a gentle mouth, a narrow straight nose, and dark gray eyes, something like Morgan's. The hair was short and curly, blonde and pulled back from a broad forehead. Her dress was gold, and on the full and elaborate sleeves were embroidered two red leopards. The insignia of the Treverlys.

"An ancestor of mine," said Morgan abruptly, from behind her. "About six generations ago or more. I have not figured it all out yet. There are books in the library on the family genealogy. However, I have been so busy restoring the woodwork, taking up carpets and replacing the draperies, that I have not had much time to read."

"She has a lovely face, full of character," said Deborah, studying the portrait.

"She was married at fourteen to a man twice her age," said Morgan. "She gave him six children, of whom three died before the age of two. She herself died in childbirth at the age of twenty-five."

"How—how sad," whispered Deborah. Twenty-five. Just her age. And this lady had been married eleven years, and borne six children!

"You might be interested—another day—in seeing more of Treverly. The art objects would probably interest you." He spoke with such cool indifference that she could not express her enthusiasm at the thought of seeing his home.

"Alice—Alice said you had brought back many lovely objects from your travels." She lifted the cup and swallowed the liquid as though it were a bitter brew.

"She is very gentle and sweet." His voice softened when he spoke of Alice, and her heart sank further.

"Yes, she is wonderfully good-natured," agreed her sister.

"And you raised her, I believe. Your mother was too ill to care for her," said the disembodied voice behind her. She wished she could see his face. Was he interested, or merely making conversation?

"Yes, Mother was ill from the time of Alice's birth. I took care of her as well as I could. Then, when Mother died—well, you know what happened," she added in a low tone.

"You seem to have a stern conscience where your family is concerned. I am sorry for any man who might love you and wish to marry you. Your family always comes first with you."

Deborah gasped. He was deliberately insulting her! "I am sorry you feel that way, my lord. My sister is now grown, and should marry soon. I am no longer responsible for her, for my brother-in-law has kindly taken on the care of Alice and me. He is very good to us."

"So good that you are now obliged to bring up his children for him!" Morgan appeared at her side and poured her another cup of hot tea, adding some brandy. She could not see his face, as he bent forward to pour.

She was trembling. "I am but obliging them

while I live there. And I do not see what concern it is of yours!"

"Oh, it is not, except that everyone in Lowbridge is my concern as Viscount Treverly," he said, with a cold sneer. He came to stand in front of her, brandy glass in hand, and leaned against the side of the mantel, staring down at her as though mocking her wan looks, her shapeless black gown, her disheveled state. "I understand the schoolmaster wants to marry you."

"Then your understanding is far greater than mine, my lord!" she snapped, her eyes flashing. "He has never said so, nor have I encouraged him."

"No? You merely sit out most of the dances with him, and everyone couples your names. Monsieur Rigaud was most desolate at the talk. He had considered that he had made a conquest of you himself. He said he admires your—mind—and your talented fingers!" His gaze openly mocked her, as though he were thinking that there was little else about her for a man to admire.

"He is most kind, my lord." She lifted the cup, drained it, and stood up. "I am going now," she said abruptly. "You have been most courteous." She could not truthfully say more, for in fact his courtesy had ended when they entered the house. He must find it impossible to be civil to her. "Pray, do not bother to accompany me."

He caught her arm. "Stubborn as ever," he said. "You'll go nowhere until I say you may!"

Roughly he yanked her to him, and she felt the warmth of his body against her own. She gasped, looked up at him, and felt the shock of his lips against her cheek. He pulled her closer, his hard arm like an iron bar behind her.

His mouth closed on her opened lips, and she felt his breath as her own. He kissed her with anger and fire and dislike, she thought. He was so rough with her, his mouth made her lips sting.

She tried to turn her head, but his hand caught in her hair and brutally held her still. His mouth roved over hers, fastened again on her lips with a hard pressure that took her breath away.

He held her long, until her struggles ceased, and she leaned against him, her hands helplessly clutching his sleeves. Her breasts were crushed against his hard chest. In pent-up fury, his mouth took its toll, forcing her to receive his kisses.

Then he put her from him, holding her at arms' length while he gazed down at her, his eyes still blazing with anger.

"There, miss, you can think about that!" he said, as she blinked and stared up at him in bewilderment.

A knock sounded at the door.

"Come in!" he called, and set her farther from him.

"The carriage is ready, my lord," the footman said, looking curiously at Deborah, her crimson cheeks and trembling mouth.

"Very well."

He picked up Deborah's cloak from the chair. "It is still damp. When you get home, I advise more brandy and a long rest before the fire, Miss Stanton," he said very calmly, as though he felt no more than ordinary courtesy toward her.

114

She followed the footman in silence. At the door, Morgan handed her old black bonnet to her. She fastened the ribbons with shaking hands; she had forgotten all about her bonnet, but was now grateful for its shelter.

Morgan followed her out to the carriage. She had thought he would leave her to the coachman to be driven home. But no, he was following her into the carriage, helping her up with a strong hand at her elbow. She sank back on the velvet squabs, feeling as if she had been turned upside down, shaken thoroughly, and set back down very hard.

During the drive home he made polite conversation. The rain would do the fields good. He would come over in a week for a conversation with Squire Frome concerning the common fields. She must be sure to take more care and not walk in the rain again. He might return to London with his guests.

He let her out at the door, but refused to come in, explaining that he was too wet, and besides, he must return to his guests.

She managed to thank him. "You have been most kind, my lord, though you should not have troubled yourself." She could not raise her gaze to his face. She knew his eyes would be mocking her.

"Not at all. It was my pleasure, Miss Stanton," he said, and bowed as the butler opened the door to her. He was gone, leaving her to wonder if he did mock her, or whether he had truly found some pleasure in her company, in the kisses he had forced on her lips.

She went inside, dazed. Fortunately Gertrude

was upstairs changing her gown for dinner, the squire was engaged with guests, and Alice was nowhere in sight. She made her way alone up to her room, to strip off her still damp dress and sit for a while in her dressing gown, absorbed in wonder.

He had kissed her. In fury? In dislike? Surely it was so. Yet had he felt some other emotion for her at the same time?

She knew only that she loved him more than ever, despite his harsh words.

She thought of those words. Meek-spirited. Doing whatever her sister ordered. And he had not believed her when she had said that Alice would be left alone if Deborah had not taken care of her.

Her slight elation vanished as the effect of the brandy died. She brooded before the window, gazing through the dusk and still-falling rain toward Treverly Hall. She had been there, a mere hour ago, with Morgan.

Did he still despise her? Did he fail to understand her at all? Could he truly believe she was so weak that she had let her sister rule her life?

Or was it true, what he said? Again she examined her feelings. Gertrude was selfish, yes, but would she truly have left her youngest sister alone, in the care of a stranger? Would the squire have allowed it? Or would their knowledge of what the neighbors would think have forced them to take Alice in? Could Deborah have compelled them to remember their duty to her? Would her father have cared enough to annul her marriage, had she acted against his wishes?

She held her aching head in her hands, and did not know any answers at all.

CHAPTER SEVEN

Deborah began to regain her strength once more. She took brisk walks every day, and sometimes Alice accompanied her.

Her younger sister seemed to have acquired a glow, a bloom, and her eyes were often dreamy. She was now given to strange silences. Deborah eyed her uneasily, fear growing in her heart. Had Alice fallen in love? And if so—with whom? Was it Morgan who had managed to capture her girlish heart?

She wished the best for Alice. However, she had not recently observed Morgan with her young sister. If he truly loved her and Alice loved him, it would be a fine match, thought Deborah, trying to stifle her own pain at the idea. However, if Morgan was merely playing with her, or meant to marry only for the sake of having an heir, then—then—

Oh, it was so hard to know what was right and best! Deborah would walk in the garden, pacing up and down absently, scarcely seeing the early tulips and daffodils, the first buds of the lilacs. She thought of Morgan's kisses on her mouth. Had he kissed her only in anger, or did some feeling for her remain?

On Saturday Gertrude told her that Lord Treverly and his cousin were coming to call that afternoon.

"I think dear Alice has an admirer," beamed Gertrude, clasping her hands excitedly. She looked quite blissful. "He has not returned to London, he no longer even speaks of going back for the season! And his guests have departed; he and his cousin are alone."

She contemplated the mantel with much satisfaction. Alice and Deborah had gathered some early flowers and set them in porcelain vases.

"Deborah, would you make some of your special cakes for tea? It only wants that to be perfect. Lord Treverly is still quite thin, you know, and has an enormous appetite, I've noticed. Poor dear, he was quite badly fed in the wars, I believe."

Deborah was glad to retreat to the kitchen and make some almond cakes, which she knew were his favorites. She also made some chocolate cakes and some cream-filled pastries, for the others. Alice came to help her, and decorated them skillfully.

"Do you not think Mr. Vaughan is quite handsome, Deborah?" she asked suddenly.

"Mr. Vaughan? Oh yes, quite." Deborah sent a quick look toward her sister.

"He makes me laugh," said Alice softly. "I feel quite at ease with him. He is devoted to Lord Treverly, and told me of many kindnesses done him by his lordship. His family has only moderate means, and he is the third son besides. Lord Treverly has set up the two older brothers in trade and will finance them until they are on their feet. But Lord Treverly requested that William come to live with him, to assist him in managing the estate."

"They do seem very close, and to have much regard for each other." Deborah was interested in this information about Morgan, which confirmed her opinion that he was good-hearted and helpful to his relatives, as well as to those who looked to him on the estate.

"Lord Treverly told me that William had twice saved his life," went on Alice, with a flush in her cheeks. "I think he is very noble, don't you?"

Deborah was not sure which gentleman she referred to, but felt safe in saying, "Yes, of course. Very noble."

"I shall wear my pink muslin today," said Alice, after a pause. She set the last cakes in the oven and closed the door on them. "There! Will you take them out, Deborah? I want to sew a fresh ribbon on my gown."

"Of course, my dear." Alice ran off, and Deborah looked after her wistfully. She was so sweet and gentle, one could not help loving her.

When Deborah had finished the cakes she checked briefly on the children. She found them in the nursery, demurely drawing and painting. She praised their work, settled them to their luncheon, and went swiftly to change to her new lilac muslin with the purple ribbons. As she brushed her hair carefully into curls, she looked anxiously at her face. Surely she looked more rested now, surely she did.

Luncheon was a rather hasty affair; Gertrude was anxious to have everything in order when the gentlemen called. And her haste was rewarded, for the guests arrived quite early, about two-thirty, in a fine black phaeton drawn by two magnificent horses. Squire Frome hurried out of the house to admire them.

"Oh, they must not linger out there," muttered Gertrude, rushing from window to door and back again. "Oh, dear, why does he not bring them inside? They did not come to discuss horses, I am certain!"

Ten minutes sufficed for the horses, then the groom took them back to the stable. When the gentlemen came indoors, Gertrude at once came forward to greet them, followed by Alice. Deborah hung back a little, recalling her latest meeting with Morgan.

Did he seem conscious of her, embarrassed? No, she did not think so. He looked quite relaxed. He wore a fine plum jacket today, with buff trousers and high black boots polished to a gleam. How handsome he was. Did he limp so much? She thought he still seemed to favor one leg more than the other.

She finally came forward as he turned to her. He took her hand and bowed above it, but scarcely looked at her.

"Good afternoon, my lord." Once she had called him Morgan, had lovingly placed her hands on his cheeks, and kissed him. Did he remember also? She glanced up to his gray eyes and found only distant courtesy there.

"Good afternoon, Miss Stanton. You seem well today," he said in a level tone.

"Yes, I am, thank you." They turned away to the drawing room, and Morgan took the seat on the sofa beside Alice. They began to chat about his houseguests who had just left, and who had sent their best regards to Miss Alice.

William Vaughan looked longingly at the straight chair on the other side of Alice, but very properly seated himself beside his hostess. The squire sat down in the huge chair he favored, opposite them, and took out his pipe.

"Well, well, sunshine at last," he said genially.

The weather took up quite ten minutes of conversation. Then Gertrude asked after his guests, knowing they had departed, trying to conceal her joy that they were gone.

"And do you go up to London?" asked the squire. "Proper season they'll have."

Gertrude looked as though she would have liked to kick her much-loved but blundering husband.

"We may do so, it is not decided," said Lord Treverly coolly. "Much depends on how matters go here. The estate has been left neglected for too long, but William is giving me a hand with it." And he gave his friend a smiling, appreciative look.

Poor Deborah would have given much for such a look. She folded her hands in her lap, wishing both to participate in the conversation and to shrink away, unnoticed.

The talk was general, and Morgan and the squire showed no indication of wishing to speak in private. Deborah was afraid they would remove to the study at any moment, and she would scarcely see Morgan again that afternoon.

"What a fine garden you have," said William Vaughan presently. "I noted when I came in how the flowers are blooming. It is most charming, with the trellises and the small gazebo."

"Thank you very much, I am sure," said Gertrude, much gratified. "Of course, it is not so large, nor so magnificent as the gardens at Treverly. Everyone admires Treverly so much. However, it is fine in its small way, and Alice is always arranging some flowers for us. She has a delicate touch with flowers."

Lord Treverly looked down on the blushing Alice and nodded. "I would have thought so," he said softly.

"I noted," said William Vaughan, determined not to be left out of the conversation, "that you have some rose bushes. We're thinking of planting a large rose garden at Treverly. And I think you should have a summerhouse, Morgan. It would be splendid, down near the lake."

"It has been on my mind," said Lord Treverly. "The gardens have been neglected for some time. However, other matters came first. Perhaps this summer we might take time to expand the gardens."

"Miss Alice could probably give us much advice," said William Vaughan. The squire concealed a smile behind his hand.

"You will have expert gardeners," said Gertrude. "However, Alice or I should be happy to give our opinions, should they be required. I myself think roses are the most splendid of flowers."

"I have always loved roses and carnations," said Alice. "However, Deborah favors the wilder flowers, columbine and violets, lilies of the valley and larkspur. Tell them, Deborah, how you have painted them."

But Deborah could say nothing, frozen into stillness by a single look from Lord Treverly. A look of scorn, of mockery.

The squire deftly turned the conversation. "Should you like to come outside and see the gardens? It is too fine a day to remain indoors."

Though his wife frowned at him, he had his way, and all the company moved outdoors to the gardens. Gertrude was mollified by Lord Treverly's praise of her plots and walks. Alice explained the varieties of roses and told which would bloom first, which did not flower until late summer. Deborah trailed them silently, miserably aware of Morgan's marked indifference to her.

"Why don't you show Lord Treverly and Mr. Vaughan the farther gardens?" suggested the squire presently. "Eh? I must return to my study for a time, but I shall join you for tea. Go ahead, you young people, have a nice long walk."

"That would be pleasant indeed," said Lord Treverly, and took Alice lightly by the arm. "Are you warm enough?"

Gertrude looked pleased by his solicitude. Deborah would have gone back into the house when the squire and his wife did, but Mr. Vaughan took her arm and urged her to accompany them on their tour of the garden.

"You must show us the flowers you love to draw," he said in a friendly fashion. "Have you painted many of them? Do you allow people to see what you have accomplished?"

She was forced to follow the first couple, now many strides ahead of them. It would not be proper for Alice to go off alone with a gentleman, so she must play chaperone for her sister and the man she loved. Deborah could scarcely speak pleasantly to Mr. Vaughan, so miserable was she.

"Here are the columbines," she pointed out to him. "They will become tall spikes of pink and lilac and blue, many varieties. They make charming arrangements to paint. And here are the patches of violets, see how they hide under the thick leaves in the shade." And she bent and tenderly brushed aside a thick leaf to reveal the budding purple violets beneath.

Lord Treverly and Alice had paused in their walk, near enough to hear Deborah's remark, and Alice turned back to see the first violet buds of the season.

"It seems a pity," said Mr. Vaughan thoughtfully, "that such beautiful flowers are hidden under great green leaves. No one can see them or appreciate them there."

"Oh, I think that is often true of nature, and of people also," said Deborah quickly. "The obvious are not always the most admired, are they? Nature has a way of concealing her beautiful flowers and plants from all except those that will take the trouble to seek them out. So it is with some people. A kind nature is not always noticed, unless there is trouble and help is needed. How much we value our friends who have been dear to us in difficult times, and do not regard their exteriors."

She turned her gaze from William Vaughan, to see Morgan regarding her somberly, his feet apart, his hands clasped behind his back.

"A pretty sentiment," said Mr. Vaughan, and turned to Alice. "And what is this rose bush, Miss Alice?"

Mr. Vaughan took advantage of the moment to draw closer to Alice and take her arm; Deborah remained with Morgan. He indicated the path by a jerk of his head. "Shall we accompany them, Miss Stanton?" he inquired.

So Deborah found herself following her sister and William Vaughan, accompanied by Morgan, who walked a proper two paces away from her whenever the narrow path permitted.

"You are fond of gardening, Miss Stanton?" he finally remarked, with obvious indifference.

"Yes, my lord." He did not even remember the times they had strolled in the garden of her own home. He did not recall when he had come to visit and caught her in an apron and gardening boots, tying up some vine or trimming a bush or removing small insects from the roses.

It was as though all that had happened seven years ago was erased from his mind, including his deep love for her. Engrossed in her bitter thoughts, she did not attempt to make conversation.

His shining boots became muddy as they walked on, following where Alice and William led. The light chatter ahead of them was interspersed with laughter. They walked through the garden, and beyond, to the wilder hedges and fields. Deborah thought of her light slippers, and of Alice's, but did not regard them. If Alice was happy—

Another burst of laughter came to them. Morgan remarked drily, "They seem quite in tune today. I wonder what they find amusing?"

"They—they seem to enjoy each other's company," Deborah managed.

"William Vaughan is a splendid fellow. Not a deep thinker, but you would go far to find anyone more good-natured and thoughtful of others."

"He seems so."

Another long awkward silence followed. She cast about frantically for another topic of conversation, but her mind seemed a blank.

"I understand," said Morgan, "that you are acquainted with a boy named Matthew Summersby."

She could not think for a moment, then she remembered. "Oh, yes. Mr. Irving has spoken of him to me. He seems to believe that the boy has great potential. In mathematics, there has been none to match him in the school."

"Mr. Irving—ah, yes. It was Reverend Plummer who spoke to me of the lad. He seemed to have some possibilities. I shall have him tutored and sent up to Oxford or Cambridge, as he likes. His parents are hardworking, but have little funds to draw on."

She turned to him impulsively. "Oh, that is very good of you, Morgan! I thought you would understand! The boy is so fine and intelligent—he needs help so badly—"

They had paused on the path. She gazed up at him, her eyes shining. He looked down at her as though from a great distance.

"Ah yes, Miss Stanton," he said curtly. "I believe the schoolmaster will also be greatly pleased."

"Yes, of course—my lord," she said faintly. She realized she had, in her agitation, called him by his name. She turned and walked on, her knees weak.

"You have lived in Lowbridge all your life, I believe, Miss Stanton?" he inquired presently, in a bored drawl.

"Yes." He knew quite well that she had.

"You should travel about a bit. It might amuse you, give you more to sketch and paint. I understand you and Miss Alice traveled some with your father on his holidays."

"That's correct."

He gave up then and walked on in silence, to where Alice and William stood. Both had a fine color in their cheeks. "Should we turn back? Miss Alice has muddied her slippers," said William anxiously, as though her possible discomfort mattered a great deal to him.

"Yes, yes, we have gone a distance." Lord Treverly offered his arm to Alice and began to stroll back with her. Mr. Vaughan must then give his arm to Deborah, and they followed.

Mr. Vaughan had a fund of idle chatter which occupied them both on the journey back to the house. Deborah was grateful to him, for she was busy berating herself for her stupidity. She had had all that time alone with Morgan, and had been unable to think of anything to say to him. Morgan, with whom she had talked by the hour! Morgan, whose mind had been attuned to hers, who had talked to her of books they loved, of history, of faraway countries. She had even once imagined herself traveling with him to Paris, Rome, Athens, exploring with him the wonders of Persia. How far apart they were now.

They returned to the house; the girls hurried to their rooms to change their muddy slippers. Alice was already back in the drawing room when Deborah came down; she could scarcely have wasted a moment, Deborah thought. Alice was chatting spiritedly with Lord Treverly, who actually had a slight smile on his face as he listened.

She had no trouble speaking to him. He did not feel awkward and silent with *Alice*.

Gertrude indicated that the tea tray should be brought in, but it was Deborah who poured for them all, glad to busy herself with the trays of pastries, the cups and milk and sugar.

"Alice made the cakes for you. Is she not clever?" said Gertrude.

"Very clever," said Morgan, and Deborah could detect no note of mockery in his voice. She had the satisfaction, however, of seeing that he ate her own almond cakes as greedily as a schoolboy. The squire got out a bottle of his finest brandy, and they finished their tea with that in high good humor. The talk was of horses, of the estate Lord Treverly was restoring, of Lowbridge and the changes in it.

Mr. Vaughan had given up all pretense of indifference to Alice. He sat on one side of her, his cousin on the other, and the three carried on a lively conversation. No loss for words there, thought Deborah. She was becoming increasingly uncomfortable when suddenly the nursemaid came quietly in and bent to whisper to her. "Mr. Tommy is crying for you, Miss Deborah. Could you come, please? It is his tooth."

She was very glad of the excuse to leave the company. The gentlemen stood when she got up to depart, and Morgan remarked drily, "You are in much demand—with the children, Miss Stanton."

"They are accustomed to me, sir. Pray forgive me for leaving you." She curtseyed and left the room, to speed up to the nursery where Tommy was crying wretchedly over his aching tooth.

She pressed Tommy's head to her aching heart. She ran her hand over the soft hair. There was little prospect that she would ever have children of her own, thought Deborah. The man she would have married despised her, and she saw nothing ahead but a bleak future. She would continue to care for Gertrude's children and assist in the running of the household. Clarence and Gertrude liked her, they would always be kind.

If only she could leave Lowbridge! How could she bear it, to remain here, the sister of the Viscountess of Treverly! For surely that was what Alice would become. She herself would be forced to see Morgan often—the loving husband of her sister!

"I could not bear it—Oh, it is evil to feel so jealous of my own beloved sister!" she whispered. "I do not want to feel like this!"

But she ached with suppressed desire. She longed for him, for his hard arms about her. She thought of his fierce kisses that afternoon before the fire. He had held her and warmed her with his body, until her blood had raced wildly in her veins, making her dizzy. She wanted him, wanted him to hold her again, wanted to become his wife and know all his passion.

Must she give him up again? This time, for Alice?

CHAPTER EIGHT

Deborah accompanied the family to church the following day and had the satisfaction of seeing Morgan ahead of them, with his cousin, in his family pew.

After church, she was busy with the two older children, as usual. Morgan glanced at her, then away again, but he spoke amiably to Clarence before turning his attention to Gertrude and then to Alice. He did not approach Deborah.

She stood, holding the hands of the two children, and felt miserably that she might as well be a maid in the household. Mr. Vaughan had given her a smile and a bow, then turned eagerly to Alice. Alice, so lovely in her pale blue bonnet, with her shining eyes and delicate face.

Deborah was silent on the way home as the others chattered. She felt almost desperate. Must she see him daily, and be ignored?

"Lady Horatia Torrington calls this afternoon," said Gertrude, with satisfaction. "And then Lord Treverly comes later. I cannot help believing there is some attraction in our home for his lordship!" And she laughed, and sent a teasing look at Alice, who was blushing.

"Who, Mama? What, Mama?" the children demanded.

They were immediately shushed, and the topic of conversation changed by Clarence. Alice hastened to put on an even more becoming gown at home, and Gertrude asked that luncheon be served at once.

They were gathered in the drawing room, awaiting guests, when the butler showed in Lady Horatia Torrington's French acquaintances. Gertrude frowned slightly, but went forward graciously to greet them.

"How pleasant to see you! We have not met for several days," she said.

After greeting Gertrude and the squire, Paul Rigaud came over at once to Deborah, took her hand and looked deeply into her eyes.

"And I have not seen *you* for a long time. It seems like months," he said in a low, significant tone. She felt rather flushed and surprised at his attentions. "It is a shame that you must be confined when the children are. Do they not have a nurse?"

"Oh, yes." She removed her hand gently, firmly, from his. "However, she took care of the two who were well, while I remained with the ones who were ill and kept them from the household."

"I missed you immensely," he said quietly, and she felt he was sincere.

"You are most kind, sir."

Marie Andreossy seated herself beside Deborah, with a rustle of her deep blue taffeta skirts. "My dear Miss Stanton, you are an angel of goodness.

I do not know how you manage to accomplish all that you do," she drawled. Her eyes flicked over the simple lines of Deborah's lilac gown. "Lady Horatia was gracious enough to allow us to view the portrait you have begun of her. Amazing! It is a magnificent likeness already."

"Oh, it is not nearly completed. It is but a poor study yet," began Deborah, surprised at Madame Andreossy's attentions.

"One can tell it is good," said the Frenchwoman decidedly, nodding her head in the huge blue bonnet. "One is gifted or one is not. And you, my dear Miss Stanton, are greatly gifted."

"You are very kind," said Deborah, in a low tone. She noticed that her brother-in-law was overhearing them, a thoughtful look on his kind, ruddy face.

Bernard Houdon said from his chair across from them, "I understand that your good father also possessed much talent, Miss Stanton. I hear he made portraits of many of the navy's finest officers."

"Yes, sir, he did. He was much in demand until his—his accident. He drew ports and ships. He was fondest of scenes of naval life."

"And do you have these scenes still? The oil paintings? They must enhance your home, Miss Stanton."

She hesitated. Gertrude had given away most of the oils, and the navy had the rest. "I regret we have few left, sir. The navy kept most of them. They are in ships' wardrooms, on various naval vessels, and in the Admiralty in London."

"You must be very proud of your father," said Paul Rigaud gently, daring to touch her hand which was nervously playing with a purple ribbon at her waist.

"Yes, sir, he had a magnificent talent."

Gertrude was impatient with the conversation. "How do you enjoy Lowbridge by now?" she said abruptly. "It does not offer much to entertain one, does it? You must miss London and the excitement of society. How kind you were to come to our ball."

"Not kind. We enjoyed ourselves very much. Such kindness, such courtesy to us poor strangers," murmured Marie Andreossy.

"I should not say I was amazed, however, I *was* taken aback several times to be addressed in French!" said Bernard Houdon. "Even in London, few are as fluent in French as in Lowbridge. I thought it a great compliment to us and to our former nation that many of the good citizens of Lowbridge have troubled to learn French, to continue to read French, and speak it to us."

"Good of you to say so," beamed the squire. "We are not so backward, then, are we? Yes, yes, country folk we may be, but you will find some well-read citizens among us. And Deborah here, she could teach French, she does so well."

"Indeed! Yet another talent, Miss Stanton?" Bernard Houdon turned his sharp gaze to Deborah. He always spoke so formally that Deborah was never sure whether his compliments were genuine or mocking.

"My brother is good to say so," she murmured.

"Let me try you," Paul Rigaud urged eagerly. "Miss Stanton, how do you do today?" he asked in French.

She blushed, but managed to reply, "I am very well, sir, and you?"

"Ah, a very nice accent. She probably learned from someone from the north, near Paris," remarked Bernard Houdon. "Miss Stanton, tell us of your talent in art. In France, if you went there, what would you sketch?"

Again in French, she replied, "I should like to sketch the charming cottages of which I have heard, the fascinating dress of the peasants, the harbors, the ships—"

Marie Andreossy was kind enough to compliment her again on her accent.

"Madame, pray excuse me if I blunder. I have spoken little French recently. If I make a mistake in my accent," said Deborah in her slow French, "please be so kind as to correct me. I would consider it a thoughtful gesture on your part."

They were still exclaiming that it was not necessary to correct her, she spoke so very well, when a carriage drew up, almost unnoticed, to the house. Clarence jumped up and looked out the nearest window.

"Bless me, it is Lady Horatia, earlier than she said." The squire started for the door.

"Are we in the way?" inquired Bernard Houdon. "Perhaps you expect many guests. We should have inquired before. However, manners in the country do not seem so formal as in the city."

Deborah begged him to remain. "Lady Horatia

will be happy to see you, I am sure. And of course we are less formal in the country. It is a pleasure to have guests."

Lady Horatia Torrington swept in, a vision in a gold crepe full-flowing gown, with a massive purple turban on her graying head, a brooch of gold in the form of a star on the turban. On a smaller person, or one with less self-esteem, the costume would have been overpowering. On her, it looked quite natural.

She greeted everyone politely, then turned to Deborah.

"How are you, my lady?" Deborah held out her hand, but was swept to that imposing bosom.

"My dearest Deborah, it has been too long!" and she kissed each cheek affectionately. "I have come myself to see why you do not call upon me! I heard about the children. Have you been ill also? I miss your visits. When shall you come again?"

"I long to come, Lady Horatia. I should like to resume the sittings tomorrow, if it is convenient for you."

"You may depend upon it! Come at ten, as usual. I shall send my carriage for you. Such gossip from London, and everyone else is bored with hearing me! I shall bend your pretty ear while you paint me."

She sat down and gave the company a commanding stare. "And what have you all been doing? What is the conversation? Have I missed any news?"

"Miss Stanton was displaying her command of the French language," said Paul Rigaud, having seated himself again beside Deborah. "You told me that people outside London were as cultivated as those within, but I doubted you until I met Miss Stanton. She could grace the finest society."

"Pray, Monsieur Rigaud—say no more, sir!" Deborah was embarrassed by the unaccustomed praise.

Paul Rigaud smiled down at her with an understanding look. In a low tone, he said in French, "Your modesty becomes you, mademoiselle! It but makes you the lovelier."

Lady Horatia's expression was bland, but Deborah was sure her friend missed nothing. "What is the news? What is the news?" she repeated, and Deborah was grateful to be the center of attention no longer.

"Well, my lady," Clarence was beginning, when the sound of yet another carriage came to them.

Gertrude was in a delighted fluster. So many guests, such distinguished ones, so many carriages rolling up! She did not know when she had been so happily excited. The squire had no pretensions; he strolled to the window and gazed out.

"Bless me, it is Lord Treverly and Mr. Vaughan, early also. We *are* popular today, my dear," he said to Gertrude. He went outside to greet the two gentlemen, his hearty laugh echoing in the April air.

Deborah's face grew pale and she clasped her hands nervously in her lap. Paul Rigaud noticed her uneasiness and pressed his hand on hers. "You are troubled, mademoiselle?" he murmured in French. "Pray tell me why."

"No, monsieur. It is nothing." The man was too keen.

Everyone stood as Lord Treverly entered, except Lady Horatia. He greeted his hostess, then turned at once to her ladyship and kissed her hand.

"My dear Lady Horatia, how do you do? You look in fine spirits. I had heard you were much depressed and had threatened to quit Lowbridge." His teasing voice seemed to make Lady Horatia a little cross.

"Indeed! How rumor exaggerates!" she said sharply. "I did but remark a few times that it had grown quiet. And I missed the visits of my dear Deborah, who is doing my portrait, you know. It seems too bad that she must be nurse to her nieces and nephews, with her fine talent."

A brief awkward silence followed, during which Lady Horatia glared up at Lord Treverly. He had a slight, polite smile on his lips, but Deborah thought he looked rather hard.

"Miss Stanton is indeed fond of her relatives," he said, and turned to greet Deborah. He bent briefly over her hand, and shook hands with Paul Rigaud, who once again took his seat next to Deborah. In the general flurry of greetings, the other remarks seemed to be forgotten.

The gentlemen and ladies were all seated. The squire turned the conversation to Lowbridge matters, a subject in which the Frenchmen were plainly uninterested. Paul Rigaud turned to Deborah and began a low conversation in French.

Lady Horatia leaned forward to hear. "What? What? I cannot hear you, Paul! Speak louder. You said to Deborah that you have come to detest politics? Why do you say so? You were keen enough in London, not so long ago."

"I did but say," Rigaud said patiently, "that it seems politics has become the evil demon of our age. Why cannot people live in peace with each other? Why must a difference of government separate us and make us go to war? I have begun to think deeply about this."

"That is *your* influence, Monsieur Houdon," said Lady Horatia, shaking her black lace fan briskly at the older Frenchman. "You are a deep thinker and have corrupted this nice young lad who was once so charming and flirtatious!"

They all laughed politely at her heavy humor.

Gertrude leaned forward and hissed to Deborah, near her, "What did they say?"

Deborah translated for her, and they all switched back to English. But soon, as they began to argue about politics and the influence of government upon people's everyday lives, they became heated, and the Frenchmen reverted to their own language once more. Marie Andreossy seemed less engrossed in the topic, and was attempting to flirt over the top of her ivory fan with Lord Treverly.

But he had begun to frown a little as the trend of the conversation reached him. "If you wish to keep politics from ruining people's lives, you had best refer to your Napoleon Bonaparte," he said abruptly. "The man is hungry for power. After the Revolution, you would have done well to limit the power one man can have."

"What could we do? We have had to flee our country, we have lost our lands, our votes," Houdon said, his palms raised expressively. Deborah noted how shapely his hands were, how white and graceful, not like those of a man of action, but a man of letters. Next to them, Morgan's hands, large and tanned, seemed roughened by work in the sun and riding without gloves.

"The government formed was that of councils," said Marie Andreossy, unexpectedly entering the conversation. Her sometimes melancholy face seemed to come alive. "We had high hopes. We thought we could return to France when the terrors were over. But no, our lands were taken. Those—those peasants wanted everything, yet they could manage nothing! The land lies in weeds—little grows. My own vineyards, oh how I weep for my vineyards! No wine shall come from those grapes again."

"Not wine, but blood," murmured Bernard Houdon, his dark eyes hooded. His voice sent a shiver down Deborah's spine. "The terrors are not over. Napoleon craves power, and he shall rise until all Europe trembles."

"I cannot understand," said Gertrude pettishly, "how a mere corporal in the army could rise to such power. What is happening in France? Is it customary to rise through the ranks? It would never, never happen in England!" Her tone implied that the English were too civilized to permit such an occurrence.

"The Bonapartes are an unusual family," Houdon said. "Much hated, yes, but with an uncanny ability in the military and in politics. I look for them to seize much—in lands, in nations, in thrones. No, I do not admire, but I comprehend. I have seen the man at a distance, and it seemed to me that though he is short and not handsome, still there is something—yes, there is something. Some dynamic power that draws men to him, yes, and women also."

"You believe he has designs on England, then?" asked Lord Treverly, stretching out his fine long legs. Deborah stared at his shining boots, to avoid looking at his face.

Houdon shrugged. "How can we know? We have been away from France for years now. All we know, we hear. Rumors heard from friends who have also had to flee France. No one can remain who does not swear devotion to Napoleon Bonaparte. The First Consul is becoming more powerful, that is certain, but he moves behind the scenes."

"But the rumors—do you hear that he might invade England? He has said that he might," said Lady Horatia. "Idle threats, perhaps? We have always feared invasion from France."

"That kind of talk comes up every ten years," said the squire, determined to be cheerful despite the gloomy subject. "We shall be prepared. If he tries to invade us, he will be in for a surprise. England has never been conquered!"

"Except by William the Conquerer," murmured Lord Treverly. "From France."

There was a little shocked silence. William

Vaughan looked at his cousin in some apprehension. Alice and Gertrude were the only ones showing signs of boredom, and only one who knew them well would recognize the signs, the fidgeting with ribbons, the side glances at the windows, at the clock.

"Well, well, that was long ago," said the squire briskly. "And we no longer run about naked! No, no, we have changed a little!"

"Squire!" His good wife was shocked.

He chuckled heartily, and the gentlemen had to join him. Yet the conversation continued.

Rigaud leaned toward Deborah. "What did he say?" he asked in French, for he had missed his host's remark.

Deborah translated for him, whispering almost into his ear, to avoid disturbing the general conversation. She caught the icy look Morgan gave her as her head came closer to Paul Rigaud's. She blushed, and moved back to sit erect once again.

"Is it true that French troops have been seen across the Channel, apparently gathering opposite Dover?" Houdon asked, his dark eyebrows drawn together in a frown. In his usual black velvet, he seemed rather gaunt, almost demonic, Deborah thought fancifully. She would have liked to paint him as a demon in a religious scene, or as the devil tempting Faust.

"They have been seen about Boulogne," said Lord Treverly. "Whether they are on maneuvers, as seems likely, or are indeed serious about an invasion one does not know. We probably shall not discover the truth until the French troops begin to move. However, I think they would find a

Channel crossing very difficult. Storms come up quickly, and their small boats would be swamped." Deborah thought he seemed rather unconcerned, considering the seriousness of the subject.

"If I were Napoleon, which I am not," laughed Rigaud, "I should choose a more comfortable crossing point than the English Channel! I beg your pardon, but I was extremely sick during my crossing, and I should not care to attempt it again. I am quite happy in England, even though it is not my France. Indeed, my France is quite gone and may never come again."

A shadow crossed his face, and Deborah touched his arm impulsively. "I am so sorry, Monsieur Rigaud, for you and your friends. To be forever alien to your own country! That is hard indeed."

"It would be difficult indeed, Miss Deborah," Rigaud murmured, "if it were not for the many kind friends who have made our lives easier. How grateful I am to them—and to you, for the sympathy in your beautiful eyes."

Deborah was confused by the intensity of his gaze and his speech. She drew back, grateful when the maid came in with the tea tray.

Gertrude rose gratefully. All this talk of politics irritated her. There were so many more interesting topics that could be discussed, such as fashions, London, matrimony—

She poured, and the conversation took a lighter turn. Lady Horatia was asked when she meant to return to London.

"For the season? Oh, I shall not go," she said.

"I am bored with it. It is not the same without my dear uncle. No, no, I shall make other plans for the season."

"And you, Lord Treverly?" Gertrude managed to ask demurely, as she handed him a cup of tea. "Do you mean to leave us for the season in London?"

He accepted the cup and moved to the mantel to stand, leaning against it gracefully. Deborah thought he looked splendidly aristocratic, yet very much the soldier too, in his high, shining boots.

"I have been unable to make definite plans until recently," he said deliberately. "William and I have been working hard on the estate, and it shows progress now. So we may go to London for the season, after all. William begins to feel dull in the country, so I may have to liven him up a bit, eh, William?"

William, sitting near Alice, seemed struck dumb. He stared into his teacup so intently he might have been reading his fortune, thought Deborah. She herself had turned cold with dismay. Why did Morgan want to go? Was there some female in London he wished to see? Why the slight smile on his lips?

"As for me, I like it here in Lowbridge," said Paul Rigaud. He smiled at Deborah as he handed her cup of tea to her. "With cream and sugar, yes? You see, I am beginning to know your tastes. I mean to become better acquainted!"

He had lowered his voice a trifle, but Deborah was sure several people must have heard him. Color washed over her cheeks, leaving them warm.

"I like it here also," said William Vaughan. "It is *you* who have become restless lately, Morgan. We shall do as you say, however. If you wish to kick up your heels in London, I shall assist you. Through thick and thin, as I told you!"

"And which is London?" laughed the squire, disregarding his wife's anguished look. He drained his glass of port.

Lady Horatia turned to Deborah. "My dear, may I truly count on your coming tomorrow morning?"

"Yes indeed, my lady." Deborah collected her thoughts. "I hope to accomplish much work on the portrait."

"Good, good. Let me make my farewells then. I must make another call this afternoon. No, do not accompany me to my carriage—indeed, Squire Frome, you pamper me *too* much!" But she was clearly delighted by his attentions. She paused to kiss Deborah's cheek. "I am happy to see you again, my dear child. You look well. And we shall have a good long chat tomorrow. Prepare to stay the day. Gertrude must let you stay!" And she gave Gertrude such a kindly smile that Deborah's sister could not protest.

Lady Horatia might no longer be a power in London society, but she was a formidable woman in her own right, and in Lowbridge she was second only to Lord Treverly in wealth and influence. Her friendship was not to be sneezed at, and Gertrude was not in the habit of affronting those who ranked above her, in any event.

In the stir of Lady Horatia's departure, the French party also left with much kissing of hands, bows and flourishes. Marie Andreossy said to Deborah, "If at any time you wish to study more French, come to me, my dear. I shall remain in Lowbridge for a time, and it would delight me to introduce you to some of my favorite authors. Do say you will come to me!"

Deborah did not wish to do so, but she smiled and murmured, "You are most kind, Madame," without committing herself.

The room seemed almost deserted after the four had departed. William Vaughan was seated again near Alice, and seemed content to gaze at her demurely excited face. Lord Treverly had resumed his position near the mantel and gazed into space. Gertrude rang for more tea, but no one wanted any. Squire Frome wanted to hand around the port, but no one wished it.

There was a brief, uncomfortable silence. Deborah's self-esteem had been much restored by the kind attentions of Lady Horatia and the devotion of Paul Rigaud. How lavishly they had praised her skill at French, her artistic talent. Had Morgan noticed anything?

How desperate she was, that she could take comfort in these crumbs of hope! She wished him to think well of her, not to regard her as an idiot who followed meekly in her elder sister's wake. Once he had loved her; he no longer did. However, she still wanted his respect—not the cold contempt she sometimes saw in his eyes.

She became aware that Morgan was thoughtfully studying his cousin, William Vaughan. William was speaking softly to Alice, causing the pink to come into her cheeks. She tossed her head teasingly, making her blonde curls dance about her shoulders. He looked at the curls nearest him, as though he longed to touch them.

Morgan turned abruptly from them, caught Deborah's gaze, and held it for a long moment. But he did not seem to see her; he seemed to be thinking deeply. Then he turned to Clarence.

"Yes, yes," he said, as though continuing a conversation only momentarily abandoned. "I think we shall repair to London in May. There is much going on. A reunion of my regiment—I should like to attend it. A change from Lowbridge should bring us back here in the autumn with fresh spirits to continue the work. Eh, William?"

"As you wish, Morgan," said William, looking with affection at his cousin. "You have been working like a trooper. You need a holiday. Besides, there have been letters to you with perfume on them, and you are longing to go up to London, to visit their senders, I suspect." And he laughed teasingly.

"You are too astute, my lad," Morgan said severely. "I hope you are not given to reading addresses on envelopes?"

"Not deliberately," said William. They both laughed, but Deborah thought there was something besides amusement behind their laughter.

They soon made their farewells. The high-perch phaeton was brought around by the respectful groom, who admired the handsome black horses as much as the shining black carriage with the crest on its doors. The gentlemen thanked the

Fromes for a splendid afternoon, and departed.

Gertrude stared after them, sighed deeply, drew her shawl about herself, and went back into the drawing room. "Oh, my poor Alice!" she exclaimed. "Lord Treverly cannot be serious about her! London, and perfumed letters. Oh, my poor Alice!"

CHAPTER NINE

The stately black barouche called promptly for Deborah the following morning. She felt very grand as the elderly coachman solemnly handed her in.

She seated herself, settled her hold-all beside her, and gazed out the low windows as they set out. She was glad to be away from the squire's residence for the day.

The atmosphere in the house was heavy. Alice had come down to supper the night before with pink swollen eyelids, and Gertrude had sighed in sympathy throughout the meal. Alice excused herself early, and Gertrude shut herself in the study with her husband for quite two hours. The rise and fall of their voices had reached Deborah, seated alone in the drawing room with only her sketch pad for company.

Were they all to suffer because of Morgan? It made her quite angry that he should pay such marked attentions, then drop her sister so quickly that her hopes were dashed. So she alone was not to suffer, but Alice as well, and by extension Gertrude! She wondered, with a savagery foreign to her gentle nature, if his recent houseguests had also departed with broken hearts. Did he *deliberately* flirt with them all?

That Morgan should be fickle had never entered her mind before. It seemed to her that fickleness was the opposite of his character, which had always appeared to her sturdy, thoughtful, and considerate of others.

Perhaps he had changed in the years since she had known him. Did a person change so much that he became the opposite of what he had formerly been? It seemed to her, limited as her experience had been in life, that people remained much the same throughout their lives. As children, their characters were formed by their ancestors and by the events that happened to them. As young people, the nature of their characters became more evident. As they grew older, the nature deepened, became consistent and clear.

She frowned thoughtfully at the greening fields, the dark earth freshly plowed up, ready for the planting. It was April, the season of hope. Her heart rebelled at loving forever one man who ignored her. She would not! She would overcome this passion for him. He had certainly overcome his presumably deep feelings for her.

No, there must be other things in life than this hopeless passion for one man. She would live for her art, her family. She would forget him, especially if he proved false in his nature.

With this firm resolution, Deborah felt cheered. She was further pleased with the sight of fresh spring flowers along the roadside as they slowly made their way to Lady Horatia's house. She leaned from the window eagerly and fancied she could catch the fragrance of the lilacs even from the barouche on the dusty road.

This was what I needed, she thought. A touch of spring! Yes, yes, as much as medicine, I needed the spring to get over the winter gloom! Love is a sickening passion when it is not returned. I shall recover, with spring as my doctor and flowers as my strong medicine! Why, by autumn, when *he* returns I shall scarcely know him, and will be able to see him from far or near without a heartstring to stir at the sight.

Deborah was further cheered by the eager welcome she received from her hostess, and when they entered the drawing room, it was to find the draperies opened wide and blowing in the fresh breeze.

"It is spring," said Lady Horatia dramatically. "I am so happy—look, I have arranged flowers for the first time in months." Her broad hand gestured to the vases on either side of the mantel, which she had filled with tall spikes of larkspur, grasses, pussy willows, and ferns. "And you in blue today. How young and charming. Come in, come in. Do you wish to set to work at once?"

"I think so, my lady. I am eager to set hand to brush," smiled Deborah. Indeed, she did feel eager to work today. Morgan was shaking the dust of Lowbridge from his heels, and he must be forgotten. Another life must be made; she would begin today.

Her easel was already standing near a window, her paints and her palette were nearby. She donned the sturdy dark blue work apron that was splashed with the paint of years.

Lady Horatia took her place on the sofa, resuming her pose eagerly, as though she too had missed their sessions. "Shall you mind if I talk, dearest Deborah? How I have missed our conversations."

"Do go on, but do not mind if I am too absorbed to answer you. I shall hear you," said Deborah, standing before the easel.

Lady Horatia began to chat then, her long nose fairly quivering with various bits and pieces of news from London, from Bath, from Brighton. She spoke with animation, and Deborah patiently observed her expressions.

She wished the portrait to seem as intensely alive as Lady Horatia was. She began to work on the face, the most difficult part of the portrait, because today she felt confident that she would paint well. She brushed in the mouth, began to work on the nose, the difficult, alert eyes of piercing gray.

She worked for over three hours, with only brief pauses for Lady Horatia to get up and walk briskly about the room and for Deborah to shake her arms and extend her fingers, stiff from holding the brushes so long.

The golden clock over the mantel chimed a silvery half-tone when one-thirty came. "There, there, we must pause for today," exclaimed Lady Horatia. "Enough, my dear! You must be exhausted. Do let me see what you have made of me."

She came around as Deborah stepped back from the easel. Deborah too gazed at the portrait, but she was so weary she could no longer see it clearly.

Lady Horatia stared and stared at her painted image. Finally she proclaimed, "Deborah, I think you have got me! I think you have. It is me to the life. Yes, yes, it is me."

The maid who came to announce luncheon was made to give an opinion. "Oh, my lady, it is indeed you, it really is. Oh my, how did she do it!" and the maid stared in admiration at Deborah, then back at the portrait.

"It is beginning to take shape," sighed Deborah. "A few more sessions, then I shall work on the hands. After the face, they are the most difficult to do properly."

"For today, you have earned your luncheon. I do hope you will be pleased with it. I told cook she must prepare something special for you."

The lunch was indeed special. First was served a delicate broth with fresh spring vegetables floating in it.

"It is the French style," pronounced Lady Horatia. "A clear broth with just a few vegetables. Delicious and refreshing."

Deborah agreed, and took note of the novel notion. Every day in Lady Horatia's company was an education.

Next came the fish course, splendid trout in an orange sauce, with tender green asparagus beside it. The meat course consisted of lamb served with tiny green beans from the garden.

Deborah could scarcely want a dessert, but she must have it. The cook had prepared it especially, and it was cautiously carried in by the maid. A quivering mound of pale almond, with the smallest cookies she had ever seen. And the taste! A delicate almond-flavored pudding, cold and soft to the taste, with the crisp cookies as contrast.

"Lord Treverly is most fond of this dessert; I always serve it when he comes," said Lady Horatia complacently. "He has formed a taste for almond. I enjoy it myself."

"It is most delicious," said Deborah faintly. Why must she be reminded of Morgan again, when she had practically forgotten him for four hours!

They had coffee in the drawing room, where the French doors had been opened to the breeze. They sat, and sipped, and talked, and another four hours passed with amazing quickness.

"Now, will you come again on Wednesday this week?" asked Lady Horatia with evident anxiety, as Deborah declared she must depart.

"I shall be happy to come, my lady. Indeed, we could make it a morning session only, and you need not serve me luncheon! And I can walk, the weather is so fine—"

"No indeed, I shall send for you and make *sure* you come. I am lonely, my dear, for companionship of your kind," she confessed, and only her noble looks saved her from seeming pathetic. "It is the one thing I miss of London. I had friends with whom I could converse by the hour. Here in Lowbridge, only you and Lord Treverly save me from utter boredom. You have the books I wish you to read?"

"Yes, they are here in my hold-all. I shall be most happy to read them. I feel as though I am being educated by the gentlest, kindest teacher in the world! If you knew how I hungered for such education—"

"So do all we females with any mind," Lady Horatia assured her. "It is not only the men of this world who need education; it is we females! And one day," she said, looking fierce, "it shall be as natural for women to have a complete education as for men! I may not see it in my lifetime, but perhaps you shall in yours."

After their conversation about Byron and other poets, about the opinions of Thomas Paine versus the French Revolutionists, about Benjamin Franklin's influence on Parliament, it was a decided jolt to Deborah to return home and find Gertrude talking of bringing Alice out.

She stared blankly at her elder sister at the supper table that evening. Gertrude was flushed and brightly determined.

"You see, Deborah," she explained anxiously, "Alice must have her chance! If even in Lowbridge she attracts noble suitors, what would she do in London!"

"Oh, Gertrude, nobody would notice me in London," murmured Alice, sounding rather frightened and desolate. "And noble suitors pay flattering attentions, then go away again. I would rather continue here."

"And whom will you marry, I ask you, miss? Whom will you marry? A farmer, a digger of ditches?" asked Gertrude, sounding nearly overwrought.

"However, my good wife, this is all beside the

point," sighed Clarence. "Much as I would enjoy launching dear Alice into society—and who would grace it more?—frankly, I cannot afford it. We have done the figures again and again, and a London season would cost over three thousand pounds."

"Three thousand pounds!" gasped Deborah. "That is the entire amount of our legacy—oh, Gertrude, it would not do!"

Gertrude frowned at her. "It could be put to no better use," she said firmly. "However, I have another thought. If not London, why not Bath? It is still elegant. Many people go there for the waters. If we go in the season, in June and July, we shall no doubt meet many eligible men. Alice must have her chance!"

"Bath," breathed Clarence, with something like relief. "I could hire a house in Bath without emptying my pockets."

"Of course, Bath is not London," said his good spouse with fervor. "But we shall have our dressmaker make up some fine gowns, simple and elegant. Our Alice looks her best in simple elegance. She would not need so many ball gowns as in London. Gowns for concerts, yes, some gauze dresses for the Assemblies—"

Deborah sat numbly while they planned. Alice was beginning to perk up, though her pink lids betrayed that she had wept much the past twenty-four hours.

Gertrude expounded on the virtues of Bath all evening. She sketched out what they would need—the rental of a town house, a carriage of more recent date, the attentions of a cook, two maids, two grooms, their butler, and two footmen. They would leave the children here in Lowbridge, of course. Reverend and Mrs. Plummer would keep an eye on them. The undercook would prepare their meals, the nursemaid might have an assistant, a footman would do service for them in the house, and one groom in the stables for the horses they left. The gardens might be neglected except for one elderly gardener.

Gertrude spoke so convincingly that they were all nearly assured that a summer in Bath would be scarcely more expensive than staying in Lowbridge. The squire finally retired to the study with his wife to work out the cost in greater detail.

Alice and Deborah remained in the drawing room, Alice dreamily drawing threads on her embroidery, Deborah working at her sketch pad, but without giving much attention to the work. She had much to occupy her mind.

Was Alice so readily appeased, so easily placated, did she have so little feeling for Morgan that a husband-hunting expedition to Bath would make her happy? It seemed so. She sat with a contented smile on her pretty mouth, as though nothing disturbed her but choosing the right shade of pink for her embroidered rose.

Alice glanced up, caught Deborah's worried look, and smiled with her usual sweetness. "Did you have a splendid time with Lady Horatia, Deborah? I quite forgot to ask you. She seems so formidable, I should dread being alone with her. But you seem to enjoy her company."

"Oh yes, she is immensely kind to me. And so

flattering about her portrait. She quite likes it, I believe. And the luncheon—" Deborah went on to describe it, and the artistic treasures she had examined that day.

"She has traveled widely, then; I do not see how she manages without a man to guide her," said Alice. "I should be frightened out of my wits to travel even to London without a gentleman to assist me."

"She is quite different. She is bold without being excessively daring, and strong without being impudent. And the traveling she has done—" Deborah's eyes glowed. "She describes a ride on a camel in the desert as casually as though it were a carriage ride to church! The savages there are but simple-hearted children, to hear her tell it!"

Alice shuddered delicately, and the conversation occupied them through the evening.

The next day the decision was announced. Clarence had agreed to sponsor Alice for a season in Bath. Alice was gleeful, and Deborah was happy for her.

At once the house seemed to have been turned upside down. Maids scurried about, examining gowns, seeing which ones would do, which must be replaced. Footmen carried down trunks and valises and set them in bedrooms. Clarence wrote at once to an agent, asking him to look for a house to rent for three months in Bath. They would depart at the beginning of May.

"We can afford a modest coming-out," said Gertrude complacently. "And I am sure, Alice, that with your beauty and modesty and goodness, you will attract a gentleman of some means, of good character and breeding. I am sure of it."

The squire looked somewhat fussed, and muttered about leaving the farms for so long, but he must adjust to the idea, Gertrude told him privately. "It is important for Alice to be launched. She shall not be wasted on Lowbridge! I am determined on that."

Of course, the word soon went about Lowbridge. Nothing could be kept secret in the village. And the fact that the squire would be departing soon, for an absence of some three months, caused wonder and speculation. And to Bath—the ladies and the squire were going to Bath for the season!

During their Wednesday session, Lady Horatia questioned Deborah with much interest. They talked of it in the afternoon, after a full three hours at the easel had left Deborah pleasantly wearied.

"And my dear, *you* are not unhappy?" inquired Lady Horatia. "You are quite recovered from Lord Treverly? Forgive my impertinence in asking."

Deborah managed a smile. "I must forget him, it seems. He does not mean to settle on me, that is quite evident. As for Alice, his attention seems to have wandered from her as well. Ah me, perhaps there is some fine lady in London." She checked a deep sigh and stared into the fire, as though to find some answer there.

"Well, well, you are so intelligent and have such talent, if he does not appreciate you, others will, I am sure of it!" And Lady Horatia tactfully changed the subject.

To the household's amazement, Lord Treverly

and his cousin appeared again on Friday afternoon. Squire Frome was still out on his estates, and the three Stanton sisters were toasting their toes before the fire on a blustery April day which threatened rain. Clothes were the topic, a consuming passion for clothes. Deborah had sketched a charming ball gown for Alice, and they discussed it earnestly. Should it be set so low about her shoulders? Should style be followed, or modesty be allowed to dictate? It was an important matter, for even so small a detail could change the course of Alice's life.

When a carriage was heard pulling up outside, Gertrude hurried to the window to peer out. "Bless me," she said, unconsciously imitating her husband. Deborah had noted how much alike they were growing. Marriage seemed to have that effect on some couples, she reflected. "Bless me, if it isn't Lord Treverly and Mr. Vaughan! Whatever—and the squire not here!"

The butler showed them in. The gentlemen were wind-blown and a trifle flushed by the weather, but in high spirits, to judge by their smiles at Gertrude and Alice. Morgan gave Deborah a quick look, then turned away.

"Come in, come in. Is it blowing up to rain?" Gertrude nervously took refuge in the subject of the weather. "The squire is not yet home. If it rains, he must come home soon, for I will not endure his having another cold this winter!"

"The rain is coming, but not yet," said Lord Treverly in his usual decisive way. "Forgive our bursting in upon you like this. You make us feel so welcome that we come at any time, as if we were family."

It was an unusually gracious remark for him. Gertrude stared at him, flustered. "So good of you to say so. Of course, you are welcome at any hour, my lord! Pray be seated. It is cold—will you have tea? Or shall I order some port?"

"Tea, if you will. There is nothing like tea on a cold windy day—don't you agree, Miss Alice?" And Lord Treverly stretched out his hands to the blaze in the fireplace and smiled down at Alice.

The squire came in wearily about an hour after they had arrived. He brightened up when he saw who was there, for he loved company, and enjoyed nothing more than a great bustle about him. But when Gertrude looked with obvious annoyance at his muddied boots, he was forced to make an apology for his appearance.

"Come in as you are! We did, and your good wife did not rebuke us," said Morgan, and Deborah knew he must delight in teasing Gertrude. "How go your farms?"

"Well, well, except for the south fields. I have had to speak to Jensen yet again," and the squire frowned. "I fear he may have to be dismissed. He has no more idea how to plow than a donkey. Indeed, a mule would have more notion of how to go about it, I am convinced."

They laughed, and the uncomfortable moment passed.

"I hear you are so confident of the orderly management of your farms that you plan to leave them for three months," said Lord Treverly, still standing before the fire, his teacup beside him on the mantel.

"Rumor creeps about," laughed the squire. "Yes,

yes, my wife and I shall go to Bath. Alice shall have a coming-out. A modest one, but it shall serve. Who could look at Alice without admiring her? A fine little woman, a fine housekeeper."

William Vaughan had been sitting across from Alice, his gaze intent on her. Now he started and looked at his cousin anxiously.

"What attraction has Bath? You must persuade me," said Lord Treverly smoothly. "I had heard it was going down sadly. I have a house there which I have not seen since I was a youth. And then, never thinking I should inherit, I gave little notice to its condition."

"Oh, Bath is splendid," said the squire vaguely. "Tell him, Gertrude."

"There are assemblies, and concerts at all seasons," said Gertrude. "Many ladies and gentlemen come for the waters, even though they are not at all ill! It was formerly all the rage, and even now it is fashionable enough."

"I really ought to see to the house there," murmured Lord Treverly, and crossed to the tea tray to have his cup refilled. Deborah poured out for him and offered him the cake tray. She knew he would choose one of her almond cakes, as indeed he did.

"Of course, you made these?" he said to her.

She nodded, so startled that he had actually addressed her that she could not speak. Her throat had quite closed up.

"Delicious as ever," he said, and it seemed he would remain talking to her, but Gertrude called his attention back to herself.

"You have not seen your own house, my lord? You should not allow a property to be neglected so! Of course, you probably have an agent to manage it, however—" She paused, struck by her own daring.

"You are quite right, Mrs. Frome," he said smoothly, and deliberately seated himself beside Deborah on the sofa. "I would ask you to look at it while you are there, but that would be too presumptuous. I have a mind to go myself, except that we have already planned to go to London." Deborah sensed he was gazing at her, but she dared not look up.

"We should be happy to do it for you," began the squire.

"Oh, I think we should go for a time ourselves," broke in William Vaughan anxiously. "It is important to see for oneself how things are managed, is it not? I could go for you, Morgan!"

There was a little pause, and Morgan said to Deborah, "And will you take your sketch pad with you, and your paints, Miss Stanton? I remember that you were fond of sketching scenes of houses and people and shops."

"I—I hope to," she said faintly.

"Lady Torrington is most pleased with her portrait, you know. It is a splendid thing to be able to do something well, is it not? A great satisfaction."

"Yes, it is, my lord. A great satisfaction. It is a great relief to be able—" She stammered to a halt, realizing what she was saying, and blushed deeply.

There was a little silence between them. Mr. Vaughan was speaking to Alice about Bath and what she might see there. He recommended the libraries, the museums, the walks.

"Yes, yes, you are quite right, William," said Lord Treverly suddenly, as though coming out of a daze. "But I should see to the place myself. Should you mind very much if we decided on Bath for the season, rather than London?"

William's good-natured face lit up. "A splendid idea, Morgan," he said. "I should like it above all. To go to Bath—and have—have such good friends there—what a time we shall have!"

"Do you mean it?" gasped Gertrude, doubting her ears. The squire was eying Lord Treverly with a shrewd look. "You would give up the London season?"

Deborah prayed she would not add, *and those females who write you perfumed letters!* In an agony, her hands clasped, she prayed for her sister to be discreet. The squire interrupted smoothly.

"Delighted, delighted," he said easily. "How very pleasant to have one's friends about, instead of all those strangers. Not but what we should meet many people! Alice will draw them like honey, I am sure!" And his infectious laughter made everyone smile.

"Indeed, I am convinced of it," Lord Treverly agreed. "When Bath learns that three such beautiful ladies are in their midst, society will not be slow to become acquainted. I predict a path worn smooth to your door. And I hope to find myself and William often welcomed to your home. Have you yet found a house to suit you?"

The squire spoke at length on the problems of

finding the right place, with enough bedrooms, a
drawing room, in the right area, not too far from
the spas, with pleasant walks. . . . Lord Treverly
offered to write his own agent, if Squire Frome
was not satisfied with his agent's efforts. Gertrude
sat squirming with pleasure.

She had dared to dream, and now her determination was bringing to pass everything she could
have wished. They would go to Bath, not to London—yet Lord Treverly should be there also!
Now—now she could hope again. Alice should have
her chance!

CHAPTER TEN

Gertrude found an opportunity to speak to Deborah the very next day. "You see, Deborah, what it is to plan. I could not be more pleased with the way matters go on. You observed Lord Treverly's renewed attentions to Alice?"

"Yes, I did," said Deborah, bending her head over the cook's proposed menus. Gertrude was abandoning all her housekeeping to plan for the move to Bath.

"You see, he does not mean to let her slip through his fingers after all," said Gertrude. "However, I am concerned about the children, very concerned. I do not at all like leaving them alone for three months."

Deborah began to stiffen, her pen poised above the paper. "Oh really, Gertrude?"

Gertrude gave her sister a rather uneasy look. One never knew, any longer, which way Deborah would jump. And she had that set look on her face which Gertrude mistrusted.

"There is really no reason you must go to Bath, is there?" she asked brightly. "If you would consent to remain with the children, I should have no further worries in the world, and so I told Clarence. I would trust you with them forever! As I said to Clarence, no one could take better care of them, in sickness and health. And Clarence said that you were surely the most dependable female in the whole world!"

Gertrude rattled on, for Deborah said nothing. "And that would mean the more money for gowns for Alice. You do want Alice to be a success, I feel sure. How fond of her you have been through the years, what care you have taken of her. I do not know what she would have done without you!"

"She would have been left alone for *years*— when you are unwilling to leave your own children for even three months!" Deborah said sharply.

"Nonsense! Nothing of the sort! What a vivid imagination you have, Deborah. But you have always been fond of her, and so very concerned. I know you will want Alice to have every chance."

She rustled away before Deborah could gather her wits to reply. She laid down the pen and propped her chin on her hands to gaze moodily out the window.

Not to go to Bath! Not to go to assemblies and balls and concerts, not to see the smart people, even from a distance. Not to observe when Alice cut her dash, not to see Morgan as he paid court to her—

Ah, perhaps it would be best not to go, after all. She pressed her hand to her weary eyes. If these last weeks had been painful, what would it be to observe Morgan's regard for Alice grow, as he escorted the girl about, danced with her, smiled down at her—

She brooded about it for a time, while Gertrude took it for granted that Deborah would do as she wished.

Alice said gravely, "You are not going to Bath, dearest Deborah? But I depend on you so. To whom will I confide my innermost thoughts?"

"I have not yet decided," said Deborah, to Gertrude's displeasure. "I must think about it."

"But Deborah, I need you here with the children. I shall be most distressed if you do not have charge of them."

"I must consider the matter," Deborah repeated.

Gertrude showed her displeasure in small ways. She sent Deborah up to the nursery before dinner was well begun, because she "was sure Jenny had been coughing." She took Alice with her to the dressmaker's, but said there was no need for Deborah to go; she was quite capable of choosing gowns for Alice herself.

On Sunday, Lady Horatia Torrington greeted her little friend after church and eyed her keenly. Deborah was standing alone except for Frederick and Jenny, who tugged at her hands.

"Ah, here you are, Deborah. Why do you stand here? Where is the nursemaid?"

"She is in the carriage with the two little ones," said Deborah wearily.

Lady Horatia's mouth set in a tight line. "Dear me," she said quietly. "Deborah, you must come over to me for several days. I hear all is in confusion at the squire's. Do come tomorrow with a valise and your drawings. I have longed to see more of your work. And did you not promise to show me some of your father's sketches?"

"I should like to very much. However—" Deborah hesitated, gazing down at the two children who danced about and pulled at her arms. "Do be still, Frederick. Jenny, you must not dash about so. You know we will be leaving shortly."

"Mama always talks so long," sighed Frederick.

"Oh, do let them run about. Someone else can chase after them," said Lady Horatia. She nodded imperiously at the children, and Deborah did let them loose and watched them run for the churchyard. "Now, my dear, do say you will come to me. I can send the carriage for you tomorrow morning, as usual. But one day is never long enough! You must stay for three or four, as you will."

Deborah hesitated. Gertrude came over and said suspiciously, "Why are the children running loose, Deborah? You know we will leave soon, and I dislike for them to get so muddy!"

Lady Horatia smiled at her brightly. "I am persuading Deborah to come to me tomorrow, to spend several days. Do say she may be free of her duties with you, and come to me! She is looking quite weary, and she will be ill if she goes on this way."

Her clear bell-like tones drifted across the churchyard. Many turned to gaze curiously at them, including Lord Treverly and his cousin.

Alice and William Vaughan started toward them. Gertrude flushed vividly at all the attention.

"But Deborah is free to do as she wishes," insisted Gertrude, giving her sister a frosty look. "Of course, she may come when she chooses. We are not usually so busy. It is the preparations for going to Bath, you know."

"Indeed, I am sure," said Lady Horatia. "Then it is all settled. I shall send the carriage for you tomorrow morning at the usual time, my dearest Deborah! And you shall come for several days. Do be sure to bring the sketches. We shall amuse ourselves talking of ports and ships and faraway places."

Deborah gave her a grateful smile. "You are so gracious to me, Lady Horatia," she murmured. "I shall be happy to come."

Lord Treverly had almost reached them now. Alice offered to go for the children, now dancing about the gravestones with no thought for the solemnity of the place. William Vaughan hastened to assist her, and they soon brought Frederick and Jenny back.

"And where is it you go, Miss Stanton?" Lord Treverly was saying.

"To Lady Horatia's for a few days," she murmured, daring a fleeting look at his grave face. How handsome he was in his plum coat, the high white stock, his blond hair uncovered to the April wind. His gray eyes seemed warmer today.

"Perhaps we shall see you there," said Morgan, and bowed upon leaving them all.

Gertrude was quite cross, but could not insist

that Deborah cancel plans that had been made so publicly. So Deborah set out thankfully on Monday morning, with three valises settled beside her in the grand barouche.

She felt as if she had been let off a leash. No hurrying to the nursery to look after the children. No getting up in the night if a child so much as coughed or groaned. She was settled into a grand bedroom next to Lady Horatia's, with a pretty dressing room of her own—so much space that she marveled at it.

The large bedroom was decorated in lilac and pale gold, with satin draperies at the large windows, and a huge fourposter bed with a canopy of lilac silk trimmed in gold braid. The mirrored dresser was large enough for three people, and her few toilet articles looked lost on its shining surface. In the corner was a huge rosewood desk, on which she spread out the sketches, her own and her father's, to study which she would show to Lady Horatia.

They spent the first morning in the usual fashion, and considerable progress was made on the painting. Today Deborah worked carefully on the folds of the robe, the details of the face, and finally she began the difficult work on the hands. They were so expressive, yet so strong. She decided on the pose, one hand in the lap, one held up in a commanding yet charming gesture for attention. Lady Horatia admired her work when the morning was over, and then they had a long luxurious luncheon.

In the afternoon, Paul Rigaud came to call.

When the butler informed Lady Horatia who was there, she raised her eyebrows in surprise but bade him show the man in.

"He knows you are here, Deborah," she murmured teasingly. "He does not come to see *me*, I'll warrant!"

Deborah blushed, and her cheeks showed a pretty color when the Frenchman entered eagerly. He bowed to his hostess and kissed her hand, then turned to Deborah and kissed her fingers slowly, his mouth lingering. Deborah, conscious of her hostess's bright eyes watching every move, wanted to yank her hand away. Yet it was very flattering to have such attentions paid by a handsome young man.

"So, you have heard about my charming guest," said Lady Horatia, "and have hastened to visit me."

Paul Rigaud looked disconcerted for a moment, and Deborah thought his discomfort appealing; sometimes he seemed almost too sure of himself. He laughed and admitted it. "I had heard Miss Deborah was here, yes. I could not resist calling! One encounters so many visitors at the squire's, I hardly have an opportunity to speak to Miss Deborah."

Deborah knew his charm was of the practiced variety, yet she thought his compliments sincere. How reassuring it was to know that a handsome Frenchman, who had met so many women of the world, would seek her out! Perhaps, thought Deborah, I am not so "sadly aged" as *someone* seems to think!

He talked with them for a time, thankfully accepted tea and cakes, and when Deborah brought out the sketch folders, he examined them with great eagerness, both hers and her father's.

"How fine it is," he murmured again and again, holding up this sketch and that. Lady Horatia was examining them critically through her lorgnette. He looked closely at the details. "Yes, yes, I can see the likeness, yet the difference. You have the exactness of line and attention to detail that one admires in the elder. Yet there is something—" He almost seemed to be talking to himself.

Deborah was a little amused and very pleased that he showed such interest. He finally sat back and let her take the folders from him and set them on the side table.

"Yes, I see the difference," he said, his brown eyes glowing. "Your father is all detail and exactness, every line is there for a purpose. In your work, Miss Deborah, I can see that you have learned to show a ship with every sail in place, every rope precise. Yet there is more. There is feeling. In your port scenes, one catches a glimpse of a sailor and sees in the lean of his body, as he observes the shore, how he longs to be on land once more with his loved ones. In the face of a captain, one senses the loneliness of command, the sternness of self-discipline. I prefer your work, I must confess."

"Very prettily stated," said Lady Horatia, giving him a keen look. "I think you do not flatter; you are quite sincere. And I agree with you. Her father is a fine draftsman, but Deborah goes further; she gives the deeper feeling of the place. Yes, Deborah, you are a fine artist. You must never give it up. But you need to travel about, to see more people and places."

"I could not agree with you more, my dear Lady Horatia." Rigaud gave her an engaging look. "I think we do not praise our Miss Deborah too much, despite her blushes and shaking of her lovely head! A true critic in London or in Paris would feel the same. We must encourage her to go on to greater efforts and not confine her talents to her home."

"You are both doing me too much honor," Deborah protested. They both seemed so serious! "My poor talent—not like my father's at all. After all, he was employed by the British Navy—"

"Tell me about it," said Rigaud, settling back and accepting another cup of tea. "That is, if I am not disturbing you ladies by remaining so long. I know that you are great friends, and you may wish to converse by yourselves—"

"No, no, you must remain," said Lady Horatia. "We are not so mean as to wish to send away a handsome young man who amuses and delights us! Do tell us, Deborah, about your childhood, and how your father came to take you about with him."

She told them her story, shyly at first, then more readily as she sensed their sympathy and interest. She told how her mother had died when she was eighteen. Even before then, her father had taken her, and Alice, to the many ports and spas of southern England.

"He was much interested in the navy. He was not strong, for he never fully recovered from a

wound received in his young years. But because of
his ability as an artist, the navy kept him on to
draw and paint."

"And then he taught you also—"

"Yes, later he did, when he saw I had talent. At
first, a governess encouraged me, and my mother
was always suggesting that I spend several hours
a day on my paintings and watercolors. Later,
Father took an interest, finding I had inherited his
great talent in a modest way."

"Modest! No, no, you are too deprecating!" said
Paul. "I think your talent exceeds your father's!"

The argument went on, and Rigaud did not
leave until late afternoon. Even then he was obviously reluctant to go.

"Dear me, I should have asked him to dinner,"
said Lady Horatia. "However, I did long to have
a chat with you alone."

"And I with you," said Deborah. Indeed, she
felt rather weary of the Frenchman's smiling attentions, flattering though they were. She felt on
edge with him, as though she had to make a great
effort to continue to charm, to smile, to listen, to
protest his flattery.

Deborah enjoyed the comfortable evening with
Lady Horatia, for the woman was a mine of information about many topics, yet she never made her
guest feel ignorant. They finally retired about
eleven o'clock, and Deborah reveled in the luxury
of going to sleep without a final trip to the nursery
to quiet the children and make sure all was well.
She felt truly free. Well, that was the way it should
be for her, if no man wanted to marry her. Lady

Horatia did quite well by herself—why shouldn't Deborah?

Marriage was not the only state in the world. If a girl could not marry the man she loved, then why marry at all? Why not travel and write and sketch, do as she wished?

It was a breathtaking thought, and Deborah wished she could remain awake long enough to consider it seriously. But the day had been full, and she was weary. She soon dropped off to sleep.

Something awakened her. Some sound, unusual in the night. Was it a bumping of some object? Did she imagine she heard a voice? Forgetting where she was, she sat upright in the wide bed. Had Jenny cried out? Then she remembered where she was and why.

Suddenly she heard a scream, full-bodied and female! She leaped from the bed and raced across the room. Her door was open, yet she distinctly remembered closing it before she retired. Shapes moved along the hallway. Dark shadows.

Men! Moving along the hallway—two of them—They held something in their hands—she could not make it out. Lady Horatia screamed again, and a light bloomed from her bedroom along the hall from Deborah's. Deborah began to scream also, losing the cold fear which had gripped her. Lady Horatia's house was being robbed!

Someone brushed past her and tried to enter her room. Deborah pulled at his jacket, but he broke away from her and headed toward the dressing table and the desk at the window.

She rushed toward the fireplace in her bedroom,

grabbed a poker, and faced the dark shape. "Get out!" she cried, more fiercely than she would have imagined possible. She faced the dark figure, his face hidden behind a scarf. "Get out at once!" She swung the poker ominously before her as he approached her.

He tried to wrench the poker from her, but she fought him for it with the strength of surprise. He flung her back, and she struck her left shoulder sharply against the mantel. The poker fell from her hands with a clang on the tiles. She screamed again and again.

A deeper, masculine voice joined the yelling in the hallway. The butler and a footman had entered the fracas. The man before Deborah hesitated, glanced toward the desk and the dresser, then ran toward the window. He smashed it open and jumped out onto the small balcony. She saw him balance there, then drop the one story to the ground.

She ran out into the hall once more. "He is gone! He jumped out the window—" she panted, as Lady Horatia, formidable in a crimson dressing robe and white mobcap, came toward her.

"My poor dear—what a fright!" she said. "They got my rubies! Oh, I am furious for leaving them out! And in Lowbridge! I had not thought to find thieves here—"

The butler was racing down the stairs, amazingly fast for one of his age and bulk. He flung open the door and ran outside.

Soon he returned, his white hair ruffled, to report, "Them fellows has all gone, my lady. Two of them, I think."

Lady Horatia shuddered. "Let them go, then. I'll have the law after them! Two great louts—I can describe them well."

Deborah started to protest. The man who had confronted her in her bedroom had seemed slim and lithe, not too much taller than herself. But her shoulder had begun to throb, and with a moan she put her hand to it.

Lady Horatia was all concern. She applied hot cloths, and gave Deborah a little laudanum to help her sleep. Deborah had nightmares in which men with blank, black faces came toward her in the darkness, and she woke about noon the next day with a throbbing head and a pounding pain in her arm.

The doctor was summoned to examine her. The shoulder was dark with bruises, and the arm wrenched. He put it into a sling and advised frequent applications of hot cloths and salve. Lady Horatia sent her back to bed, and sent word to Gertrude about her sister.

"I shall keep you here for several days," she announced commandingly. "You shall not return home. They would have you up and working in no time. Here you shall rest."

And rest Deborah did, in bed for two days, then dressed and lying on the comfortable chaise longue in the drawing room. Lady Horatia refused all visitors, insisting, "You must have rest, Deborah. I can never apologize enough that this has happened to you in my home."

Deborah was sorry about her hostess's edict against visitors only when she heard that Morgan had called and expressed his concern for her. She would have liked to see him, but not the way she looked, so pale and wan, with her shoulder throbbing badly.

Deborah could do no more on the portrait until she had recovered. So Lady Horatia read to her guest in a lively and animated style and talked to her for hours, then left her to rest when she seemed weary.

And later in the week, she began to talk to her seriously.

"My dear Deborah," she said the day before her guest was to return home. "I must talk to you about your future. It seems to me that you shall continue as nothing more than unpaid nursemaid and governess to your sister's children if you do not make up your mind now to refuse to do so."

"What else can I do?" asked Deborah, not without bitterness. "What else is there for a female to do? My education is unremarkable. I can paint and sew and cook. I have little looks to commend me. I might marry someone such as Mr. Irving. He has expressed some shy interest in me. But oh, Lady Horatia, I do not want that kind of life! I want to love and to be loved! Am I too impossibly romantic? Should I be more practical, and settle for what I can have?"

"Nonsense," said Lady Horatia, fire in her fine gray eyes. "No woman of your intelligence and talent need settle for what is only practical! I am sure your sister would be quite willing to settle your future for you. Well, do not allow her to do so. Decide what you want, and go ahead and do it. You can earn your living, and in an interesting fashion."

"How?" asked Deborah bluntly, sitting up against the cushions. Her hostess had money and influence; it was all very well for her to speak of freedom!

"I have been considering that," said Lady Horatia, pouring more tea for them both. "First, there is your artistic talent. You could set up a studio in London. I know a neighborhood where you could rent a house with a studio on the top floor to provide excellent light. I think your paintings and watercolors would sell."

Deborah gazed at her wide-eyed. "Even though I am a woman?"

"Even so. I should buy them, for one, and so would my friends. And others who admire my taste would follow my example."

"And live alone?" Deborah's voice quavered.

"Well—you would hire a companion, or live with some female in similar circumstances. Or there is another possibility. Someone like me would enjoy your companionship. You could live with me, and travel about as my friend. We would travel to the Orient, to the Continent—wherever we pleased. It might be an interesting life for you. I myself no longer care to live in London; it has some bitter memories now," and she frowned slightly. "Once I was all the fashion, and everyone was eager to come to me. When I entertained for my uncle, no one refused me. Now—ah, that is a different matter. I have no influence now." And she seemed to lose herself in memories for a time.

There was a comfortable silence between them. Deborah leaned back and thought. Lady Horatia was a good friend, indeed. Before her ladyship had arrived in Lowbridge, there had been no one to share her thoughts, to show concern for her. Alice was too young and, despite her sweetness, was shallow. And she looked on Deborah as her mentor, the comforting presence she had leaned on most of her life.

Gertrude liked to use her, but did not treat her as an equal. The squire admired Deborah, and they could talk easily, but he was a busy man, and his first loyalty was to his wife. And Morgan—but she turned her mind from him. Morgan was not for her. Nor she for him. Lady Horatia was right. She must begin to consider seriously what to do about her future. If she could not marry Morgan—and that possibility had now faded forever—she would not marry at all. Far better to be alone and independent than the wife of someone she did not admire or respect.

So she must consider Lady Horatia's advice and begin to think of some course she could follow. She might teach, perhaps in the field of art or literature. Would a school accept her on her scanty education?

The thought of living as an artist in London terrified her. Yet, with Lady Horatia Torrington as kindly patron, she might manage, and with time gain courage to do it.

Then there was the suggestion, delicately hinted at, that Lady Horatia might take her on as a companion. They would travel and meet many interesting people, and fill their lives with adventures around the world. It could be an interesting, even fascinating, life.

Yet the notion of continual traveling was wearisome. And at the moment her shoulder pained her. Her head too had begun to ache, in a persistent throb. Thinking just now seemed too much of an effort. Later she must gather her wits about her, but for now she wanted to rest and be spoiled by attention. She wanted to do nothing at all.

Perhaps it was because of her weakness, but tears came into her eyes, and she blinked them back. If only she might lean on Morgan and let him take care of all her worries, he would have them gone in a trice. Morgan—how strong he was, how gentle he could be. She closed her eyes and remembered his kisses, the warmth of his lips.

Deborah lay with her eyes closed, dreaming. Lady Horatia got up quietly and went to the door to stop the butler from entering.

"No, we will see no one," she whispered. "Miss Stanton is sleeping now. We cannot receive today."

Deborah wondered who the caller might be, but dimly. In her dreams, she was sinking into a pleasant state, walking through a sunlit field with Morgan beside her, swinging her hand, and flowers bloomed about their feet. She turned up her face to the sun. It was warm and soothing, and the pain would go away. Yes, with Morgan's hand in hers, the pain would go away very soon—very soon—

She slept, her head deep in the pillows, smiling in her sleep.

CHAPTER ELEVEN

Deborah returned home in the barouche, with Lady Horatia to escort her. The good lady made no bones about informing Gertrude that Deborah must continue to rest.

"The girl has had a great shock, and her arm is badly wrenched. Be sure no one troubles her for some days, until her shoulder is healed." Lady Horatia issued further commands about the proper treatment for the arm before sailing grandly away with her scarlet turban bobbing.

After the lady had left, Gertrude gave vent to her fury. "What right has she to tell me how to handle my household! And she would not even let us visit you when you were injured! Indeed, I feel very humiliated. As though we did not know how to treat our own sister!"

Deborah murmured something placating and went up to her bedroom. Alice came to her soon, to find her lying on the bed with a light coverlet pulled over her.

"May I come in?" and she entered without waiting for permission.

Deborah lifted her aching head, then let it fall

back on the pillows. "Yes, dear, of course." She closed her eyes again, hoping Alice would not remain long. How coddled and spoiled she had been at Lady Horatia's. It had quite ruined her, she thought.

"Whatever did happen? No one seems to know, except that Lady Horatia's jewels were all taken," Alice said eagerly. "And you were injured. How did that happen? Why was the robber in your room?"

"It was her rubies that were stolen—she had been wearing them and had left them in a small box on her dresser. And I expect the robbers must have been strangers to Lowbridge. They thought I might be wealthy also, and were about to take what jewels I might have about."

"It did seem strange," said Alice, "and Morgan —that is, Lord Treverly—thinks so also. Why would you be attacked? We were all concerned. He went over to see you but was not admitted. He was quite angry about that."

"Indeed? Lady Horatia would admit no one. She wished us to rest from the shock."

She thought about Morgan coming to see her, and being angry when he was turned away. Her heart leaped a little, then calmed again. No doubt it was only the affront to his arrogance that had made him angry.

Alice was eager to continue her queries but saw that Deborah was truly weary. She kissed her forehead gently and drew up the coverlet. "You must rest, dearest. How glad I am to have you back again! Gertrude does not truly understand me, kind as she is. It is only you to whom I can open my heart, my darling Deborah. I do hope you will not be gone again for so many days."

She tiptoed away. When Deborah would not go down to luncheon, preferring to rest, Alice brought her a tray of tea and toast.

Deborah felt better the next day and managed to dress and come down to breakfast. But she looked so pale, and the bulk of the bandage showing through her muslin dress was so alarming, that all felt concerned. Gertrude was most anxious about her and insisted she must rest in the drawing room, with the family about.

Deborah's rest had given her the opportunity to think a good deal. She must begin to assert herself, as Lady Horatia recommended. Therefore, that evening after dinner, she brought up a subject she had been avoiding.

"I have decided about Bath, Gertrude," she said.

Gertrude looked up warily from the coffee pot. "Indeed, Deborah, I think it would be best for you to remain here and rest. You may not be recovered for a time."

"Oh, I am improving daily," Deborah said coolly. "I have decided I will go to Bath with you. After all, Lady Horatia plans to go and open a house there. We have become good friends, and I shall miss her sorely if I do not go."

There was a little shocked silence as Deborah's calm decision entered their consciousness. Clarence studied her intently, as usual seeing more than others thought he did. He drew on his pipe in silence.

Alice said impulsively, "Oh, Deborah, I'm so glad! I would miss you sorely. To whom would I talk about—about everything?" She ended with a blush and an anxious look at Gertrude.

"I will always be happy to hear your confidences, Alice," said Deborah warmly. "And I am sure we will enjoy going about together."

"But what about the children?" burst out Gertrude. "I shall not rest if they are to be left alone here!"

"We must discuss this further, my dear," said the squire firmly. "Later, in my study. I am sure that Deborah would profit much by a journey to Bath. Just think how many new subjects she will find for her sketches."

Gertrude gave her husband a stricken look, then closed her mouth at his warning gaze. The rest of the evening was rather uncomfortable, for she chose to look offended and grieved.

Deborah retired early, her shoulder still throbbing. Alice attended her to her room and made her comfortable with a hot compress on the shoulder.

"Poor darling, I hope you will be easier tomorrow," she said anxiously. "Do you know, this is the first time I have been able to do anything for you? All these years you have acted the mother to me." She bent and kissed Deborah affectionately, tears misting her eyes.

Deborah returned her kiss. "Thank you, darling. I am feeling better and better. And you were always a pleasure to me, never a burden. How beautifully you have grown up! You will make a splendid wife to some fortunate man."

Alice blushed and beamed, a happy light in her

eyes. She left Deborah then, with just a candle at her bedside. Deborah finally blew it out and lay back to sigh and lie awake for a time. Alice thought of her as a mother! And so had she been. She felt old before her time. Yet she could not be sorry. Her sacrifice had not been in vain. For Alice was a blooming, happy, lovely girl.

The next morning she slept late, and wakened to find the spring sunshine flooding in her windows and the fragrance of spring flowers emanating from a pretty glass vase on her dresser.

She lay looking at it. Alice's welcome home, she thought, and smiled gently to herself. Her family did love her and needed her. Was that not enough?

No, she must go on, as Lady Horatia said, and make a new life for herself. Perhaps in Bath she would find the answer she sought. She might find the courage to break away, to go to London and be an artist. Or she might take up some occupation which paid her enough to support herself.

She must decide in the next months what to do, then firmly follow that course.

To her surprise, Gertrude came to her as she still lay in bed. She knocked lightly, then entered the room. "Ah, my dear, you are awake. We were concerned about you."

"Thank you. I shall get up presently."

"No, no, we are going on to church without you. The squire says you must continue to rest. He is quite alarmed at your pallor. I'll send up a breakfast tray for you, then a maid shall help you bathe and dress. I know people will inquire after you at church, but we shall deal with them."

Gertrude was so amiable that Deborah could

not help feeling a little suspicious. Her sister lingered, looked at the vase on the dresser, and plucked out a drooping flower.

"The squire and I have decided to take the children with us to Bath," she finally said. "I should not feel easy without them, I have decided. It will be simple to take the nursemaid with us, and there will be plenty of room in the house that Clarence has hired for three months. There, it is all settled! You shall come along with no fears about anything."

She beamed down at Deborah, who stared at her, a little dazed. "You will—take the children to Bath?"

"Of course! It is the ideal solution. I would worry about them, being apart from them for months. And Clarence is pleased with the idea. You will enjoy it, too, I know. And I'm sure you will not object to helping us with the children at times— when you are free, you know."

"Oh—I see. How splendid, indeed," Deborah said mechanically.

"I knew you would agree," said Gertrude, twitching back the draperies with an impatient hand. "Dear me, these are dingy. They must be washed while we are gone. Yes, we shall all go, and leave but a few here to do the housework and tend the gardens. You shall have another dress or two also, the squire says."

She waited for Deborah's expression of gratitude, and after it came she smiled and departed on a wave of violet perfume.

Alone, Deborah laughed aloud a little, and shook

her aching head. One did not easily defeat Gertrude! She would have it her way, one way or another.

Deborah herself felt quite deflated. She had braced herself to defy them, and all for nothing. She would end up with the care of the children after all—in Bath.

Bath, with its gracious walks, its assemblies, its concerts and balls—and Morgan. And Deborah would be walking with a child at each hand; she would be expected to remain home evenings if one of them was sick. She would see little of Morgan, or of anyone else, for that matter.

She shut her eyes. What was the use of struggling? She was trapped in this loving but smothering household. How could she blithely go off into the frightening world, and make her own living? No matter how much she wished to be free, how could she cut herself off when Gertrude with her cunning wit, and the squire with his cool generosity, would always see to it that she lacked for nothing?

She might as well resign herself to her fate, no matter what Lady Horatia advised. She did not have that lady's steel-like will nor her independent means, nor the backing of influential relatives.

A maid came up with her tray. Deborah struggled to sit up comfortably, but her head was aching worse than ever. The household was very quiet; she was alone with her thoughts, and they gave her little pleasure.

A maid came to help her dress in her lilac gown, and she bound back her hair with a lilac ribbon.

She felt quite unable to wind it up in its usual severe style, her arm ached so.

She did go down to luncheon, and greeted the family with composure when they returned from church.

Gertrude was full of messages of concern from everyone. Reverend Plummer had even mentioned her and Lady Horatia Torrington in his prayers, and hoped their fair village was not to be plagued with burglars. Lord Treverly had paused to inquire after her health, and Bernard Houdon and Paul Rigaud had been quite fierce in wishing they had been there to give those scoundrels a fine accounting!

"Indeed, I think they would have," said Alice blithely. "I can easily picture them with swords, can you not, Deborah?"

"I imagine they know one end of a sword from the other," the squire said from his end of the table. "They probably had to learn to handle them in that awful Revolution."

Yes, Deborah thought, to see one's friends and neighbors slaughtered, imprisoned, tortured, and that horrible guillotine taking so many lives—she shuddered at the horror.

"We do not know what they have suffered," said Deborah softly. "I should feel very bitter and lost, I know."

"Not you, Deborah," said her brother-in-law. "You are too strong for that. You would mourn for a time, then pick up the pieces and begin a new life with energy and imagination."

Deborah looked at his shrewd, kindly face in

near amazement. Compliments always took her by surprise, and this was praise indeed. "Thank you, Clarence, I am sure. You are most kind—"

"No, I think I know you now, my dear Deborah. You will not allow life or its disappointments to defeat you, I believe."

The others at the table looked startled. Alice looked at Deborah as though trying to imagine what had made the squire say such a thing. Gertrude looked rather troubled, but brushed her uneasiness away. The squire was only flattering dear Deborah, to make her feel better. She had been so pale, they were all quite frightened for her.

Deborah decided to rest on the chaise longue in the drawing room that afternoon. "We may have visitors. Everyone is curious about you," Gertrude warned her.

"Never mind. If I tire I shall go to my room," Deborah said, smiling at her older sister as she solicitously laid a rug over her legs. "Thank you, Gertrude, you're very kind."

"Nonsense, I am not kind; I am worried about you. You must take care and become well again soon. It is not like you to be ill. I always said you were strong as a horse, no matter how frail you might appear." And Gertrude patted Deborah's head as though she were no older than Jenny.

Deborah was no sooner settled than the sound of a horse's hooves drew the squire to the window.

"Bless me, it's Lord Treverly, and alone," said the squire, and hastened out to greet the gentleman.

Deborah felt a mixture of wild happiness and

alarm. Would he be angry, or formal, or gentle? She knew that whatever he felt, he would be proper in his manner. But she would see his true feelings in his eyes.

He came in, greeted Gertrude and Alice, then came over to where Deborah lay against the cushions.

"My dear Miss Stanton," he said, and bowed over her hand. He did not take it quite to his lips. She looked into his eyes; they were cool and dark and cautious.

"How do you do, sir?" She matched his formality.

"That is not the question. How do *you* do? We have heard all kinds of wild stories, and were not assisted in our quest for the truth by Lady Horatia, who hid you away from us all."

His eyes were very gray and chilly. Yes, angry, thought Deborah, and withdrew her hand.

"You are too good. Lady Horatia meant to spare me any inquiries which might make my headache worse. I am much improved, thank you."

He seated himself beside her, with Alice hovering nearby. He ignored Gertrude at the coffee tray.

"You will tell me what happened," he commanded. "I am most anxious. Do you think the scoundrels were strangers to Lowbridge? They took some jewels of Lady Horatia's, I believe?"

"Her rubies, sir, which she had left on her dressing table."

"And one came into your bedroom? What was he like? Lady Horatia described them all as large and burly."

Deborah hesitated. "Well—he did not seem so to me. I thought him slim and not much taller than myself. And he moved as quickly as a panther."

Alice shuddered prettily, and made a sound of distress. Morgan's gaze never left Deborah's face.

"So? Not tall, but slim and light of foot. A professional burglar perhaps?"

"I thought so, though on this subject I am sadly ignorant, thank God," and Deborah tried to laugh in the face of his cool questioning. "He did move very quickly, and when the butler and footmen were shouting in the hallway, he ran directly to the window, smashed through it, leaped from the balcony to the ground, and was away. It seemed to me that he must know exactly what he was doing."

"Indeed, a very scoundrel," the squire was murmuring. "Right here in Lowbridge! Disgraceful!"

"And you did not see his face?" Morgan asked. She thought he seemed uncustomarily nervous, fidgeting in his chair. He glanced from her face down to her shoulder, where the bandage showed thick and white through the thin muslin dress. His face grew even grimmer. "Did he strike you there?" He indicated her shoulder.

"Oh no, no. I did not see his face. It was covered by a kind of black scarf or mask. He approached me when I screamed. I grabbed the poker from the fireplace and threatened him—"

"Oh, Deborah, you did not! I should have fainted!" Alice cried in dismay.

"Really, Deborah, you could not have hoped—" began Gertrude.

"Yes, it is like you," said Morgan coolly, a glint of humor softening the hardness in his eyes. "So, you attacked him with a poker. Then—"

"Well, he grabbed it from me, and thrust me against the fireplace. I struck my shoulder, and my head. Then the butler yelled, and the footmen. He looked toward the opened door, seemed to judge it too far, and leaped for the window. No—first, he looked about the room, as though wondering where I might keep my jewels—"

"He stopped to look about the room?" asked Morgan keenly.

Deborah nodded, then frowned and pressed her hand to her forehead, as her head began to ache again. "Yes, he looked about, then leaped from the window," she repeated wearily.

"Oh, do let us talk of more pleasant matters," urged Gertrude. "When I think how close Deborah was to being murdered in her bed—"

Alice clasped her hand to her mouth in horror.

"Yes, let us turn the subject," the squire said hastily. "I think the sheriff has all the details to work with. Let us hope the scoundrels are well gone by now!"

Deborah lay back thankfully against the pillows. The inquisition was over. Morgan turned politely to the squire, and they began a lighthearted discussion of what might be done with some wild forest lands on the edge of Morgan's estate.

She could lie there and gaze up from time to time at his profile. She could glance at him naturally in the course of the conversation, and no one would notice, because both Alice and Gertrude also looked at him, then at the squire, as they spoke.

Gertrude sent for more coffee, and the conversation continued, to touch on village matters and the trip to Bath.

"When do you depart for Bath?" Morgan inquired. "Our own departure may depend on yours. I have the promise of the labor of a man recommended to me, who will come and remain while we are gone, and I am wondering what date to give him."

Gertrude struggled to conceal her triumph, and only the glitter of her eyes showed how she felt. "We hope to leave in about two weeks, my lord. I think all will be in order by that time, will it not, Squire?"

Her husband nodded. "I think so, as ready as it will ever be. I have appointed a man to take charge for me, and I believe it will be possible to leave about the fifth or sixth of May."

"Splendid. That will suit me perfectly. Might we not go up together? I shall take about three carriages, and have two of my men go before me to open up the house."

He glanced at the three ladies, a slight smile on his lips. "And are you all eagerness? I think you are, at least, Miss Alice. There is a look of anticipation on your face."

"Oh, yes, will it not be splendid!" she said. "And how much better to know people already there! Lady Horatia goes, you know, and you will be there and—and Mr. Vaughan?" She gave Morgan a questioning look, and he nodded.

"Yes, William goes. I could not leave him behind. I think he would follow after! He was quite angry with me today that I departed before he was ready. He threatened to follow me here."

Alice looked self-conscious. "And—does he come, then?" She glanced toward the windows.

"Oh, perhaps later," Morgan said carelessly, and turned to Gertrude. "And you, madam, are you eager to go?"

"Oh, naturally. But there remains much work to be done. The children go also, you see. At the point of leaving them, I could not do it, so we shall all go. Yes, it will be exciting for us all. Quite a holiday."

Morgan turned last to Deborah. "And you, ma'am? Are you anxious to depart? Or have your recent adventures taken your spirit from you? Perhaps you are not feeling quite the thing."

His keen gaze seemed to assess her languid posture on the chaise longue, the way her head lay back on the cushions.

"Oh, I shall be well enough in a day or two. I am only tired, and the pain has sometimes kept me awake."

His gaze softened. "Are you in much pain?" he asked gently, his deep voice lowered so only she could hear.

She nodded. "It was bad for a time. My brain felt quite addled," she said, with an attempt at lightheartedness. "However, I shall soon be quite recovered."

"Your will is stronger than your body," he said, still softly. "Sometimes I think I have misjudged you. You have a strong, stubborn will. I wonder that you bend to anyone else's commands or wishes."

Their eyes met, and she felt curiously weak. What did he mean? He had once accused her of bending to Gertrude's wishes too meekly. Had he discovered he was mistaken? That it had been necessary for Deborah to assume the care of Alice? Or did he mean that she was rigidly stubborn and mulish?

Tea was brought in, and Gertrude busied herself with the tray. When Alice rose gracefully to assist her, Morgan's look went to the girl's slim, beautiful figure as she bent like a blue lily to the table, taking the cup from her sister.

"Your duties to her are done, I think," said Morgan.

"Yes, I agree. She has grown up beautifully. She will—probably marry before long."

"And you will be free—to do what? Lady Horatia has told me some wild story about your going up to London to paint. Whatever did she mean?"

Deborah stiffened at his lightly mocking tone, and sat up straight. "She has faith in my ability to paint," she said finally, trying to keep the hurt from her voice. "She is encouraging me to—to strike out on my own. She is convinced I could make my living as an artist."

"And does she know just how difficult an occupation that is?" he asked impatiently. He stared down at her, and she could not meet his implacable look. "Men have starved, trying to do just that. One is always dependent upon the good will of patrons, the whims of society. Are you willing to starve in an attic for your painting? I think not! You have lived comfortably—"

"What are you two talking about?" asked Gertrude uneasily. "Will you have tea, my lord? Deborah is looking so weary—do you wish to retire, my love?"

"No, no, not at all. I am quite thirsty," Deborah said, and took a cup from Alice. She sipped it, trying to think what Morgan could mean by the anger in his tone. Was he concerned only because he had once known her well? Did he think so poorly of her talent?

He too accepted a cup of tea, then looked at it as though wondering why it was in his hand. A few moments later he set it aside, half-empty.

"I will speak to the squire," he finally said to Deborah, still in a low tone. "He is no scatterbrain. I think he should know what you are considering. He would not be so thoughtless as to allow you to do this."

"I wish you would not. I have not made up my mind yet," she said with dignity. "It is up to me to consider what future I shall carve out for myself. I must ask you not to speak to him." She met his gaze serenely, but with the pulse beating hard in her throat. He studied her eyes, the set look of her mouth.

"Well, I see you are determined on having your own way," he said. "I wonder at you. Sometimes I think you are just the way you were when I left you. Other times, I am convinced that you have grown hard and cold toward those who love you."

"*Never* hard, *never* cold," she said quickly. "I

love them all dearly. I would do anything for my family."

"As you have proved," he said, with an ironic glance down at her.

So he must remind her again of how she had refused him. Color rushed to her cheeks. "I would do it again," she said softly. "I am still convinced it was necessary. Now—now Alice is grown. My duty toward her is done."

"I wonder why you are whispering so in the corner," cried Gertrude impatiently, her curiosity overriding her good manners. "What do you ask, Lord Treverly? Do you still wonder at her adventures with the thieves?"

Deborah could have shaken her sister. This was one of the few times she had been able to talk intimately with Morgan. Almost he had expressed concern—almost worry for her. Was the concern that of a friend? Or of a former lover? Or of someone who still considered her well-being of prime importance to himself?

"I beg your pardon," said Morgan stiffly. "We but spoke of some events—long ago, no matter. Miss Alice, I think your sister looks weary. Will you walk with me in the garden while she takes some rest? I fear I have made her more tired, urging her on to speak."

He stood as he spoke. Alice too rose and accepted his arm, though she looked back questioningly at Gertrude.

Gertrude nodded and smiled at them. "The sunshine is lovely. Do not go far, however. We may have more visitors today, Alice."

So the conventions were observed. Morgan

bowed Alice out the French windows, into the gardens, and Deborah could see them walking slowly, always within sight of the drawing room.

Deborah leaned back with a sigh and closed her eyes. "Will you go upstairs, Deborah dear? I think you are very tired," Gertrude said anxiously. "I will give you my arm up the stairs."

"No, no, not yet. I must not allow myself to be so weak," she said, half to herself. Not so weak as to imagine Morgan's interest in her was personal. Not so weak as to remember the clasp of his arms when he held her, the warmth and passion of his lips when he kissed her—long ago, so long ago. And recently, when he had been angry with her—his mouth crushing hers, his arms holding her against his lean, hard body. She shivered at the remembrance. If only she might feel him yet again, the touch of his hands, his arms, his lips.

"Oh, very well then, but if you tire, I shall take you up," said Gertrude, rattling the teacups. "Did you notice, Clarence, how early Lord Treverly came today? He *is* interested in Alice, I know he is. And how particularly he asked about our plans!"

"It would seem so," said Clarence, giving Deborah a long, keen look.

"Oh, it is famous, it is famous. He has practically declared himself. He does not wish Alice to go to Bath without him! He asked most precisely when we should depart. Did he not, Squire?"

"He did indeed, Gertrude. Most particularly. In fact, he wishes to drive down *with* us. That will take some planning," he mused.

The squire and Gertrude rambled on about the

move to Bath. Deborah gazed out into the sunshine. There she caught a flicker of blue—Alice's skirt. They were as far as the rose arbor. The early roses would be coming out, the first primroses. And the lilacs were nearby. A romantic setting, and Morgan would have Alice's hand on his arm, his head would be bent devotedly to hers—

A pain went through her that had nothing to do with the ache in her shoulder and her head. She must accustom herself to this sight, to the thought of them together. She must grow hard and not let it disturb her, or life would be unbearable. She must grow a shell, like a small sea animal, hiding herself within until the outside world no longer mattered.

CHAPTER TWELVE

Morgan and Alice had not been long in the garden
—though it seemed long to Deborah—when the
sound of a carriage was heard. Gertrude darted to
the front window anxiously.

"Dear me, if it isn't Lady Horatia! I do hope she
has not come to give me further orders in my own
house! Oh, Mr. Vaughan comes with her. How
strange!"

The butler announced them, and Lady Horatia
swept in, grand in cream silk, and came directly
to Deborah, ignoring the others. "My dearest Deborah, should you be up? Whatever are they thinking of? When I called upon Lord Treverly this
afternoon and learned he had come *here*, I determined to come myself, and Mr. Vaughan accompanied me. Are you not attempting too much?"

"Not at all, my dear friend," Deborah said with
a smile and a squeeze of both the grand lady's
hands. "As you see, I am lying about like a sultan
in his harem!"

William Vaughan had gone over to the window,
where he caught a glimpse of Alice disappearing
around the hedge and his cousin strolling after her.
He frowned and turned back to the room.

Lady Horatia seated herself near Deborah. "Will you be able to make the trip to Bath?"

"Yes, of course. We plan to go in about two weeks."

"I shall leave in about a week. I have much to do to put my house in order before I entertain. Well, well, we shall have a splendid time of it! Let me tell you what assemblies are planned. I have had word from friends there—"

She proceeded to entertain them with an account of the summer before them. Gertrude listened eagerly, quite forgetting how irritated she was with Lady Horatia, and they all talked gaily until another carriage drove up. "It is those French people," Mr. Vaughan said gloomily, as though he had reached the end of his tether. Lady Horatia gave him a quick, speculative look.

The squire rose to greet the party as they entered, and once again Deborah was forced to answer questions about her health, to smile and reassure them. Her head was aching. However, she was so amused to see them all together that she would not have left for the world. She thought Lady Horatia was also entertained, for she occasionally arched an eyebrow at Deborah as Paul Rigaud pointedly ignored William Vaughan, and Mr. Vaughan turned his shoulder to Monsieur Rigaud.

Once Deborah's health had been dealt with, the robbers were taken apart and put back together again, their ways and their motives dissected in a manner that would have done credit to a chemist in his laboratory. Finally that also was put aside, and Bath became the topic of conversation.

Deborah had leaned back, listening rather than contributing to the conversation. William Vaughan presently seated himself on the other side of her from Lady Horatia. He bent over to whisper to her under cover of the conversation, "*They* have not come in. They must have seen the carriages approach and know we are here, yet they do not come to us."

She wanted to smile, but the unaffected gloom of his face roused her tender spirit. "They will come presently; they wanted some air. They had just gone out when you arrived with Lady Horatia."

"Do you think they are serious?" he wanted to know, still in a gloomy whisper.

She shrugged, and was sorry for it. Her shoulder began to throb again. "Perhaps. I don't know," she said cautiously. Why should she confide in him?

He gave a deep sigh. "I thought she liked me quite well, for a time at least. But he is more attractive to her, after all. He has a title, a splendid estate—what have I to offer?"

"You are too modest, sir," she said gently, in the whisper he seemed to wish. "I know you will make your way in the world—Lord Treverly has every confidence in you. Look at how he insisted on bringing you with him as his manager."

"Yes, he is too good to me. I do not deserve it. I envy him—yes, I am not ashamed to admit it," he said miserably, his shoulders drooping. "I have come to admire—no, to love Miss Alice. She is so lovely, yet so modest. She blushes when one praises her and will have none of it. She is so gentle with the children. One cannot help thinking how she would be with little ones of her own."

"You are quite right. She has never a mean thought in her head but is all concern for others. She has such beauty, she could turn men's heads, but she has no wish for such trivial triumphs. She will make a splendid wife and mother."

His eyes glowed at her tribute, and he pressed her hand fervently. "How good you are to say so! And you, her sister, who have known her always! I *thought* she was all you say, but some females strive to cover their real natures with men, and one does not recognize a shrew until one has married her!"

She had to laugh a little at his remark, yet she acknowledged the truth of it. "She is no shrew, I assure you. And Gertrude has trained her well in household matters. She is thrifty, yet not penny-pinching."

"Just the wife a man would long to have," he sighed.

"You must not despair," Deborah ventured to say.

He glanced significantly toward the windows. They could no longer see Alice or Morgan. "You think not? I cannot even struggle—I owe him too much! She must choose, and I can do nothing. Nor have I nearly so much to offer her as he does."

"You must not think in just material terms, Mr. Vaughan. You know your cousin as well as we do, even better. He is a viscount, yes, and has much of wealth and home to offer to—to a woman he makes his wife. But he himself is of a noble nature, generous to a fault. Inheriting Treverly has not changed him, no, it has merely provided him the instrument to carry out what he would have wished to do."

William Vaughan eyed her curiously. "He said— I have heard—" he began slowly. "You once were fond of him, and he was close to you. Ah, Miss Deborah, perhaps you suffer as I do!"

She shrank from him, the smile frozen on her face. "I—sir, you presume. I did not mean—"

"No, no, I would not offend you for the world!" he said quickly. "I have but guessed your secret. You love him still, do you not?"

"I *admire* him, Mr. Vaughan," she said with coolness. "I understand his nature a little, I believe. Yes, we once knew each other, but we went our separate ways."

He ignored this, lost in his own thoughts. "You know, I do admire you deeply, Miss Deborah," he said earnestly. "Almost as much as I admire Alice. You are much alike in nature. Too good, too fine to be left without partners for life!"

"Indeed, sir?" she said faintly, beginning to feel rather hysterical. Was she going to laugh or cry?

"We could comfort each other," Mr. Vaughan said, leaning closer to her, speaking confidingly. "I can see something of Alice in you, and perhaps you see something of my cousin in me! We could confide in each other and find some comfort. When they marry, we could do likewise, and have the consolation of each other's presence."

"Good heavens," said Deborah, and felt truly weak. She glanced rather wildly about the drawing room. Was there no rescue from this highly unconventional proposal? She caught the earnest gaze of Paul Rigaud, and the desperation in her look appealed to him. He rose at once.

He approached her and bowed. Lady Horatia had risen to admire the gardens, discussing them at the window with the squire. Paul Rigaud took her chair, drawing it close to Deborah.

"I have not had an opportunity to inquire personally for your health, Miss Deborah," he said, taking her hand tenderly in his.

Vaughan glared at him, but Rigaud ignored the other man.

"You are most kind," she said.

"Not kind. I have been most distressed by the episode. How could anyone get into the house? Was it not locked? You were not safe there! You must not go again!"

"I cannot imagine it would occur again, Monsieur Rigaud, though I thank you for your concern. The servants will be on guard. Someone will patrol the house every night from now on; Lady Horatia has made sure of that."

"I am glad of it," he said warmly, pressing her hand.

Lady Horatia returned to her seat to find it taken. "No, no, I am not offended. I shall sit beside Mrs. Frome. We have much to discuss." She proceeded to engage Gertrude in conversation, while Gertrude's attention wavered between Lady Horatia and the scene in the garden. Alice had wandered about for quite an hour, unchaperoned, with Lord Treverly. And one did not scold a viscount.

And there was Deborah, looking quite attractively flushed and pretty, with a handsome young man on either side of her, each scowling jealously at the other. Whatever was going on? Deborah? She had counted on keeping her sister with her.

Her husband, who had been conversing with Bernard Houdon, suddenly raised his voice. "Gertrude, my dear, have you heard this? Our friends here are also going to Bath!"

Gertrude gasped and looked at Marie Andreossy for confirmation.

"Yes, we have discussed it. Lowbridge without our greatest friends—we could not endure it. And we have heard so much about Bath, we must go there."

"Dear me, how splendid!" said Gertrude, her head whirling. She looked again at Deborah, who was gazing at Paul Rigaud. "Deborah, did you hear that?"

"Yes, indeed, what lovely news. We shall have our own society there, and shall not even need to meet another person!"

"Yes, indeed," Gertrude echoed weakly. What had she begun! She had decided to take Alice to Bath, and now she was dragging all Lowbridge with them! Wildly she wondered what she would do if the Reverend and Mrs. Plummer decided to go, and old Mrs.—But there, she was growing lightheaded.

Paul Rigaud lost no time in asking, "And shall you take your sketching with you, Miss Deborah? I shall offer my services at once, to accompany you to the Crescents and the many walks, to hold your pad for you and your pencils, as you stare and admire and are admired in turn. I must go along with you, to protect you from the bold beaux who might disturb you."

William Vaughan interrupted, more rudely than was his wont. "*I* shall be happy to accompany you, Miss Deborah. You need look no further for an escort. I plan to call on you often, if you will permit me, and any time you wish an escort for your walks, you may command me."

The squire looked from one to the other in some amusement. Bernard Houdon looked thoughtful, and Marie Andreossy raised her slim eyebrows at Monsieur Rigaud.

Gertrude said hastily, "I am sure we will be happy to welcome *all* of you whenever you will come and call upon us."

Paul Rigaud bent tenderly toward Deborah, and adjusted the shawl over her. When his hand brushed lightly against her breast, he did not appear to notice, but the touch seemed to burn through her. She leaned back among the cushions, confused and embarrassed, wishing she had had the sense to go upstairs when Morgan had left the room. Whatever was going on? She had always been content to remain quietly in a corner and observe. So much attention flustered her.

"I believe Bath is quite near Bristol," remarked Paul Rigaud. "How I admire your father's work at the port of Bristol! Would you consider making an oil of that work?"

"It is an interesting thought," she managed to say. "I am not sure how much time I shall have for painting—" She thought again of the four children accompanying them. Would she have time for these "beaux"?

"But you must make time!" exclaimed Rigaud. Such talent must not be allowed to go to waste!"

"Speaking of painting," Lady Horatia interrupted, "will you feel well enough to come to me tomorrow, Deborah? You must not work long, yet I should like it so much if my portrait were finished before we proceed to Bath."

"A few more hours should suffice," said Deborah thoughtfully. "Yes, I should like to come. Perhaps by next Wednesday we might complete it."

"Good, good, I shall send my carriage for you at the usual hour," said her ladyship, ignoring Gertrude's frown. "I wish to take the portrait to Bath with me, to have it framed. We shall have it set in the drawing room, that all may admire your talent, Deborah."

"Is it so good?" asked the squire mildly.

Several voices combined to assure the squire that it was not only good, it had captured Lady Horatia splendidly, that it was equal to any portrait they had ever seen, that Deborah had a magnificent talent, that Lady Horatia had never been so well represented.

In the midst of all this, Alice and Morgan returned, practically unobserved. Deborah noticed them first, standing in the French window, the handsome man and the lovely girl both flushed with their energetic walking. She noticed, also, the rose in Morgan's lapel. It was pale pink, Alice's favorite.

Her heart sank, despite all the flattery still being

heaped on her. A rose, a token of love. She scarcely noticed the cold look Morgan gave to her, the frown that encompassed William Vaughan and Paul Rigaud.

Rigaud was still earnestly proclaiming that Deborah's talent was singular. "It is unusual, it is unique. Yes, I am excited by Lady Horatia's idea that she shall become a professional artist. Why not? *Men* would envy the talent she has. She shall have commissions to paint, more than she could find time to complete."

"What are you saying?" Morgan demanded in amazement, leaving Alice standing in the doorway.

The men had stood up promptly when Alice entered the room. However, both William and Paul resumed their seats next to Deborah, and Alice gave both of them a puzzled look. Morgan loomed over them, scowling down at Deborah.

"What is this?" he repeated. "We left the room so that Miss Deborah might rest. Instead everyone has descended upon her. Miss Deborah, do you not wish to retire to your room?"

She had wished it, but now that he had practically commanded her, she felt defiant. "No, sir, I am comfortable," she said with composure. "Have you had a delightful walk? Are the lilacs not splendid?"

He gave her a haughty look, and she returned it in kind; now she had nothing to gain, nothing to lose by defying him. All chance was gone. William Vaughan stared at the rose also, and the look of gloom on his handsome face intensified.

"I think you should retire!" Morgan continued,

as though issuing a command to an unruly private.

"And I think I should not," she said. Paul patted her hand and chuckled softly.

"When the ladies take that tone, one may as well give in to their whims," he said. His brown eyes twinkled with enjoyment of the byplay.

"Her *whim*, if indulged, will compel her to her bed, and she will be quite unable to go to Bath," said Morgan, in a harsh tone. His gray eyes were like chips of ice in a wintry pond, thought Deborah. "And this talk of her becoming a professional artist is absurd. Surely there is no need for that? Squire, she is not leaving your household?"

The squire smiled. "Oh, Deborah has a home here for her lifetime, and well she knows it," he said comfortably. "But if she wishes to try the life of an artist, she shall. We will support her in whatever she wishes to do," and he gave Morgan an inscrutable look.

"Oh, that is all nonsense! Deborah shall not go to London alone!" Gertrude cried, unable to keep out of the conversation. "We shall not allow *that*, that is too much! I should not sleep nights, knowing she was alone! Deborah, tell us you are teasing!"

Deborah only laughed, which seemed to appease her older sister. Gertrude's face relaxed, and she said brightly, "Just think, Madame Andreossy is going to Bath also, and the gentlemen. What times we shall have!"

Morgan's expression became stormier still. His walk did not seem to have improved his spirits, thought Deborah, watching as he paced over to the fireplace and glared down at Bernard Houdon.

"Oh, shall you take a house also?" asked Alice brightly, as she rang for more tea.

"No, not a house. We shall take lodgings, I believe," said Monsieur Houdon. "We are not in funds to do that. But rooms shall suit us. And you may depend on us to bother you almost daily with our calls. We have not been so amused in years, eh, Marie?"

Marie Andreossy smiled in her wistful fashion and murmured, "How charming everyone is. I should have come to Lowbridge years ago. In London everyone is cold unless one has jewels and money."

"I think we should have been happier here," Paul Rigaud agreed. "Here is where the true spirit of England reigns, where courtesy and hospitality are generous, where the hard worker earns his bread, and no one is idle. This is the heart of this great country."

"How right you are, how right you are!" the squire cried enthusiastically. "Yes, the heart of England is in her countryside, the farm lands, the fields and forests. Here you will find the basis of her economy and the strength of her arms. London is only the surface, the perfume of the profits. Here in the country beats the heart of England."

Monsieur Houdon stood and bowed to the squire. "Here beats an honest heart, and words to go with it. I honor you, sir. Now, we must take our leave. In spite of protests, our good Miss Stanton shows herself very weary. If we leave, she may retire gracefully. Mademoiselle, may I wish you a speedy return to health."

Lady Horatia had been listening with intense

interest all this time, remaining unusually quiet. Now she jumped up also.

"You are right, Monsieur Houdon. We shall leave and let our Deborah rest. You are too hospitable, Mrs. Frome! We come and remain for hours, little thinking how we must strain everyone! Deborah, remember I shall send my carriage for you tomorrow, but if you are not feeling quite the thing, send back word that you cannot come. I shall be disappointed, but know that you are resting."

Morgan looked intensely disapproving again. "She does not go jaunting about tomorrow, surely? That is too much!"

"I wish to finish Lady Horatia's portrait before we remove to Bath," said Deborah, though in truth she felt little like painting.

"Your resolution does you credit." Rigaud bent to kiss her hand once more. "May I wish you a speedy return to health? And may I call upon you again very soon?"

"Thank you, you are always most welcome, Monsieur Rigaud," said Deborah, smiling up at him. He might not be serious about her, but his charm and attentions had quite restored her spirits. When the other visitors had departed, Morgan lingered only a few minutes before saying, "We will leave too. Come, William. I will call upon you during the week, Squire—shall we say Thursday? We will make our plans to go to Bath together."

"Splendid, do come when you will, my lord." The squire watched keenly, without seeming to, as William Vaughan kissed Deborah's hand as lingeringly as had Rigaud.

"Remember what I told you," he murmured to

her. "We shall speak further of this. It may be the solution for us both."

He fairly ran after his cousin, as the viscount strode out to the hallway, displeasure in every line of his tall body. Gertrude ran to the window to watch them bid farewell to the squire. "I think Lord Treverly is angry with Mr. Vaughan," she said with interest. "He is frowning, and scarcely waited for Mr. Vaughan to mount his horse—there, they are off. Dear me, what a very exciting afternoon, to be sure! All those guests! Dear me, I don't know when I have been so upset! All these people going to Bath!"

"And all these beaux hovering about our two beautiful sisters," teased the squire, entering the room in time to hear her. He reached for his pipe, his face crinkling up until his grin reached from ear to ear. "Dear me, I *have* been amused! Yes, bless me, never so amused. This is better than a game of chance!"

"Whatever are you talking about, Clarence?" asked Gertrude.

"Only that we shall have an amusing time in Bath. Much better than I had imagined," said her husband with a laugh. He turned to Deborah. "Now, my dear, I shall escort you upstairs. I think you must be dragging with fatigue. Alice will bring you a tray for your supper and help you to bed, eh, Alice? Yes, you must be weary." And unaccountably he laughed again.

Deborah eyed him dubiously. She knew the squire well enough to realize that his understanding and intelligence were greater than they seemed. Behind the jolly twinkle and jovial good will toward all, there was a shrewd comprehension of human nature. Had he guessed her secret, that she loved Morgan? Or was he merely amused at all the beaux, as he said?

She went up to bed on his arm, thanked him gratefully, and sank down to await Alice's attentions. Yes, she was weary, and she had much to muse about as she waited.

CHAPTER THIRTEEN

Lady Horatia's portrait was completed in two more sessions, and the painting left to dry. Lady Horatia eyed it with great pleasure.

"I do not usually care to contemplate my phiz," she said with a little laugh. "But you have done something, Deborah, something I like immensely. Yes, you have given me character. I know I shall like to live with this painting."

Deborah was more than gratified, she was intensely pleased by the praise. This was the most ambitious project she had ever undertaken. She had thought to do a modest job of it, and hoped that Lady Horatia, familiar with the great artists and portrait painters of the day, would forgive her her faults.

Instead the grand lady seemed sincerely pleased with it, turning it this way and that, setting it in the proper light to study how Deborah had painted her face, her hands, the folds of her silk gown.

"Yes, I shall have it framed in goldleaf, and set it in my home in Bath. Everyone will admire what you have done, and you will have more commissions, mark my word! Now tell me, how do plans proceed for Bath?"

Deborah turned away slightly from Lady Horatia's keen look. "Oh, they go well, I believe. Alice and Gertrude are again at the dressmaker's, and all will be completed within a few days."

"And you? Do you have enough gowns made for all the grand affairs?"

Deborah could not help looking downcast. "I shall feel a dowd, I'm afraid. Oh, forgive my frankness, my lady," she said, laughing a little at herself. "At my age! To long for fine garments and attentions from beaux!"

"My dear Deborah, I have been meaning to speak to you about this matter."

"About beaux? I am not serious, as you probably know."

The lady looked very thoughtful and determined. "Well, about beaux—I do not know. That is your concern, I am sure. However, one's clothing is a matter of much concern to me. I have had an idea. Upstairs there are boxes upon boxes of fabric which I brought back from my travels. I shall never in the world use them all to make dresses and cloaks for myself. I asked my maid to take out a number of them. Dearest Deborah, no money in the world could repay you for the beautiful portrait, or for your friendship. Do say you would consider accepting several lengths of cloth to be made up as garments for you!"

Deborah looked her astonishment. "Lady Horatia, I do not know what to say—"

"Then wait until you see the fabrics," Lady Horatia interrupted, with a commanding smile. "First luncheon, and then you will see the cloths. I do hope you will find something suitable there."

Deborah did not know what to say. Tact prevented her suggesting that the colors Lady Horatia usually chose would not suit her at all.

Following luncheon, Lady Horatia made a little ceremony of presenting Deborah with an envelope of money, far exceeding what Deborah would have dreamed of, to pay for the portrait.

"It is a modest amount, scarcely what a London painter could command, but you must accept it, Deborah."

"It is far too much. I cannot! I meant the portrait as a gift."

"It would please me immensely if you should accept it—" And Lady Horatia had her way, as she usually did.

Then the maid brought down lengths of cloth, one after another, with the help of a footman. The cloth was wrapped in crisp, rustling rice paper, exotic in itself. Unfolded, it revealed strange fabrics, marvelous designs, the most glamorous colors Deborah could have imagined.

There were none of the brilliant scarlets and purples which she associated with Lady Horatia. Instead, the maid unwrapped first an exquisite cream silk brocade with a subtle pattern, cunningly interwoven, of chrysanthemums, shadowy and mysterious. Deborah stroked the fabric with a reverent hand. It was as soft as a baby's breath.

"Oh—lovely," she breathed.

Lady Horatia looked highly pleased. "It is an exquisite fabric, but too quiet for me. I thought it would suit you. It somehow looks like you, ladylike yet exotic, unexpected."

Deborah gazed at her in wonder. "Is that how—"

Then her attention was caught by the next piece. The maid carefully unfolded the lengths of rose velvet.

"I thought—an evening cloak, with a high collar trimmed in pearls," announced Lady Horatia.

Deborah could only gulp. The rose velvet shimmered in the soft light of the oil lamps. She could picture herself in the cream silk, with the rose cloak flung about her, curls to her shoulders— would Morgan notice her then?

More fabrics were unfolded, a green tulle that matched a transparent green gauze with a spider-web pattern of gold woven into it. "An evening gown with overdress," announced Lady Horatia. They set it aside.

There was pale golden shot silk, green velvet for another cloak, plumes of ostrich and peacock feathers. Fur muffs, feather muffs. A shawl of India cashmere, so soft one could crumple it easily, yet warm and strong. There was more than enough for many seasons to come.

Deborah sat bewildered with the fabrics spread about her, feeling transported to an Oriental bazaar, with Lady Horatia a spell-binding magician persuading her she really must have still another gown.

"But—but there will scarcely be time to have them made up—" she finally managed to protest. At the same time she could not bring herself to release the latest fabric laid before her dazzled eyes, a striped silk from Damascus of the most delicate hues of blue and white.

"My maid shall make up two or three of them,

and the rest can be turned over to a dressmaker in Bath," said Lady Horatia firmly. "I shall take them with me, with your measurements. After you arrive, there will be a final fitting. Now, about bonnets—"

"Oh, this is too much—too much—"

Lady Horatia pretended not to see the tears that gathered in Deborah's eyes. "Nonsense, you must be fashionable in Bath! Think of whom you may meet there!"

She chose satin to make frills on a straw bonnet, ribbons of silk and velvet. Deborah's measurements were taken by the maid, and all was noted down. "I'll manage everything," said Lady Horatia. "I am so pleased the fabrics shall be used at last."

She waved away Deborah's stammered protests and turned again to the maid.

"Bring down the sultan's robe, the cream silk with the gold trim, the one that is too small for me," she commanded. The robe was brought, and Deborah found herself arrayed in an exotic garment which covered her from shoulder to foot, and managed to look both dramatic and feminine. Lady Horatia nodded in satisfaction.

"You shall be *ahead* of the fashions," she declared. "Oh, I look forward to the comments on my little protégée. And when all hear you are as talented as you are beautiful—"

"Beautiful! I am not even pretty—"

"Of course you are not *pretty!* Mere prettiness fades. You have bones that are excellent. You shall be beautiful into old age, mark my words!"

Deborah thought, going home in the huge old

barouche, that Lady Horatia was better than a
dozen tonics. With her invisible wand she had produced dramatic fabrics, flattering phrases that yet
rang true, and a confidence in Deborah that the
girl was determined would not be worn away. Lady
Horatia knew the world. She said that Deborah
could succeed in society and as an artist. What
more could she want?

The coachman helped carry in boxes of muffs,
bonnets, lengths of ribbon, swansdown edging,
and so on. Gertrude herself met them at the door,
eyes wide with curiosity and agitation. Deborah
had never looked so excited.

"Whatever have you been up to, Deborah? Late
for tea, and with all these boxes! Did you not finish
the portrait?"

"Finished, and she is most pleased with it, Gertrude!" caroled Deborah, her eyes sparkling. "Oh,
Gertrude, she praised it to the skies! I cannot come
down to earth! And all these fabrics—she insisted
that she would never use them. Bonnet trims—
there is a blue perfect for Alice—"

The bundles and boxes were opened. Alice came
to see and exclaim. Gertrude was first amazed,
then wary. What did all these favors mean? She
stared at the sultan's robe.

"But you could never wear it in company, Deborah!" Gertrude finally exclaimed. "Lady Horatia
can wear outrageous costumes, but you cannot!
She is Lady Horatia Torrington!"

Deborah stroked the silk fabric lovingly. "She is
sure it will do for a concert, over a muslin gown
of white trimmed with gold," she said in a dream.

"And—oh, she is having others made up by her maid, and some to be made in Bath!"

Gertrude did stare at her sister then, and even Alice looked puzzled.

"But Deborah, did you not tell her that Clarence would pay for all?" asked Alice, in her sweetly serious manner. "It does not seem fitting that Lady Horatia should pay for your clothes. Indeed, I am not sure—"

Clarence Frome came from his study, to blink at the exotic array laid out in his cheerful parlor. "A church bazaar?" he asked rather dubiously. One never knew what the ladies would be up to next.

"No, no, some items that Lady Horatia has foisted upon Deborah!" said his wife. "Clarence, do tell Deborah it will not be fitting for her to wear—that!" She pointed at the sleek sultan's robe which Deborah had pulled about her shoulders. Clarence stared at her flushed cheeks and sparkling eyes, at the willful set of her mouth, at the soft silken robe cloaking her slim form.

"My, my," he said inadequately. "The newest style, eh?"

"It's from some Oriental place! And probably full of diseases," said Gertrude wildly. "Just look at those furs! A fur bonnet, if you please, and a muff! How she will wear them in Bath in the summertime, I do not know!"

"Oh, no, these are for next winter," said Deborah, stroking the fur lovingly. "She has many items in her trunks, and indeed, she seemed relieved to be rid of some of them. I think she buys on impulse on her travels, and then does not know what to do with all the fabrics. She herself likes strong colors."

Alice swept her hair up with one hand and struck a pose as she thrust a peacock feather into the mass of blonde curls. "There, how do I look? Is it not grand? Imagine us at the assemblies!"

Deborah and Alice laughed and chattered happily over the feathers, the furs, the swansdown which they draped about their throats. The shawl from India was a curiosity, and they took turns sweeping it about their slim shoulders.

"Oh, so warm and lovely," cooed Alice. "But not my color. This must be yours, Deborah. How happy I am for you! Tell me the fabrics she is having made up!"

She listened with wide eyes as Deborah told of silk brocade, rose velvet, striped Damascus silk. Gertrude grew more and more troubled and finally drew the squire back to his study.

"I do not like it, Clarence, I confess I do not like it! You have been generous with Deborah, she has two new dresses for Bath. The green muslin is modest, the gown for balls is all she could wish— she said so herself. Has she complained that we treat her shabbily? What must she have said to Lady Horatia! To give her fabrics, as though to a maid!" Gertrude was working herself into a frenzy.

Clarence reached for his solace—his pipe—and filled it carefully. "I do not know what to make of it. I know little of fashions," he said cautiously.

"But Deborah is past the age for marrying!" cried Gertrude, too agitated to conceal her true feelings. "Whatever is she thinking of? I thought she would be content to live with us always, helping with the children!"

Clarence silently drew on his pipe and watched the smoke ascend to the fine wood-beamed ceiling.

Gertrude paced the room, her skirts swishing about her, her hands tightly clasped. "Lady Horatia is spoiling Deborah! All this talk about becoming an artist, going off to London—I could not endure it! Deborah is not a—an abandoned artist. I should worry myself to death, should she go off to London and live in a garret. Why does that female put such peculiar ideas into her head? I am sure Deborah has been quite content with us. She was grateful to us for giving her a home, she has said so many a time. She was sincere, I am sure of it!"

"Now, now, Gertrude, no need to agitate yourself. Deborah has not gone off to London; she is going to Bath with us."

"Why?" asked Gertrude bluntly, coming to a pause before her stout, placid husband. "I ask you, why? And why have those young men come calling on her so much? She never used to be interested in young men. She is old, she is twenty-five! Can she be thinking of marriage, at her age? I thought she was quite settled with us."

Clarence's eyes narrowed, but his expression remained bland. "Indeed, indeed," he murmured.

"All those silks and satins and velvets," wailed Gertrude. "If only they were right for dear Alice, or even for me! But the colors will not suit!"

"No, they are Deborah's colors, more than Alice's," said Clarence. "Yes, I think she will be quite happy with them. Sounds as if it will be an interesting time in Bath. Did you hear, we have set on a date? We shall start out Wednesday next, with Lord Treverly's carriages before us and one pair of outriders to follow, in case of highwaymen. Yes, I'm glad he thought of traveling together. Much safer these days."

"Clarence, I did ask you about the clothes—"

"My dear, I know little of clothes. Just so you are all happy," he said, and patted her shoulder gently. "We are happy for Deborah, are we not, that she has made such a friend as Lady Horatia? Deborah has a good mind, and her ladyship exercises it energetically. Do not worry about what has not yet happened. I am sure Deborah will always dress modestly and do us credit. And dear Alice is always a good girl. Yes, yes, you may be proud of your sisters."

The squire had managed to change the subject. Gertrude glared in exasperation as he settled down to his papers once more, then flounced away to see whether dinner was proceeding as it should.

Deborah and Alice, with the help of a maid, had carried everything up to Deborah's bedroom, where they giggled over the sultan's robe, and entertained plans for refurbishing old bonnets with the many feathers. Alice was all in favor of new bonnets, however, especially when Deborah showed her how much Lady Horatia had paid for the painting.

"All that!" she gasped. "Oh, Deborah, you are rich! Shall you give it to Clarence to invest?"

"No, I shall spend it," said Deborah decisively. "I shall buy more canvas and paints, and I shall turn my mind seriously to painting. Surely, in Bath there will be many subjects to catch my attention. And Monsieur Rigaud has urged me to do some port scenes in oils. Who knows, perhaps I *shall* become famous!"

"Oh, my dearest Deborah, I know you can do whatever you set your mind to," said Alice with conviction. She hugged her sister, and they began another fascinating discussion of how many rows of frills should trim the hem of the new cream silk.

Life was full of excitement, it seemed, and very soon they would all be proceeding to Bath. Who knew what would happen then, in the next three months? Anything could!

But in the midst of the excitement, Deborah's thoughts turned to Morgan. She had to admit to herself that her pleasure in the new garments would be much lessened if he were never to notice what she wore. It was Morgan she longed to charm, to attract. If he did not see her, or if his gray eyes were like ice when he glanced in her direction, none of it would matter much.

If Morgan did not care, it was all for naught.

CHAPTER FOURTEEN

In coaches, carriages, and high-perch phaeton, with alert outriders ahead of them and behind them, the party proceeded to Bath on a fine day in early May.

All was excitement. Morgan held the reins of his phaeton, with Alice perched up beside him. William Vaughan drove Deborah in another carriage from Treverly. Squire Frome sat in the back of his carriage with his wife and two younger children, while a coachman drove them. The two older children were with the nursemaid in another coach. Other coaches carried the luggage. In all, eight vehicles proceeded in state, all the way to Bath.

There was even room for the French party. Marie Andreossy sometimes shared the seat on Morgan's phaeton. But her bonnet blew about, and her skirts, and she soon declared she would be more comfortable in a carriage.

Deborah longed for the seat beside Morgan, but it was not offered to her. She told herself the attentions of Mr. Vaughan and of Monsieur Rigaud ought to have satisfied her, but it was no use.

They stopped for luncheon, and a change of

horses, at an inn where Lord Treverly had made arrangements in advance. Tables were set for them, and the landlord and girls ran about eagerly to wait upon the fine company. They hungrily ate chickens roasted to a turn, and fresh new strawberries in thick cream.

Then they were on their way again. Lord Treverly had insisted on an early start, and his urging kept them going. As he had predicted, they arrived at Bath in the early evening, as dusk turned the sky to lavender, and the lights began to twinkle in the valley of the Avon River where the city lay.

Deborah's first sight of Bath, from the high seat beside Mr. Vaughan, caught her in silent rapture: the curve of the river, held gently by the folds of the hills about, the impressive sweep of houses, the spires of churches and chapels. At once she picked out the massive gray Abbey, dominating all from medieval times.

Eagerly she gazed, and gazed again. She heard the voices of the others, their laughter, their eager queries, as if in a dream. Bath—where society reigned, where music would be heard, and books were available in great numbers, where dances were held often, and her future might lie.

Morgan saw the squire's party to their door, where the servants were waiting to welcome them. He refused their invitation to alight.

"No, no, we will go on. I am expected, and dinner will be waiting. We shall see all of you tomorrow. If you hear of rooms to let, let us know. I shall have the pleasure of the company of our French friends such time as they choose to stay! Farewell—"

His bow included them all. They saw him off, then turned into their own rented house.

The squire insisted on seeing the entire house that night, from ground to attic, and pronounced himself well-enough pleased. The agent had done well by them. Gertrude sniffed dubiously, wondering if she smelled dust and mold. Tomorrow's daylight would show whether they indeed had a bargain, or cause for regret.

Dinner was served to the weary company, and soon after they were in bed. Deborah stretched out in the bed beside Alice, for they shared a second-floor bedroom. She was situated far from the children—the nursemaid must see to them now. She was intent on finding her future! Almost too excited to sleep, she lay awake long after Alice's even breathing told her that her sister slept.

The next day began with the delivery of a huge bouquet from Lady Horatia, praised even by Gertrude. Massive carnations and ferns, of wondrous color and scent, were set in an exotic Chinese vase.

It was given pride of place in the formal drawing room, and was soon joined by bouquets from Lord Treverly and Paul Rigaud. But wonder of wonders, a Master of Ceremonies called on them scarcely before Gertrude had put on her white lace morning cap and settled herself to coffee.

She told her sisters about the visit when they came down later. "Only imagine, he called simply to welcome us, and goes from us to Lord Treverly! It is the custom. He invites us to the assemblies, tells us of the theatre, the circulating libraries. Clarence is so good, he will subscribe everywhere—"

She was glowing and jubilant, all her doubts set aside. They had come to Bath and had been called upon at once! Her campaign for Alice would succeed, and they would all have a glorious time as well.

Alice winked slightly at Deborah, and Deborah smiled fondly back at her. They soon set out to discover a few of the delights of Bath, a coachman stalking behind them as escort.

But soon they would need no escort, Alice whispered, for Mr. Vaughan had already searched out the circulating library nearest to them, and when they entered the shop, it was to find him poring over the latest newspapers from London. He looked up, stared in delight, and dropped the papers to come to them and bend over their hands.

"It is too much!" he cried, and other gentlemen looked up alertly, to gaze with pleasure at the new faces before them. Approving looks darted from the blue dress and blooming young face of blonde Alice, to the smile and sparkle of the older girl in her rose muslin.

"I did not dream you would arise so early. I was coming to call upon you as soon as I dared," Mr. Vaughan said ingenuously.

Alice withdrew her hand gently from his, but he released it reluctantly. "And we find you reading the news!" she mocked him gently. "Do you read of your regiment, Mr. Vaughan?"

He flushed a little, and nodded. "Action, and I have no part in it," he sighed. "Come, let me show you the books here. The latest of novels! Will you read Mr. Walter Scott?"

Alice soon pounced on *Castle Rackrent* by Maria Edgeworth. "Oh, what is this? It sounds wonderful!" and she opened the first volume to scan the pages.

Deborah gazed wistfully at the paintings on the walls. Could she ever attain such mastery of oils? How splendid that one was, of a stag in a Scottish highland scene with the gloom of a storm behind him and his head alert to the sound of the wind. She turned to contemplate a placid scene of a ship at sea.

The voice behind her startled her. "Do they please you, Miss Stanton?" Morgan said, his voice gently mocking. As she jerked about, he added, "I beg pardon for not announcing myself more carefully. I fear I made you jump."

"No, no, it is nothing." She turned slowly to face him, and managed to look up as far as his intricately folded stock, his firm, hard chin. "I have to thank you for your care of us yesterday. Never was a long journey so enjoyable."

"You rested well, I trust? Mrs. Frome is satisfied with the house?"

"She is pleased, sir. And we are all delighted with Bath and long to see the city."

"You will wish to call upon Lady Horatia, of course. Permit me to escort you there, if you wish to go this morning."

"Is that done?" she asked anxiously. "I do not know the customs of Bath as yet."

"Oh, there is a ritual, but you need not heed it if you do not choose to," he said drily. "Early in the morning, those who wish go down to the old Roman baths and partake of the healing waters. Then they eat lightly, and receive callers. Then they dress and stroll about, and eat an enormous number of pastries, and comment wickedly on all they saw the evening before. Then the afternoon is spent in calls, the evening in dinners, whist, or dances at the Assembly Rooms. Reading, gossip, pleasure, all stop at eleven o'clock, and so to bed. The next day, all begins again."

Alice and Deborah listened wide-eyed, and began to giggle as his recital ended. "He is gammoning you," said Mr. Vaughan with a smile.

"No, no, I am not!" Morgan insisted. "Watch and wait! You will see I am right. But it is all amusing enough, and sometimes the plays are good. And the music can be excellent—you will enjoy that, Miss Deborah."

At his friendly tone, she flushed, and did not know where to look. Her heart began to beat more wildly. Was he going to be friends with her again? If only they might be friends, could she wish for more?

"Where are your guests? Are they searching for housing?" asked Alice, fingering the Edgeworth book longingly.

"Yes, they are setting out at once. I told them to wait a time, but they have heard of other French émigrés settled in Bath—there is an entire colony of them here—and they were eager to make their acquaintance and speak their own tongue for a time." He smiled at Alice then. "Have you made a choice, Miss Alice? Allow me to take it for you. I insist; I have my card ready."

He glanced at the title, smiling at her choice.

Then he asked Deborah to choose. She shook her head, somehow reluctant to be indebted to him.

"Not yet, sir, I have not chosen. I should like to call upon Lady Horatia, if that is the accepted practice."

The two gentlemen assured her it was, and they all set out, Mr. Vaughan with his hand under Alice's elbow to assist her over the curbs and around the horses and Bath chairs. Morgan did the same for Deborah, and she felt as if the pulse in her throat would choke her as his hand tightened to guide her around an obstacle.

He pointed out the chemist's, another circulating library he recommended, pointed up the hill toward the New Rooms of the Assembly, where dances were held. They were usually contra dances, and one might stand up with whomever had been introduced. "There is little formality about meeting anyone. No private parties are permitted in the dances," he explained. "It is the custom here in Bath that merchants and lords, young and old, doctors and lawyers and artists"— and he gave Deborah a significant smile—"all are equal and must be easy with each other."

She returned his smile, with more ease than she had felt in some time. If only Morgan would be like this always, friendly and smiling. His serious face seemed lighter today, his gray eyes warm and smiling. His blond hair curled below his ears in a careless, handsome fashion. Oh, he was so fine and elegant, no wonder ladies stared at him on the street, and gentlemen looked at him as though wondering who he was.

When they arrived at Lady Horatia's, she welcomed them as though they had not met for a year. She immediately showed them into her drawing room, where Deborah's portrait of her was set on a table against a wall. She would have it framed soon, but for now she could not bear to part with it.

All examined and praised it. Deborah waited eagerly for Morgan's opinion. He picked it up and held it to the light. Lady Horatia watched him alertly, as if ready to spring to Deborah's defense should that be necessary.

"It is very good," he finally pronounced, and set it down. "I had allowed for the natural prejudice of Lady Horatia, with her fondness for Miss Deborah. But one need make no allowances. You have a fine talent, Miss Deborah. This is a splendid portrait."

She let out her breath in a sigh, unaware that she had been holding it in. "Thank you, sir," she murmured, wishing only that his opinion did not matter so much.

The visit soon over, they returned home for luncheon. The gentlemen left them at their door, with a promise to see them the next day. William Vaughan would have accepted Gertrude's cordial invitation to dinner, but Lord Treverly hurried him away.

"They have guests," Deborah told Alice, who seemed to droop with disappointment. "They cannot accept our invitation when their guests will be there."

"I shall invite them all here tomorrow," said Gertrude. "Dear me, I did not dream we should be so busy so very soon. Do you know, I had two more callers this morning? A lady who knows Lady Horatia came with her companion—dear me, we shall be a success, I am sure of it."

The next morning, Alice and Deborah, out of curiosity, went to the Pump Room. Deborah especially was amused at the company, those who gravely drank the mineral waters, those who gossiped and drank tea, those who stood about and observed the others. They proceeded to the library, where Clarence had taken a subscription, and Deborah chose some volumes to take home.

The next evening was their first dance. Lady Horatia's maid had delivered several new gowns for Deborah, who finally chose the green silk with the green gauze overdress shot with gold. She added a thin gold chain about her throat. Alice looked delightful in a misty silk chiffon, cut modestly about her throat, showing her long graceful arms, her delicate slim-waisted body.

Alice was presented that evening by the Master of Ceremonies, who also danced with her. Gertrude was enchanted with the ceremony and afterwards pronounced that it was far better than being presented at court. She preferred the informality and friendliness of Bath. Alice was vastly popular, and her blue eyes were radiant with her success.

Deborah also enjoyed her share of attention, though she was not presented; it was tactfully taken for granted that she had been presented long ago. She was introduced to a cloth merchant and his oldest son, and stood up with the son. She met a writer who was gloomy and abstracted, an artist

who seemed somewhat Bohemian in appearance.
(She did not tell him that she also painted.) But
she stood up with Morgan only once, and he was
again coolly formal with her.

The days passed serenely. Deborah began to
make time for her sketching. She drew the silvery
Avon River, the dots of houses nestled in its bends.
She drew sketches of Bath from the hills surround-
ing it, where Mr. Vaughan would take her and
Alice in the Treverly carriage, and wait patiently
while she found just the scenes she wished to draw.

On rainy days, they sat in the drawing room.
While Alice embroidered and Gertrude presided
over the tea table, Deborah would take out her
sketch pad and work in pastels or watercolors.

On one of those afternoons, Gertrude fretted, "I
do believe we have not had above a dozen callers
this week. Whatever can be wrong?"

"My dear," said Clarence mildly. "Were we at
home in Lowbridge, you would have been amazed
to have a dozen callers! Here in Bath, you fret to
have only half a dozen a day! Whatever shall we
do when we return home? I shall have to beg the
whole village to call daily!"

They all began to laugh, even Gertrude. "Truly,
I *am* spoiled," she admitted. "And the children are
so happy here. And Alice—what a success she is!"

Alice blushed, and looked down. Her needle
paused above her work. Deborah gave her a searching look, then with a little sigh returned to her
sketching. Morgan had been more and more attentive to Alice. His flowers came frequently. Was he
serious about her? They had seen him on the

streets of Bath with other females, but he came most often to the Frome house—everyone said so.

About two-thirty in the afternoon a knocking sounded at the door. Gertrude brightened up, and the butler hastened to answer.

"Dear me, I heard no carriage! Do look, Clarence, is it—"

No need for the squire to bestir himself, for Lord Treverly's suave tones were heard and William Vaughan's eager ones.

Gertrude and the squire rose to greet them. They came in with wet coats which the butler hastened to remove.

"Forgive us," said Lord Treverly with a genial smile. "We were about to drive past when we concluded that you would not mind too much if we called upon you again, wet as we are. If we could but dry ourselves—"

Lord Treverly looked over at Deborah, but did not approach her. "The artist at work," he said, but he did not sound as cynical as usual.

"Indeed, sir, Bath has inspired me. My sketch book is filled, and I have begun another."

He came then to gaze over her shoulder and leaf through her book. He paused at one scene, an elderly plump woman wrapped to her ears, being carried home in a chair following her morning bath. He gave a hearty laugh, which startled her; she had scarcely heard him laugh in so long.

"Oh, splendid, Miss Deborah! You have her to the life. Ah, I like this one—" He paused at a soft sketch of Bath from the hills. "You should do this one in color."

She nodded, excited by his interest. "I hope to, sir." She was so delighted by his attention that she was sorry when other guests arrived.

Among them was Paul Rigaud, who eagerly told Deborah of other French émigrés he had met in Bath. There was now a sizable colony of them. When that subject had been exhausted, he began to turn over the pages of her sketch pad as Morgan had done, pausing to exclaim over one or another.

"However—you will not be offended, Miss Deborah?—I liked best your port scenes, those of ships and sailors. It seems to me that you have a natural sympathy for that subject. Did you bring that portfolio to Bath with you?"

She had, so she went to her room to fetch it. He went slowly and appreciatively through the sketches.

"I am so fond of the sea, I should have been a sailor," he sighed. "Now I am only a drifter, knowing not where I shall end. Ah, how much I like this one—" He paused at a scene of Bristol port. "I wish you would continue in this vein," he said seriously. "I feel sure you could sell paintings made from scenes such as this."

"You mean it, I believe. Well, I shall try," she promised. She turned over the pages with him, their heads close together over the sketchbook. The others gazed at them and smiled significantly.

"I have seen the Bristol Channel," Rigaud said. "How handsome and busy it is! Someday I might persuade you to make some sketches for me. I wish I were wealthy enough to buy them all from you! They are the finest I have ever seen."

"You are too kind, sir," she said, with reserve. She felt herself drawing back a little from his eagerness. He seemed to wish to take the portfolio with him! But she cherished it for the memories it held, as well as for the samples of her growing talent. The sketches reminded her of sunny days with Alice and her father, in the years before the accident had changed him to a tired, frustrated man.

She closed the portfolio, but not before Rigaud had her promise to continue to draw sketches of ships and ports, and other scenes from memory. "You must not be so busy with the Bath scene, it is frivolous and beneath you," he said, with a slight frown. "I long to see your work hung in the local libraries. All should know of you."

Deborah glanced at Morgan and met his cynical gaze. Evidently he had heard the comments. She had only a small talent in his opinion, of that she was sure. Perhaps she should merely exercise it in amusing the company. How could she hope to have her work hung?

She set the sketches aside and turned her attention to William Vaughan, who came over to sit on her other side.

The guests left late, the last one lingering until after six. Gertrude was radiant at her success as a hostess in the fashionable spa of Bath. Who could ask for more! And next week would be best of all. Lord Treverly was having a grand dinner party for fifty persons, and Alice would be the guest of honor, having just come into society.

And all this accomplished in only two weeks in

Bath! thought Gertrude with immense satisfaction. Deborah wished she could feel an equal satisfaction. For despite the pleasures the city offered, she could see little change in her own prospects. Perhaps she had hoped for a miracle, she thought bitterly. If so, the more fool she!

CHAPTER FIFTEEN

The following evening they all went to a concert in the Upper Rooms of the Assemblies. The squire had urged them to go early, because it would be crowded. They dutifully did as he suggested and arrived in time to take chairs toward the front of the room. The orchestra members began to arrive, taking out their instruments. Deborah enjoyed watching them begin to tune up, the violinists working intently on their strings so that they might be just so, the flutist trying tentative little notes, the pianist grandly sweeping up and down the keys.

"There is Mr. Vaughan," Alice whispered, a blush accompanying her words. "They have just come in the door."

Deborah dared not frankly turn about, but she wondered at Alice. She had said, "Mr. Vaughan," when she could have said "Lord Treverly," for it was Morgan's party which had entered. Paul Rigaud spotted them first, and eagerly came toward them. The empty seat beside Deborah attracted him, and he motioned to it questioningly. She nodded and smiled, and he seated himself beside her. She noted then that Lord Treverly hesitated, and finally found seats for Marie Andreossy and others of the party, while he continued to stand near the wall toward the back of the room.

"I knew you would be here," Paul whispered into Deborah's ear. "I believe you are as fond of good music as I am."

"I like it immensely," she whispered back. Their heads were close together, and Morgan was eying them gloomily, she noticed when her head was slightly turned toward the back.

If only *he* had taken the empty chair beside hers! But that would have been too much to hope for. Now if the empty chair had been beside Alice, that would have been a different matter.

"I saw you out sketching today on the Parade," whispered Paul. "The sun was brilliant, and you looked so charming with the wind blowing your curls."

"You flatter me too much, sir!"

He laughed softly, as though she had said something witty. "How I enjoyed our visit yesterday!"

"And I also," she felt compelled to say.

The conductor came out, a plump, commanding figure, and all were hushed. Paul settled back, folded his arms, and gave his attention to the music. The musicians proved to be in fine fettle, and it promised to be a beautiful evening.

During the slight pause that followed the first piece, Paul leaned toward Deborah again. "You have thought of my words? You have started a painting?"

"Yes, I have, sir, of the Bristol port you admired."

"Ah, how happy you make me! I long to see it—" His brown eyes glowed. "If only I had the direction of your career—"

The music began again, and Deborah leaned back, rather startled at his presumption. Direct her career? Indeed he would not! She valued him as a friend, and his kind criticism encouraged her. But to direct her career—they were scarcely *that* close.

After the next piece, from Handel's Water Music, Squire Frome stood up, stretched, and left his seat between his wife and Alice. Deborah thought Mr. Vaughan must have been watching the seat like a hawk, for he promptly slid into it, beside Alice, and turned to speak to her eagerly. Deborah wondered at him. Should he not have waited to see if his cousin wished the place?

Lord Treverly saw that a footman brought them a tray of cool drinks during the intermission, and Deborah accepted hers gratefully. Morgan paused near them, and leaned across Rigaud to say to Deborah, "I do not need to ask if you enjoyed the music. Your face speaks for you. It is splendid, is it not?"

"It is very fine, yes. I am enjoying it immensely, sir," she said. "But I wish you had a seat, sir. It is too bad there are not enough places—"

"It does not matter. I rather enjoy watching the entire room," he said. "I have spoken to the squire. Everyone will return to my house for some refreshments after the concert. You will come, I hope?"

"Of course, I shall be delighted." To see his home! She had thought they would have to wait until the dinner he gave for Alice. And he had spoken directly to her, not to Alice or Gertrude.

He smiled and withdrew. Deborah leaned back in a daze of pleasure and scarcely heard Paul's whispered comments on the next piece to be played.

When the concert was over, Clarence Frome gathered his women together, as he cheerfully put it, and swept them all down to their coach. Together they drove downhill, and around corners, and uphill and around again, until the coach drew into a fine circle where other carriages stood. Lights flared in the beautiful windows which extended from the ground floor nearly to the roof. Deborah alighted with great anticipation in her heart.

She was dazzled, when they entered the huge hall, to see gray flagstones extending all the way to the back of the deep house. Doors were open along the way, and the butler showed them into the first drawing room where a rather large company was already gathered.

Morgan detached himself from a group and met them at the door with every evidence of delight. "You have come after all. I feared you had lost your way," he smiled down at them.

Deborah took off her cloak, to have it whisked away by a maid. Morgan's gray eyes seemed to approve of her slim, rounded figure in the smart Damascus silk. Yet he looked with equal approval on Alice, in white crepe.

Marie Andreossy was seated on a sofa, resplendent in her usual red chiffon, her dark hair swirled high in a chignon which set off her beautiful face. She gave them a gay little wave of her fingers.

"We know most of the company," commented Gertrude in a low tone of immense satisfaction. "We have met them already!" And she swept forward, as became a matron, to shake hands with all she knew.

William Vaughan came up to Deborah and Alice to take their arms with easy familiarity and escort them about the large room. Morgan kept glancing at them, as if to make sure they were at ease, and were being introduced all around. His attention was being held by a tiny dowager with a tiara on her white hair, an imperious voice, and an ear trumpet held to her ear.

"Lady Willoughby," whispered Mr. Vaughan. "A relative of His Royal Highness. You will meet her presently."

Alice glanced at Deborah, her blue eyes sparkling. Royalty—or as near as they were likely to get!

Lady Horatia found them in the corner, staring at everyone. "My dearest girls," she boomed at them happily, "I thought you would be here. Come, let me introduce you to Lady Willoughby. She is much impressed by Deborah's portrait of me!" And she swept them with her to meet the formidable woman.

"You painted the portrait?" demanded Lady Willoughby, her voice nearly a shout because of her deafness. Deborah nodded. "Incredible! You don't look like a Bohemian! An artist and a lady! Amazing! What would you make of me?"

Deborah hesitated, not knowing what to say. Lady Horatia shouted into the other woman's ear trumpet. "You should make an appointment with Miss Stanton for sittings! Terribly popular, have to wait!" She gave Deborah a sly wink as she said it.

"I never wait, I never wait. Have to make appointments at once. What about Thursday? Come on Thursday, Miss Stanton. You shall do the sketches at once!" Deborah looked around, rather aghast, to meet Morgan's amused gaze.

"I will come," she said loudly and distinctly into the ear trumpet. "Where—"

Lady Horatia gave her a dig in the ribs. "I'll send my carriage. My coachman will know; he will take you about," she muttered rapidly. "Give her two hours, then leave. Any longer would exhaust you!"

Deborah gave her friend a grateful smile, and Lady Willoughby moved on to greet someone else, to Deborah's considerable relief.

She found Paul Rigaud scowling at her elbow. "Why did you give in to her? Your other work is far more important," said the Frenchman. "Portraits! Paugh, anyone can do them! It is not everyone who has your talent for scenes of the sea."

"Her future is more secure with portraits," said Lady Horatia decisively. "I advised her to do it, and I shall find others who wish to be painted. Bath shall be the beginning of a splendid career."

"Her forte is the sea!" insisted Paul, with barely controlled anger. "This is her heritage, her strong talent!"

"I would suggest," Morgan said in a deep drawl, "that Miss Stanton should be allowed to choose her own subjects. And she should not take on more than she chooses. She is here on holiday, after all. Miss Stanton, do not allow yourself to work all day and night, as your *admirers* would insist! Enjoy yourself; you have worked hard for years. It is time to relax now, is it not?"

A little dizzy at his attention, she managed to nod and accept the glass of wine that a footman held before her on a tray.

"To Miss Stanton and her career," said Lady Horatia firmly, giving Morgan a cross look.

"To Miss Stanton and her brilliant work in her father's footsteps," said Paul, and drank rapidly.

"To Miss Stanton and her happiness," said Morgan quietly.

Deborah could only smile faintly, but no one seemed to notice her silence, for they were all glaring at each other.

Alice drew her aside. "What was all that about, Deborah? What did that terrible little woman want?"

"Her portrait," Deborah whispered. "And now Monsieur Rigaud is annoyed because I had promised to do the painting of Bristol Channel, and Lady Horatia is annoyed—dear me," she ended with a sigh.

There was no time to explain further, for Morgan took Deborah's glass from her and firmly took her arm. "You two must meet some of the other guests," he said, and drew Alice with them. He led them about the room, and they chatted with one group and another. Everyone stared curiously at the two lovely sisters, escorted by the handsome new Viscount of Treverly. Whispers flew in their wake, like bubbles on the ocean waves after a ship passes.

"Which of them—"

"Handsome, both of them—"

"Which does he favor? Or is it—"

"Young girl is damned attractive! Pretty as a picture!"

"Older girl more character, I hear she is an artist. Smart as paint, that—"

"Sponsored by Lady Horatia Torrington—"

"Saw the portrait—fine work—"

Deborah's cheeks were soon scarlet. Morgan glanced down at her, a wry smile on his mouth. "Your success is more than you had hoped, is it not?" he murmured in her ear.

She nodded ruefully. "I thought little of my talent. I still cannot believe—"

"And this is Mrs. Hortense Crawley. You will be happy to hear her impressions of Bath, she writes splendidly," said Morgan smoothly, at the edge of another animated little group.

They realized they were in the presence of a noted gossip writer for one of the London gazettes. Alice was tongue-tied, but the woman quizzed Deborah hopefully, her sharp eyes studying every inch of her slim figure, the smart gown, Alice's pretty features, the way Lord Treverly held each girl's arm.

After they had left that group, Lord Treverly murmured, "We shall have to watch the London gazettes now for mention of you. I trust it will not be spiteful. You were quiet and polite, I think she will not claw you to pieces."

"Oh, would she do that?" asked Alice anxiously.

"Only if you are too high in the instep," he said, a quirk lifting one corner of his mouth. "Her favorite occupation is hauling down some poor soul who aspires too high. All pretensions are pricked like a bubble by her sharp quill. But she is a fair enough judge of character, and she did admire your portrait of Lady Horatia, Miss Deborah, so fear not. I think she will enhance your reputation."

"Who would have thought, Deborah, when you did the portrait, that all this would come of it?" said Alice delightedly. "I am so happy for you! You have worked so hard for years—no one knows better than I how much you gave up for us."

"Hush, my dear," said Deborah, uncomfortably aware of Morgan's hard look at her. "That is all in the past."

"Yes, you were always ready to do everything— for your family," said Morgan gravely.

Deborah gave him a quick look. "It was all a sister could do, and a daughter. If one is not prepared to help one's family, how can one look in the mirror of a morning?"

"Yes, so you said," he answered abruptly. "But not everyone shares your devotion to family. Of course, Alice has grown to be a lovely woman, thanks to you."

"It is gracious of you to say so," she said in a muffled tone. Alice had turned when someone spoke to her, and she and Morgan were alone in the crowd. She gave him a pleading look. Did he truly understand her? Did he forgive her for her actions in the past?

His gray eyes were brooding, but not cold. He met her look intently for a moment, then turned abruptly when Marie Andreossy appeared at his side and tapped him lightly on the arm with her black lace fan.

"My lord, here are some guests who are anxious to greet you." She acted exactly like his hostess, thought Deborah in dismay.

He looked past her, saw the guests, and murmured an excuse to Deborah. She nodded and tried to smile. The first time they had talked intimately for so long—and then he had been called away.

She suppressed a sigh. It was probably hopeless, this yearning she had felt for so many years. He showed little regard for her beyond courtesy. But she had no opportunity to become lost in her thoughts, for Lady Horatia appeared at her side.

"There, I have not been so amused in years!" the woman said.

Deborah turned to face her friend and tried to smile. "Amused, Lady Horatia? I am glad of it, but may I ask why?"

"Oh, dear me, everything is going in circles," said Lady Horatia obscurely, her eyes snapping in satisfaction. "One and two and three, yes, yes, it all adds up."

Deborah gazed at her in astonishment, momentarily forgetting her own pain. "Whatever are you talking about?"

"Never mind, never mind!" Lady Horatia laughed and tapped her hand lightly. You shall be a great success, my dear, whatever you choose! Bath is greatly amusing, don't you think? I am so glad we all came here!"

There was a murmur among the newest arrivals; then William Vaughan broke away from them and approached the squire. His face was pale, his mouth working. Deborah caught his words, "Have you heard the news, Squire? Dreadful, yet inevitable—"

The words caught at her. She began to move toward Clarence, and Lady Horatia followed her. "What is it? What is it?" people were asking.

Lord Treverly raised his hand to the company, and they fell silent. "We have just had word from the latest gazettes—our country has again declared war on the French!"

There was a hush, and Deborah looked toward Paul Rigaud, who had turned pale. His hand clutched automatically at the back of a chair. Her sympathy went out to him, and to the other French émigrés. In the babble that followed, she heard William Vaughan's voice.

"I must re-enlist! I must rejoin my regiment! No other course is possible—"

"No, no," whispered Alice, near enough for Deborah to hear her. "He must not—"

Lord Treverly made his way to William and clapped him on the shoulder. "Do not excite yourself, William. It may come to little—"

"I must go. Our chaps will be the first to go—you must see it, Morgan!"

"No more now, you are upsetting everyone," Morgan said in a low tone, but Deborah heard him clearly, and the mixture of sympathy and authority. "We will speak of this tomorrow, after reading the gazettes. No more tonight."

"We should leave, sir. There is much to worry about," Deborah whispered to the squire.

"You are right, my dear. Come, I will gather up Gertrude—where is Alice?"

Their party came together at the doors, where Morgan stood to see them off. Others had begun to stir and leave. Deborah saw Paul Rigaud looking pale and anguished.

He stepped forward to help her into the carriage. "Come to us tomorrow," she said encouragingly. "Do not take it so to heart. We should have known the peace could not last."

"You are too good, Miss Deborah. I shall come— and thank you." He raised her hand to his lips and kissed it passionately.

She had never liked him so much, nor felt so close to him. She pressed her fingers to his. "Be comforted, sir. None will hold it against those of you who had to flee France. You shall not be the worse for it. Perhaps one day you may return to France, when that monster Napoleon has been defeated."

"But he seems unconquerable," said Paul.

Morgan approached them. "Do not fight the war tonight, my friends," he said lightly. "Come, Paul, come inside and enjoy some of our fine brandy smuggled from France. We shall be friends, though our countries are not. Miss Deborah, sleep well, and do not dream of frightful things."

He took her hand and kissed it, and she felt a wild surge of excitement. Did he hold her hand longer than necessary? He gave her a smile, but in the light of the midnight torches his face was partly hidden in shadow. Then the coachman sprang to his seat, the horses were started, and the sound of their hooves rang on the cobblestones and drowned out the called farewells.

"I had thought all that nonsense was over," said Gertrude, a distinct quaver in her voice. "War yet again! Shall we ever be at peace?"

"Not until Napoleon is overset," said the squire, with unusual gravity. "I fear that man; he has uncanny military powers. And we know how he has been gathering troops on the Channel opposite Dover. Word comes of more troops, and they are building boats to invade England."

Gertrude and Alice gave little shrieks and gazed about in wild dismay, as though to see the monster himself on horseback, leading troops right into Bath.

"I am sure our military will be more than ready to meet them," said Deborah, with unusual firmness. "Think of all our regiments, and our navy! Surely our navy is on the alert in the Channel, and all about the French coast. Napoleon's men shall not come near us, be assured of that."

"Bravely spoken, Deborah! But we must be alert," said the squire. "I think we must have more drilling at Lowbridge when we return."

"They would not come so far as Lowbridge!" breathed Gertrude, her hand clasped to her heart.

"No, no, but our men may be sent to help along the coasts," said the squire, and then, seeing she was very upset, he added, "But come now, war has just been declared. Formalities only, my dear! Do not fret, our fine military shall protect us. Why, England has not been invaded for eight hundred years! I warrant you—"

But Gertrude would not be calmed. The squire drew Deborah aside when they arrived home. "When that young Frenchman comes tomorrow, Deborah," he said quietly, "let him not affright Gertrude and Alice. I will not have hysterical women about! If it is a fine day, perhaps you could walk out with him. Though it's no wonder the poor chap is upset, away from his homeland, feeling a stranger here."

"Yes, I shall do my best, sir."

"Whatever are you talking about?" asked Gertrude, approaching them. "Must we set the footmen on guard tonight?"

Her husband gave a great bellow of laughter. "Not for Napoleon's men, my dear! If you speak of the many beaux who pant after our two sisters, that is another matter. How serious are they, do you warrant? Shall we have to lock the doors and bolt them against these impassioned young men?"

"Oh, Clarence, do not be so foolish!" Gertrude scolded him in a more normal tone.

"No, no, I am not foolish," he insisted, his hand under her elbow to escort her up the stairs. "I saw the hot looks directed at young Alice and our Deborah! Yes, yes, we must be on guard!" And he turned and gave Deborah a broad wink and a grin.

She had to laugh, and he was satisfied. Alice, however, was very troubled, and Deborah managed to distract her only by talking about Mr. Vaughan and how attentive he had been at the concert.

"And is not Lord Treverly's house grand? Almost as fine as his manor at Lowbridge," said Deborah encouragingly. "Just think, in little more than a week, you shall be guest of honor there! What shall you wear?"

Talk of dresses continued until Alice drifted into sleep, but Deborah lay awake a little longer.

She shuddered at the thought of Morgan going off to war again. Surely his high position, as well as his wounded leg, would prevent his going. He had done his share; surely he had done *more* than his share.

CHAPTER SIXTEEN

Paul Rigaud appeared early the next morning, and Deborah had all she could do to calm him. He was still pale and distraught.

Mindful of the squire's admonition, she tried to turn the subject. Failing in this, and realizing that Gertrude was becoming upset, she said, "Do let us walk out, now that we have a gentleman to escort us, Alice. I shall take my sketchbook, and perhaps M. Rigaud will escort us to the Parade."

Rigaud seemed to regain a little of his composure. "You are too good to me in my despair," he murmured as they set out. "I fear I have taken advantage of your kindness."

"Not at all, sir. Your feelings do you credit, I am sure."

The wind was strong that May morning, yet the sun shone golden, and Deborah looked about absently for a scene to sketch. Such perfect weather, and the silvery Avon winding below them.

The sound of fife and drum reached them as they approached the Parade.

"Oh, they are drilling this morning. Do they not

look splendid?" Alice exclaimed as they came into view of the grounds. Battalions of men in red and white, with gold flashing in the sunlight, marched and wheeled. The occupants of Bath had come to watch by the hundreds.

Paul Rigaud politely pushed them into the crowd, and deftly made room for them near the front. He indicated the sketch pad, and people smiled and made way for Deborah and Alice to go forward. They stood at the railings above the Parade and watched in fascination as the soldiers drilled smartly, wheeling and turning to the commands, snapping their muskets to order.

Deborah opened her sketch pad, and Rigaud nodded enthusiastically. "A fine sight," he murmured. "England will not be easily conquered!"

Deborah took a brown pencil from the box Rigaud carried for her, and began to sketch the sight. The hills beyond, the Parade, and the ranks of men took shape on the paper. Others in the crowd peered around to watch her skillful hand at work.

Finally the drill was over, and someone called for a cheer. Three good shouts went up from the crowd into the clear morning air. Then the crowd dispersed, with more to talk about over their morning coffee and their glasses of mineral water.

Paul seemed more cheerful as they strolled on. "Splendid, splendid," he kept murmuring. "Yes, I am more reassured. The British will be prepared. Now, tell me, Miss Deborah, what would you like to do today? Lord Treverly said I might command one of his carriages at any time. Shall we ride out into the countryside—and Miss Alice as well?"

She hesitated. She did not wish to be further obligated to him, nor to Morgan. Did he care so little if she went out with Monsieur Rigaud? Evidently. "No, I had best return home by luncheon. Gertrude has guests coming. But if you would accompany us to the library, I would be most grateful."

"My dear Miss Deborah, I shall accompany you wherever you choose!" he said, with a glowing look at her.

Alice gave Deborah a wide-eyed look. Deborah blushed and glanced away uneasily. He was a handsome and charming young man, and she cared not a whit that he had little to live on. If she loved him, she would marry him if he wished. If only— if only she did not still have this foolish, hopeless yearning for Morgan! *Morgan* had been within her reach. *Lord Treverly* was far beyond her. She had to keep reminding herself of that.

And Paul was so kind, so handsome, with a past he might forget if he had a family in England to help him settle down. He was concerned about her career, too; he thought always of her welfare. She was sure that if she encouraged him, he would be much more than a friend.

He accompanied them to the library, and then back to the Fromes' house, but Deborah hesitated over asking him to luncheon. When he came in with them, however, Gertrude promptly invited him, and Paul accepted with flattering alacrity.

"You are so kind to me, Mrs. Frome," he said earnestly. "Even though my countrymen are at war with yours! Here indeed is Christian forgiveness."

"Nonsense," she said, quite pleased by his compliment. "What is one more at table? And you must know I could not fail to ask you if I wished to please Deborah. She is determined you shall be happy in England." She sent a coy glance at her blushing sister.

The guests around them prevented him from saying anything further. Yet later on, when some had left following the excellent luncheon, Rigaud approached Deborah.

"I keep thinking of what your good sister said to me," he said quietly, his glowing look telling her that he was serious. "If only I might believe that you are—a friend to me, a good friend!"

"But of course I am, sir, you know it. And—and others are also. I know Lord Treverly thinks of your comfort and that of those with you."

"He has been very good to us. However, we have at last found some rooms to let, and are moving tomorrow. We must not impose further on his hospitality—though he is most reluctant to allow Marie to leave," he added, with a little laugh. "Marie says to me, she must allow him to miss her! She is clever, that one, and with a great understanding of men. Her first husband was my dear friend." His face darkened. "Killed by savage beasts—ah, how many horrible memories—"

Deborah laid her hand on his arm lightly. "Oh, sir, if only the past might be dead for you! You must make a new life for yourself—I hope with us here in England."

He was quick to cover her hand with his. "With

your aid, I believe I could do it swiftly," he said solemnly.

She withdrew her hand, blushing. "Sir, I did not mean it so personally—" Her voice quavered a little.

"I wish I could hope that you did."

Uneasily she turned the conversation to the sketches. "I must thank you for your aid this morning. We should not have seen the Parade, and I would not have been able to sketch—"

"I so much admire your talent, as you know! May I be permitted to see your oil painting of the harbor very soon?"

"Of course," she was glad to promise. "However, I have promised to do a portrait of Lady Willoughby, and then Gertrude has asked my aid in planning several dinners. Bath is such a busy place, sir!" she said with a smile.

He gave her a thoughtful look as they stood near the windows, a little apart from the others. "Forgive me yet again for interfering in what must be your own decision—as Lord Treverly reminded us," he said, "but if I had the managing of your career, you should paint only the sea and the ports, and other scenes of the naval life your father knew and thought so highly of. You *know* this area. Your talent is here, I am convinced of it."

She looked at him in a troubled way, loath to hurt him, yet unwilling to give him the direction of her life. "Sir, I am new to all this; I must try various types of painting and find what I like best, and also I must decide if I wish to make a career of it. If I become a professional artist, then I must

paint what my subjects wish. That would probably
be portraits. It would be my way to make a living."

"And if I assured you," he said lightly, "that you
would make a great deal of money indeed, painting as I directed you? Painting those scenes of the
sea which you do so splendidly? What would you
say then, Miss Deborah?"

She answered him playfully. "Oh, then I must
do as you direct, I am sure! No, no, do not tease
me. I must grope and find my own way."

"I shall convince you one day!" he said significantly, and put his hand gently on hers. "One day,
I hope to have the *right* to direct your career, and
you will trust me enough to listen to me!"

She flushed deeply and looked away from his
intent gaze. He went too far too fast. And yet she
wanted to believe she was important to someone,
that she was not the foolish chit Morgan believed
her to be—throwing away his love.

"I have not offended you? You will think of what
I have said?"

"I will—think of it," she promised, and then Alice
rescued her, sent by Gertrude, who feared they
had talked together long enough to excite gossip.

The talk became general, and they spoke of the
ball that evening, which promised to be a splendid
one. Paul Rigaud finally took his leave.

"You will save several dances for me, Miss Deborah?" he said in parting.

"Of course, you know I will," she said with a
smile.

When he had left, Gertrude teased her a little.
"The Frenchman will not let you alone, Deborah!
What were you discussing so long?"

"Oh—the war—and painting," she said vaguely. The squire gave her a keen look.

"Does he still insist that you should paint only the sea and harbors and sailors?" asked the squire with a laugh. "One would think it was his own career at stake, rather than your hobby!"

"He is kind and concerned," she said absently, stung a little, after all the praise she had received, that the squire should speak of her painting as a hobby. What if she did make a career of it? What if she became a well-known artist and made a great deal of money at it? What would her relatives say then? They would be the last to admit she had great talent, she thought, and then was sorry for her lack of charity.

But Clarence had been kind to her, and Deborah was assured a home with them always. With compunction, she offered to take care of the children for the rest of the afternoon, and remained with them until almost six o'clock.

Then she hastened to her room to change for the evening. She and Alice both had gowns they had not worn before. Alice wore her favorite blue, a handsome brocade with a delicate silver pattern woven through it, and a matching blue feather in her blonde hair.

Deborah wore rose, a delicate shade as soft and deep as the inside of the flower itself. She had dressed her hair in long curls to her shoulders, and looked as young and vibrant as she had at Alice's age. Flowers had arrived for them all, sent by Lord Treverly, and she boldly wore his offering, a soft crimson rose, at her bodice, among the chiffon folds. She looked regretfully at the lilies which Paul had sent. Their fragrance was too strong. Besides, the rose suited her gown. He would surely understand.

Another rose was placed at her slim waist and fastened carefully with threads. Alice drew an admiring breath, and said, "Deborah, you look like a rose yourself! How the men will flock about you tonight!"

"I shall say the same of you!" Deborah helped her set the creamy white rosebuds Mr. Vaughan had sent at her waist and throat. Morgan had sent crimson roses to Alice and to Gertrude as well, but only Deborah wore hers. She wondered if the gesture was too obvious.

Squire Frome nodded his satisfaction, and his beaming face said more. The carriage was brought around, and all carefully mounted the steps, mindful of their fragile gowns.

At the Assembly Rooms, the footman helped them out. The squire told him to come at ten minutes till eleven to avoid the crush when the ball was over. Just three hours from now, thought Deborah with a sigh. What did the evening hold for her? The rooms were already so crowded that Deborah looked about in dismay. Would she even be able to find Morgan?

She jumped when a hand touched her own gloved hand. "My dance, I think—because you wear my roses," said a deep, familiar voice.

"Oh—I did not see you—" she said faintly, and allowed herself to be drawn into the line forming for the contradance. She noticed vaguely that Alice was smiling up at Mr. Vaughan, but she did not see Paul Rigaud.

Then her attention was on Morgan, who moved so gracefully. He wore his colors tonight, plum and gold, and his white knee breeches were molded to his fine legs and thighs, his plum coat opened to reveal a silver and gold embroidered waistcoat beneath, and a frilled white shirt of linen and lace. For once he was smiling frankly down at her, as though the sight of her pleased him immensely.

After the dance, he returned her to the table the squire had taken. She wondered that he had been able to find a table, but he soon confided that Lord Treverly had sent early to reserve a place for them. The large table seated them all, Morgan and his cousin, the squire and his ladies.

Paul Rigaud hastened over to them, looking reproachfully at Deborah's roses. "You did not wear my flowers," he said quietly, as they moved to the line of dancers.

"I regret so much, but you see, the squire had bought us gowns especially for this evening, and they did not suit. But I must thank you for the beautiful lilies. How lovely they are." She did not add that they had been placed in the drawing room, their scent being too powerful for her bedroom.

"They are a symbol of France, you know," he said with a deep sigh. "And I have been thinking much of my poor country these days."

The dance separated them. She smiled, drew back, turned, and returned to him again. "How beautiful you are," he said fervently. "And how much happier I am after our conversation!"

"I am glad for it, sir," she said.

They parted, and returned again. "What a crowd

there is tonight," he said. "I had longed to talk with you. May I come tomorrow?"

"I regret so much—I would like it, but we have guests. And the next day," she hastened to add, "I go to Lady Willoughby."

His glance darkened, but he said nothing. "And on Friday?" he asked finally, when they met again in the movement of the dance.

"Pray do come and see us. Perhaps we could walk out," she said with a smile.

His brow lightened at once, and he smiled again. Was he becoming so serious about her? she wondered. He returned her to the table, and once seated, she was anguished to see Morgan going to Madame Marie Andreossy, radiant in emerald silk, with a plume setting off her magnificent black hair. Was the woman a serious rival for Morgan's affections? She must be older than he, yet more sensible men than he had fallen for a widow with experience, beauty, and a tragic past to lend her an air of romance.

The squire escorted Deborah to the dance floor after a brief intermission, and happily sent her through the vigorous measures of a lively dance. When they returned to the table, laughing and breathless, she found Morgan waiting for her, holding out his hand, in silence, for the next dance. She placed hers in it, and felt an exquisite thrill as he once again drew her onto the dance floor. How natural it was to be with him; she yearned to be ever closer.

He did not talk much through the movements, though his eyes spoke for him, admiring her gown, the roses at her throat and waist. He smiled when he held her waist; she could scarcely look at him when they parted. Was his hand holding her more tightly than before? Surely it was.

They returned to the table, where Gertrude at once said, "How kind of you to think of Alice's birthday, my dear Lord Treverly."

"Not at all." He turned to Deborah to explain. "I learned but yesterday that Alice has a birthday early in June. Rather than give a dinner for her next week, we have postponed it until her birthday." He smiled at Alice. "I shall do all I can to make it a memorable occasion."

Deborah's heart sank, then she immediately rebuked herself for being so hateful as to deny Alice any pleasure.

"That will be splendid," she managed to say, and smiled when Paul Rigaud came to her yet again. Glances followed the couple as they moved away.

Gertrude leaned toward Lord Treverly. "I wish we knew more of that young man, my lord. I am sure he is serious about our Deborah. Yet how can we find out more? He is alien even to his own country."

"I have wondered that myself," he said slowly. William Vaughan had taken Alice's hand and led her to the dancing. Lord Treverly leaned over and spoke earnestly to the squire, with only Gertrude to overhear. "I had not realized they were so serious about each other. Is—Miss Deborah truly interested in him?"

"It would seem so," said the squire, looking troubled. "I like the chap myself—charming, polite, intelligent, and all that—but what do we know of him? He tells us his family is dead, but for the lady, Madame Andreossy, and his cousin, Monsieur Houdon. They vouch for each other. Who else knows of them? I have spoken with some of the other French people in town, and they know nothing of our friends."

"I should like to make further inquiries—quietly, you may be sure—if you will permit me, Squire."

"Oh, as you will, as you will! I should do it, but with your connections—"

"I shall be glad to undertake the task, Squire," said Lord Treverly firmly. "All we know of them is that they came to Lowbridge with Lady Horatia Torrington, and she tells me she had only just met them in London. There will be ways of discovering their background. Leave it to me. We want the best for Miss Deborah, do we not?"

There was an ironic twist to his handsome mouth. The squire looked at him keenly, then nodded. "Right you are. The matter was beginning to trouble me."

"But whom will you ask?" Gertrude broke in. "If no one knows their past, how can you find out—"

"Pray leave the matter to me, ma'am," said Lord Treverly firmly. "I have sources of information. But say nothing to anyone. Our friends might hear of it and be deeply offended. I confess, I have been curious—" He broke off, and his gaze followed the progress of Marie Andreossy, now smiling as she chatted with Monsieur Houdon in his smart, somber black.

"Of course," said Gertrude, feeling relieved. She did not *really* hope that he would find out something horrible about them, but perhaps a little disgrace? Something to put his lordship off Madame Andreossy, and encourage Deborah to give up Monsieur Rigaud. That would solve everything nicely.

Deborah and Paul Rigaud were slowly returning to the table. His hand was on her elbow, his free hand gesturing vividly. She appeared to be listening intently.

"You may depend on me," Lord Treverly repeated, watching them grimly.

Alice was also returning, with Mr. Vaughan holding her arm protectively in the crush.

"Oh, Alice, there is a splendid art exhibition Monsieur Rigaud has been telling me about. We must see it on Friday," Deborah said when they reached the table.

"Allow me to take you there," urged Rigaud. "I want to point out my favorites and hear which ones you approve." It was obvious his words were for Deborah alone.

"Why don't we all go? We can make up a party," said Morgan smoothly. "Shall I come for you about ten o'clock, Miss Deborah? Will that suit the others?"

Rigaud gave him an angry look, clearly upset that the matter was being taken out of his hands. The squire watched in quiet amusement, and Deborah squirmed at the predicament.

"That is settled, then," Morgan concluded.

Monsieur Rigaud drank a glass of wine with

them, then departed reluctantly. Bernard Houdon had signalled to him, and presently he stood up with another young lady from the French colony gathered in Bath. Morgan rose and held out his hand to Deborah.

As they moved onto the dance floor, he said, "Are you angry with me, Miss Deborah?"

"Angry, sir?"

But the dance began then, and they were separated. She had to wait for his answer until the steps brought them together again.

"For spoiling your solitary outing with the— other gentleman," he said.

"Of course not," she managed to say. "It was not solitary—"

Back again, and then forward. "I am glad to hear it," he continued. "You do not want to arouse the gossips, I'm certain."

He put his hand on her slim waist to guide her through the next steps. His other hand held hers firmly, and she glanced up to find his eyes deep gray and fathomless. But not icy and cold. Not tonight.

Her heart beat more wildly, and she wished the music would never end.

But it did end, and presently the squire, yawning, said the carriage was surely waiting, and they must go before the mad squeeze began. Morgan saw them through the crush and to their carriage. He kissed Gertrude's and Alice's hands, then turned to Deborah. The others were now in the carriage, and she waited to be handed up.

She had removed her gloves, and when he bent

over her hand, she felt the burning touch of his lips not on her fingertips, as was proper, but on the inside of her wrist. And then he straightened, so swiftly she thought she had imagined the caress, and assisted her into the carriage.

"Good night then. We shall meet again on Friday morning," he said, his voice quite controlled and cool.

And poor Deborah was left to wonder, as the carriage rattled through the night, what he had meant by *that!*

CHAPTER SEVENTEEN

On Thursday morning Lady Horatia's carriage arrived to take Deborah to her appointment with Lady Willoughby, and she set out rather apprehensively.

The carriage stopped at a magnificent house set a little apart from its neighbors, in a fine garden of roses and green hedges. An elderly butler showed her to the elegant drawing room, even larger than Lady Horatia's, where Lady Willoughby waited for her.

"Oh, here you are, here you are!" cried the lady. She wore a dainty gown of palest gray, and her face seemed weary.

Oh dear, thought Deborah, she looks so faded. How can I paint a portrait of her that will satisfy her and yet be true to her face and figure? Lady Horatia had such a commanding posture, her face was engraved with so much character—this lady was a different matter.

Deborah found the lady to be as nervous as the artist.

"I really dread having my portrait done," she confided, with a little droop of her rouged mouth.

"I look so old. Now when I was young—" she sighed, "the finest of artists painted me, and they were so splendid! I do not look like that anymore."

Deborah asked to see the portraits, and Lady Willoughby was pleased to show her two. Deborah looked thoughtfully at the frivolous hats, the fashionable dresses of forty and fifty years ago, at the gay, sweet face that peeped from under the rose-laden brims.

"These are very lovely, Lady Willoughby," she said sincerely. "But I hope to show in the portrait what splendid dignity you have now, and poise. The years have taught you much, and if I could but show—" She hesitated, then mused over the portraits again.

Lady Willoughby was silent, letting her think. Then Deborah nodded more decisively.

"Yes, yes, I think I know what I wish to do. Will you sit for some sketches first, my lady?"

"Oh, yes, whatever you think best," said Lady Willoughby, eying her with more respect.

Deborah directed her to a graceful Queen Anne chair, with her small dainty feet on an embroidered footstool. One hand rested in her lap, the other held a small book of poetry. Deborah tried several quick sketches, then decided on one in which the woman was gazing at the book musingly, as though she thought of the past.

Before the session was over, Deborah had set the canvas on the easel, and sketched in charcoal the pose she wanted. She gave thought to the colors she would use.

"Do you have a gown of violet silk?" she asked Lady Willoughby.

"Yes, yes, I have a favorite dress of violet, with a lace collar. But it is old, I have not worn it for some time."

Deborah asked to see it; the maid brought it down. She knew by the way Lady Willoughby caressed it that it held memories for her. The style was of about ten years before.

"It is the gown I wore to the last ball I attended with my husband, before he died," she finally confessed. "I will always remember how he looked at me and said, 'My love, you grow more beautiful with the years.' Of course, it was not true, but he seemed to mean it. We had three children—two are dead, and my son is away in India. My grandchildren are in the north of England, with their mother. I do wish I might see them more often." Her fragile hand caressed the lace on the bodice.

"Would you wear it the next time I come?" asked Deborah gently.

"Oh yes, my dear, I shall enjoy that. Will you come again soon? Perhaps on Tuesday?"

Deborah agreed, and went away relieved and touched at the confidences of the elderly dowager. To see her in public, so confident and arrogant, shouting her questions at all, listening to conversations through her ear trumpet, one would not guess at the sadness that lurked in her eyes, the loneliness of her life now, even with friends about.

Deborah went out to the carriage almost half an hour late. She was shocked to find Lady Horatia patiently waiting for her there, along with the coachman.

"Lady Horatia! You should have sent inside for me!" Deborah was horrified. Lady Horatia had been kind enough to lend her the use of her carriage and coachman, and then had been kept waiting.

Lady Horatia patted her hand and gave her an impish smile. "Nonsense, my dear. I was sure you were finding Lady Willoughby enchanting. Is she not a dear, under that formidable exterior? I have always loved her. When her husband died, all spirit seemed to die in her. Now she has come alive again."

"She is a courageous lady," Deborah agreed.

Lady Horatia then explained that Gertrude had invited her for luncheon, and so the conversation begun in the carriage continued through the long meal. Finally the butler came in and murmured discretely to Gertrude.

"Oh, we have callers already," she announced. "Pray, let us remove to the drawing room, and have our coffee there. There is a guest for you, Deborah," she said with a significant look at her sister. "Monsieur Rigaud has come to call."

Deborah stifled a sigh, and pretended pleasure. But she was a bit tired of his frequent visits. Still, he had endured so much . . . she brought a smile to her lips with an effort, and managed to greet him with every evidence of cordiality.

Lady Horatia sat beside her on the sofa, and looked keenly from Deborah to Paul Rigaud. She said little, however.

Presently other guests arrived, and Rigaud tore himself from Deborah's side with a reminder that he would meet them at the art exhibition the next morning. "I wish to escort you about personally," he reminded her. "Pray, do not allow anyone to interfere with our arrangements."

Recalling that Morgan was escorting them, she felt some irritation. Perhaps if Paul did not cling to her side, she might have the pleasure of Morgan's company at the exhibition, viewing the paintings together and listening to his comments.

"We shall all enjoy the exhibition, Monsieur Rigaud," she said firmly. "I look forward to seeing you there."

He bowed, gave her a keen unsmiling look, and said his farewells to Clarence and Gertrude.

"He is most persistent, dearest Deborah," murmured Lady Horatia, after he had departed. "He seems very fond of you. Does he cause you to forget—others of the past?"

Deborah flushed. "I might hope he would," she said. "For others do not care much for me, I assure you! If only I could respond to his liking—"

"If only *others* were finally out of reach," ended Lady Horatia, and patted her hand. "Well, well, do not despair. You look very charming today, and grow more lovely each week. You seem younger to me, do you know it?"

"Do you mean it, Lady Horatia?"

"Of course I do. You are much rested, and happier. Prettier than ever," she added with a smile. "And now I must say my farewells."

Lady Horatia's words gave Deborah renewed hope, and she was full of anticipation at the thought of spending Friday with Morgan.

Promptly at ten o'clock he arrived with two carriages to take their party to the large hall where the art exhibition, "Scenes of the British Sea," was being shown.

Paul Rigaud was waiting impatiently for them at the entrance. He waited while Lord Treverly purchased their admission tickets, then possessed himself of Deborah's arm and urged her inside.

"I am longing to show you my favorite paintings," he said.

Inside, they found quite a crowd of persons, among them Marie Andreossy and Bernard Houdon. Morgan did not go to them, however, Deborah noticed. He and Alice remained close behind her.

"I wish to witness Miss Deborah's impressions of the paintings," Morgan said, as if in explanation.

This did not please Monsieur Rigaud, but there was little he could do. Deborah refused to be hurried from one painting to another; she wished to see them all. She only wished she might return alone, so she might gaze in silence. As it was, Monsieur Rigaud distracted her by pointing imperiously to whatever he wished her to notice, what had pleased him best, asking her opinion of a picture before she had had time to look fully at it.

But it was he who had told them of the exhibition, after all, and she chided herself for feeling so impatient with him.

They made the rounds of the large rooms, viewed each painting quickly, and were on to the next one. Deborah grew impatient, and tried to stifle her feelings when Gertrude complained audibly of the crowds, the heat, and her boredom.

It was close to noon when Morgan approached Deborah with a suggestion. "I am sending the squire and Mrs. Frome home in a carriage. Will you and Miss Alice remain longer with me? I think you have not looked your fill."

She turned gratefully to him. "Oh, I should like that so much," and she glanced about for Monsieur Rigaud.

"Monsieur Rigaud is taking his leave," Morgan said flatly. "I told him we were leaving shortly. Or did you wish him to remain at your side?"

"Oh no!" she said quickly, then blushed for her rudeness. "I mean—I should like to look alone at the paintings. Pray thank Monsieur Rigaud—"

"He is here," Morgan said, and turned politely to the Frenchman. "You have seen enough, monsieur? Miss Deborah was just expressing her gratitude to you for showing us the paintings." Was there mockery in his deep voice? Deborah was not sure.

"Not at all. I wish I might accompany you home, Miss Deborah," he said, giving her a wistful look.

"No, no, Lord Treverly will take us," she said, feeling deceitful. "Thank you again. We shall see you soon?"

He bowed over her hand and left reluctantly. Deborah drew a sigh of relief as the French party departed.

"I ordered our carriage for an hour from now," Morgan said. "Miss Alice, you look fatigued. Do sit down here in the corner. There is a breeze from the windows."

Alice smiled. "Thank you, my lord. It's just that my feet hurt," she confided childishly. "Do let me sit and rest, and you go about looking. I know you longed to look at the paintings alone, Deborah."

Deborah left them with a smile, and wandered about happily. The crowd had diminished abruptly as the noon hour approached, and she nearly had the hall to herself.

Finally she returned to Morgan and her sister, who sat conversing quietly, their heads together. The sight gave her a pang which she roughly suppressed. She managed to smile brightly.

"I cannot thank you enough for allowing me another look," she told Morgan.

"Which did you admire most?" he asked idly. "I noticed you stood quite fifteen minutes at that one," and he indicated a painting about three feet wide and two feet high, of a ship at anchor, with the sunset behind it giving a red glow to the sails.

"Yes, that is my favorite. If I could but achieve a tenth of his effects, I should be happy. It gave me an idea on how to proceed—"

Morgan gave them each an arm to the carriage, and escorted them home with every evidence of being pleased to be in their company.

Over their late luncheon, Alice confided, "How much easier he is in his manner to me! I quite felt at home with him today, he was so easy to talk to. Do you not like him, Deborah?"

"He is a fine man," said Deborah, and listened

while Alice rambled on happily. The pleasure of the morning began slowly to dissipate.

Deborah had begun to grow rather weary of the social round Bath offered. When would it be over? That evening, when she saw Morgan at yet another ball, he noticed something amiss.

"You look weary, Miss Deborah. Too much sight-seeing today?"

"No indeed. Perhaps too much excitement—Bath has so much to offer."

"Monsieur Rigaud is not here tonight. He has left town for three days," he informed her coolly. "Is that why you look so downcast?"

"I had not heard the news," she replied, a little startled. "Where did he go, to London?"

"No one knows where he went. Do you mind that he did not inform you of his movements?"

"He is not obliged to do so, my lord," she said stiffly, annoyed at his mocking persistence. After his friendliness and consideration that morning, it was a shock to have him turn cold yet again.

She went home with a sore heart, and a head that pounded mercilessly. And when she was re-minded that the next evening they would attend a supper party at Morgan's house, she felt she could not bear to be with him again.

By the next evening she felt more composed, and dressed carefully in the smart Damascus silk, which made her feel sophisticated, and more confident of herself.

"I enjoy going to Lord Treverly's," said Gertrude in the carriage. "I always know everything will go so smoothly. The food will be exquisite, the decorations perfect, the guests amiable. You know, I find it difficult to remember a time when we did not know him and enjoy his attentions."

"You have grown accustomed to the high *ton* of Bath," teased the squire. "How you will settle down to Lowbridge, I cannot imagine!"

"But Lord Treverly will be there," said Gertrude.

"He may go off to London," said the squire. "He spoke of it only last night. June is the height of the season, you know."

Gertrude fell silent, her mouth downturned in the dim flare of the street lights. Alice looked serious. Deborah, however, felt her world had been turned upside down.

Morgan—go to London! Would he? She had taken for granted that he would remain in Bath while they did. If he departed, all the joy, many of the delights of Bath would go with him. It was the thought of possibly meeting him at the library that made trips there more than a pleasure. When she and Alice took walks her gaze was constantly searching the street for a glimpse of him. If he departed—

There were only about twenty that night, "a smaller group," Gertrude said later, and was promptly teased by her husband. They were all acquainted, and sat about a beautiful rosewood dining table set with gleaming silver. A low silver epergne was filled with fruit—apples, oranges, and figs from the Mediterranean. A different wine was served with each course, and Deborah and Alice sipped cautiously. They were all so heady, but delicious.

After dinner they adjourned to the two drawing rooms where card tables were set up. Some played whist, others were content to chatter and gossip.

Marie Andreossy and Bernard Houdon were not there, and Deborah wondered at their absence. Lady Willoughby claimed her attention for a time, as they quietly discussed the portrait. Lady Willoughby confided that she "knew it would be splendid, for Deborah understood her."

"You are not playing cards, Miss Deborah." Morgan appeared at her side.

"No, not yet."

"Then come with me. There is something I should like to show you, a painting I have just purchased. You must give me your judgment of it."

Deborah hesitated, glancing about for one of her sisters. Neither was in the room.

Lady Willoughby had turned to another acquaintance. Morgan said softly, "Come along, I shall not seduce you in my study. Or are you afraid to be alone with me?"

Deborah blushed vividly, but rose to accompany him. Could he never speak to her without mockery?

They walked down the wide hallway, filled with fine portraits and landscapes. She would have liked to pause and study them, but he drew her on, past cabinets displaying ivory, jade, and porcelain. "Another time for the art tour, Miss Deborah," he said, evidently reading her thoughts.

He showed her into his study, then shut the door halfway behind them. She gazed about slowly, trying to envision him alone in the room, with its massive desk and bookcases extending from floor to ceiling.

He leaned against his desk, his arms folded. She was uneasily aware of him in that intimate room. This was where he worked, wrote letters, thought out matters of concern. It seemed full of him; she even caught the fragrance of the light masculine scent he used.

"Do you like it?" he asked.

"Oh, yes, it's a splendid room," she said absently, her brain whirling at being alone with him.

"I mean the painting," and his nod indicated the wall behind him. She looked past him, and her eyes widened. She stepped closer, moved past him to examine it. It was the painting she had admired so at the exhibition—her favorite.

"Oh—you bought that one! How I envy you," she said. "I did not know you meant to have it."

She stepped closer still, to gaze up at the scarlet sunset on the sea, the sails furled, the ship at anchor, poised, calm yet alert. Like him, she thought. Quiet, yet instantly ready for action.

"If you had married me when I asked you, years ago, the painting should be *ours*," he said, with a cruelty that took her breath away.

She turned slowly to gaze at him, her hands closing to fists at her sides. "You taunt me with *that*?" she whispered.

"I but remind you of a truth," he said, seemingly casual, but she noted the hard white line about his mouth.

"It is unworthy of you," she said, her hand going to her throat, where a pulse bounded unsteadily. She could not seem to catch her breath.

"The truth is unworthy of me?" He stood away from the desk, looming before her. His eyes glared down at her. "You like pretty pictures, all smooth and serene. You like neat gardens, carefully tended. I presume you like your truth in similar form. I must suppose you find Monsieur Rigaud of such interest because he is charming, handsome, and never disturbs your calmness. If he were older, scarred, sometimes abrupt, you would turn from him, isn't that so?"

She drew herself up to her slight height, her chin up. "You suppose wrong, my lord!" she said. "I like and admire Monsieur Rigaud. I am sorry for the ills he has suffered—"

"And you enjoy the attentions he lavishes upon you, cheap though they are! A few pennies for flowers, a few hours spent walking you about, holding your sketch pad devotedly—oh yes, I have seen you on the Parade! He is all devotion and smooth words, and like all women you cannot see anything beyond the boyishly handsome face. You do not care where he comes from, who he is, where he has gone for several days without informing any of his friends!"

She stared at him in bewilderment. "I do not understand—" she began, then hesitated. "But what matter is this to you?" she went on, striving for control in the face of this unexpected attack.

"Matter? I am one who is concerned for my true friends, those I have known and admired for years. The squire is concerned that you allow him too many liberties, your sister worries over you. But you—you go on allowing him to take you about freely, you expose Miss Alice to his charms—"

"Sir, I cannot permit you to say—"

"You cannot permit! You cannot permit! My word, Deborah, I wonder at you! You have no idea of the danger you are in!"

"Danger? From Monsieur Rigaud? He has always been a gentleman—"

"Who spoke of him? I speak of *myself!* You defy me, you are cold when you wish, you turn your shoulder to me when I speak to you—" He had stepped closer. Emotion seemed to choke him; he reached out and caught her arms as she would have turned away. The shawl slipped from her shoulders.

"Let me go—Morgan, let me go!" she breathed. She began to struggle, a little afraid of this stranger whose gray eyes blazed hotly down at her.

Ice? No ice there. He was furiously angry, and she was bewildered. *Why* was he so angry?

He yanked her to him, wrapped his arms about her, and pulled her close. She turned her face to his shoulder. One hand slid under her hair, turned her face up by pulling roughly at her curls. It would all come down, she thought dazedly, the fragile curls, the light ribbon—

His mouth crushed down on her soft, surprised lips. He kissed her, as though he would vent his fury on her, punish her for some unknown sin. His arms held her closer, his fingers ruffled through her soft curls. When she would have turned her head, his fingers closed more tightly, holding her firmly. His lips roamed from her mouth to her cheek, over her ear, teasing her ear lobe, then to the vulnerable base of her throat, where her pulse raced beneath his lips.

She felt faint, and could not struggle. This was where she had longed to be, close in his arms, but tenderly held, not in this hard, cruel grip. Yet his lips were not hurting her now. They teased the pulse of her throat, caressed her white shoulders.

She was dizzy, unable to move. He must feel the surrender in her body. She was so tightly held to him that he must be aware how she throbbed to his kisses. Her body was bent to his as he held her, his hard-muscled thighs urgently pressed to her slim rounded body. Drums beat in her ears—drums? No, the beat of his heart against her ear, as he pressed her head against his chest.

He moved his head, and the warmth of his lips came again to hers, holding her so she could not move or breathe for a long moment.

Her shaking hand went to his sleeve, clutching it. Always she would remember the feel of his silk coat under her fingers, the hard arm beneath it, silk over iron.

There were voices in the hallway, near them. Deborah started and tried to pull away. His hands still held her, then slowly, reluctantly, they loosened their grasp. She raised her gaze shyly to his. The glint in his eyes frightened her. He was still angry.

He released her, and she stepped away from him quickly. When the squire and another man entered the study, she was staring unseeingly at Morgan's new painting.

"Ah, so that is the painting you purchased," said the squire. "Deborah is entranced with it, aren't you, my dear? Noticed it myself in the collection."

She excused herself from Morgan without meeting his gaze, and returned to the drawing room alone. She wished she could walk out into the cool night air, be alone to think and dream.

Morgan had kissed her—savagely, then tenderly. What did it mean? What would he have said if they had been alone for a few minutes longer?

She hated returning to the crowd playing whist, but she must do so. To her relief, the tables were full, and she smilingly refused the offer of a place. Instead she took a seat beside Lady Willoughby once again, and did not hear a word the good lady said to her.

CHAPTER EIGHTEEN

Deborah bloomed with hope. She could not bear the wait until she could see Morgan again; perhaps he would explain himself then.

She burned with shame, then hope. He would not kiss her like that if he did not feel some strong emotion toward her. Surely he was not merely angry. Could he be jealous of Monsieur Rigaud's attentions to her? If so, she would be glad of those attentions which had come to annoy and distress her.

It was foolish, yet she must be foolish. Without hope, the heart would die. She felt as though she had been in winter darkness during the years without him, and now the sunlight dazzled her, blinded her. Could it be that he might still love her?

Sunday was turbulent with thunderstorms, Monday misty with fog, but by Tuesday the weather had cleared. Deborah had to bring her thoughts back to practical matters, for she was to begin in earnest on Lady Willoughby's portrait.

She encouraged the woman to talk and caught the changing expressions of her wistful face, the animation in her violet eyes, the gestures of her hands. Lady Willoughby had found a book of poems which her husband had loved, and she read aloud from one poem.

She had promised to stay for luncheon, and enjoyed the conversation immensely. Lady Willoughby was not lost in the past but conversed tartly and expertly on the present. She knew everyone of note in the government, she spoke of generals and politicians, and even His Royal Majesty, with calm familiarity. She told stories with a flair, and had Deborah chuckling often.

Lady Willoughby reached over to tap her hand. "Ah, you have a bright, quick mind, my dear. Lady Horatia told me I should enjoy you immensely. She is quite right; I must tell her so. I thought because you were so quiet you might be dull. Why do you not speak up more in company?"

"I—well, I feel I have little to say—"

"That does not stop those with empty minds!" Lady Willoughby said with bright malice.

The coachman called for her at three o'clock, and Deborah went home to find Paul Rigaud there, silent reproach in his eyes that she had not been there to greet him.

"Oh, we have missed you, sir," she said brightly, to please him. "Where have you been these days? But forgive me—it is not my concern."

Paul began to smile charmingly and caught both her hands in his. "And did you miss me?"

Gertrude overheard and frowned a little.

"Of course we did," said Deborah.

"I mean, did you, yourself, miss me?"

"Of course I did," she repeated with a blush. He seemed satisfied.

He seated himself beside her and said, "I had to go to London on some foolish business. It took twice the time I had intended. I would have returned on Sunday, but the storm kept me."

"Wasn't it horrid? I was quite frightened," said Deborah, to make conversation. Actually she had not been frightened, but had rather enjoyed the sensation of being in a snug house, watching the lightning play about the hills, hearing the thunder echoing like the voice of some angry god.

"Then I wish I had been here to comfort you," he said softly.

Alice distracted them innocently. "I hope you were not out in the storm, Monsieur Rigaud."

"Well—part of the time I was, and I got soaked." A curious look came over his face. "But I found shelter in a tavern and drank some hot rum to warm me. What a civilized thing it can be, your rum," he said with a smile, then turned the conversation.

"We have hired a carriage for a month," he said. "I wonder if you would give me the pleasure of going out with me, Miss Deborah? With your sister, of course. I long to show you some places I have discovered outside Bath, some charming scenes you might wish to sketch along the river."

"I should enjoy that," said Deborah, and they fixed on the next afternoon.

On Wednesday, he came promptly after lunch, and they set out. It was a shining day, and the storms had washed everything bright and clean. Flowers bloomed around every hedge, yellow primroses, soft pink field roses, cornflowers blue as the sky, larkspur, and even a field of lavender heather.

Deborah longed to draw a country scene, for the flowers attracted her, but Paul insisted on driving on. "No, no, I have a special scene for you," he said, laughing mysteriously.

He finally drove around a corner, across a bridge, and drew up. "There, what do you think of that?" he asked triumphantly.

In a tiny square of common, just outside a village, some men were drilling. They wore only their everyday clothing, and in charge of them was an elderly sergeant in an equally elderly uniform. But he was drilling them smartly up and down.

Deborah stared, rather shocked. Was this what Paul thought of her, that she wished to draw such a motley band of soldiers and volunteers?

"Is it not splendid?" he insisted anxiously. "It seems to me that this is the brave spirit of England, that even the occupants of a village drill daily to repel invasion from any source. Won't it make a fine picture?"

Aware of their audience, the group was drilling rigorously, wheeling and turning. Deborah hesitated; the scene seemed both pathetic and ominous to her.

"It is—a touching scene, yes," she said finally. Obediently, she took out her sketch pad.

She managed quite a good scene of them, in spite of Paul standing over her. At least he was quiet, as was Alice, who sat patiently in the afternoon sunshine.

When the men stopped drilling, they dispersed

with many a curious look at the girl drawing them. The parson and the elderly sergeant came over to them importantly. Deborah rose to shake their hands, and immediately Paul urged her to show them the sketch.

"Right as rain, to the uniform and the buttons," said the sergeant. "And you but a young lady!"

"My father served all his days in our navy," said Deborah quietly. "That was where I began to sketch. You drilled them very well, sir, if I may compliment you."

His elderly face wrinkled into a smile. "Should do so, miss! I been in the army for His Majesty since I was a sprig of ten years!"

To Deborah's surprise, Paul was patient and gentle with the old man and the elderly parson. He accepted for them all the offer of a cool drink at the village pub. Deborah hesitated a little, but was reassured by the parson.

"I assure you, Miss Stanton, no one will disturb you or make a rude remark. I shall accompany you myself."

Glasses of cool punch and cups of hot tea were soon set before them at the tavern, where Deborah and Alice sat down rather timidly in the open doorway, on a crude bench with a rough table before them. One of the former drillers served them, and everyone was curious about the sketch. Deborah willingly passed it round.

"Look, there's me," said one red-faced man from the mercer's shop next door. "Why, it's me to the life! Ain't it a wonder!"

"I should be pleased if you would keep it," said

Deborah impulsively to the group. She tore the sketch carefully from the pad and gave it into the care of the sergeant.

He handled it reverently. "Bless me, if I ain't been drawed by a true artist," he mused, staring at the sketch.

Paul was frowning. "Deborah, you cannot give away your work!" he said urgently into her ear.

"I wish them to have it," she said with a smile. "They have been so cordial."

They soon departed, driving home as the sun was beginning to sink in the west. "Forgive me for speaking out," said Paul as they reached the outskirts of Bath. "But if you give away your work, you will be sorry. A professional artist keeps his, and sells it dear! You could make an oil from that scene—it would be splendid."

"I still may, Monsieur Rigaud," she said quietly. "I can reproduce it tonight, if I will. It is strongly in my mind. Such scenes are not soon forgotten."

His brow relaxed. "You could do it again?" he echoed.

"Yes, of course. I still remember scenes from my childhood; I have sometimes sketched a ship years later. And ports—Father took us to many ports, and much later, I could sketch one as though it lay before me."

He smiled at her. "I misjudged you," he said apologetically. "I keep thinking you are a little lady, all silk and frills. Yet you are an artist as well, with a keen mind and memory."

Her talent was put to the test again on Thursday morning, when she went to Lady Willoughby.

The work was going amazingly fast; another three or four sessions would see it done. Lady Willoughby was reluctantly delighted with the portrait, though it made her "look old," as she said.

"But I do have character," she said, with resignation.

Deborah laughed softly, and wished she dared kiss the wrinkled cheek. But the woman was too regal for such a gesture.

Deborah was tired that noon and dreaded the thought of Paul Rigaud coming yet again. At the end of luncheon, she said to Alice, "Do let us walk out alone. I long for fresh air and quiet."

Alice nodded understandingly. "Paul Rigaud is a little—overpowering, is he not? He seems to wish to command you. And somehow, I find it disagreeable when *he* does it," she said reflectively.

Deborah looked at her gratefully. Sometimes she felt she underestimated her younger sister. "Yes, that is it exactly. Let us go for a walk alone."

She took sketch pad and pencils as usual, and she and Alice walked out before guests could arrive, though Gertrude protested a little peevishly.

They found a sheltered place in the busy streets, where a curve in the road led to some older shops. Settling down on a worn bench, Deborah began to draw the women shopping with market baskets, the carriages, a shopkeeper bringing an item to the sunlight of the open door to prove its quality to a customer. An elderly shop owner with a bolt of silk fabric caught her attention; he held it lovingly in his old hands, as a woman in a regal bonnet eyed it critically.

Alice watched for a time, contentedly. "Do you not like Mr. Vaughan?" she asked suddenly.

"Um, yes, very much," said her sister absently, sketching in the lift of the shopkeeper's arm, the expression on his face, both anxious and proud.

"I think he is the finest gentleman I have ever known," said Alice. "He is of such a generous nature, so sweet-tempered. I have never known him cross or out of sorts."

"No one could be cross with you, my dear." Deborah added a small gray cat sunning itself in the bow front of a smart shop, among the gay bonnets and ribbons.

Just as she was completing her sketch, a carriage pulled up right in her path. Rather annoyed, she looked up with a frown—to meet the amused glance of Morgan, stepping down from his phaeton.

Alice did not notice him for a moment, for she was looking in another direction. Morgan strode toward them, having slung the reins to a boy in the street. As he came up to them, Alice started and blushed. Deborah hoped she did not look so self-conscious as her sister.

"Working again?" he asked softly. "Are you never without your pencil?"

"There is so much to see and sketch here," she managed to say.

He turned to greet Alice. "I have been to your sister's, and told her that when I found her errant sisters I would carry them to Lady Horatia. The good lady is most upset that she has not seen her dearest friend for a week."

"Oh, I have missed her also. But the days seem to pass so swiftly."

He seemed in such a cordial mood that Deborah almost held her breath for fear that something would happen to destroy it. "Have you completed your sketch?" he was asking, reaching out for the pad.

He looked at the sketch keenly, then nodded. "Excellent. You improve daily. It is a shame that so many years passed when you could not work at your art."

"Oh, I did work at it, though not so much, sir," she protested. "I often kept a pad in the kitchen and one in the drawing room, so I might sketch when I had some minutes free."

"But she worked so hard, my poor Deborah," said Alice brightly. "I have found her nodding to sleep over the pad, and had to coax her up to bed."

"Those days are over," said Deborah firmly. "The squire has been marvelously kind to us." She refused to be pitied, if that was the look in the gray eyes gazing down at her.

"Well then, come and be idle with me," he said lightly. "You are not afraid of my high-perch phaeton, I hope?"

Alice looked dubious, but Deborah shook her head. He laughed and handed them up, accepted the reins, tossed a coin to the young man, and they set off. They did seem awfully high off the ground, and the wind whipped their bonnets, but to Deborah, seated so close to Morgan that their legs touched, the ride was all over too soon.

When Lady Horatia came to greet them, however, with both hands outstretched, Deborah was delighted to see her friend.

"You are as good as your word, my dear Lord Treverly," Lady Horatia said approvingly, and greeted them all fondly. When they were all settled with cups of tea, she turned to Morgan.

"You were out of town for a time, I believe?" she said.

"Yes, I had to go to London on business for three days," he said pleasantly. He volunteered no further information, and Lady Horatia looked curious. Deborah too wondered what his business could be. However, he had many interests and many properties, and the visit could have concerned any of them.

"What news did you hear there, my lord, what news?" Lady Horatia asked. "Is there much talk of the war? Is there any hope that it may blow over?"

He looked grave. "Much talk, more action, Lady Horatia," he said. "They believe—even the Prime Minister—that Napoleon will make an effort soon. Some say as many as eighty thousand troops are grouped across the Channel from us, and boats are being built. The talk is common; I reveal no secrets. They keep much of it from the gazettes, though, for fear of panicking the people."

"The British will not panic," said Lady Horatia sharply. But she seemed to have gone rather white under her rouge. "Where will he attack, do they surmise?"

"There are several possibilities, of course. The most obvious is near Dover. That is the shortest route. However, Napoleon is not always obvious."

"Where else could he attack?"

Deborah was thinking of the military drills in the common, the elderly sergeant, even the parson readying himself. Her hands trembled, and she set down her teacup for it rattled betrayingly in the saucer.

"The Irish are rebellious and willing to make trouble against us. Some say the attack will come from there, across the Irish Sea and into many ports. There is also mutiny in some ships, and at least one admiral believes this is instigated by the Irish." He sighed. "It is bad enough to be attacked by Napoleon. When our own men turn against us, it is heart-rending."

"Yet the sailors have a cause, sir," Deborah could not refrain from saying. "I have witnessed—inadvertently, to be sure—the lashing of a common seaman, and I was appalled. The brutality of it— They do not wish to remain under such conditions. Some commanders of ships are fair, others delight in their cruelty."

Morgan looked at her intently. "You are right, I am sorry to say. I too have witnessed such cruelties. There must be discipline, and whipping seems to be the only way to ensure it. Yet I have seen a man die of it, and for a minor fault."

"It seems to me the fault is that men have no more pride in their military calling," said Lady Horatia, her chin high. "I am ashamed that our men rebel and mutiny! What a black spot against the honor of our navy!"

"They are human beings, and rebel against misuse, Lady Horatia," said Deborah with gentle firmness. "And you know as well as I that many do not go willingly into the navy. They are impressed off the streets and docks. I have seen press gangs sweep up whole streets of able-bodied men while their women and children shrieked and wept and begged. Now the Americans are complaining that our sailors go aboard American ships and impress men from them! I believe they speak the truth, and it is wrong, wrong!"

Morgan sighed. "If you had your way, all the ills of the world would be set right at once," he said with a gentle smile at her. "It does your good heart honor, Miss Deborah, but the world does not work that way." When he saw her stiffen slightly, he said, "To return to our former topic, some say Napoleon may even attack by Bristol Channel, too near to us for comfort."

They were all silent for a time, their faces somber. Bristol Channel, with its gay ships, its sailors whistling about their tasks. There they had happily spent holidays with their father. Bristol, to be invaded!

And from Bristol, the invaders would swarm ashore, cutting a bloody path from there to Bath, to London! It was too horrible to contemplate. Perhaps those earnest farmers and pubkeepers and their brisk sergeant might one day have to go forth, with muskets and brooms, against the drilled soldiers of Napoleon.

"We must change the subject; it is too brutal for such a lovely day," said Morgan quietly, and he turned the talk to the next ball.

Morgan continued to be charming but impersonal. Did the recollection of their last meeting affect him at all? The afternoon passed pleasantly, but when Morgan escorted the sisters home, Deborah still had no answer to that question.

CHAPTER NINETEEN

The next week raced past, and Alice's birthday arrived. In growing excitement the sisters dressed. Rumors had been coming to them all week of the grandeur of the party. All Bath gossiped about it. Those who were invited were exultant, those not invited were cast down.

The squire had laughingly warned them to take all the rumors with a grain of salt, but nothing could dampen Gertrude's excitement. She *had* done the right thing in bringing Alice to Bath. Only one thing was lacking to complete her happiness. If only Lord Treverly had asked for Alice's hand, the engagement might be announced tonight. In that alone, Gertrude was disappointed.

By six all were ready to depart for Morgan's house. The squire looked them over proudly, shaking his head in wonder.

"All of you so handsome and fine. Gertrude, you have never looked so splendid. Deborah, you are very smart. And dear little Alice, all grown up and radiant."

The women preened for him, laughing and happy. Gertrude was indeed handsome in a sweeping gown of lavender brocade with purple plumes in her beautifully arranged blonde curls. Deborah wore a new gown from the hands of Lady Horatia's maid. It was deep rose with an overdress of rose gauze, embroidered with silver butterflies. The gown was low-cut, showing off her handsome shoulders and long neck. And Alice—Alice was so radiant that they all gazed in wonder. She was in deep blue tonight, with a silver gauze overdress, and blue plumes in her soft golden hair. And about her a glow of loveliness that made all her previous appearances as previews. Her eyes sparkled bright blue, her mouth was rosy, her cheeks deeply pink with excitement. When she laughed, her small teeth were pearly white against the rose of her mouth. Her rounded chin was dimpled.

The squire was smartly attired also—too smartly, he thought, as he eased his fingers around the high white stock. He wore a purple velvet coat, silver knee breeches, silver-buckled black shoes, and his stock was fastened in a waterfall of lace.

Morgan had asked them to come early, so they might be presented to the guests as they arrived. He himself came out to help them from their carriage.

"How splendid you all look. Miss Alice, you are truly beautiful. May I congratulate you on your birthday?"

"Thank you, my lord. And how very kind of you to have this lovely dinner for me," she said with composure. Only her flushed cheeks and sparkling eyes betrayed her intense excitement.

He showed them in, and a footman took their

cloaks. Then they formed a receiving line in the hallway. As the other guests began to arrive, Morgan presented them first to Alice, as the guest of honor. Deborah heard the numerous whispers as guests moved away from the receiving line.

"They say he'll offer for her any day now," went the murmurs. "He has given the dinner just for her. So young and pretty. Do you think he will really marry at last? Much sought after, you know —injured in the war—noticed his limp last week— but so handsome, my dear—"

So it went, and Deborah was both proud of her sister and heartsick for herself. No, Morgan spared her no more glances than anyone else in the crowd. For Alice, he was all attention, all kindness. Was she tiring? He must introduce her to Lord Rigglesdale. Lady March had always wished to meet her —and on and on. And around Alice's wrist was yet another sign of his devotion—the silver bracelet, set with sapphires, which had arrived that morning with his card.

Dinner was served at a series of long tables. Morgan had honored Alice's family by making each of them the head of a table, Alice at his own table, Deborah at another, Gertrude at a third, and the squire at a fourth. Deborah felt miserably that she would have given anything to be at Morgan's table, the most insignificant of his guests. As it was, she did not see him for quite two hours while the dinner was served. She scarcely knew what she ate, only that it was beautifully presented.

The meal was finally over, and they all moved

to the ballroom in the back of the large house. As Deborah passed through the rooms and halls, she noted the fine murals of scenes of Italy, the ivory and porcelain figures gracefully arranged on tables. The ceilings were painted in the Italian manner, like a sky alive with cupids, angels, and goddesses.

The ballroom was lit with three immense chandeliers and wall sconces whose candles were reflected in the many mirrors. The floor had been so highly polished that the ladies' gowns were reflected in them like so many flower petals. The musicians sat in a gallery above the heads of the dancers, and the music went on until past two in the morning.

As the room warmed, the French windows were thrown open, and one could walk out into the splendid gardens, fragrant with roses and jasmine, honeysuckle and stock.

Morgan led Alice out in the first dance, and they danced alone on the polished floor, he so handsome and she so lovely, even the jealous mamas could not help smiling.

Then all joined the dancing. William Vaughan was quick to ask Alice, and Paul Rigaud made his way to Deborah.

"I had hoped to be at your table tonight—I have a bone to pick with his lordship. That is right, is it not? To pick the bone, when one wishes to quarrel?"

"Oh, I hope you do not wish to quarrel, Monsieur Rigaud," said Deborah, smiling brightly despite her aching heart. "Everyone is so happy tonight. I do hope you will be happy also."

"If *you* wish me to be happy, I shall be." And

he clasped her close in the dance, before reluctantly giving her up to another partner.

It was quite two hours before Morgan came to her, and requested her hand. By then her lips were stiff with smiling.

"You have been so popular tonight, I have scarcely seen you," he began politely, a glint in his gray eyes.

When she did not reply, he looked down at her questioningly.

"You are silent, Miss Deborah."

She forced herself to speak. "You are most flattering," she said.

"All ladies like flattery, do they not? You enjoy the flattery of Monsieur Rigaud?"

"Of course," she said, and could think of nothing else to say. They circled the room in silence, and he bowed and left her with the squire, who happily bounced about the room with her, then paused to wipe his wet brow.

"Bless me, what a crush tonight!" he said. "Who would have thought it? All for our Alice! Well, I shall be glad to go home, when all this is done. Gertrude loves the fuss—she will be bored when we return to Lowbridge. However, it is for the best, is it not? For the best."

She was not quite sure what he was talking about, but it did not seem to matter. All that mattered was that Morgan had once again gone to Alice and was leading her out in a spritely contradance. Her dress floated about her; the gauze fluttered as lightly as her steps and the laughter on her lips.

A baronet, slim and languid, bowed before Deborah and requested the pleasure of a dance. She managed a bright smile and went with him.

"I understand you are the Miss Stanton who is an artist? Is that so?"

"Yes, I do paint. Not well yet, I fear," she said with an immense effort.

What did all that matter? She loved, and ached with loving. She longed fiercely for a day to come when she might be quite indifferent to Morgan—to all men!

"My mama longs to have my portrait painted for her. She understands that you would do a splendid job of it. What d'you say, Miss Stanton? Shall I sit for you?"

She looked at the elegant young gentleman as he drew back in the dance, fluttering his handkerchief from long thin fingers that probably did not work from morning to night. He had a reputation for sensuality and for an addiction to cards; it showed in his red lips and his restless gaze that tended to linger too often at the low neckline of her gown.

If she became a professional artist, she might have to accept commissions from such men as this popinjay before her, to be prey to his gazes and perhaps his hands. She might have to hire a maid to remain with her constantly as she painted.

She quivered a little with revulsion. "My time is much taken at present. But perhaps we might speak of this another time?"

She did not cut him off altogether. If she went to London, she must resign herself to doing portraits of such people. But she left him with a sense of relief when Monsieur Rigaud returned to her, and her smile at the Frenchman was more welcoming than she realized.

He was frowning. "Do you like *him?*" he murmured, indicating the languid baronet. "He has quite a reputation. Indeed, I am surprised he is here tonight. Otherwise, the company is quite select."

"His mother is well-liked, I believe," said Deborah with reserve. "And he has a title."

"A title? And does that matter to you, Miss Deborah?"

"Not to me," she said firmly. Only gray eyes, icy or warm, a tall distinguished figure, a quick mind, a slow smile, sensuous lips that had sometimes pressed hers—only those mattered to her, and those were beyond her, far beyond, she assured herself wearily.

"I am glad to hear it," Monsieur Rigaud was murmuring in her ear. "I had a title once in France, but it did not save my lands nor the lives of my people. I have come to despise titles. If only I might recover my own property, how happy I would be. Then—then I might dare to ask—someone—to be my wife, and how proudly I would take her to the altar!"

She glanced up at him in surprise. Did he mean her? Surely not. She had not meant to encourage him.

"Monsieur, I am sure if the lady loves you, she will regard neither title nor property," she said calmly. "It is the man himself, what he is and what he thinks, that is important."

"I should like to believe that," he said forcefully. "How much I should like to believe it!"

Troubled at his intensity, Deborah did not choose to continue the conversation. She smiled vaguely, and when the dance was over she managed to return to the squire, and remained near him until the almost unendurable evening was over.

She left with the others about two in the morning. Alice was dreamy and quiet when she undressed and went to bed.

"The best birthday ever, Deborah," she murmured when Deborah slid into the large bed beside her.

"I am so glad you enjoyed it, darling," Deborah managed to say. "You deserve every happiness."

"That is what *he* said—Lord Treverly. I told him about the early days, how you looked after me when Mama died. And about my birthday—when I was thirteen, do you remember? Papa was at sea, and Gertrude and Clarence were away. I cried for a doll, and there was no money for a new one."

"I remember," said Deborah softly.

"I told Lord Treverly how you took my old doll and cut up one of your own dresses to make new garments for it, and wrapped it in pretty paper you had painted yourself, and that was my birthday present. Do you remember?"

"Oh, Alice, you did not tell him—those old stories—" Deborah bit her lip. She did not want his pity.

"Oh, yes," said the sleepy voice. "I told him how you had been mother and father to me, how cold and distant Gertrude had been. Was that wrong? He seemed so interested, I am sure he would not repeat what I said."

The sleepy voice went on, while Deborah was silent from sheer mortification.

"I told him how, when I needed a dress, you cut down some of dear Mama's for me, and always I had the finest bonnets and ribbons you could devise. How Papa was always absent, and so cross when he was not well. He said he had not known how difficult it was for you, and asked if Clarence had not helped."

"Oh, Alice, you should not have confided all this! Family matters should remain private."

"But Deborah, he was so interested, and so sympathetic. I do not know why I always thought he was cold and aloof. No one could have been kinder than he was tonight. To give such a party for me!"

Alice sighed, turned over, and was soon asleep, her lips smiling even as she slept.

Deborah felt numb the next day. The talk was all of the party, and of the certainty of Lord Treverly soon making an offer for Alice. Gertrude was lost in a dream. Her own little sister, mistress of Treverly! Yet she was not so insensitive that she failed to notice her other sister's pallor. Poor Deborah looked quite plain today. The white dress she wore did not suit her, and the great shadows under her eyes made her look a ghost. Too many goings-on, that was the trouble. She should give up the painting; it was too much with their active social life in Bath.

As soon as Alice's engagement was set, Gertrude

resolved, they would all return home to Lowbridge
to plan the wedding, and settle down again. Deborah would make herself ill, going so hard. That
kind of life did not suit her. No, she would speak
to Deborah soon.

CHAPTER TWENTY

On Monday morning Deborah and Alice went out early into the garden, before the heat of the day, to cut fresh flowers for the house. They would surely have many guests today, after Alice's great success at the birthday dinner.

Alice paused to consider the roses as though she did not quite see them. Deborah eyed her anxiously, scarcely knowing what she herself hoped. If only all might go well—but what did that mean? All she knew was that she had somehow lost Morgan, had never really had him, for life had come between them, and her own duties. That bright June morning seemed as bleak as a winter night.

"Deborah," said Alice suddenly, and sat down on a garden bench, holding the flowers in her hands and looking like an impossibly beautiful portrait of youth incarnate. "Deborah, I must talk to you."

"Yes, dear?" Deborah looked blindly at a honeysuckle vine. Could it be placed in a vase, or not? It did not seem to matter. She snipped off a fine length. "What is it?"

"When—when I first met *him*, I thought he was

so old, and—well—gaunt and hard," said Alice frankly. "His manners were oppressive and formal, and he seemed to smile so cynically. Not like younger men, who were charming and gentle."

"Oh—really?" Deborah bit her lip to hold back anguished words, and kept her tone calm and encouraging.

"I thought—at first—that he was impossible. I could never live up to anyone like that! He seemed so stern sometimes—do you think he's stern?"

"His—responsibilities have been heavy," Deborah managed to say.

"Yes, so heavy." Alice smiled dreamily at the roses in her hand. "I could lighten his life for him. He said my youth seemed like sunshine to him."

Deborah flinched, and pressed a spray of honeysuckle to her nose, as if to lose herself in the scent. She could not speak. Alice did not seem to notice her agitation, for she was lost in her own thoughts.

"I could not seem to think of myself as a *wife* to him. I don't know why—I thought he was so severe and cold. But now that I know him better, why, I wonder at myself! He is all courtesy, he thinks only of one's happiness. Don't you think so, Deborah?"

Deborah managed a mumble that satisfied her dreamy sister.

Alice drew a deep sigh. "I have been thinking, Deborah. If he asks for my hand—and I think he will do so—I shall say yes. He is lonely, I think. He needs a wife. Sometimes he looks so—alone and aloof. If he were married, and had children, he would be happier, don't you think so, Deborah?"

Alice was blushing becomingly, and she looked young, untouched, yet womanly. Deborah remembered her own face in the mirror that morning. White, gaunt, anguished—"sadly aged." No wonder he had turned to Alice.

Alice did not seem to notice Deborah's silence. She went on, "And he is so very wealthy, that he does not even consider it! I would have all the new gowns and bonnets I could wish! And," she added hastily, "I could help you, Deborah. I could set you up in a little house of your own, perhaps very near to us. You should never know want. I know that Morgan feels as I do. You have sacrificed so much for me that you should be repaid. You shall live in comfort all your days."

Deborah shut her eyes against the sunshine. She swallowed, and knew the gall of unwanted charity. She had never wanted to be helped. She had wanted to do her share, to have the hand of a partner in hers, to help her as she helped him. Not this, not this—

"That is all in the future," she managed to say calmly. "I am sure Clarence will see to it that I am never in want. And I can—repay him with care of his children."

"Oh, of course, the children adore you," murmured Alice, her thoughts elsewhere. "And I shall have his children. He wants a son, especially. Can you imagine such happiness, Deborah? I should love to give him a son."

Deborah could not bear much more of this. She hastily began to clip flowers, any that her fingers touched.

"And the title," Alice went on. "Plain Alice Stanton become Lady Treverly—the Viscountess Treverly! Can you imagine it, Deborah? Me, a viscountess! It seems absurd, but it would be true!" She gave a delighted giggle.

"You would—make him very happy," Deborah managed to say. "We must take the flowers indoors, Alice. I am sure we will have guests today."

"Oh, yes, yes, and I am dreaming on." Alice jumped up and gave her sister a bright smile. "How pale you look, darling! Is it the heat? Do let us go in," she urged anxiously, and led her sister affectionately indoors. "I will arrange the flowers while you lie down for a time."

But Deborah could not rest. She must get out of the stifling house or go mad. The heat seemed to enclose her, and the voices of her sisters, endlessly talking over the party, Morgan's attentions to Alice, whether he might come today, how soon he would ask to see the squire—

She hurried downstairs, and saw the surprise on their faces. "I must go and see Lady Horatia; there is something I had forgotten that I must consult her about," she managed to mumble before running out.

"Where are you going? You are not walking! The squire has the carriage—wait until he returns —wait—" Gertrude cried after her, quite distracted. Deborah had looked so pale, so distraught.

Deborah would not wait. Alone, defiant of convention, she walked rapidly along the streets, ignoring the looks cast at her. Some called after her curiously; she did not heed them. An acquaintance was brushed aside as she walked blindly past the booksellers and up the hill to Lady Horatia's. Her one friend in the world, she thought.

Fortunately Lady Horatia was at home, and alone. She came out from her private sitting room, her hair still in curl papers, her dressing gown a frightening purple and crimson Chinese silk with dragons roaming about her feet.

"My dearest Deborah—my dear—whatever is it—" Even the formidable Lady Horatia was alarmed. "You are alone? I did not hear your carriage—"

Deborah managed to get her breath and regain her composure. She was at home here; Lady Horatia would advise her.

"I beg pardon for my abrupt arrival, but I must speak to you alone."

"Of course, of course." She ordered coffee, sent the maid away, and led Deborah to a comfortable sofa of rose and purple. She eyed her friend anxiously, shrewdly. She had some idea of what had disturbed the girl.

Deborah pressed her hands to her cheeks. Her flight from the house had left her hot and disheveled. "I beg pardon again," she said weakly.

"Never mind begging pardon!" said Lady Horatia brusquely. "I am glad you think enough of me as a friend to come to me. Catch your breath, and then you shall tell me all."

Deborah leaned back and closed her eyes. The room was cool and quiet. The maid returned with coffee, but Deborah set the cup down untasted.

She wanted nothing but the quiet friendship and sympathy of Lady Horatia.

"Now, my dear," said Lady Horatia after a time.

Deborah opened her eyes at last. "You must think me gone mad," she managed to say.

"I wondered," said Lady Horatia, and gave her a smile. "What has happened?"

"I—I must settle my future. I must get away from here. I do not think I can bear it."

Lady Horatia considered her response with care. "Has Lord Treverly offered for Alice?"

"Not yet. But Alice means to have him. She has said so. And at the party—he was so attentive—I think he means—" Deborah's voice broke, and she strove again for composure. "I must be happy for her. He will be a gentle and—loving—husband. He —he has spoken of his wishes for a—a wife and— a son—to her—"

Deborah's voice caught and a sob escaped her. Shocked at her own deep feelings, she pressed her fist to her mouth.

"Let us carefully consider the possibilities," said Lady Horatia, setting down her cup with a decisive click. "Whenever I am unable to make a decision—rare, I admit—I consider all the various possibilities, the advantages and disadvantages of each. Then I decide which is the best course. It works amazingly, my dear."

Deborah wiped her eyes carefully with her handkerchief, blew her nose, and felt better. Lady Horatia's brisk practicality was like a splash of cold water.

"Yes, I am sure it must be. How—how shall I consider?"

"Good girl. Well, first I am sure you have thought it your duty to return to Lowbridge with Mrs. Frome and take care of her brats, however many she has."

At the scorn in her tone, Deborah smiled weakly. "Yes, I think Gertrude wishes me to do this. And the squire has always been so kind."

"He is a good soul, yes. He would make sure you were not overworked—maybe. However, your older sister is not so concerned. She is willing to fob off onto you all the work possible. You are too intelligent a woman, with too many talents, to be nursemaid to her brats."

Deborah picked up her coffee cup and began to drink. She must begin to deal with reality, rather than her hopeless dreams.

"Second, there is the possibility of marrying someone else. Are you fond of Mr. Vaughan? Or Paul Rigaud?" The keen eyes watched her sharply.

Deborah trembled a little. "I do not think—I could consider marriage to anyone else," she said simply. "I have tried to think of Philip Irving—we have interests in common—"

"That dolt! He would have you dressed always in black, and slaving away for the entire village! No, do not think it."

"What else, then? I might be an artist. Lady Willoughby's portrait is completed. She gave me a hundred pounds, as you suggested. I felt as though I cheated her, yet she seemed so pleased with the portrait—"

"Nonsense! It was little enough. She is showing it all about, and will pay another fifty pounds to have it in a gold frame!" Lady Horatia smiled with pleasure. "That should bring more commissions for you. Her word is much respected, and the portrait is a charming one."

"So—I might go to London," said Deborah. "The only thing is—I believe I am a coward. The thought of being alone in London, depending on commissions—and the sort of persons who wish to be painted. The baronet at the party—I would be afraid to be alone in the room with him," she confessed simply.

"Lord, no," said Lady Horatia. "That would be a mistake! You must hire an abigail to be with you at all times. Yet some arrogant lord might take it into his head to dismiss her, and you *would* be in a fine pickle. No, no, let me think."

Deborah was content to let her friend do just that. She sank back, rather exhausted, against the violent purple cushion and closed her eyes. She felt as though she had not slept deeply for years.

"There is another possibility, a strong one," said Lady Horatia, with an eager note in her voice that made Deborah open her eyes and sit up straighter. "I have for some time been considering a journey to Egypt. It is a fascinating country, Deborah. History abounds there. There are strange pyramids and gigantic figures of stone that you would be amazed to see. And the journey there by ship would be marvelous, long days and nights on the open seas, charming ports when we weary of traveling. And my dear Deborah, you would be the perfect companion!"

Deborah stared at her friend, and in spite of her misery her spirits rose in sheer delight. To travel—to see the world outside England! To stop at charming ports—to travel on the high seas as Morgan had—as Morgan had—

"Ever since our conversation some while ago, Deborah, I have been thinking what a charming companion you would be—a paid companion, of course. I should deem it an honor if you would consider the post. After our journeys, when we tire of strange lands and different peoples, we would return to London and take up residence there. You would enjoy my townhouse. There you could paint, and you would be a novelty in society. People would flock to you to have their portraits painted, and you would never lack a chaperone. Yes, I think it would be delightful. What do you think, Deborah?" The vivid flow of words stopped, and she gazed rather anxiously at Deborah. "I know I am years older, yet we have so much in common."

"You are too kind, too good," Deborah began to stammer, rather bewildered.

"Nonsense. I suit myself, as I always have! However, what suits me may well suit you, also. I think we might cause a little stir in London," and she smiled complacently. "The first females to travel alone in Egypt! Yes, we shall be quite the thing!"

Deborah hesitated. She wanted to say, yes, yes, let us go away, let us be off at once. But something held her back. Would traveling thousands of miles away dull her longing to be near to Morgan? Was it better to wonder where he was and what he did, or to be nearby and see him sometimes, however coldly courteous he was to her?

"You need not decide at once," said Lady Horatia. "We shall read books on Egypt—I have several in my library. I think you will be enchanted with what you learn. And what paintings you shall make of it! I quite long to see them. Think about it, Deborah. Oh, and let me find the books—"

She was up and darting to the library, to return with four heavy tomes. She dusted them off carelessly with her napkin and laid them before Deborah, who opened the first one to find an engraving of a triangular-shaped building set in the midst of endless sands.

"A pyramid," said Lady Horatia knowledgeably. "And look on the next pages, at that odd creature in the sand, with the face of a woman and the paws of a lioness."

Deborah turned the pages slowly, enraptured by the thought of the strange place, these odd sights. When the maid announced luncheon, they went in, still talking animatedly. They discussed earnestly the possibility of taking a ship from the south of England down to Lisbon, where Lady Horatia had friends, then on to the coast of Africa. Africa! And then into the warm blue of the Mediterranean Sea, along the coast, the wild coast of Africa itself, and on to Egypt.

They had continued their talk in the drawing room, over coffee, when the maid appeared, to ask if she might bring in Monsieur Rigaud. Lady Horatia sighed and said yes, she could not turn him away.

Monsieur Rigaud entered, to look at their animated faces. "My dear Lady Horatia," he said.

"I came to call upon Miss Deborah this morning, to find she had fled! After luncheon, I was easily persuaded by Mrs. Frome to come here and discover what had happened to you."

"Well, we are planning a trip to Egypt together," said Lady Horatia complacently. He looked immensely startled, picked up one of the books she indicated, then managed a chuckle.

"You are teasing me! You mean only to read a book together about that wild country. It is no place for ladies—there are wild barbarians there." And he set down the volume in relief. "You had me terrified that you meant it!"

"We do mean it," said Lady Horatia.

He looked grave as he heard of their plans and and said finally, "But surely you, Miss Deborah, are not seriously considering this great venture? It would cause a strong man to quail, I assure you!"

She was having some doubts of her own. However, the thought of the journey, and of living pleasantly in Lady Horatia's London townhouse, had whiled away the difficult day. She smiled. "We are thinking of it, sir. Do not be surprised to hear of us sailing away to the South! Would it not be splendid to be able to sketch such scenes as this?" And she indicated the page opened to the engraving of the pyramid.

He shook his head. "The English have such a sense of humor, I never know when they are serious or only having a gentle tease. Do convince me that you do not mean it, Miss Deborah!"

"We are thinking about it," repeated Lady Horatia. "But pray keep the news to yourself for a time, my dear Monsieur Rigaud. I do not wish it bandied about. You are such a close friend, we felt we could tell you anything. However, we have only just begun to make plans. I am sure Deborah's sisters will be distressed if they hear of it too soon. Let her tell them in her own way."

Paul Rigaud looked very serious, and presently he offered to escort Deborah home. She consented, and left with a grateful smile for her friend.

Rigaud was rather quiet as they walked, but as they neared the squire's house, he said, "Miss Deborah, you are indeed a close friend of Lady Horatia, are you not? I know she admires you greatly."

"Yes, I am proud that she considers me a friend."

"But you would not set out soon, without giving this journey careful thought, would you?"

Deborah shrugged, feeling rather depressed after the day's excitement. "Why not? There is nothing to keep me in England, once my sister is—is engaged. She may become engaged soon, sir."

They had reached the door. Rigaud paused, still holding her arm as they stood before the steps. "Miss Deborah, I beg you not to do anything so reckless without first consulting me—or your estimable brother-in-law, the squire. Pray, let us advise you. I—I should hate for you to rush off to some unknown place."

"You are most kind, sir." She had no intention of consulting him, but she smiled brightly. He had indeed been kind to her, and often had soothed her wounded feelings.

"I should like to be more than kind to you," he said softly. The butler was coming to open the door; they could hear his stately footsteps in the hallway. "I beg you to think how much I should miss you. I long to speak further to you of this. May I come this evening?"

She was uncomfortable under his serious regard. "Oh—not this evening, pray—perhaps tomorrow or Wednesday?"

He looked upset. "You will do nothing further about this—" he was beginning. The door opened. The butler looked surprised to see the two of them standing there as if reluctant to enter.

"Pray come tomorrow or Wednesday, sir; we shall be glad to receive you." And Deborah slipped inside, in great relief. She had feared he might begin to propose to her on the very steps of her brother-in-law's house, with neighbors strolling past!

She went inside and paused at the drawing room. She found guests there, some distant relatives of the squire who had come for tea and dinner. She had forgotten all about them.

She made a quick excuse and ran upstairs to brush her hair and compose her expression. Later, when she joined them, she made trivial conversation, but all the time was thinking, thinking.

To be a paid companion was not her ideal in life. Yet Lady Horatia was a kind friend and a fascinating woman. Would she always be conscious, though, of being a *paid* companion?

Yet her art could flourish, with the traveling, and Lady Horatia would introduce her to many in the *ton;* she would have a hundred subjects for her portraits. It might be that in time she could afford a place of her own, be independent. And it would be an interesting life, gay and social.

Why, then, did she feel so depressed and bitter? Much as she admired and liked Lady Horatia, the life of a paid companion was not what she had dreamed of all these years while Morgan was away. Well, if one could not have what one wanted, one must make do with the next best.

Gertrude whispered to her once, "Wherever did you go? Why were you gone so long? I was worried to death!"

"I will tell you tomorrow," whispered Deborah, forcing a gay smile to her lips.

Gertrude looked at her suspiciously. Deborah had been pale and wild-eyed when she left; now she was pink-cheeked and giddy. Whatever was going on? Was it that Frenchman, Monsieur Rigaud? If there had been anyone else to send for Deborah, she would have done so. Oh, to think that Deborah should be so difficult now, when once she had been so meek and helpful! Gertrude resolved to give her a good talking-to tomorrow. All this artistic nonsense had given her notions above herself.

With that firm resolution, Gertrude returned to her guests and managed to give an impression of a happy matron, immersed in the many social duties of Bath.

Deborah dreamed on, scarcely hearing when spoken to, and earning many a dubious look from the squire's relatives. Clarence gazed at her thoughtfully. If only females were not so devious and strange! He wished they were honest and straightforward, like men.

CHAPTER TWENTY-ONE

Alice tried to question Deborah that night as they readied themselves for sleep. Deborah firmly refused to answer her anxious queries.

"Tomorrow, Alice. I am weary, and I have much thinking to do. Tomorrow I will talk of my plans."

"Your plans! Deborah dear, you talk so strangely! What plans are you speaking of? What do you mean to do?" Alice gazed at her older sister as though she had never seen her before. The girl who had been like a mother to her seemed a stranger now, flushed, defiant, distant.

"Tomorrow, Alice." And Deborah would say no more. When Alice slept, she lay awake for a time, confused, yet strangely calmed.

She slept finally, and so deeply that Alice, waking early, eyed her in a troubled way. Alice rose quietly, washed and dressed, and crept downstairs. She told Gertrude, "Deborah is still asleep. I did not wish to awaken her—she seems so weary."

"Of course, of course. What did she say last night?"

"Nothing, she would say nothing," sighed Alice. "Shall I cut some flowers?"

"Perhaps you had better. Deborah must be allowed her own way, I suppose. I hope she is not going to turn strange, as some spinsters do."

"Oh, no, no, Deborah is not *mad*. It is just that—well, I don't know." And Alice wandered out into the garden, her mind searching in perplexity for a reason for her sister's odd behavior.

It was noon when Deborah arose. The night's sleep had strengthened her certainty that she would be better off away from Morgan. Lady Horatia's offer had come like a gift from heaven, and she had best grasp it.

Deep sleep had brought back the color to her wan face. She put on a gay cream and red silk gown that Lady Horatia had given her. She wound her curls in a more sophisticated style than usual and fastened them with a red ribbon. Defiance brought a sparkle to her eyes, and the cream silk suited her. It was bordered with an odd pattern about the long sleeves and the deep hem, a peculiar design that made her think of Egypt, with its animals and flowers and trailing vines.

She came down in time for luncheon. Gertrude, about to question her sharply, paused at the look in her eyes. Well, the squire had been warned; he could speak to her later. Gertrude moved uneasily in her chair, scarcely able to concentrate on the bright gossip about her, as Alice took up the conversation, chatting with Clarence about friends in Bath.

"Do you expect any guests today?" Gertrude finally asked Deborah pointedly.

"Today? No—that is, Monsieur Rigaud said he

might come. I told him he might call upon us on Tuesday or Wednesday." She spoke with cool composure, almost indifference.

"Ah, you are becoming serious about Monsieur Rigaud?" The squire ponderously tried to tease her.

"Not a bit of it," said Deborah, finishing her pudding. "This is excellent, Alice. You are becoming quite good with desserts."

"Thank you," said Alice, quite taken aback. Usually Deborah complimented her with warmth and delight, not in this cool tone. She eyed her dubiously.

"Do let us have coffee in the drawing room, before guests descend upon us," said Gertrude hastily. If they were going to quarrel, and she had an ominous feeling that they were, it might as well be in private, not before the curious footmen.

They withdrew to the drawing room, where the butler wheeled in the coffee tray. Deborah went to stand at the window. Finally Gertrude's voice penetrated her thoughts. She heard her sister say, "Does Lord Treverly call on us soon, Clarence? I had thought he would offer for Alice one day quite soon."

"He has said nothing to me," said the squire comfortably. "Has he hinted to you, Alice my dear?"

"Hinted, yes," said Alice, and Deborah turned about to see the delightful blush on her sister's face. "But he has said nothing to me. I am sure he is so proper he would come first to you."

"And you do not wish me to turn him away, heh?" laughed the squire.

"Oh, sir, you would not do that!" cried Alice anxiously.

"He is but teasing you," smiled Gertrude. She caught Deborah's strange look, fixed on the squire. "Deborah, my dear, you must never worry about *your* future. You may not care to marry. Indeed, I should think it strange if you did! You are indifferent to Monsieur Rigaud, yet I am sure he is most charming," she said complacently, sure now of the cause of her sister's peculiar behavior.

Deborah approached the coffee tray slowly, her shoulders stiffening. Now was the time to tell them, before strangers and guests arrived.

"I am not worried about my future now, Gertrude," she said, and bent to receive her coffee cup. She sat down on the sofa. "I have been speaking with Lady Horatia about that."

"Lady Horatia!" cried Gertrude, spilling some coffee on the tray. She set down the silver pot with a clatter, her hands trembling. "How can you go to her about something so—so intimate? She is not family!"

"She has been a good friend to me," said Deborah quietly, and sipped cautiously at the hot coffee.

The squire sat up straighter and set down his pipe. Deborah did indeed look and sound odd; Gertrude was not exaggerating, for a change.

"You know you have a home with us always, Deborah," he said comfortably.

"Yes, yes, after Alice is married, you must remain with us," said Gertrude, giving her husband a grateful look. "You know how fond we are of you."

"Yes, and I am fond of you, and I do hope to visit you from time to time, as our journeys permit," said Deborah. She took a deep breath, looking about the circle of faces, Gertrude's anxious, the squire's thoughtful, Alice's wide-eyed and curious. "Lady Horatia has done me the honor of asking me to be her paid companion. We plan to take a trip first to Egypt."

They were speechless, as though she had spoken a strange language and they needed an interpreter.

The silence in the room was unbroken as the three kept staring at Deborah.

She sipped her coffee, chose a cake, all in complete silence. She noted a little worn place on the carpet; the sofa should be moved to cover it, she thought dimly. But no, it would not matter. Alice would soon be engaged, and they would all return to Lowbridge to prepare for the wedding. No need to move furniture about; it was but a rented house and they would soon leave. She wondered who would move in. Some other hopeful family with a marriageable daughter? Someone like Alice? Would they find a suitable husband for the girl, a marquis perhaps, or—or someone like Morgan, who wanted a wife and a son to make his comfortable life complete?

She had to break the silence. "Lady Horatia has kindly implored me to accompany her to Egypt. We go from the south of England down to Lisbon, where she has friends. Then we continue on by ship into the Mediterranean—"

The squire said harshly, interrupting her, "What nonsense is this? France and England are at war!

You must be aware that our ships have set up a dangerous blockade all about the ports—all along the coasts. France may attack at any time!"

"Lady Horatia is aware of all the news, Clarence," said Deborah, in cool despair. Nothing seemed to matter. What if they *were* fired upon, even killed? It did not matter. Her heart was already dead.

"She must be an idiot, then. I am surprised at her!" said the squire heavily, knocking the tobacco out of his pipe before it was half-finished. "It would be exceedingly dangerous to journey anywhere— but to Egypt! I know! She was only teasing you. She is a great tease."

"She meant it, and so did I. She knows many politicians and persons in the army and navy. I am sure she is aware of the situation," said Deborah, with a calm that seemed to enrage them.

"You are both demented!" cried Gertrude. "To think of going to Egypt at a time like this! And Alice about to become engaged! We shall need you at home for the wedding. How do you think I shall manage alone? And you must attend Alice's wedding, or what will people say?"

"I no longer care what people say," said Deborah, her lips set in a stubborn line. "I am going to please myself, for once in my life. For too long, I have danced to the tunes others played. First Mother and Father, then you and Clarence. No, I am going off to be happy. I shall travel and sketch and paint. We shall return to London, and be part of a circle of smart, interesting persons. Lady Horatia said so."

Gertrude caught her breath, deeply shocked.

Alice put her face in her hands. The squire said, very coldly:

"Have a care, my girl! You are not free to do as you please, you know. Your father would be exceedingly shocked to hear you speak so. He took every care of you—"

"Oh, yes," said Deborah sarcastically. "Every time he came home from sea, that is. Each year we saw him for a full three or four weeks! Yes, yes, every care! While I worked in the garden, worried over Alice, sewed our clothes, nursed Mother until her death—every care, indeed! How can you speak so? Don't you know the truth? Don't you know why I was so exhausted when Father finally died? I was worn to the bone! I worked every day from early morning, I rose before light to heat the kitchen and prepare tea for all."

"Deborah, Deborah, do not speak so! How you hurt me!" cried Alice, quite frightened. She had never heard her sister speak in such a fierce, terrible way, nor seen her with fists clenched and body taut with rage.

"I am sorry, Alice, it was not your fault. You were young and needed care. So did Mother, poor soul. Poor soul, indeed, married to an indifferent, callous man who cared only for his navy career and his painting! He did not even bother to come home when she went into her final illness! Do you know I sat up with her dead body that night, quite alone, bathed her and prepared her for burial with my own hands? Do you know that I was sick at my stomach, a girl myself, to have to do that? I could not eat or sleep for days and nights—"

"We would have come to you," said the squire,

more quietly. He stood and came over to her, his hand heavily on her shoulder. "Do not upset yourself with thoughts of long ago, Deborah. That is all over and done with."

"Yes, all over and done with," Deborah said, twisting her hands in her lap. "All is pleasant now. But I cannot forget those memories. I gave up—" She caught sight of Alice's horrified face, and amended her words. "I gave up my youth—to take care of Mother, then Father, and Alice. Now, only Alice is left, and she will soon be married. Now I am free, and I shall go away and please myself."

"I never knew you felt like this." Alice put her slim hand to her throat. "I thought you loved me! The one person in the world on whom I could depend."

"And so I did," said Deborah gently, unable to resist the pleading look and tone. "And so I still do. But you will soon have a husband to love you and take care of you. You no longer need me. Gertrude needs me only to help with her—children." She had almost said "brats," like Lady Horatia, but caught herself in time. She loved the children; it was only that they were not her own. She turned from that thought also, with determination. "I shall not live on your charity any longer. A nursemaid will be sufficient. I mean to be interestingly employed by Lady Horatia."

The squire released her shoulder and began to pace about the room in agitation. Gertrude shook her head angrily.

"You are ungrateful, ungrateful!" she cried. "After all we have done for you—Clarence has

342

been more than generous to you! You should be willing to remain with us always, and help us when we need you. Is it so much to ask? Any loyal sister would do as much, especially when she is too old for marriage and not attractive to men. How long do you think Lady Horatia will be amused by you? She quarrels with everyone. How long—"

"We do not quarrel," said Deborah quietly. She had anticipated a battle, but not like this. She had let her tongue run away with her, for the bitterness of past memories had risen up like gall and she had had to speak or gag on it. Now, seeing Alice's shocked, appealing face, she was sorry. Nor would she forget Gertrude's cruel words. A sister's loyalty, indeed!

"You might quarrel in time," said the squire, halting before the mantelpiece. He spoke heavily. "Deborah, think carefully about this. I did not know you felt so bitter—we will speak in private about this another time. But I pray you, do nothing in haste. Think carefully before you venture into the unknown. You are letting pride and anger rule you, and that is unlike you, Deborah."

"I beg your pardon, Squire; you have been very good to me and to Alice. But I shall not be ruled by anyone but myself from now on. I shall do what seems best to me, and that is to travel about and enjoy myself—"

"You are thinking of being a loose woman!" said Gertrude. "Deborah, you are mad! I think we should never have let you come to Bath with us. The attentions to you and your silly paintings have quite gone to your head!"

"My silly paintings—" And Deborah found herself on her feet. "My silly paintings—the one of Lady Willoughby alone has brought one hundred pounds! And I can do it again, and again. And I shall do it. No one shall stop me!"

"Your ingratitude hurts the more deeply," shouted Gertrude over Deborah's stormy voice. "You have no sense of gratitude, to me who gave you a home and every care—to Clarence—"

Alice burst into tears, sobbing into her handkerchief. The squire tried to speak, but had to shout over the din.

"Cease this, cease! It does no good; you are all overexcited! Come now, come now—"

No one heard the butler at the door. Lord Treverly pushed past the startled servant and into the drawing room, surveying the scene with amazement.

Gertrude saw him first, and stopped in the middle of a word. How ghastly, to have this stupid family quarrel overheard! Alice was sobbing bitterly and still did not see him enter.

Deborah gave him a furious look. He blinked and finally said, "What in the world is going on?"

The squire said heavily, "I regret—a family argument—pray excuse us, my lord—"

"It is not his concern," said Deborah angrily.

Morgan gave her a strange look. "I think it may be," he said quietly. "What is the matter?"

"She is ungrateful, inconsiderate, unladylike," cried Gertrude, reaching for her lace handkerchief. "To think that all these years—and our care of her—"

"Enough!" said Deborah. "We shall not continue now, since Lord Treverly has seen fit to come in without permission. I shall go to my room."

She made for the door, to be halted by his hard arm. He jerked her about rudely and made her stand before him.

"What a tempest," he said, with a half-smile. "Come now, Deborah, what is it? What has put you in such a temper?"

"She is going to Egypt!" wailed Alice, lifting her swollen face briefly. "She is going mad!"

"Which? Or both?" he asked with a grin. Deborah could have struck him.

"We shall continue our discussion another time," said the squire hastily, striding up and down the room again. He wiped his flushed face. "I beg your forgiveness, my lord. Such a scene, quite unlike us —do forgive—"

"But I should like to know what is going on. What has Deborah done that is so dreadful?" He spoke as though he were humoring a child, she thought furiously.

She drew herself up to her slight height and lifted her chin. "I merely informed them that I am becoming a paid companion to Lady Horatia Torrington. Our first voyage is to be to Egypt, and we shall leave soon. That is all, my lord, and none of your concern!"

"You do not mean it," he said flatly, losing his smile.

"I do mean it. We have discussed it seriously." She wrenched herself from his grasp and went over to a table. "You see? Here are some books on

Egypt. We shall see the pyramids, and I shall
sketch. When we return, we shall live in London
and be very gay. I am tired of Lowbridge, I am
tired of being a nursemaid, I am tired of thinking
of others before myself. I shall go off and do as I
please!"

Alice began to weep softly again. Morgan looked
from Deborah to her, then to Gertrude and the
squire, who shrugged helplessly. He turned back
to Deborah. "You would not be so insane," he
said forcefully. "You have too much sense to do
such a thing."

"Not at all, my lord," she said, calming herself.
She hugged the heavy books to her bosom as
though defying anyone to take them from her.
"I *am* going to Egypt! And no one shall stop me!"

His mouth tightened. "That is a pack of nonsense. We have blockaded the coast, the French
are expected to try to invade! And you and that
wild Lady Horatia are talking of going to Egypt!
I cannot believe you are not teasing yourself, or
us. There is no way you can go to Egypt now. It
will not be permitted."

"Lady Horatia is wise to the ways of traveling.
She says we can go. She will find a manner of going. I trust her completely."

"Then I shall speak to Lady Horatia," he said
with cold displeasure, and fury in his gray eyes.

"Yes, do so," said Deborah tersely, her brown
eyes flashing sparks.

"I shall! And if she is serious, you will do well
to listen to me, then. It is sheer madness to consider such a trip, even if the time was ripe. The

journey is long and tedious, full of dangers for men. And for two females, innocent and lacking sense—"

"You just said I had sense, Lord Treverly! Can't you make up your mind?"

"Deborah! You will not speak so to his lordship!" urged Gertrude, in agony. She was beginning to realize what this scene meant. If Lord Treverly thought he had misjudged the family, he might back off from his devotion to Alice. And if he thought they were fools enough to let her go—

The squire had given up. He stood with his back to the room, staring out the window, mentally rejecting them all, one might judge by the angle of his shoulders. Alice still sobbed softly. Morgan seemed to take hold of himself.

"Well, yes, we shall talk later. I believe you have other visitors," he said. "Meanwhile, I shall call upon Lady Horatia—"

"You will not interfere in my concerns, Lord Treverly," Deborah warned him ominously. "You are not a member of the family yet, and even if you were I should not listen to you. Leave me to decide my own fate!"

He stared at her. The doorbell rang, and voices were heard. Alice started up. "I cannot—talk to anyone—" she stammered, and dashed for the stairs.

"And I shall go up to my room and read about Egypt," said Deborah, and swept from the room after her sister.

Morgan looked after them both and drew a deep breath. He shook his head as though dazed and looked at the squire. The squire looked back at him and ran a hand over his head.

"Females," said the squire feelingly.

Morgan nodded. "Females," he said deeply. They turned politely to meet the guests coming in.

CHAPTER TWENTY-TWO

All the tears and excitement and quarreling had exhausted Deborah. On Wednesday morning, she decided to go over her sketches and begin work on a harbor scene. That would take her mind off the cold atmosphere of the household. Gertrude and Alice had gone out calling, as Gertrude had insisted they must, and the squire had accompanied them. Probably they hoped that Deborah, if left alone, would "come to her senses," she thought. But she still burned with anger at Lord Treverly's interference, and the reactions of all the others.

She sat down in the large drawing room and spread out her portfolio of sketches. She would work on the Bristol port scene that Paul Rigaud had liked so much. Perhaps she would paint that next.

She started through the portfolio, but did not find it. Frowning impatiently, she went through them all again more slowly. No, it was not there.

Furthermore, as she went over them, she realized other sketches were missing. She had never counted them; however she remembered some that should be there—one of a port on the

Dover coast, two others in Bristol Channel. One in Cornwall and another near Brighton.

How could she have lost them? Some of her favorite, most detailed sketches! She must have put them upstairs in a drawer, though she could not remember doing so. Impatiently, she went up to the bedroom she shared with Alice, went through all the drawers, peered in the wardrobe, and finally decided she might have left them in the squire's study.

She went downstairs again, searching her memory in vain. Vaguely she heard sounds at the door, the butler's smooth voice. She slipped into the study; she did not want to see visitors unless she had to; she was too distracted.

She searched around the study. Nothing on the desk but the squire's papers. Nothing in the top drawer, where she had sometimes slipped a sketch she was working on. Nothing on the bookshelves. The sketches were large, some of them twelve inches by fifteen. They could not very well be hidden from view. Had she given any away? No, she would not do that, not when she intended to use them for paintings.

She sighed. She must be losing her mind—perhaps Gertrude was right. When had she seen them last? Had she taken them to show Lady Horatia recently? She searched her memory, but it was no use.

Silently, on heelless slippers, she went back to the drawing room. She walked in, not expecting a guest, to find Paul Rigaud rapidly going through her portfolio. He had taken out three of them and set them aside.

She stared at him. He did not see her at first, so intent was he on the sketches, and his charming face was set in hard lines. He was working rapidly. Even as she watched, he made a tight roll of several sketches and inserted them into his hollow cane!

She gasped, and he glanced up. For a moment, she was afraid. He looked so different—

She had no time to think. He smiled, put the cane aside, and came forward, catching her hands and swinging them.

"I am caught out!" he said engagingly. "And I so wanted to give you a wonderful surprise!"

"A surprise? You have taken my sketches?" She could not adjust herself to the thought.

He nodded, his eyes sparkling with mischief. "And wait until you hear what I have done! You will thank me over and over again. I told you I could sell them for a high price, did I not? And that there is a marvelous market for your paintings of the sea? Did I not tell you so?"

"Oh, Monsieur Rigaud, what have you done?" she laughed breathlessly. He stopped swinging her hands, drew her closer, and dropped a kiss on her forehead. She felt a tingle of—what? Not pleasure, but a sort of warning. She drew back. He was going too fast for her.

"Come, come, and I will show you!" He swept up the portfolio, tucked it under his arm, picked up the cane, and drew her with him, an arm about her waist. "Where is your bonnet, your cloak?"

She sent a maid to fetch them, and they were brought at once.

"Tell Madame we shall return presently," Rigaud

said gaily. "Now for the surprise. Come along, Miss Deborah!"

He drew her with him out into the drab June day. The sky had darkened, but he had a closed carriage waiting. "You will not get wet; do not worry."

He handed her into the carriage, climbed in behind her, and the coachman swung up to his seat. "There!" He sat down beside her, taking her hand. There was an odd, tingling excitement about him. "Presently you shall know all. How I have longed for this moment, to reveal the secret!"

"But what is it? Where are we going?"

He grinned down at her. "To meet the man who is going to buy all the paintings you can possibly do, all the sketches! He will be enchanted to meet you, I know. And you need not worry; I shall be right beside you. You are my protégée!" And he squeezed her hand encouragingly. "Are you quite warm enough? The day is cool."

"Yes, yes, but do tell me where we are going!" The carriage was moving rapidly along the cobblestones. As Paul talked, Deborah sensed they were leaving the city. The traffic was less, the calls of the street vendors had died behind them.

He ignored the question. "I only wish we could have brought your father's sketches as well," he sighed. "Oh well, we can send for them. The buyer will be entranced with them. But it is your work he will love, I know it!"

"Who is this mysterious person? Do I know him? And how do you know he will like my work? Has he seen it?"

"No, but he trusts my judgment." And Rigaud laughed aloud. "He will be immensely pleased with me that I have found such a treasure!"

She began to be uneasy. Paul was talking so wildly. And if the "buyer" of her sketches had not seen her work, how did Paul Rigaud know the man would want them? It was all so strange. And why were they leaving Bath?

"He lives in the country?" she asked.

"Sometimes," he said provokingly.

"Really, Paul—Monsieur—"

"Call me Paul," he murmured, his face suddenly close to hers. "I find I like the sound of my name on your lovely lips."

And he slipped his arm about her waist, held her close, and kissed her mouth. She stiffened and tried to shove him back. "Please—don't!"

He laughed a little, as though to himself, and leaned back in the comfortable carriage. He let her go, to her relief, and began to hum lightly, as though he could scarcely contain his elation. Even in the dim light of the carriage, she noted how his eyes glittered.

Deborah reached out and pulled one curtain away from the window. She saw that they were approaching the lovely common where she had witnessed the drilling of the little village troop. It was quite a distance from Bath, and she had told no one where she was going. And she was alone with Paul Rigaud, with no chaperone, not even her young sister!

"Monsieur Rigaud, this has gone far enough," she said with dignity. "I appreciate your wish to help me with my career. However, I must return to Bath. My sister will be worried about me."

"Not yet, my dear," he said. "I have my heart set on taking you with me to meet a buyer for your wonderful work. You will thank me, I promise you! When you see the amount he pays for the sketches, you will open your lovely eyes quite wide." He patted her hand and leaned toward her.

She drew back from him. He had not been drinking; she could smell no liquor on his breath. But the puzzle of his unusual behavior was disturbing her greatly. He had always been so respectful and kind. He always thought of the conventions, of what society would say, and seemed anxious to be in everyone's good graces and careful of Deborah's reputation. What had changed him today?

She mused back over the scene this morning. The sketches had been missing, and Paul was frank in admitting he had taken them. He was prepared to take more—in a hollow cane! Was that the way one presented artistic work to a potential buyer? No, it was more like secret work, like something illegal and furtive . . . like spying.

And Paul Rigaud had said nothing of taking her work. When had it disappeared? The last time she could remember seeing it was when she had taken out the portfolio about a week ago, at a general gathering for tea at which Lady Horatia and Monsieur Rigaud had been present. They had insisted on her showing her work to a lovely young baroness, whose husband wished her portrait painted. Deborah frowned slightly, gazing into the distance toward the Malvern Hills, the silvery streak of the Avon River.

What had she done with the portfolio that day? Lady Horatia had been the last to leave; Deborah had accompanied her into the hall and they had spoken for a time. No, Monsieur Rigaud had remained. He had been last to leave, coming from the drawing room to kiss her hand devotedly and thank her for a marvelous afternoon.

"I do not understand this," she finally said, in a small voice. "Where are you taking me, Monsieur? I demand to know!" She said it very firmly, sitting rigidly beside him. "I wish to return home at once. This is not—not the conventional behavior that I would have expected from you."

He was watching her keenly from his languid position, resting against the squabs. "My dear Miss Deborah, you must trust me. I know you will be overwhelmed when you meet the buyer."

"Overwhelmed? Is he—royalty?" she asked rather fearfully, glancing down at her simple muslin dress. "I am not dressed properly—"

"You need not worry. He is interested in your work only."

She was silent for a time, her hands twisting in her lap. It must be past noon, and she was vaguely hungry, but far too worried to think of when she might eat next.

"How long is the journey, Monsieur?"

"Why do you not call me Paul, as you just did? It sounded delightful from your lips!"

"Please, Monsieur, do not tease me," she said in a stifled tone. "I should like to know how long the journey is to be!"

"It is not very long as one counts journeys."

She drew a deep breath. "I do not wish to go

on a journey, long or short, today," she said with an attempt at calm. "Pray return me to my sister's home."

"Oh, you are quite ready to go to Egypt, but you will not go a quarter of that distance with me!" he said laughingly.

"A—quarter of that distance? How far?" she asked sharply. "What are you doing? Where are we really going?"

Her voice had risen. He leaned forward swiftly. "Be quiet. We are about to go through a village!"

Now Deborah was really alarmed. Seeing houses begin to appear ahead of them, she reached for the handle of the carriage door. She would cry out, jump from the carriage. It would have to slow down on the dusty village street.

Paul Rigaud pulled her back. "Don't do anything foolish," he warned her, and his voice, cold and hard, was scarcely recognizable. "Come back here—"

He yanked her against him, took a fold of scarf, and before she was aware of what he was doing, he had wrapped it about her mouth, effectively stifling her cries. Then, as she struggled the more fiercely, he took another scarf and fastened her hands together before her. Bending, he bound her ankles together with yet another scarf, and when she was tightly tied, he leaned back, breathing rather hard.

He said nothing, but leaned forward once again and drew the curtains of the carriage so that no one could see inside. The carriage had slowed for the village, and Deborah attempted to kick out against the door. He held her back, and in a furious whisper warned her, "You will be quiet, or it will be the worse for you! Do not compel me to use force on you! This venture is too important for me to hesitate at striking you unconscious!"

Deborah's heart seemed to stop beating for a few seconds. Then a rush of blood to the head made her wild and frenzied. She struggled against the bonds, attempting to cry out in a muffled tone. He lifted his hand, struck a blow to her jaw, and she knew nothing for a time.

She wakened very slowly, with a fierce headache, and the sensation of being rocked back and forth, back and forth. She felt weak and nauseated.

"I think she is wakening," said an accented voice, and a smooth hand moved over her forehead. Deborah reluctantly opened her eyes, winced at the bright lamplight before her, and narrowed her gaze until she could bring the face before her into focus.

"Madame—Andreossy—" she whispered. The woman smiled compassionately.

"Poor child, you must feel so ill," she said in a gentle voice. Then a man's hand touched her shoulder, and she obediently moved aside.

Rigaud took her place and leaned anxiously toward Deborah. He held her hand tightly in his. "Deborah, how do you feel, my dearest?"

She blinked at him in bewilderment. The last thing she remembered, she recalled slowly, was his binding her up, putting the cloth in her mouth, warning her to be silent. And, oh yes, that blow to the head—had he really struck her?

She tried to speak. "Did you—where—"

"We are on a ship, my dear," he said quietly, a gleam of triumph in his eyes. "We are going on an adventure. You wanted travel and adventure, did you not, my sweet? Well, you shall have them! We are off to France."

"To—France—" It must be a nightmare; she must be having a horrible dream. Alice would waken her presently if she but cried out.

"Let her have something to eat and drink," said Madame Andreossy quietly. "The poor child is bewildered."

"Presently," said Rigaud, waving his free hand impatiently to silence her. "Listen, Deborah. What would you say if I told you we are going to meet the greatest man in the world?"

"The greatest—" she whispered, watching the queer gleam in his eyes. He looked a stranger, hard, and even cruel.

"Yes, the greatest man in the world—Napoleon Bonaparte!"

She stared blankly at him. He gave a low laugh.

"You are transfixed! No wonder! It will be a tremendous honor! And wait until the great one sees what we have brought him! Sketches of the many ports of England! Ships of England! And the very girl who can draw for him any port he wishes, any ship! It will make his invasion infinitely easier! You shall tell him all you know about the British navy, their regulations, their customs—" He gave a little laugh at her incredulous stare.

"But—but Napoleon Bonaparte—he is a monster!" said Deborah weakly. "He is our enemy! He would invade my country! You cannot mean—"

"Nonsense! How dare you speak so of him!" Paul's mouth tightened. He half-lifted his hand, menacingly.

Marie Andreossy warned anxiously, "She believes all that foolish talk in England, *mon cher*. Do not be angry with her. Wait till she meets the great one himself. She will forget all that nonsense. You know she will!"

Somehow Deborah gained the impression that Madame Andreossy was fearful of Paul's anger, was trying to soothe the man, and that made her all the more afraid. She must try to guard her tongue. Oh, how could she have gone so obediently, so trustingly with Monsieur Rigaud? A Frenchman, whom no one knew—

Her eyelids drooped. "I am so tired—so confused—" she murmured. "I don't know— When will I return—to my home?"

Rigaud made an impatient sound and shook her slightly. "Keep awake! Listen to me! We sail with the morning tide, a few hours from now. We are on our way to France! If anyone stops us, you shall say that you go willingly with us to America—"

"To America! You cannot mean—" gasped Deborah, in horror. "All that way—"

"No, no," soothed Marie Andreossy quickly. "We are going to France. But our vessel looks like an American one—we fly the American flag. So we will probably not be stopped when we leave Bristol Channel. It will not be a long journey—"

A movement at the door caught Deborah's attention. A dark figure entered. For a moment she hoped for rescue; then her heart sank again. It was Bernard Houdon, his gaunt face more bleak than ever.

"Is she awake? What does she say?" he asked abruptly.

"Perhaps a little confused," said Marie Andreossy. Rigaud waved her to silence and spoke to Houdon arrogantly.

"Leave her alone. She will do as I say. You must marry us soon, and then she will come with us willingly enough. After a little persuasion she will do all I wish. She likes me very much already. A few nights in my arms and—" He snapped his fingers and grinned down at Deborah, his gaze traveling over her slight figure in the thin muslin gown. She shrank from him, her tortured brain scarcely able to comprehend what he said.

"Best come up then, and we shall see that the sailors have their proper orders," said Houdon coldly. He turned on his heel and left the small cabin.

Rigaud hesitated, then bent and kissed Deborah carelessly. "*Cherie*, I shall return presently, and we shall talk. Look after her, Marie."

And he went out, shutting the door behind him. The latch clicked. He was locking them in.

Deborah raised her hand to her forehead. Her head ached abominably. Yet she was thinking, thinking hard. How could she escape from them? She must escape. They were all monsters!

Marie Andreossy sat down beside her again with a rustle of her black skirts. In her hand was a bowl. "Some soup, my dear," she said. "I will feed you."

Deborah wondered if it was drugged. Marie put

360

the spoon to her lips, and Deborah tried it cautiously. It was so good, she could not resist. She ate it
slowly, watching Marie from under her lashes.

Marie said in a whisper, "Do not defy *him*,
Miss Stanton. It will do no good. It only makes
him angry, and when he is angry—" She shuddered,
and fear flashed in her sad features.

"What does he do?" asked Deborah, the nightmare going on and on.

"I have seen him—kill," whispered Marie. "He
becomes so enraged—and Bernard is the same.
Bernard was a priest once. He beat a woman who
resisted him, and was defrocked. He is my cousin,
but I too fear him. They have no mercy, those
two. Do not cross them."

"And all of them—all of you—are spies for Napoleon Bonaparte? You work for that—that—"

"Do not say it!" Marie threw a quick look over
her shoulder. "We lost all our lands, our houses,
in the horrible Revolution. Napoleon promises we
shall have them back if we do as he says. We have
worked for him many years, and he has been very
generous. Yet we do not have our land back. I do
not know how long we must work and wait. Paul
thinks this will be enough. With you married to
him—"

"By a defrocked priest—" said Deborah drily.

"Yes, yes, he will do it. Bernard claims he was
unjustly—but then, do not speak of it to him. Do
not anger him. Listen, my dear, do what they
wish, draw what they order. It could do us much
good, and you will live in luxury one day. I think
I can promise you that!" She spoke in a livelier

manner, her cheeks flushed, her dark eyes sparkling. "We will go home again, to our beautiful Lorraine. And once again we shall live in grand houses, and all shall bow down to us once more!"

Marie rambled on, as steps sounded on the deck over their heads. The sailors were moving about; it must be almost dawn. And with the dawn and the morning tide, the American-disguised vessel would leave port, would move out to sea, and freely pass the blockade—to France!

And once there, Deborah would truly be a prisoner of these spies, these agents of the barbarous Napoleon. They must have a wealth of information for him by this time, for they had moved freely in British society, read the gazettes, talked to important persons close to the government—

She thought of her dear Lady Horatia, and tears burned her eyes. Would her friends guess what had happened? Could they follow her and rescue her from the heart of enemy country? Or would she be forever lost—used by Paul, to be discarded and perhaps murdered when her usefulness was ended?

He returned to the cabin. "She has eaten? Good," he said more cheerfully, a glow in his cheeks. He had been drinking; she could smell the wine on his breath as he bent over her. She closed her eyes, pretending to be very sleepy, and he laughed softly.

"You will not sleep soon, my dear, when you are married to me! You will stay awake all the sweet nights, while I have my first tastes of your innocence and loveliness. I think you shall enjoy it also. I am a fine lover, am I not, Marie?" He laughed as Marie flushed vividly.

Deborah did not try to answer him, but watched him warily. He moved to a small desk fastened to the wall of the cabin. He opened her portfolio of sketches, took the other sketches from the hollow cane, and put them all together, to gaze at them in great satisfaction.

"Yes, yes, he will be pleased," he muttered, nodding at the portfolio. "And when I tell him my dear wife can reproduce all he wishes in such vivid sketches, he will be more than pleased. Marie, did you tell her of my home in Lorraine?"

"I have not yet described it, dear Paul," said Marie with composure, but Deborah noted the white knuckles of the hands clasped tightly in her black satin lap. Marie had learned how to get along with her "cousins." She wondered now what their real relationship was. Evidently at least Marie and Paul had been lovers, perhaps Bernard Houdon also. She felt half sick with her new knowledge of them.

"There is plenty of time for descriptions. You have the notes?"

Marie nodded, got up, and fetched a notebook. She offered it to Paul, who sat down at the desk to look it over.

Deborah guessed that the notebook contained all the information the spies had gathered, and she would be forced to provide more. She would be made to draw anything they demanded, and would be forced to give information on the men she had come to know, friends of her father, his superior officers, their natures, their habits, anything that would help the French to take over England.

She did not know how she might accomplish it, but quietly, in the murmur of the French voices, Deborah made a resolution. She would die before she would give them any more information. There must be some way—

A knife, a pistol—

Or rousing Paul's anger, so that he killed her!

Somehow she must find the courage to do it. She could not betray England.

She thought of Morgan, with desperate longing. He would probably never know what she had done. But she would keep faith with her love for him, for her family, for England. She would not be forced into betrayal.

She would die first.

CHAPTER TWENTY-THREE

Lord Treverly was pacing up and down the drawing room of Lady Horatia Torrington's town house. She watched him with shrewd, knowing eyes. William Vaughan looked from one to the other of them, troubled but silent.

"You are both mad," Morgan said flatly, his gray eyes flashing fury. "To even consider going to Egypt at this time! Madame, my opinion of you used to be very high indeed. You have disappointed me sorely. To encourage that girl to go off on travels at a time like this!"

"Dear me, Lord Treverly," said Lady Horatia mildly. "You speak very strongly. However, as my dear Deborah remarked, it is scarcely your concern. You are *not* a member of that family—as yet! Your attentions to Alice do not include Deborah, and surely Deborah has earned the right to do as she wishes. Or do you, also, think that she should remain as unpaid nursemaid to her elder sister's children?"

She noted the dull flush of his cheeks, but he flung out his hands impatiently. "All this is beside the point. What she does with her life—of course she should not be a nursemaid. She will marry; surely she will marry. But at this time, to think of going off to Egypt—"

They had argued all through luncheon. Lord Treverly and his cousin had arrived about ten o'clock, to find her ladyship serenely contemplating several books on Egypt and the islands of the Mediterranean. It had set off a minor explosion, and the butler went about on tiptoe as he brought in coffee now.

Lady Horatia thanked him with a smile and set about pouring coffee, as Lord Treverly strode up and down again.

"You must surely see the danger of it," he said, with an air of forcing himself to be patient with a person of low mentality. "You have lived much of your life in political circles. You have read the gazettes. Napoleon has gathered troops opposite us. The blockades that England has set up—"

"You begin to repeat yourself, my lord," said Lady Horatia, her pursed lips the only sign of her resentment of his attitude. In truth, she was enjoying his lack of composure. It showed promise— yes, it showed promise.

"Damn it, woman!" he said, coming to a halt before her. "If you will not be sensible, I shall use force of law. You will be halted if you attempt to leave the country with that innocent girl! Leading her astray, taking her from the bosom of her family—"

A loud knock on the front door startled them all. The butler jumped and looked to Lady Horatia appealingly.

"I am not at home to anyone this afternoon," she instructed. "Lord Treverly is busy losing his manners, forgetting he does not swear in the presence of a lady. I would not wish any guest to hear of this!"

Morgan's flush deepened, and he glared down at her as she offered him coffee. "No thank you, madam!" he said curtly.

The butler hastened from the room, but a moment later, Squire Frome burst in. "Is she here? Is Deborah—" He gazed from one to the other in growing dismay. "She is not here?"

"Deborah?" Morgan barked, striding toward the squire. "Where is she then?"

"I do not know." The squire took out a handkerchief and mopped his red face. "She has disappeared with that damned Frenchman!"

Lady Horatia set down the cup with a clatter that spilled her coffee. She sprang to her feet. "What are you saying?" she cried sharply.

"Deborah—she has gone! Our man told me that Monsieur Rigaud called while we were out. Deborah went out with him at once, with her cloak and bonnet and some sketches. The damned Frenchie was talking about a buyer for her work. And she hasn't come back! Not a word to anyone! Demme, she has forgotten about society completely! Can't disappear like that, with a man!"

"With the sketches?" Lady Horatia put her hands to her face. All color had fled from her cheeks. "Dear God," she said quietly. "I should have warned her—oh God, I should have warned her—"

"Warned her?" Lord Treverly caught her up sharply. "What is it? What do you know?"

She turned to him, and her hand went out to his pleadingly. "My dear Lord Treverly, go after them, I beg of you. I have information that the three French people we know may be spies of Napoleon. That is the reason for Paul's interest in Deborah's sketches! They have been seen aboard an American ship in Bristol Channel, the *American Eagle*. He must have taken Deborah there—"

"And I could find out nothing about them from my contacts in London!" Morgan said bitterly. "If only I had known— Where is that ship?" he demanded.

"Off Bristol. I will show you on a map." Quickly she moved to a desk in the corner, took out a map, and indicated on it where the ship had been seen. "Pray do not pause to ask questions, my dear sir. If I were a man, I would come with you—"

"I shall come," said Mr. Vaughan at once. "Pistols in the carriage, dear fellow? And our swords— I will get them."

"Right—we'll be off at once—" Morgan started for the door.

"Get help from the navy forces in the harbor!" she called after him. "The entire ship is French, all the sailors trained for emergencies. Call on the captain of the *Valiant*, Captain Trent. He is a personal friend of mine—use my name—"

The squire followed them out. "I should come also," he said.

"No, I thank you. Go home and try to keep your wife and sister calm. I shall bring Deborah home to you, though all the forces of hell try to stop me!" said Morgan, so savagely that the squire blinked. He was still blinking as the two horsemen set off, the carriage following them, to bring Deborah back.

They rode furiously, but it was almost dawn when they reached the port. Stars had begun to dim, and a faint light shone in the east. When they reached the docks, Morgan's keen eyes surveyed the ships. He drew a deep breath when he saw the lean black ship flying American colors, still out in the Channel.

Then he located the *Valiant,* and he and his cousin raced to the dock nearest the British ship. Several sailors yawned there, exchanging sleepy gossip.

They sprang to attention as the two gentlemen, their expressions urgent, appeared and demanded to be rowed out to the *Valiant.* There was something in Morgan's tone and bearing that denied the possibility of their refusing.

They rowed him out, and he was up the rope ladder as one accustomed to quick action, in spite of his fine velvet clothes and polished boots. He sprang onto the deck and demanded to see the captain.

They exchanged quick greetings, and Morgan wasted no time in explaining the situation. "Lady Horatia Torrington asked me to use her name, to assure you of the seriousness of this matter. An English girl is being held on the French ship—"

"French ship?" echoed Captain Trent, gazing at him curiously. "What ship is that?"

He was cautious rather than skeptical. Morgan said impatiently, "The one with the American colors. The *American Eagle*. It is full of Frenchmen. They are holding an English girl, who is able to draw and sketch harbors—her father was in the navy—"

"Her name?"

"Miss Deborah Stanton!"

"Ah—yes, Lady Horatia told me of her. We have been keeping the ship under surveillance. So that is why they waited here!" The captain hesitated no longer, but turned and spoke to his second-in-command. Soon the ship came alive with seamen running here and there, hauling out the guns, straining at the ropes until they snapped and the sails billowed out in the morning breeze.

The ship sailed imperiously into the Channel. At the same time, the *American Eagle* had put up sail and was drawing into their path.

Aboard the disguised French vessel, Paul Rigaud said, "Those damn fools! Why must they play their games today of all days? Get Deborah up here; she'll speak her piece if she has to!"

Deborah was brought up, looking small and fragile in the company of the rough French sailors.

"You'll say what I direct you," said Rigaud, his hand gripping her elbow. "Wait, and speak only when I say so."

She said nothing, resolved not to speak a word. She would die for it, but better death than betrayal. She raised her eyes to the heavens, saw the pale blue sky of morning and the billowing white sails of the British vessel moving deliberately into their path, blocking their access to the open sea.

She prayed silently for strength to face the end. She thought once of Morgan. It was not meant to be; it had never been meant. At least she could die with dignity.

"Damn them, damn them," Paul whispered savagely. "They will stop us, will they? Call out to them, Bernard! Ask them jovially to get out of our path. We have no time for games today, tell them!"

The suave voice of Bernard Houdon called out, in clear English. "Ahoy there, *Valiant*. We wish to be on our way! Clear the lanes, if you will be so kind!"

To their shock, the voice that came back was that of Lord Treverly!

"You will go no farther, Houdon! Surrender peacefully, or we will blow you out of the water!"

Paul Rigaud hissed between his teeth. Marie Andreossy caught Deborah's arm and drew her under the shelter of the overhanging quarterdeck. "Come—I think they mean to fight—we must go below—"

She hurried Deborah into the cabin below, in spite of the girl's protests. Her face was ghostly pale. "Oh, God," she was saying over and over in French. "God deliver us. They were so sure— how did *he* come to be on that ship?"

They had little time to wonder, for a gun boomed, and another, and there began a round of firing so deafening that they clapped their hands over their ears. And then there was a great cracking and splitting overhead. One mast had gone down, shattered by the cannon fire.

A thump of footsteps sounded on the deck overhead, shouts and the firing of small arms. The door was flung wide, and Paul Rigaud stood in the opening.

His jacket was gone, his white shirt torn. He looked wild, desperate. He caught Deborah by the arm, and his sword was at her throat.

"Come—" he snarled. "You shall be my passport, my little one—" And he shoved her ahead of him up to the deck.

Men lay in their own blood. Deborah's slippered feet inched a path between them. She slipped once in the blood and was caught up by Rigaud's hard arm. He shoved her again, out into the sunlight of the morning.

Facing them on deck was the commander of the *Trent,* in blue uniform, and beside him—Morgan. A sword was in his hand. Behind him stood William Vaughan with a pistol poised to fire.

The French sailors stood meekly in line, their hands up in surrender. The British sailors were watching them alertly. Bernard Houdon lay on the deck, his face blank, his eyes open. It was a moment before Deborah realized he was dead. She shuddered and looked away, to Morgan's face.

He glanced at her only briefly before his attention was again on Rigaud. "You are unharmed, Deborah?"

"Yes, Morgan," she said quickly. Rigaud's hand closed on her arm; he held her steadily before him, his sword point ready at her neck, poised to kill.

"Miss Stanton will not live if you persist!" Rigaud snarled. "You will allow this ship to pass, or she dies!"

Morgan was silent. The captain looked from one to the other.

Deborah said quietly yet so clearly that all could hear, "I am not afraid to die, Morgan. Do not let him go. He would betray us to Napoleon!"

The point pricked her neck. She flinched, then stood erect again, her head held high. She prayed her courage would not desert her.

"You hide behind a woman's skirts?" drawled Morgan in a deadly tone. "I am surprised at you, Monsieur! You always bragged of your bravery. Your cousin died with courage. But you wish to live—at any price!"

"You will not taunt me to my death!" answered Rigaud. "Let us proceed, or this woman dies!"

The sword pierced her skin, and blood ran down onto Deborah's dress, staining the white muslin. She felt rather faint, but kept her chin high.

There was a brief but intense silence on the ship. The sailors looked curiously from one antagonist to the other. This was outside their experience of war.

"You shall go free," said Morgan finally. "But only if you will fight me yourself. If you manage to defeat me with your sword, you shall have your freedom and the ship to go with it. My word on it." He looked at Captain Trent, who hesitated, then nodded.

"No, no," whispered Deborah.

Rigaud seemed to consider, darting a quick look about. "Your word as a gentleman?" he asked. "Why should I trust you?"

"Why indeed?" asked Morgan with a shrug. "It is your life, after all. If you do not care to gamble—"

Paul gave Deborah such a shove that she fell to the deck, against the corpse of a sailor. She shuddered and sat up, her hand clutching her throat as the men faced each other. The sailors backed off, gazes eager. This was better than battle!

Rigaud sprang toward Morgan, his sword flashing in the sunlight. His grin was a grimace of hatred. They moved cautiously. Deborah wondered why, as they circled around and around. Then the sun glinted off Morgan's face, and he blinked. They were both trying to get their backs to the sun, and Paul had succeeded!

He moved forward like a panther, his sword swinging in little circles before him. He was intent now, all concentration on Morgan. The bigger man moved slowly; scarcely did his booted feet shift. He merely turned as Paul moved toward him, and somehow the sword was always ready to protect the body behind it. Deborah could scarcely draw breath, could do nothing but wait. A wounded man groaned behind her, and she started. But the two swordsmen did not heed the sound. All their attention was fixed on one another. Each watched the other's eyes.

Slowly they circled. Then Rigaud lashed forward, and Morgan's sleeve was rent to the elbow.

A faint cry sounded from the line of British sailors. The French sailors began to grin triumphantly. Their fellow would win! They were sure of it now.

Captain Trent of the *Valiant* made himself watch, though with intense disapproval. This was not in any regulations; in fact, it was probably enough to get him court-martialed! Damn it, why had he let his lordship dictate to him? Damn it, he was captain of his own ship, wasn't he? Why had he listened to the man?

The men moved again, and it seemed to Deborah that Morgan was moving more slowly, breathing heavily, while Paul's face gleamed with triumph. Then the Frenchman leaped forward, his sword darting. With effort, the British sword parried the thrust, and they moved apart once more.

Only Mr. Vaughan watched serenely, his brow confident. He had seen his cousin in action many times. Yet he stood ready with pistol cocked—just in case—

Paul moved in again, the sword thrust keenly inside the guard. Just as the point was at Lord Treverly's breast, Morgan moved swiftly around, and his sword went into Rigaud's shoulder. The Frenchman wavered, his sword dipped as though too heavy to carry, and he fell to the deck, groaning.

Marie Andreossy gave a little scream and ran forward to kneel beside her cousin. "He is dead, he is dead!" she wailed, and her hand went to his face.

"Not dead, but out of commission," said Morgan. He was not even breathing heavily. He dropped his sword, went to Deborah, and picked her up, to hold her close. She clung to him.

"Oh—Morgan—Morgan—" Her head fell forward against his chest, that had been so near to death, so very near—

He picked her up and carried her over to the side of the ship, grandly ignoring the officers and crew. Captain Trent snapped out orders, and his sailors went into action, moving to take over the French vessel and its crew, and to sail the ship back into port, this time as captive.

Captain Trent watched the little launch as it carried Lord Treverly and Deborah Stanton back to shore. He wondered what he himself would have done had the outcome of the duel been different.

In spite of his bleeding arm, Morgan carried Deborah inside the nearest tavern on the dock, where he demanded a private room. He sent for the surgeon from the *Valiant*, but while they waited he examined the wound on Deborah's throat, cursing softly.

"They did not—harm you otherwise?" he asked her gruffly.

She flushed, and shook her head weakly. "They —they only threatened. And Madame Andreossy stayed at my side. She was there when I wakened on board ship."

"Wakened? Were you drugged?"

"No. Paul Rigaud—knocked me unconscious." She indicated the purple bruise on her chin, and Morgan's face tightened.

The surgeon arrived, and William Vaughan let him into the small room. Briskly the doctor opened his bag, examined the wound, and swabbed it with some stinging liquid which made Deborah want to scream. She clenched her teeth. She was so grateful to be alive, she would not cry or faint, she vowed.

She almost did faint, however, when she saw Morgan's wound. He removed his shirt and allowed the surgeon to examine his arm, wash it in more stinging liquid, and bandage it. Then he shrugged into his torn shirt once more. William helped him carefully into the dusty velvet jacket he had worn to call on Lady Horatia, a mere twenty-four hours before. Then Morgan left the room to consult with Captain Trent, who had brought the prisoners back and was holding them in another room.

William Vaughan had tea brought in, and saw that Deborah drank some and ate some meat and bread. She managed to ask him, "What will happen to Monsieur Rigaud and Madame Andreossy?"

William shrugged. "Taken to London under guard, questioned. Prison then."

She looked at the table. William had rescued her portfolio of sketches. Morgan's still-bloody sword lay across it, leaving a dull rusty-red streak on the fabric. She shivered. It had been so close.

"I don't understand what happened. How did you come so quickly?" she asked wearily.

Morgan returned to the room. "No more talk now. Deborah, after you have recovered, someone will come to question you about the matter. For now, we shall take you home."

Home. Her eyes brimmed with tears, but she fought them back. She had thought never to see home again, her sisters—and she had quarreled so with them!

It was past noon when they set out in the carriage. Deborah shivered again and again, huddling in her lightweight cloak. As they left the docks, she saw the fallen mast across the slim black vessel, *American Eagle*. She might have died there, and Morgan—he had been so close to death at the hands of Paul Rigaud! She shuddered again. Morgan reached for a carriage robe and tucked it about her.

"Is that better?" he asked in a gentle tone that was nearly her undoing.

"Yes, thank you," she whispered. "I cannot—thank you enough—I still do not understand how you came. I am so grateful—so foolish of me—"

"Never mind that now. Plenty of time for talk later," he said, and leaned back in his corner with his eyes closed.

He despised her! She had caused such trouble, he had nearly had to die for her! In her corner, screened by the wide brim of her bonnet, she finally let tears trickle down her cheeks. She was so weary, so exhausted after the terrible events, the horrible emotions. Behind her closed lids, she could see the dead and wounded sailors, the spectacle of Morgan and Paul Rigaud circling each other in the bright sunlight.

She reached up furtively with her handkerchief to wipe away the tears. Morgan saw her. "Now Deborah," he said softly.

She sniffed. "I am—so sorry—" she sobbed.

"Foolish child!" He reached out to untie her bonnet ribbons, and eased her head down on his shoulder. "There now. Sleep if you can. It is a journey of some hours back to Bath."

She relaxed against him. This might be the only time he would ever hold her so. She closed her eyes, for the tears still flowed. Gently he wiped her face with his lace-trimmed handkerchief, then softly stroked her hair.

William Vaughan watched them with a bright, knowing gaze. He thought he had learned much these two days, and he felt happier than he had for a long time. He gazed out the window at the green and fragrant fields, and hummed a little to himself.

Deborah slept, her head on Morgan's shoulder. She wakened briefly when they paused to change the horses, then heard Morgan's deep voice in her ear, "Sleep on, Deborah."

She curled more comfortably against him, and slept on.

She wakened only when the carriage halted in front of the squire's house in Bath. Lights streamed into the night darkness, and Clarence was running out to greet them.

"What is it? What has happened? Where have you been?" he cried, and gasped as he saw Deborah's bloodstained white muslin. Morgan helped her down.

"Get her to bed! All shall be told tomorrow. She needs rest and care. I shall order my doctor to come round in the morning," Morgan said. "She is unharmed but for the wound on her throat. Still, she has had a great shock. And not a word to anyone, Squire, outside the family! I must warn you most urgently about that."

But the squire would not let it rest at that. They had been too anxious and upset. He must have Morgan and William come in and tell him the story in the privacy of his study.

Meanwhile, Gertrude and Alice took Deborah up to her bed. They exclaimed anxiously over her throat, her exhausted condition. But they knew she could not answer questions in her present state, and left her to sleep.

Deborah slept the clock around, not wakening until the doctor was shown in. He examined her throat, put ointment on it, warned her to be careful of any infection and to send for him should it trouble her. Then he bandaged it again and made to depart.

She stopped him timidly. "Doctor—you have seen—Lord Treverly?"

"Yes, this morning."

"And his—arm?"

"Doing well. Don't you know you can't keep the man down?" The doctor grinned, and departed.

Deborah sank back thankfully and slept once more, relieved.

The next day Lady Horatia came to call upon her, and was shown up to her room. Alice and Gertrude were shut out, to their disgust. Lady Horatia spoke to Deborah in great confidence.

Quietly, with no boasting, she told her, "For many years now, I have been an agent for His Majesty, reporting information helpful to the Crown. I have long been suspicious of my supposed friends from France, yet I confess I was at first taken in by them. Pretending to be in such need, to be such enemies of Napoleon, when all the time they worked for him!

"I cannot forgive myself that you were in such danger! I had but recently learned of their activities and realized they meant to leave England soon. My contacts told me they had gone several times on board the *American Eagle* and had heard French spoken there, fluent French, when none thought strangers about. Putting the matter together, I was about to act. Our French 'friends' have gathered much information concerning our efforts to repel any invasion. They know the number of our ships in the English Channel, in Bristol Channel, and en route to the Mediterranean and the Caribbean. It is a shame that sailors—even officers—write home so freely that what should be secret is common gossip among their wives and families!"

"And my sketches—" Deborah said. "Paul Rigaud would have exchanged my sketches to regain his home and lands. He meant to marry me—at least for a time," and she shuddered even in the warm room.

"Yes, that was one thing that made me suspect him. He was not such a great lover of art as he pretended; I caught him out on that!" nodded Lady Horatia, head bobbing in her brilliant purple turban.

They talked on for a time, until Deborah grew weary. Then Lady Horatia stood and said she must depart. After she had gone, Deborah managed to get out of bed and with uncertain steps went over to the desk. She opened the bloodstained portfolio and with a shudder began to tear up every sketch of a port, a harbor, a sailor.

She cast them all into the fireplace. Alice came in as she was doing this and gave a little cry.

"You are up, Deborah! The doctor did not say you might arise! What are you doing? What are you doing?"

Deborah threw the last sketches on the fire, and watched the fine blaze they made. "I am quite sick of harbors and ships," she said fiercely. "They make such trouble! From now on, I shall paint only pretty garden scenes, and portraits, and such like."

Alice looked at her as though she thought her sister delirious. She said nothing, but helped her back to bed and brought some light beef broth, and fed her as though she were a child.

CHAPTER TWENTY-FOUR

Deborah lay abed through Saturday and Sunday. When visitors arrived, Gertrude and Alice and the squire received them. When Deborah inquired who had come, she learned that Lord Treverly and Mr. Vaughan had not been among the callers.

Where had they gone? Or were they so disgusted with her and, by extension, with her family that they had gone off to their own pleasures? Somehow she could not think that.

On Monday morning, she rose and dressed. She said firmly that she felt much better, as she donned a white muslin gown and arranged a blue scarf casually about her throat, to hide the bandages. She went down early and cut some flowers with Alice for the vases. Life seemed to have returned to normal.

They were still in the garden when the Treverly carriage drove up. Deborah felt rather faint when she saw the two men coming into the gardens.

"Ah, so you are here," said Morgan. "How do you feel, Deborah?"

She was greatly relieved to hear no formality,

only anxiety in his voice, to see the open, questioning look in his gray eyes. "Well, I thank you, sir," she said. "And you? Your arm?"

"It heals. I would speak with you privately. There is something we must discuss."

"And I would speak with Miss Alice," said Mr. Vaughan, and took the basket firmly from Alice's hand. His earnest look stilled any protest, and she went meekly with him to a white bench near the honeysuckle.

Deborah felt Morgan's arm at her waist as he gently turned her to the house. They entered the drawing room through the French windows. Gertrude stared at them in surprise.

The squire rose from his chair. "My dear sir, you are here again! We are anxious to know of all that has transpired."

"Later, sir, if you will. All went well in London. The prisoners are under guard. I should warn you that the affair is still secret and must remain so. Our French acquaintances have left Bath, and we do not know they've gone—that is our story, sir."

Morgan sounded respectful but a little impatient. His arm still circled Deborah's waist.

"Well, we shall be satisfied when you tell us," said the squire reluctantly. He took out his pipe. "Will you have tea with us now?"

"Later, perhaps. For now, I would request your study, Squire, if you will. Deborah and I must discuss a matter in privacy, and she is to make a statement for the authorities. If you will forgive me—"

"Of course, of course, pray use the study. There is paper there, and ink—"

Morgan thanked him and drew Deborah with him to the study. Once inside, he shut the door and turned to her, searching her face gravely.

"You are still pale. I wonder if we should speak—"

She clasped her hands tightly. "Oh, it would be best to have it done with, I am sure," she said. "I am quite strong, really, and the injury is healing."

They sat down, he behind the squire's desk, she in a chair nearby.

"I promised I would obtain a statement from you, Deborah," he said, fiddling with some blank pages. "Perhaps you would tell me what happened to you; then we will make up a statement for you to sign. Later this week, some men will come from London to question you. Do not worry, I shall be here with you."

"Thank you. You are very kind, sir."

She wanted to weep at the gentleness and thoughtfulness he was showing her. He might have shouted at her for her recklessness in going off with Paul Rigaud, and she could not have blamed him.

She began to tell him about that horrible day. He listened intently, not trying to make notes, his steady gaze on her face, watching her changing expression. He interrupted only once.

"Was it then that you realized Rigaud was your enemy? Only then? You had no suspicion of him before?"

She hesitated, frowning a little. "When I came into the drawing room and found him going through the sketches and stuffing some into the cane, I felt—oh, a sort of fear. I wondered—but then he was so charming and gay, as always—"

"You loved him?" he asked abruptly.

"No," said Deborah, just as bluntly. "I enjoyed his attentions, but I did not love him. I thought he dispensed his charms freely among many women, and no matter what he said to me, I did not believe he loved me. Later, on the ship, I found that his charming manners were a mask for his evil. A clever mask, I may say. But beneath— a villain. Madame Andreossy told me that he had killed and would kill again. She feared him as much as she feared Monsieur Houdon."

He questioned her further, and she told him all that had happened, until he was finally satisfied that he had the whole story.

"When his belongings at the hired flat were searched, we were amazed to find Lady Horatia's missing jewels," he told her. "Tracing back, and questioning his movements, we discovered that it was indeed Paul Rigaud, and perhaps Monsieur Houdon with him, who broke into her home. But your sketches must have been his main object. You guarded them too closely for him to have easy access to them, so he tried to steal them."

"He? It *was* he? He might have killed us then!" she shuddered, putting her hands to her face.

"No, no, I do not think he was desperate yet. Later, here in Bath, he gained your friendship. He was here often enough that the servants did not question his comings and goings. Then he was able to make off with a few sketches at a time, con- cealed in his hollow cane. Do you know if any were missing when we recovered them?"

She shook her head. "He admitted he had not had time to send any to his—master. He said I would be forced to sketch more scenes, all I could remember of ports and harbors and ships."

Morgan's face darkened, and he muttered a savage word under his breath. The quill he held snapped in his strong fingers. He stood, to pace restlessly before the windows. The scene he saw in the garden seemed to please him, though, for he smiled and turned back into the room.

"Now, Deborah, another matter," he said pleasantly. "Later, we will make out a statement for the authorities. For now, let us think of other things."

"Yes?"

He glanced at her face, the composed features, the clasped hands, and seemed a little less sure of himself.

"Deborah—years ago, you said you loved me. I loved you deeply, and would have carried you off with me. You refused. You could not leave Alice."

"I know, sir. I could not," she said. She had not thought he would speak of it again. Did he intend to taunt her?

"I was bitter for many years," he went on slowly, coming to stand over her. "You chose your family over me. I could not reconcile myself to accepting this. Then I returned, and you seemed aged with your cares, and weary. Still you clung to the family, let them dominate you."

"You know my situation. I told you of it."

"I did not truly believe you until finally I came to know your elder sister, and realized how her selfish concern for herself might have forced you into this action. However, if you had gone to the squire—"

"I did not know him then! I believed her when she said she would desert Alice. Oh, why must we go through this again?" she asked desperately. "You love Alice now—"

"No," he said. "Only as a sister. She is young and sweet, but shallow of mind. She has not your depth and courage, your goodness and intelligence! Oh, Deborah, I have known it for a long time, but I refused to admit it even to myself. I can live with no other woman but you!"

She stared up at him, unable to believe what she heard. Then she saw the glint in his gray eyes, saw his hands held out pleadingly for hers. She put her small hands in his, let him draw her to her feet, was clasped close to his hard, strong body.

"But you—oh, Morgan, I thought—you paid no attention to me—oh, Morgan—"

His mouth came down on hers, at first gently and questioningly, then burning hot and sweet against her lips as his passion grew. She clasped her arms about his neck, and it was like the old days, right and strong, warm and loving.

Finally she drew back a little. He would not allow her to move far from him, and clasped his hands firmly behind her waist, holding his arms about her, smiling down into her eyes. Somehow he looked younger.

"Oh, Morgan, I cannot believe this! You love me?"

"Yes, and shall forever," he said, and bent to brush his lips tenderly against her forehead. "I tried to fight it. It was infuriating that every time

I saw you, I wanted to hold you and kiss you! I wished to marry a safe, sedate, well-bred young woman, someone to bear my children. I thought I would be done with romantic love and such foolishness!"

"Morgan!" she said reproachfully, and he laughed down at her.

"All I had to do was think of you, and I was lost. I would remember how you responded to my kisses, how your eyes glowed as they looked into mine. How your beautiful face shone with love. And I could be satisfied with none other. All other females seemed bland to me, nothing at all."

"But you ignored me, or were cold!"

"I was fighting myself, my own wishes. A losing battle, my sweet!" He bent and brushed his lips lingeringly across hers. At once, a flame seemed to burn between them. Her lips moved in response, and they were kissing, holding each other, her hands desperately clinging to his neck, clasped in his hair, his arms tightening about her until they seemed one form, one heartbeat.

The joy seemed almost too great to be borne. She rested her cheek against his hard chest and listened to his heart beating, heard his murmured words, and thought that she dreamt.

"You must marry me soon, my darling," he was saying urgently. "I could not bear for us to be parted again. If anything happened—if you put your family first again—"

She smiled against his white stock and said demurely, "But my family will always come first with me, Morgan!"

She felt him stiffen against her. She pressed her

hand very gently to his shoulder, her fingers crept up to his chin, and she caressed his lips with the tips of her fingers.

"You will be my family, Morgan," she whispered. "And always, always, you will come first with me. You—and our children, when they come to bless us—"

"Oh, my love!" He caught her close again, and his mouth sought hers urgently. They kissed, and held each other, and whispered their sweet promises. And Deborah had never been so happy. Her face glowed with his kisses.

"How soon?" he asked finally, drawing back a little. She was sitting on his lap in the big chair, lying against him, their fingers entwined.

"As soon as you wish, Morgan," she said, with such sweet simplicity that he had to kiss her again.

"A month? Could you be ready in a month?"

"Yes, darling. We have waited too long already, my love," she said, with a sigh. "You will think me growing old—"

"Old? You? Never," he said, with conviction. "But we shall be married as soon as may be. Shall we be married here in Bath? Oh no, it had best be Lowbridge. Too many there would be insulted not to witness our marriage. Yes, it will be Lowbridge, and all shall come to rejoice with us."

She was smiling against his coat. He had forgotten completely his words that had stung her for so long—"sadly aged"! No, he had forgotten, and so would she.

A chiming clock reminded them of the hour. It

was twelve, and they had lingered long in the study. "We must go and announce our good news, my love," he said reluctantly. She slid from his lap to stand before him, cheeks glowing, eyes bright. He smiled as he stood. "You look a different creature than when I came in! May I suggest that Doctor Randall has improved your looks with his attentions?"

She laughed up at him. "I have heard it said, my lord, that happiness is the best cosmetic a lady can have," she told him demurely.

"One more kiss before we go in," he said huskily, and held her close, his mouth on hers for a long moment. Then he took her hand and led her from the room which had witnessed their reconciliation.

Gertrude looked up anxiously when they entered the drawing room hand-in-hand. The squire stared, then began to smile.

Morgan drew Deborah over to the squire. "Sir, I must beg your pardon for not first asking your permission to pay my addresses to your sister Deborah. She has done me the honor to consent to be my wife. We need only your good wishes to make our happiness complete."

The squire's voice covered his wife's gasp. "You have them—my very best wishes, and my hopes for your happiness!" He kissed Deborah's cheek and clasped Morgan's hand, beaming. "I cannot say I am amazed. I have watched you two with much interest! You quarrel as if you knew one another's minds."

Morgan laughed, and Deborah joined in. "But what is this?" cried Gertrude. "Deborah—and my dear Lord Treverly? But I thought—oh dear—"

Alice and William Vaughan entered the room through the French windows at that moment, hand-in-hand, looking equally contented. From the fresh air, or from some other cause? wondered Deborah, and was not long left to wonder.

"Squire Frome," said William Vaughan with a beaming smile, "may I have your permission to pay my addresses to Miss Alice? She has done me the honor—"

Gertrude forgot herself so far as to shriek aloud, "Not another—no, not another—"

Everyone began to laugh. Morgan disclosed his news to them, and Alice and Deborah kissed each other. Morgan and William clasped each other's hands like brothers.

All was talk and confusion and laughter. Gertrude forgot to wonder and said breathlessly, "Two weddings to plan! Bless me, two weddings! Oh, dear, however shall I manage? Such happiness! Dearest Deborah to be Viscountess Treverly! My dear Alice to be Mrs. Vaughan! And all to plan—dear me!"

Alice was clinging to William's arm, delightfully flushed and smiling. "We thought we might marry in the autumn," she said shyly, glancing up adoringly at her fiancé.

"We shall beat you to the altar then," said Morgan promptly. "For I do not mean to wait over a month. If our sister Gertrude cannot manage it in that time, we shall be married quietly, with no fuss—"

"No fuss!" cried Gertrude. "Indeed, there shall

be a great fuss! All the county shall be there. It will be in the gazettes—"

The squire looked on in great amusement, then finally ordered them all in to partake of luncheon. Few knew what they ate, and all talk was of wedding preparations. They must remove to Lowbridge without delay, to begin planning.

Morgan, under cover of the conversation, said to Deborah, seated beside him, "You shall have the renovation of my dull house, my dear. Can you wait until after the wedding? We shall slip away for a honeymoon—I want you to myself."

She blushed delightfully, squeezed his hand under the cloth, and nodded. "Whatever you wish, Morgan."

"That is how I like a wife to be—obedient," he whispered, his eyes glimmering with laughter. "We shall go up to Scotland, to my hunting lodge there. We can be alone and quiet."

Alice, across the table, was conversing with her William. He was so much easier to talk to than Morgan, who was sometimes grave and formal. She would have liked to be a viscountess, of course, but how much *nicer* her William was, she thought, than his stern cousin. She smiled at William, who whispered, "How lovely you are, more beautiful every day. Can we wait until autumn? Must we wait?"

"It would be nice to have everything planned without haste," said Alice teasingly. "And Deborah must be married first, for she is the elder and has her choice." And it would be pleasant to be engaged for a time, to have William courting her and bringing flowers, she decided. She enjoyed courtship and flattery and attentions. Time enough to settle down in the autumn.

Lady Horatia Torrington was their first caller in the afternoon. She arrived, looking grave and worried, to come into a radiant, laughing household.

"Dear me, whatever is going on?" She looked about in bewilderment.

Deborah came over to her. "Oh wish me well, my dear Lady Horatia," she murmured in her ear. "Morgan and I are to be married!"

"You mean, I shall lose my companion on my journey to Egypt?" cried Lady Horatia, then laughed aloud at Morgan's formidable scowl. "Now, sir, you must allow me my joke!"

"Joke! You shall involve my *wife* in no such schemes, I warn you," he said. "When France is settled down and the wars over, then we shall travel, I promise you, my dear," he added, to Deborah. "But not when there is danger about!"

"I hope you will not give up sketching entirely," said Lady Horatia presently. "You must not waste such a talent."

Deborah smiled at her serenely. "I shall have my household, Lady Horatia—" she began.

Morgan interrupted her, with a pressure of his fingers. "My Deborah shall do as she wishes about that. She shall have hours to sketch and paint when she chooses. I agree with you, Lady Horatia, that her fine talent should not be wasted. When we go to London for the season, I imagine there will be those who wish their portraits painted."

Deborah gazed up at him in amazement. "You would be willing—"

"My love, I want what will make you happy," he whispered back, with a quiet smile at her surprise. "Only I will not permit young men to pose alone with you in the drawing room! Your maid will sit with you, or I shall."

She took his hand, silent in gratitude. That she should be able to continue her painting, that he understood and would help her—her feelings seemed to overflow. Her face glowed with love, and Morgan leaned over to whisper again.

"I think we shall have to go to the garden presently, to be alone again. I am greedy for more kisses!"

His eyes sparkled devilishly, his generous mouth seemed to curve into a kiss as he looked at her.

"Whatever you wish, my lord," said Deborah demurely.

*The irresistible love story
with a happy ending.*

THE PROMISE

A novel by
DANIELLE STEEL

Based on a screenplay by
GARRY MICHAEL WHITE

After an automobile accident which left Nancy McAllister's
beautiful face a tragic ruin, she accepted the money for plastic
surgery from her lover's mother on one condition: that she never
contact Michael again. She didn't know Michael would be told
that she was dead.

Four years later, Michael met a lovely woman whose face he
didn't recognize, and wondered why she hated him with such
intensity . . .

A Dell Book $1.95

A love forged by destiny—
A passion born of flame

FLAMES OF DESIRE

by Vanessa Royall

Selena MacPherson, a proud princess of ancient
Scotland, had never met a man who did not desire
her. From the moment she met Royce Campbell at
an Edinburgh ball, Selena knew the burning
ecstasy that was to seal her fate through all eternity.
She sought him on the high seas, in India, and
finally in a young America raging in the
birth-throes of freedom, where destiny was bound
to fulfill its promise. . . .

A DELL BOOK $1.95

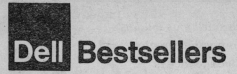

Dell Bestsellers

- [ ] **ENDS OF POWER** by H.R. Haldeman with Joseph DiMona $2.75 (12239-2)
- [ ] **BEGGARMAN, THIEF** by Irwin Shaw $2.75 (10701-6)
- [ ] **THE IMMIGRANTS** by Howard Fast $2.75 (14175-3)
- [ ] **THE BLACK SWAN** by Day Taylor $2.25 (10611-7)
- [ ] **THE PROMISE** by Danielle Steel based on a screenplay by Garry Michael White $1.95 (17079-6)
- [ ] **TARIFA** by Elizabeth Tebbets Taylor $2.25 (18546-7)
- [ ] **PUNISH THE SINNERS** by John Saul $1.95 (17084-2)
- [ ] **SCARLET SHADOWS** by Emma Drummond $2.25 (17812-6)
- [ ] **FLAMES OF DESIRE** by Vanessa Royall $1.95 (15077-9)
- [ ] **STOP RUNNING SCARED** by Herbert Fensterheim Ph.D. & Jean Baer..$2.25 (17734-0)
- [ ] **THE REDBOOK REPORT ON FEMALE SEXUALITY** by Carol Tavris and Susan Sadd $1.95 (17342-6)
- [ ] **THE HOUSE OF CHRISTINA** by Ben Haas....$2.25 (13793-4)
- [ ] **THE MESMERIST** by Felice Picano $1.95 (15213-5)
- [ ] **CONVOY** by B.W.L. Norton $1.95 (11298-2)
- [ ] **F.I.S.T.** by Joe Eszterhas $2.25 (12650-9)
- [ ] **HIDDEN FIRES** by Janette Radcliffe $1.95 (10657-5)
- [ ] **PARIS ONE** by James Brady $1.95 (16803-1)
- [ ] **CLOSE ENCOUNTERS OF THE THIRD KIND** by Steven Spielberg $1.95 (11433-0)
- [ ] **NO RIVER SO WIDE** by Pierre Danton $1.95 (10215-4)
- [ ] **CLOSING TIME** by Lacey Fosburgh $1.95 (11302-4)

At your local bookstore or use this handy coupon for ordering:

DELL BOOKS
P.O. BOX 1000, PINEBROOK, N.J. 07058

Please send me the books I have checked above. I am enclosing $_____
(please add 35¢ per copy to cover postage and handling). Send check or money order—no cash or C.O.D.'s. Please allow up to 8 weeks for shipment.

Mr/Mrs/Miss_____

Address_____

City_____State/Zip_____